SECRETS
of
STATE

INDIA AND PAKISTAN

ALSO BY MATTHEW PALMER

The American Mission

SECRETS
of
STATE

MATTHEW PALMER

G. P. PUTNAM'S SONS   NEW YORK

PUTNAM

G. P. PUTNAM'S SONS
Publishers Since 1838
An imprint of
Penguin Random House LLC
375 Hudson Street
New York, New York 10014

ISBN 978-0-399-16571-9

Printed in the United States of America
1   3   5   7   9   10   8   6   4   2

BOOK DESIGN BY MEIGHAN CAVANAUGH

For my father, Michael Stephen Palmer.

Thanks, Dad.

"I continue to be much more concerned, when it comes to our security, with the prospect of a nuclear weapon going off in Manhattan."

—*Barack Obama*

"Given current policies and practices, a nuclear terrorist attack that devastates one of the great cities of the world is inevitable. In my judgment, if governments do no more and no less than they are doing today, the odds of such an event within a decade are more than 50 percent."

—*Graham Allison*
Harvard Kennedy School of Government

"A more rational anti-terrorism policy would focus resources heavily, perhaps almost exclusively, on threats of nuclear and weapons of mass destruction terror."

—*Nate Silver*
Probability Guru

DULLES, VIRGINIA

PROLOGUE

I t is not an especially large weapon, as such things go. But then again, there really is no such thing as a small nuclear bomb, just one of which, as the bumper stickers had it, can ruin your whole day. The simple gun-type enriched uranium warhead generates an explosive force of some one hundred and fifty tons of TNT. Some of the larger thermonuclear bombs in the American or Russian arsenal, the strategic city busters, weigh in at twenty or thirty megatons. This bomb, however, belongs to one of the alphabet soup of Middle Eastern terrorist groups rather than to a superpower. For their purposes, it is more than adequate. Nor does the group's membership—those who are not themselves incinerated in the initial fireball—mind especially that they could not arrange for the airburst at three thousand feet that would have maximized both the blast damage and the radiation effects of the bomb. Their delivery vehicle is an old Ford panel van parked in front of the Empire State Building near the corner of Thirty-fourth Street and Fifth Avenue.

One second after the small explosion that shoots a subcritical cylinder of highly enriched uranium onto a matching uranium spike, a shock wave with an overpressure of twenty pounds per square inch has reached out four-tenths of a mile from the square meter of Manhattan that instantly and irrevocably wrests the title of Ground Zero from the World Trade Center. The 102-story-tall Empire State Building disintegrates. The fifteen thousand or so people who work there and several hundred assorted tourists waiting patiently for their turn to see the fabled views on what had been a sparkling clear day die instantly, vaporized by the eight thousand–degree heat or crushed by hurtling chunks of rock and metal. Other iconic buildings within the blast zone fare no better. The New York Public Library, Penn Station, and Madison Square Garden are transformed into indistinguishable piles of radioactive rubble. At midday, there are nearly eighty thousand people within a circle with a radius of .4 mile from Ground Zero. Not a single one survives.

Four seconds after critical mass, the shock wave—now reduced to a mere ten psi—has traveled nearly a mile from Ground Zero. The thermal pulse ignites thousands of fires, most of which are promptly snuffed out by the blast wave. It is a small mercy. The top thirty stories are blown off the Chrysler Building. Even so, the misshapen stump of the art deco landmark is once again the tallest building in Midtown. The glass-and-steel UN headquarters building on First Avenue at Forty-fifth Street is a multinational deathtrap. Viktor Janukovski, the newly elected Secretary-General of the United Nations, is torn to pieces by flying glass and decapitated by his own iMac. The steel frame of the building remains largely intact. Ten blocks to the south, however, Bellevue Hospital has been leveled. There are now more than three hundred thousand dead.

Six seconds after detonation, the ring of destruction reaches out a mile and a half from the Empire State Building. At the outer edge of the ring, the blast wave has dropped to five psi, enough to blow out all of the windows at Lincoln Center. Carnegie Hall is on fire. The thermal pulse is still strong enough to kill anyone in the direct line of sight. Approximately thirty thousand people perish in exactly this fashion. All together, another two hundred thousand people die in this ring.

The iconic mushroom cloud now hovers like a specter over New York City. Radioactive fallout . . .

"Damn. The system froze again." Dr. Adam Birnbaum looked up from the screen where a computer-generated image of a devastated New York City was overlaid with graphs and charts offering arcane technical details about pressure waves and radiation levels. Although he knew his way around a database and understood the fundamentals of nuclear fission, Dr. Birnbaum's field of specialty was neither computer science nor atomic physics. He was a political scientist, widely recognized as one of the world's leading academic authorities on terrorism.

"That can't happen on Thursday," said James Smith, who was the interface between Birnbaum and the source of funding for the project to which he had dedicated the last three years of his life. The Cassandra Project had started at DARPA, the Defense Advanced Research Projects Agency. When it began to produce results, the enigmatic Mr. Smith had taken over responsibility from DARPA. Perhaps the best word to describe their new paymaster was, somewhat ironically, *nondescript*. He was a gray man in a gray suit with gray hair that was neither short nor long. Even his skin had a grayish tinge, like that of a chameleon on a concrete wall. According to his business card, Mr. Smith represented a private consulting company called Agilent Industries that had the contract with DARPA to manage the project. Birnbaum had been in and around the Washington establishment for long enough to know that this was horseshit. Mr. Smith was with one of the various U.S. clandestine intelligence services with their own complex ecologies. And if his name was Smith, then Birnbaum would eat his hat. Whoever he worked for, Smith was able to provide the kind of computing power that made the project possible. Birnbaum did not particularly care if the money for the project came from Agilent Industries or the Central Intelligence Agency. In the end, what did it matter?

One of the first things Agilent had done after taking control of the project was to move Cassandra from downtown D.C. to a bland office park off the Dulles toll road. This was consistent with the division of spoils among researchers in the metro Washington region. Suburban Maryland, with the National Institutes of Health and a plethora of advanced genetics labs, had a virtual monopoly on the life sciences. Northern Virginia got the death sciences.

Birnbaum's research was at the cutting edge of modeling for complex social behaviors. There was no behavior more complex in his view than political violence. Complex, however, was not the same thing as unpredictable. The behaviors involved could be disaggregated, expressed as algorithms, and—with enough computing power—modeled. At least that's what Birnbaum had set out to prove. He was starting at the top of the Richter scale. The nightmare scenario. The Cassandra Project was focused exclusively on how different terrorist groups might acquire and utilize one or more nuclear weapons on American soil.

"What's Thursday?" Birnbaum asked.

"You're demonstrating Cassandra to the board of directors," Smith replied with equanimity. "The full dog-and-pony."

"That's in three days. We're not ready," said Dr. Dora Karamanolis, Birnbaum's primary collaborator on the Cassandra Project. She *was* a computer scientist and, in addition to designing the hardware, Karamanolis had also developed the programs that modeled Birnbaum's behavioral algorithms. The diminutive Greek was Birnbaum's physical and temperamental opposite. The corpulent Birnbaum tipped the scales at more than two hundred and fifty pounds. Karamanolis barely broke triple digits and had the delicate bone structure of a bird. Where the political scientist was pugnacious and short-tempered and—he would have been the first to admit—somewhat slovenly, Karamanolis was preternaturally calm and precise almost to the point at which it would have been considered a disorder. She was enormously proud of her brainchild. Cassandra's existence was classified. But if the project had been stacked against the competition, Karamanolis was confident that the trailer-truck-size Cassandra would be among the five fastest supercomputers on the planet.

"You will be ready," Smith said. It was not phrased as encouragement. It was a command. Everything Smith said was a command.

Karamanolis shook her head. "The hardware is ready, but we are still having trouble with the graphics software. It's just too much data, even for Cassandra. We could mock something up with stock footage, but otherwise there's no guarantee we can avoid another system freeze."

"Stock footage would defeat the purpose of the program," Birnbaum interjected. "We're modeling the real world and trying to capture all of the variables. Everything from how the bad guys acquire the weapons, to how they use them, to an assessment of the fallout. Political as well as radiological. That way, when we alter the input variables, we can model probable outcomes and assess risk. If al-Qaeda in the Islamic Maghreb gets ahold of a bomb, the mullahs are likely to use it in a considerably different way than the Haqqani network would. There are thousands of variables that we need to account for. Stock is the opposite of that. You only get out what you put in. You can't adjust the variables and there's no room for serendipity."

"The board isn't terribly interested in serendipity," Smith observed. "They understand the science, but they're not looking for variables so much as they are constants."

"What do you mean?" Birnbaum asked. In their nearly two years of association, this was the first time that Smith had said anything about the nature of the "board of directors" responsible for Cassandra's continued funding. If there was an opportunity to learn something useful about the keepers of the cash, Birnbaum wanted to seize it.

"Variables lend themselves to scenarios," Smith explained. "Constants lend themselves to action."

"But variables are what Cassandra is all about."

"Are they?"

Birnbaum looked blank.

"What's the one thing that's constant in nearly every scenario, every regression that you've run?"

"The source of the weapon," Birnbaum replied. "Everyone always assumed that Iran or North Korea would represent the biggest threat, but they are strong states. Too strong, really. They aren't going to surrender control of the crown jewels to a bunch of wing nuts with a messiah complex. Cassandra has been remarkably consistent on that point. The real threat comes from weak states that can no longer exercise effective command and control over the nuclear infrastructure."

"That's right," Smith said. "It's hard to plan for the variable, but you can plan for the constant. The primary source of the threat. Our ally. Pakistan."

ONE YEAR
LATER

00:01

I t was a good thing that the Council on Foreign Relations did not, as the black-helicopter-obsessed lunatic fringe had it, secretly run the world. *If it did,* Sam Trainor thought to himself, *the world would be forty-five minutes late for everything.* He could only hope that the CFR's alleged coconspirators, the Illuminati, the Freemasons, and the Trilateral Commission, were more efficient. From long experience, however, the Council knew how to take the sting out of the seemingly inevitable delays in its programming, even in the hyperscheduled world of Washington high policy—an open bar. Uniformed caterers circulated among the great and powerful waiting for the evening's event to begin, distributing copious amounts of free expensive liquor along with sugarcane-skewered jumbo shrimp and caviar toast points. Had this been Los Angeles or New York, the catering staff would have been a mix of aspiring screenwriters and out-of-work actors. At CFR headquarters, the drinks and canapés were shepherded by bright-eyed graduates of Ivy League and almost Ivy League universities hoping to find work as program analysts in one of the hundreds of D.C. think tanks or as legislative aides on Capitol Hill. Hard-core policy wonks.

Sam took an amber tumbler of scotch from a tray offered by a fresh-scrubbed intern who no doubt saw himself as the future ambassador to Luxembourg or some such. There was a time, Sam remembered, when he had been very much like this twenty-something, full of the kind of ambition that at its best represented a sort of naive hope that you can change the world and, at its worst, too often devolved into a mere lust for power. This was official Washington. Hollywood for ugly people. The New Rome. It was a company town in which the company was the federal government. The District of Columbia was the capital city of the single greatest power ever to bestride the globe. But it could be as shallow as Tinseltown on a bad day and as catty and as gossipy as a junior high school cafeteria.

Around him, Sam could hear the buzz of the Washington establishment playing everyone's favorite party games: Who's Up; Who's Down? and Who's In; Who's Out? The guest of honor tonight at CFR's spiffy, almost new headquarters at Seventeenth and F was most definitely both Up and In. A soft chime signaled that the lecture was finally ready to begin. Sam shuffled along with the now half-toasted crowd into the hotel-ballroom-style room that the Council used for larger meetings. The carpet was a distinguished charcoal gray. At the front of the room was a speaker's dais. Behind it, a Prussian blue background announced some fifty times in six-inch-high capital letters that this was THE COUNCIL ON FOREIGN RELATIONS. Presumably, those in attendance, nearly all of whom were either members of the Council or invited guests, knew where they were. But it looked good on television.

Sam took a seat toward the rear. In truth, he was eager to hear what the speaker had to say. Richard Newton was one of the brighter stars in the Washington firmament. He was dean of the Georgetown School of Foreign Service and the author of the year's most talked-about article in *Foreign Affairs* magazine, "The Not-So-Great Game," a thoughtful and scholarly essay on big-power rivalry in Central Asia. On top of that, he was one of the cofounders of the think tank of the moment, American Century. Like Newton himself, American Century was somewhere to the political right of Vlad the Impaler. And Newton was rumored to be in line for a senior job in the next Republican administration, if there ever was another one of those.

He was also an asshole.

Newton and Sam had been classmates at the Paul H. Nitze School of Advanced International Studies at Johns Hopkins nearly a quarter century ago. They say that people change as they grow older, but Sam had never met an asshole who had grown out of that particular condition. There was no reason to believe that Richard Newton was the exception to the rule.

Sam shifted awkwardly in the thinly padded plastic chair. He was uncomfortably aware of his belt buckle digging into his stomach. He was putting on weight. Janani would not have given him a hard time, but she no doubt would have started to "forget" the Ben & Jerry's on her weekly forays to Safeway.

It had been almost seven years, and Sam had not really moved on. Closing his eyes, he tried to picture his wife as he wanted to remember her: young and optimistic and full of life. But all he could see was his dear Janani lying in her room at Sibley Memorial Hospital with a plastic tube up her nose and an IV needle in her arm pumping the chemical poisons into her body that the doctors insisted were the only thing that could save her life. Over a few short weeks, she had grown weak and thin, wasting away as the cancer and the poison ate away at her insides, racing to see which could be the one to kill her. He allowed himself a brief moment of grief that almost, but not quite, crossed over into self-pity.

It was spring now. Time to get back on the bike and lose the winter weight. D.C. had built a fantastic network of bicycle trails and in good weather Sam liked to ride his Diamondback road bike to the point of exhaustion and forgetfulness.

It took nearly ten minutes for the guests to take their seats. Sam swished the scotch in his glass and listened to the ice cubes clink against one another agreeably.

The president of the Council, Dr. George Forrester, stepped up to the dais with the easy authority of a man used to commanding lecture halls. For all of the dignity that he sought to project, there was something about Forrester that reminded Sam of Ichabod Crane. He was tall and skinny, almost gangly, with a pronounced aquiline nose. It was rumored that Forrester had had LASIK surgery to help him with his tennis game, and the rectangular black-rimmed glasses he wore were a zero-prescription affectation that he hoped made him look like the university professor he never was. If so, his three-thousand-dollar bespoke suit somewhat spoiled that effect. Forrester was a "public intellectual," one of the Brahmins who moved in and out of government. When he was out, Forrester's home was one or more of the higher-end think tanks. The president of the Council on Foreign Relations was at the very top of that particular pyramid.

"Council members, ladies and gentlemen," he began. "Our guest of honor tonight needs no introduction." Forrester paused and there was the somewhat mischievous look on his face of a man about to tell a joke that he is quite certain is hysterically funny. "But *he* needs the introduction."

The audience laughed in self-knowing fashion. The Washington elite loved to poke fun at their own pomposity and self-importance. Ironically, Sam thought, this only made them seem somehow even more pompous and self-important. Still, Sam laughed along with the others. It was pretty funny, if only because it was largely accurate. Sitting on a comfortable leather chair next to the podium, Richard Newton smiled at the joke that was ostensibly, but not really, at his expense.

Forrester offered a brief synopsis of the featured speaker's many accomplishments and awards. Sam couldn't help but think about his own, much skinnier résumé. He and Newton had started from essentially the same place. Now Sam was in the back of the lecture hall and Richard Newton was listening to his praises being sung at CFR. Newton had made his career in Washington and Sam had spent most of his overseas. "Out of sight, out of mind" was an old D.C. axiom, but Sam was self-aware enough to know that there was more to that particular story.

"Dr. Newton has most recently turned his impressive intellect to the challenges of nuclear rivalry on the Indian subcontinent," Forrester continued, after finishing up the résumé part of his introduction. "His original and penetrating analysis has helped reshape our understanding of the volatile India-Pakistan dynamic and has focused global attention on Kashmir, the single point on the planet most likely to trigger a major regional and even potentially global conflict."

Sam leaned forward in his chair, genuinely eager to hear what Newton had to say. His interest in the subject of the lecture was deeply personal. Sam was a South Asia specialist. His graduate school research had focused on the history of peacemaking efforts in Kashmir. Richard Newton, meanwhile, had written his thesis and his first book on Soviet foreign policy. He had always been drawn to power. The end of the Soviet Union had almost been the end of his career, but Newton had found a way to reinvent himself as a foreign policy generalist, a "big thinker" as happy to pontificate on Northern Ireland as on South Africa.

On the side, he ran a lucrative international consulting business and Sam had heard from people in a position to know that the government of Pakistan was one of his confidential clients. If true, that certainly called into question his ability to express impartial judgments. Still, Newton was both extremely sharp and extremely well connected. Sam wanted to hear what he had to say about the fascinatingly complex Kashmir puzzle. He would just have to price-in a possible pro-Pakistan bias. Everyone, he reasoned, had his or her own particular blinders.

Newton had excelled at SAIS, earning his degree in a near-record four years. Sam, in contrast, had never quite finished his dissertation. In truth, Sam knew, he wasn't really cut out for the ivory towers of academia. He liked getting his hands dirty. Eventually, he had left SAIS to join the U.S. Foreign Service, spending most of his twenty-five years in the State Department bouncing around the subcontinent, including stints in Mumbai, New Delhi, Islamabad, and Karachi. It had been a good career, if not a spectacularly successful one. If he could rewind the tape, he wouldn't have done it differently.

Mumbai is where he had met Janani. She would be almost

forty-nine now. Sam was already a few months to the wrong side of fifty. He did not like thinking about that. Somehow, he had already made it onto the AARP mailing lists. They were relentless. Hell, it was probably AARP that had found Osama bin Laden when he turned fifty and qualified for a free subscription to the magazine.

"Dr. Newton is certainly among our best and brightest," Forrester concluded. "He is also, it probably goes without saying, a long-standing member of the Council on Foreign Relations. He's fallen a little behind on his dues payments and has agreed to speak to you all tonight rather than wash the dishes from the CFR dining room. Thank you for coming tonight, Richard. This should cover about six months of the arrears."

Newton laughed as he stepped up to the dais and the microphone. He looked like the power broker he was. His silver hair was gelled firmly in place. His spring tan hinted at a recent Caribbean vacation or maybe skiing in Davos. A video-friendly striped red tie stood out in sharp relief against the background of a blue suit and crisp white shirt. He spoke without notes.

"Thank you, George. I hope you know that I'm still waiting on the check from the magazine for 'The Not-So-Great Game.' I think we're square."

The audience laughed politely. Forrester nodded and smiled.

"Friends, colleagues," Newton said, suddenly serious. "You should, all of you should, lie awake at night worrying about the India-Pakistan relationship. North Korea and Iran get the lion's share of the headlines, but if at some point in the next twenty years, our world is consumed by nuclear fire, rest assured that the spark for that conflagration will almost certainly have been struck in Kashmir."

The contested state of Jammu and Kashmir was the most serious point of contention in the fraught relationship between New Delhi and Islamabad. For complex historical and political reasons, the Muslim-majority province had remained part of mostly Hindu India when the British Raj had dissolved in 1947 rather than being attached to the new Dominion of Pakistan. In the half century that followed, the province triggered at least three wars between the two giants of South Asia. That had meant one thing when the bitter rivals had been too poor to fight a truly modern war. It meant something quite different now that they were both substantial nuclear powers.

Newton offered a relatively straightforward account of the Kashmir conflict that Sam thought was somewhat vanilla and unoriginal. The audience, however, seemed to hang on every word as though the speaker were on the cusp of offering some great revelation. Maybe Sam had been expecting too much. Newton was no doubt pitching his speech to a wider audience than South Asia specialists. It may have been unavoidable that the guts of the speech felt cobbled together by graduate students or junior researchers.

"Conditions along the Line of Actual Control are tense," Newton continued. "As tense as they have been since the 1999 Kargil War. Moreover, the political relationship between New Delhi and Islamabad is at a new low. While the Pakistani government must surely shoulder its share of the responsibility, the new Indian prime minister must be held to account for his contribution to the growing crisis. Prime Minister Rangarajan has antagonized his Pakistani counterpart and has consistently rejected Islamabad's overtures aimed at securing a political solution."

"That's bullshit, Richard."

Sam looked around, wondering who had said that, before realizing sheepishly that he was responsible. For a brief moment, he clung to the hope that he had only whispered it, but the substantial number of heads turning in his direction argued otherwise. There was a boom mike suspended from a long pole hanging directly over where he was sitting. It was there for the Q&A session that was supposed to follow the lecture, but Sam realized with a creeping sense of dread that someone had left it on. His sotto voce intervention had been caught out by every Washington politician's nightmare—the hot mike.

Newton paused and looked out over the audience to spot the heckler. There were maybe a hundred people in the lecture hall. He quickly zeroed in on Sam.

"Sam, is that you?"

"Sorry for the interruption, Richard. I didn't mean to say that out loud."

"I'm quite sure you didn't. But having done so, I'd like to hear what you have to say. Ladies and gentlemen, for those of you who don't know my old classmate Sam Trainor, I can assure you that I am quite used to Sam's somewhat impolitic interventions . . . at least in seminar."

"Really, Richard, I apologize. I don't want to interrupt the talk. I was just thinking that Rangarajan has bent over backwards to accommodate the sensibilities of the generals in Pakistan. He offered President Talwar a state visit, proposed the creation of an intelligence-sharing council aimed at minimizing the risk of overreactions stemming from misunderstanding, and even quashed a move by the opposition to authorize construction of a temple to Vishnu at Ayodhya on the ruins of the Babri Mosque. That hardly sounds like the work of a guy beating the drums of war."

Even though he had pushed Sam to speak, Dr. Richard Newton seemed somewhat at a loss. Sam suspected that Newton's thinking was very rarely challenged by the sycophants who surrounded him at the think tanks. Newton, however, had been in Washington long enough to have absorbed its mores and rules of behavior. One tried-and-true D.C. tactic was: If you don't like the message, attack the messenger.

"Thank you, Sam, for that pithy and insightful riposte. Pity you couldn't have put that down on paper. Maybe you would have managed to finish that Ph.D."

Sam's ears burned at the gratuitous slap. Newton was so much farther up the food chain than Sam that it seemed completely uncalled-for.

"You may have something there, Dr. Newton," he found himself saying even as half his brain willed him to shut up and take his lumps. "I never did get the degree, but I do know that the Line of Actual Control is the effective border between India and China, not between India and Pakistan. That's the Line of Control. You're a former Soviet guy slumming in South Asia as a paid consultant for the Pakistani government. But, for those of us who know the region, the two are as different from each other as England and New England."

Newton turned beet red and the Washington sophisticates in the CFR lecture hall turned away from Sam. It was difficult to tell whether they were embarrassed for him or by him. Newton resumed speaking. Sam did not really resume listening. He knew that he had dug himself a hole that would take time to climb out of.

After the lecture, the ever-efficient CFR staff served coffee and cake in an adjacent room with a panoramic wall of windows that offered a less-than-inspiring view of the boxlike office buildings lining F Street. Sam helped himself to a cup of coffee from the samovar and decided to skip the cake as both a form of penance and as a symbol of his resolve to get back into shape. As he walked around the room, Sam marveled at the new superpower he seemed to have acquired after his ill-advised confrontation with Richard Newton. He seemed to project an invisible force field that kept everyone else in the room at a distance of at least six feet. One senior Pentagon civilian almost tripped over his own feet in his rush to avoid engaging Sam in conversation. He was radioactive at this point and he could only hope that the half-life of his professional ostracism would be mercifully brief. This was not his first experience with the consequences of pointing out the emperor's state of undress.

"Making friends fast, Sam."

"I seem to have a talent for it, Andy."

"You know you shouldn't do stuff like that."

"I know."

Andy Krittenbrink was one of Sam's favorite colleagues—former colleagues, he reminded himself—and he was glad for the company. Krittenbrink was a young analyst in the State Department's Bureau of Intelligence and Research, which in the intel world was known by the almost accurate acronym INR. He was a specialist in the Pakistani leadership. Until a few months ago, INR had been Sam's home institution as well. As the director of the bureau's South Asia office, he had been Andy's nominal boss. It was a lofty-sounding title, but, for a Foreign Service officer, INR was something of an elephant's graveyard for diplomatic careers. That Sam's evaluations were peppered with words such as *abrasive*, *intemperate*, and the more euphemistic but no less damning *outspoken* did not help his cause.

The Foreign Service, like the military, was a rank-in-person, up-or-out system. A civil servant could burrow into a position in the federal government and, assuming even a minimum level of competence, could essentially stay in the job until mandatory retirement at age seventy. The Foreign Service was more dog-eat-dog. At every grade, an officer had a fixed number of years to earn a competitive promotion against his or her peers. Fail to make the cut and your reward was early retirement. The jump from FS-01 into the Senior Foreign Service was equivalent to the jump from colonel to brigadier general. It was also where the most drastic cuts in numbers were made. FSOs called it the "Threshold." INR was not a good springboard for making the leap, and Sam had failed to clear the Threshold on his final try. After that, it was just a matter of how long it took Human Resources to finish the retirement paperwork.

"So how is life in the real world? Are things as green as they say on the other side of the fence?" Krittenbrink's Adam's apple jumped up and down excitedly when he talked. His suit was at least two sizes too big across the shoulders. It looked like something he had borrowed from his father. Andy was the quintessential career analyst. A little schlubby, socially awkward, and sharp as a razor. As one Washington wag had once observed, you could spot the extrovert in the CIA's analytical division, the Directorate of Intelligence, because he looked at *your* shoes when he talked to you.

"Not too bad," Sam replied. "I took a job at Argus Systems in Arlington. They just got a big contract with the Agency to provide intelligence and analysis on South Asia, and I'm heading up the Indo-Pak team. It's not too different from what I was doing in INR, so the learning curve's not too steep."

"I still don't understand why you didn't get promoted into the

Seniors," Andy said. "You were the best South Asia specialist in the department. It seems criminal to lose you."

Sam smiled ruefully.

"Thanks, Andy. I appreciate the support. But you said it yourself. I was a specialist. That's not a good thing to be at State. You're civil service, and they hired you to be an expert in what you do. In the Foreign Service, we're all supposed to be generalists, and there are consequences for being too specialized. I spent too much time in South Asia. My choice, and I loved every minute of it, so I can't complain."

"This wouldn't have anything to do with that time you told the assistant secretary to go to hell, would it? You were dead right."

"Maybe. But that's not the point. Look at Richard and learn something from him. You're young. You've got time. He's spread so thin that he may not know very much about the issues he speaks and writes about, but he is as smooth as eighteen-year-old scotch and he plays the Washington political game as well as any elected official. Don't underestimate that. It's a real skill. It's just not mine."

"I was sorry to see you go. You were a great boss. The guy who came in behind you couldn't find Bangladesh on a map of South Asia. Heck, I'm not sure he could find it on a map of Bangladesh."

"I was sorry to leave. But I've made my peace with it. Let me be the voice of experience. Don't fight with the new guy. Take it from me, there's no percentage in it." Privately, Sam wondered whether he really had accepted his forced retirement from diplomacy and the move to the private sector. He was ambivalent at best about taking a job at a Beltway Bandit consultancy, and he had thought hard about moving away to some small town in Montana or the Pacific Northwest and maybe finally finishing the Ph.D. He had even considered renting some fishing shack on the beach in Goa. In the end, there were personal ties that had kept him in Washington, and the job at Argus at least allowed him to stay in the policy game. It was a good holding position. Fortunes could swing rapidly in Washington. There was no telling what the future might hold. For now, he wanted to offer his onetime subordinate the best advice he could. Andy had a promising career in front of him if he could learn to play the game better than Sam had.

"I don't want to fight," Andy agreed. "But the layers of bureaucracy can wear you down. I don't really like the way the intel machinery polishes all of the sharp edges of what we write. In the end, it's all mushy, lowest-common-denominator analysis and I think that's a disservice to the policy makers."

"You're almost certainly right about that. We have a little more freedom at Argus and my team tries to take full advantage of that. It's our job to speak truth to power, but don't expect that they'll love you for it. Powerful and successful people will all tell you that they don't want to be surrounded by sycophants and yes-men and every one of them is lying."

Andy shook his head in disbelief.

"I know you're right. But I didn't come to Washington because I wanted to get ahead. I came here because I wanted to do big things. I wanted to make a difference in the world. The only thing I'm making now is condo payments."

"You will make a difference, Andy. I'm sure of it. Patience, young grasshopper." Krittenbrink had not been born when *Kung Fu* went off the air, but Sam was confident that he was geeky enough to get the reference.

The young analyst did not disappoint.

"Thank you, Master Po."

00:02

Y ou know you can't do things like that, Sam. You are your
own worst enemy."

Vanalika Chandra stretched languidly on the bed, the
sheets still tousled and slightly damp from sex. She arched her back
slightly. It was just one more thing she did that reminded Sam of a
cat. He ran his finger lightly across her thigh. Her skin was the
color of cinnamon.

"I know," Sam acknowledged. He'd just finished telling Vanalika about his unfortunate exchange with Richard Newton the
night before. "It was not my finest hour. The worst part is that I
kind of enjoyed it. Newton is living proof that you can be a stuffed
shirt and an empty suit at the same time, and I liked being the one
to expose that for all to see."

"You don't understand." Vanalika sat up and Sam let his gaze
wander idly for a brief moment over her perfect body. "All of the
people in that room feel like you made Richard Newton look. Yes,
they're arrogant narcissists, but they also suffer from imposter

syndrome. They wake up every morning asking themselves if today's the day. The day they get caught. Exposed as ignorant frauds who don't know enough or aren't smart enough or wise enough to be in the positions they're in. They're all insecure little children underneath. What you did to Newton you could have done to any of them. He just made the mistake of speaking carelessly in front of someone who both knows what he's talking about and has no idea what's good for him."

Vanalika reached for a pack of Marlboros on the nightstand.

"Now who doesn't know what's good for her?" Sam asked, as he lit her cigarette with the Bic lighter that had been set next to the cigarettes.

"I'm cutting back," Vanalika protested. "I only smoke after sex, and even then only after good sex. That means my husband doesn't know. He thinks I quit six months ago."

"And how is Rajiv?"

"Dull. And traveling a lot, fortunately."

Vanalika, the political counselor at the Indian Embassy in Washington, was married to a wealthy and powerful Indian businessman. It had been an arranged marriage, but whatever advantage their families had hoped to gain from their union had been made moot by the couple's failure to have children. A blessing, Vanalika had once confessed to Sam. She and Rajiv remained married more out of habit and duty than because either of them was really invested.

It had been almost a year since she and Sam had become lovers. It was an illicit affair. Vanalika, in particular, would face both personal and professional disgrace should it become public. Sam was not much safer. He was employed by Argus Systems, but Diplomatic Security owned his clearances. Not without reason, DS considered adulterous relationships with foreign government officials an open invitation to blackmail. If the State Department knew about his relationship with Vanalika, DS would strip Sam of his clearances—and his access to classified information—in less time than it would take to soft-boil an egg. They were careful. This weekend was one of the few they had been able to steal. The cabin in the Shenandoah Valley was a three-hour drive from the Beltway. It was rented in a false name and isolated enough that there was no cell reception.

Vanalika flicked the ash from her cigarette into a glass ashtray advertising Greenwood Mountain Lodges and leaned back against the pillows.

"You seem a little down for a man who just got lucky with an incredible exotic fox. Please tell me that what Newton said didn't get to you. He was just being spiteful because you wounded his pride."

"No, it's not Newton," Sam replied. "At least not what he said. But I can't help comparing where he is with where I am. Argus was a nice soft landing spot for me after the State Department and I came to our parting of ways. But I miss it. I'm not happy with the way it ended, and I'm not thrilled about being at a Beltway Bandit. I never saw myself bellying up to the government trough as a contractor. Somehow, I always thought I'd have a little more self-respect."

"Times change, Sam. There's no shame in what you're doing. Contractors are doing more and more of the heavy lifting in your government. Mine too, but Delhi has a long way to go before it catches up with Washington."

"That's just the point. It was one thing when federal agencies were outsourcing noncore functions. I don't especially care who runs the State Department cafeteria, for example. That's not an inherently governmental responsibility. But these contracting firms are sprouting up in the D.C. area like mushrooms or Starbucks. They've gone from running the Pentagon's shuttle-bus service to making government policy. Argus works on national security. That's about as 'core' a function as I can think of."

"In which case, the American people are lucky that you're the one doing the job. I'm sure you'll be a star. Maybe I can leak you some classified information just to make sure that you get off on the right foot."

"Got anything good?"

"Well, I hear that the Indian political counselor is having a torrid affair."

"Do tell. Is it serious?"

"Very." She giggled.

"I'm still not sure I see the harm in the contracting boom," Vanalika continued. "Governments are big and slow, and private companies can often do things faster and cheaper. What does it really matter as long as the work is getting done and getting done well?"

"Look, I know a guy at the CIA who's worked on analyzing satellite imagery for twenty years. It's pretty tedious work, but it's important and highly technical. He's the guy who can tell you when the North Koreans are getting ready to launch a missile. He'd also be the first to tell you that he was glad for the steady work and government benefits, but he did the job because he was a patriot and he was helping to keep his country safe. A few weeks ago, he left the CIA and took a job at True North, a fairly typical consultancy with a contract to analyze overhead imagery for the Agency. You know budgets are tight when even Langley is looking to downsize. This guy resigned on Friday and was back at the same office on Monday doing the same thing at twice the salary. The only difference is that now he's got a red contractor badge rather than a blue Agency badge. Oh, and one more thing. He's no longer sworn to uphold and defend the Constitution. Now he's responsible to his corporate masters and the company's shareholders. What he's doing is ultimately about profit and loss, and that feels wrong. Not as wrong as Richard Newton, mind you, but wrong."

Vanalika frowned slightly and her forehead furrowed as though she were suddenly deep in thought. She had an agile mind that allowed her to skip lightly from topic to topic, and if Sam wasn't careful, he sometimes found himself a beat or two behind in their conversations.

"Are you sure that Newton is wrong?" she asked. "About Rangarajan, I mean. I'm worried about the damage he could do to the relationship with Pakistan even inadvertently. He's young and inexperienced. Some of the decisions he's made could be seen in Islamabad as provocative. Certainly Talwar seems to see it that way. You and I have read the same intel reports. The things the Pakistanis are saying in private are alarming and unremittingly hostile. Talwar neither fears nor respects Rangarajan. We don't need both, but to have neither seems a very dangerous set of circumstances."

"Rangarajan's got to walk a fine line," Sam agreed. "But he's no babe in the woods. You don't get to the top of the Congress Party without good political instincts and an understanding of power. He knows he can't push Talwar and the clerics too hard, but neither can he afford to look like a pushover himself. That's not an easy balance to strike. I'm not saying that he's always got it right. But I think he's doing okay. And I believe he's genuinely committed to peace with Pakistan."

"God, I hope so," Vanalika said. She left her cigarette smoldering in the ashtray and laid her head on Sam's shoulder. Her hair was jet-black and thick and smelled of lavender. Vanalika was not a classic beauty. Her nose, for one thing, was just a little too prominent and a little off center, the result of a childhood horse-riding accident she had once told Sam. In repose, she was rather ordinary-looking, but she had a megawatt smile and dark eyes that sparkled with intelligence and wit. To Sam, she was beautiful and challenging, and he was grateful for the time they had together.

Vanalika sat up to retrieve her cigarette.

"I just can't image that either side really wants a war," she said, "no matter how tense things get in Kashmir."

"They don't need to want it. They just need to choose it. There are some things they'll want even less than war. When it comes to issues of pride and identity, nations and leaders can be almost unbelievably shortsighted. No one in power wants to look weak, and when leaders get caught in the kind of standoff Talwar and Rangarajan are in right now, it can be easier for them to go down the road to war than the road to peace. It sometimes seems the path of least resistance. At first. What comes later is something else. No one ever seems more surprised by war and its costs than the leaders who make that particular choice."

"Peace has its own perils," Vanalika observed. "Rangarajan has reached out to Talwar, but the clerics in Islamabad have broken every agreement they've signed so far. If Rangarajan is seen as weak, the Pakistanis will just keep pushing and taking until there's nothing left to take."

"I'm not saying you need to ask these guys to the prom. I'm just saying that Rangarajan is right to be looking for some kind of compromise. Geography is destiny, and India and Pakistan just can't escape each other."

"Not every situation is amenable to compromise. What if the European powers of the day, horrified by the violence of Shiloh and Antietam, had sent peacekeepers to America to separate the North and the South in your civil war and force a negotiated settlement? Would the world be a better place? Sometimes victory may be the best outcome to conflict even if the costs are terrible. Sometimes, maybe, it's worth any price."

"The Union and the Confederacy fought with ironclad warships and muzzle-loading rifles," Sam replied. "India and Pakistan have nuclear weapons and long-range missiles. Once you cross the nuclear Rubicon, there's no going back. You need to find a way to live together without killing each other."

"Kind of like my marriage," Vanalika suggested.

"Exactly like your marriage," Sam agreed.

"Vanalika," he said, suddenly serious. "Why don't you leave him? Move in with me. We can stop skulking around. Maybe even go out to dinner in D.C. in a restaurant with a wine list instead of a selection of light beers in a can."

"Sam, we've been over this," Vanalika replied, with a hint of reproof in her voice. "I like what we are. I don't need more. I don't want more. Rajiv is a snake, but I know how to handle snakes. He doesn't make me happy; he doesn't make me unhappy either. You make me happy, Sam. Even so, we'd never make it as a real couple. And, in any event, you're living with someone already."

"The boxes of Indian takeout piling up in my fridge would beg to differ. Who, pray tell, is my live-in love?"

"Janani. You've been living with her ghost for seven years. A mere flesh-and-blood girl could never measure up to that kind of competition." Vanalika reached over and gently stroked his cheek. "We have a good thing here. Don't spoil it by trying to rescue me from the dark knight. I don't need rescuing."

"Do you really think my motives are so simon-pure? Maybe I'm just in it for the sex."

"You do seem to have a thing for Indian girls. Am I just the latest in a string of South Asian conquests? Another jewel in the crown?" She smiled as she said this to show that she did not mean anything unkind.

"That's right. I'm a Mughal emperor and you're my barbarian princess."

"Oh, come on. Talk to me. You know everything there is to know about Rajiv, and I know next to nothing about your past. I don't mind sharing you with Janani. I just want to know what she was like. Are you with me because I remind you of her?"

"No. She was different than you."

"Different how?" Vanalika wrapped her fingers around Sam's and pulled his hand up to her lips. She kissed his knuckles softly.

"You're a Brahmin, Vee. You grew up in comfort with power and privilege. You wear it well. It looks good on you. But you wear it easily because you've never known anything else. Janani was Dalit."

He felt Vanalika stiffen almost imperceptibly at that revelation. It was so slight that she might not even have been aware of it, but with her body pressed up against his, Sam could feel it.

"Really?" she asked.

"Really."

Vanalika shifted onto one elbow. There was a gleam in her eye as though he had just told her something shocking or salacious. Sam understood why this piece of information about his former spouse would be so titillating. The Dalit were untouchables, members of the so-called unscheduled castes whose ancestors had been tanners or butchers or laborers doing work that the Hindu religion considered unclean. The structure of the caste system was complex and multidimensional, with four major castes and literally thousands of subdivisions. But however you looked at it, the Brahmins were at the top and the Dalit were on the bottom. Caste was a rough analogue to race in the United States. Officially, discrimination on the basis of caste was against the law in modern India. There were affirmative action programs in place for low-caste Indians at universities, in government ministries, and in state-run businesses. There had even been a Dalit president of the country. Life for the lower castes had definitely improved over the last twenty years, but prejudice remained, buried just under the surface. And it ran deep, especially in rural areas. High-caste families would not dream of letting their children "marry down." Sam doubted that Vanalika, who was from the highest echelons of Indian society, had many—if any—Dalit friends.

"Janani was from Dharavi," Sam explained. That in itself was a powerful statement. Dharavi was one of Mumbai's largest slums, a million people living in an area half the size of Central Park, most without running water or reliable electricity. Janani had been born into poverty and, by all rights, she should have died in poverty. But there had been a spark to her, a drive.

"Her parents died when she was young and one of the convent orphanages took her in. Somehow, she stayed in school when nearly all of her classmates dropped out to work, or beg, or marry, or steal. She had a talent for art, and the nuns helped her get a scholarship to the University of Mumbai. When I met her, she was running her own graphic-design company. It was small but growing. She had her own apartment. She had made it all the way out. There are not many who do. Most of those who make it out cut all their ties to their former lives. After we got married, Janani could have left Dharavi behind her forever. As the wife of an American diplomat, she could have essentially ceased being Dalit. She wouldn't do that. She taught art to Dalit kids and worked with various aid agencies active in Dharavi right up until she died. She was"—Sam paused as he grappled for the right word—"extraordinary." The word was a poor stand-in for how Sam felt, but it would have to do.

"I know that I'm the one who is technically married, but I can't help being a little bit jealous of Janani. I hope she doesn't mind."

"Quite the contrary. She'd like that. Janani never shied away from a little competition."

Sam reached over Vanalika for the iPhone that was sitting on the nightstand. Argus had offered him a government-standard BlackBerry, but the IT department was willing to at least tolerate his iPhone, something the more controlling State Department would never do. He glanced at the screen. There was still no reception.

"The one woman in my life I really need to talk to I can't reach," he complained.

"Lena?"

"Yeah. It's her birthday. She's twenty-four today. What does that make me? Thirty-eight, maybe?"

Vanalika laughed. "Don't worry. You're not old, Sam. You have some miles on you. But the warranty's still good." Vanalika was almost ten years younger than Sam. She teased him about his age occasionally, but always gently, as though she knew he was sensitive about it. Sam was not one of those men who felt compelled to fend off awareness of their own creeping mortality by chasing after much younger partners. He had had opportunities. Women, he knew, found him attractive, even if in something of an unconventional way. One former girlfriend had described his appeal as "nerd chic."

"I'll tell you what," Vanalika continued. "Why don't you get dressed and go get us a bottle of wine at that place we passed on the way in. There should be reception down there and you can call Lena. And I'd like a bottle of West Virginia's finest cabernet."

"You want some pâté on a crusty baguette to go with that? Maybe a moon rock or a piece of the true Cross?"

"Just go," Vanalika said, pushing him playfully toward the edge of the bed. "If you can find even a halfway decent bottle of wine, I'll find a suitable way to reward you. I promise."

Sam dressed quickly and stepped out into the crisp chill. Up here in the mountains, winter had not quite released its grip. The drive down to Mathias took no more than fifteen minutes. In honor of his daughter, Sam popped Lena Horne's 1962 album *Lena on the Blue Side* into the CD player and listened to her velvet voice as he steered his Prius down the dark and windy road. He and Janani had shared a love for Lena Horne's music, and they had listened to her so much through the course of the pregnancy that it seemed a natural choice to give her name to their daughter. In a box somewhere in the attic of their Capitol Hill townhouse, Sam still had the vinyl LPs they had played.

Mathias had a family-style restaurant, a general store, and three bars of cell reception. Sam parked in front of the general store and used his Skype app to make a call to Mumbai. It would be morning there, but Lena was an early riser. She picked up on the third ring.

"Hello."

"Hi, sweetie. Happy birthday."

"Dad. How are you?"

"Except for the part where I'm eight thousand miles away from my little girl, I'm pretty good."

Lena had moved back to Mumbai after finishing her master's degree in electrical engineering at Stanford University. She could have had her pick of jobs in the United States, but Lena said that she wanted a chance to live on her own in her mother's hometown for at least a while, not as a "dependent" of the U.S. consulate, but as an Indian. She had a job at a high-tech start-up and an apartment in a modest building only a short distance from the Dharavi slums. Her real labor of love, however, was the school she ran in Dharavi, teaching science, math, and engineering to Dalit and other lower-caste children. They spoke at least once a week, and Sam was already planning his first private-sector junket to the region that would include a stop in Mumbai.

"What's new on your end?" he asked, after catching her up on the latest family gossip and the early reports on the Nationals' spring training.

"I'm struggling a bit here, Dad, with the city bureaucracy. There's a developer who wants to bulldoze Mom's old neighborhood and turn it into a gated community for the uberrich. Uncle Ramananda and I are trying to stop it, but the developer has some powerful allies and I don't know if we're going to succeed."

Jarapundi Ramananda was the unofficial mayor of Dharavi, a con artist, an organized-crime figure of some repute, and a close friend of Sam's from his days at the consulate in Mumbai. He was also Lena's godfather. Sam liked Ramananda tremendously, but he did not necessarily trust him. He hoped Lena was mature enough to understand the difference.

"I have confidence in you, honey. But be careful with your uncle. I'm sure he has his own agenda."

"He always does. But I think there's considerable overlap between his and mine at this point."

"All right. Keep me posted. Let me know if there's some way you think I can help."

"I love you, Daddy."

"I love you too, sweetheart. Happy birthday."

After they hung up, Sam sat in the dark car for a minute or so, thinking about how much he missed his daughter. He was proud of her and the woman she was becoming. Lena was the one thing in his life, he thought, that he had gotten absolutely right.

As luck would have it, the Mathias General Store catered to the D.C. tourist trade as well as to local tastes. He found a perfectly acceptable California cabernet nestled between a case of Miller High Life and an enormous stack of Ring Dings. When he got back to the cabin, Vanalika was still in bed.

She was true to her word.

ARLINGTON, VIRGINIA
MARCH 31

00:03

Those commuters who rode the Orange Line into the District from the distant suburbs of northern Virginia referred to the experience as the Orange Crush. The metro had been designed for a more genteel time and a ridership less than half the size of the crowd who piled on at stops from Vienna to Rosslyn. Federal drones on the Orange Crush, dressed in drab trench coats with plastic ID cards hanging around their necks on cheap metal lanyards, were packed in cheek-by-jowl in a morning rush hour that seemed to expand in both directions by a few minutes every year. The rush now lasted from about six-thirty until well after nine. There was no escaping it. It was an unpleasant way to start the workday, which is why a basement-level parking pass was the ultimate status symbol in nearly every federal agency.

The reverse commute from downtown to the inner suburbs was not nearly as bad. Sam's ride in from Capitol Hill to Argus Systems headquarters in Arlington was an easy twenty-minute trip. On most mornings, he got a seat and the chance to finish the *Washington*

Post on the way in to work. Usually, he read the heavy news over breakfast and the train ride out to Ballston was for the sports page and the comics. This Monday morning, however, Sam was rereading every Washington insider's favorite gossip column, Al Kamen's "In the Loop." There was a three-paragraph report in the column about Sam's embarrassing Richard Newton at the CFR event on Friday.

Talking to a reporter about who said what in a closed CFR meeting was an egregious violation of the Council's rules, but there were few real secrets in the nation's capital. Not for long, in any event. Only a fool would say something at a Council meeting he wouldn't want to see in the *Washington Post*. Sam felt like a fool. One of Newton's competitors or enemies—and while there was a difference between the two, it could sometimes be hard to tell them apart—had evidently decided there was some advantage in outing the exchange between Sam and the powerful chairman of American Century. Anonymously, of course. Kamen could always be relied upon for discretion, which was clearly more than could be said of the CFR membership. Newton was the target. Sam was collateral damage. He was too small a fish for Al Kamen's readership to care about. Everyone read Kamen. There was no way that Sam wasn't going to hear about this at the office.

Argus headquarters occupied almost half a block of high-end real estate three blocks south of the metro. On one side of the building there was a Gold's Gym. On the other was a strip mall with a veritable United Nations of small businesses, including a Vietnamese noodle restaurant, a Korean dry cleaner, a halal butcher, and a Peruvian rotisserie chicken joint. Arlington, like much of fast-growing northern Virginia, was an eclectic mix of middle-class feds, old Southern families, and new immigrants. One of the best things about immigrants, Sam believed, was the restaurants they brought with them. He was a regular at the Vietnamese place where the former sergeant in the Army of the Republic of Vietnam who ran it referred to him unironically as "Uncle Sam." The wall behind the Formica bar in the restaurant was decorated with a mix of U.S. and South Vietnamese flags and laminated *National Geographic* maps of Vietnam that predated the fall of Saigon. Ethnic food was the second way Americans learned about global geography. The first, of course, was war.

The Argus building itself was unprepossessing, a utilitarian concrete-and-glass structure that looked like so many other similar structures spreading out from the city center. Their growth was uneven, not in concentric rings like a tree but in long tendrils interwoven with major roads that blossomed around the metro stations. The strings of office parks were like some kind of aggressive vine growing up a garden lattice and watered by the seemingly endless stream of money that had been flowing without a break since that sad September morning now more than ten years in the past.

A small sign at the front gate announced in sensible navy blue lettering that the building was home to ARGUS SYSTEMS. The "A" in ARGUS was an almost perfect equilateral triangle and the top half was a stylized Eye of Providence similar to the pyramid on the back of a dollar bill. Those like Sam who knew what to look for could see the telltale hallmarks of a building where people processed classified information. A high fence surrounded the facility. The elegant finials looked decorative but were, in fact, designed to make the fence harder to scale. Two thick wires running along the top could, Sam suspected, be electrified. He had never wanted to ask. There were numerous cameras visible and no doubt others that were not. The windows were narrow and tall and, most important, dark. There was nothing special looking about the facility, but to the experienced eye, it was far from ordinary. And far from cheap.

The guard at the gate waved Sam through with only a cursory look at his ID. Inside, Argus Systems was all about function over style. If upper management was trying to send a message to the employees through its choice of decor, it was that the company considered itself a workhorse rather than a show horse. The South Asia Unit was on the third floor. The entire floor was a SCIF, a sensitive compartmented information facility where cleared personnel could read, create, and talk about the most highly classified and tightly controlled information in the American intelligence system. The elevator opened onto a small atrium with a locked door and an armed guard. This time, the guard really did look at Sam's badge before he was allowed to key in his personal code to open the door to the analytic suites. There were a number of different units on the floor responsible for various global hot spots where Argus was under contract to the U.S. government to provide intelligence support. The Middle East Unit was the largest and, until recently, the Afghan Unit had been the most lucrative. The South Asia contract that CEO Garret Spears had signed with the CIA a few months earlier had pushed the Afghan team into the second slot. They were none too happy about it, as the office realignment had cost them a coveted location near the vending machines. Analysts, like software coders, kept strange hours and ate many of their meals out of microwave ovens with vending-machine candy bars as a chaser. There was no other way to delineate status on the third floor. Corner offices had no meaning here. The third floor had no windows.

When Sam opened the door to the unit, the buzz of conversation suddenly stopped. A tight knot of people stood bent over one of the desks. You did not need to be a psychic to know that they were looking at the *Washington Post*.

"Anything good in the papers?" Sam asked innocently.

"Boss, what did you do?" As always, Dorothy Cornett, the unit's hyperefficient admin assistant, cut right to the chase.

"Ah, nothing much. Kamen has blown it way out of proportion. It's a one-day story. No one will even remember it tomorrow. But, since it looks like we're all here, we might as well do the Monday staff meeting."

A few dramatic groans greeted this last pronouncement. The office was centered around a small cube farm where the analysts worked. Sam had a private office, but in a show of solidarity with the staff, he had had maintenance remove the door. There was a conference room that they used for meetings. The office furniture was all new and high-quality. It was also blandly generic. The staff had made an effort to decorate the space with political campaign posters from South Asia. The effect was to make the unit look like an odd parody of a teenager's room decked out in posters of rock stars or sports heroes.

The staff filed into the conference room and sat around a table that looked like it had been carved from a solid block of hard plastic. Sam considered his team. They were a mismatched assortment, but in the aggregate they were as good as any group of analysts he had ever worked with. The team had an almost implausible symmetry. Sara Zehri was a Pakistani American who was a leading authority on India, while Shushantu "Shoe" Balusibramanijan was an Indian American expert on Pakistan. The third member of the team, Ken Davenport, was a military analyst with no military experience who could not yet buy a beer in a D.C. bar without being asked for ID. They were young, wildly opinionated, and intellectually curious. Sam had grown quite fond of them in their relatively short time together.

"You've all seen the *Post* this morning," Sam began. "I've dug a little bit of a hole for myself that I'm going to have to climb out of, and I expect to get called up to the fourth floor at some point today to hear about it. So let's make sure that I'm at least smart on our issues. Otherwise, you'll be getting a new team leader, and I think I know who they'd bring in to take my place. Trust me. You wouldn't like him. Sara, why don't you start?"

Sara was smart. All the analysts were bright, but Sara was scary smart. If she had a shortcoming, it was that her intellect was unconstrained by any sense of mercy. Once she identified a weakness in an argument, or in a person making an argument, she would drill down and destroy it element by element until nothing was left. Sam had seen her do it to senior analysts from the CIA and the Defense Intelligence Agency. Men—they were all men—who were used to deference. It was simultaneously fascinating and a little repellent to watch, like looking at a school of piranhas strip a cow down to its bones one little bite at a time.

She was attractive in a rather severe way, a look she accentuated by pulling her hair back into a tight librarian-style bun that she covered with a headscarf. As far as Sam could tell, Sara's religious devotion did not go much beyond the headscarf and the halal food she brought from home. Certainly she had skipped over any verses in the Quran that advocated women being subordinate to men. A consistently stylish dresser, today she was wearing turquoise slacks with an alligator belt and a white tailored shirt. Her headscarf matched the slacks. A pair of chunky reading glasses hung on a chain around her neck.

She opened a cream-colored folder with the latest intelligence reports. Sara liked to do most of her reading on paper copies. The monitors, she claimed, gave her headaches.

"It's not good news," she said. In truth, it rarely was. At least it hadn't been in the last couple of months as India and Pakistan careened toward what many feared would be a disastrous confrontation.

"The Indian papers are pushing an anti-Pakistan, rabble-rousing line that has hardened popular attitudes," Sara continued. "Rangarajan is doing what he can, but he's increasingly boxed in by hardliners in the military. We have one report from a sensitive source that the BSP may be planning a no-confidence vote on the prime minister if he doesn't harden his stance toward Islamabad. I'll leave it to Ken to talk about the military angle on this, but the political pressure on Rangarajan is definitely building."

The Bahujan Samaj Party was the Congress Party's most important coalition partner. If the BSP pulled out, it would bring the government down and trigger new elections. In the current climate, the Hindu nationalists stood to gain the most, and the prospects for peace had the most to lose.

"Sara's right about the pressure," Ken chimed in. "And the generals aren't making it any easier for him. The Chief of the Army Staff, General Patel, is a particular problem. We have picked up a few rumors in SIGINT and HUMINT reporting about the parachute regiment under Patel's direct command developing contingency plans for the introduction of martial law, which looks like some sort of soft coup option. No word on what the triggers might be, but it's almost certainly tied in in some way with Talwar and Islamabad. I'd like to put together a piece outlining some of the possible scenarios ranging from a show of force as a tool for intimidation right up to the imposition of military rule. At this point, I don't think we can rule anything out."

Although he looked like a high school intern, Ken knew his business. He had an almost encyclopedic knowledge of the militaries in South and Central Asia, including their command structures, order of battle, hardware, and doctrine. Sam had come to trust his judgment and respect his ability to string data points together into a logical and understandable narrative. His products were easy to read and were what Sam called "senior policy maker friendly." Political heavyweights would tell you that they wanted information before making decisions, but that was not entirely accurate. They wanted reassurance. It was not information that offered this so much as a story that was comprehensible.

"Go ahead and get started on that," Sam said. "Let's aim to get something up to the fourth floor by Thursday for dissemination to the community on Friday. What about you, Shoe, what's the latest from Islamabad?"

"Like Sara said, not good." Shoe was the complete nerd package: president of the chess club and captain of both the math and debate teams in high school, B.S. in political science from Harvard, master's degree from the University of Chicago. He was one of the few people unafraid to stand toe-to-toe with Sara in an argument. They had few real professional disputes, however, and no issues stemming from their nominal ethnic and religious affiliations. The only knock-down-drag-outs in the office were over American politics. Sara was a hard-core Republican and Shoe a card-carrying Democrat. Ken, thankfully, was a libertarian who was often called on to moderate.

"Mullah Akhbar just installed himself in the presidential palace over the weekend as an 'advisor' to Talwar. That's just the latest sign that the influence of the clerics is on the rise. It looks like Barazani is on the way out at the Defense Ministry. He lost an arm-wrestling match with Yusaf Khel, who is close to the clerics. The headlines in the papers over the weekend were all about Kashmir and pretty inflammatory."

"What's Talwar's role in all this?" Sam asked. "Is he even trying to hold the line against the clerics?"

"Trying and failing," Shoe replied. "The Islamists are definitely on the ascent, helped out, mind you, by public anger at our drone-strikes program in the northwest tribal belt."

"What about recent developments in the Pakistani military?" Sam asked, turning to Ken. "Anything I should be ready to brief upstairs on?"

"There are a lot of variables," Ken cautioned. "Whatever you tell the boss, I'd hedge the bets a bit. Indications are that the religious leadership is extending its reach, particularly with the army. We've seen a rotation of senior colonels—brigade commanders—that has marginalized the most secular and put more overtly religious offi-cers in charge of critical units."

"Does that include nuclear units?"

"It does. They don't have direct control of the weapons them-selves. Those units are, for the time being, reporting directly to Talwar, but the units that control the installations where the weap-ons are based are increasingly subject to clerical influence if not yet direct control. It's really only a matter of time, however."

"You all are just a bundle of sunshine this Monday morning, aren't you?"

Shoe leaned across the table. "There's one more thing," he said in a conspiratorial whisper.

"What is it?"

"I'm worried about the intel-sharing program."

"In what way?"

"You know we have a program to share select intel with the Indian and Pakistani services?"

"Sure. In exchange for some of their reporting. It's a pretty standard arrangement."

"Well, I'm picking up echoes in our information. What we are giving the two sides is evidently volatile enough that it's getting amplified and driving the debate within their own systems. There's something of a positive feedback loop in operation. What they know about each other, or what they think they know about each other, affects what they do and the choices they make, which in turn influences what they think about each other. The program was supposed to promote transparency and information exchange in the service of peaceful dispute resolution, but it's having the opposite effect. It's making the leadership increasingly paranoid and trigger-happy."

"I'm seeing the same thing as Shoe is in Islamabad. Our intel is dominating the discussion and reinforcing the hardliners. The program needs to be scaled back in some way, because it's starting to warp the decision-making process in ways we don't entirely understand."

"I'll raise it upstairs," Sam promised. "But don't get your hopes up. Those programs are managed by the director of National Intelligence, not Argus."

Dorothy stuck her head into the conference room.

"Spears's office called," she announced. "He'd like to see you, Sam."

"When?"

"Right now."

"Tell Patty I'm on my way."

Sam took the elevator to the fourth floor where Argus CEO Garret Spears had his office. The fourth floor was more lavishly decorated than the others. The elevator opened onto a small atrium with sky-lights and tropical plants growing in oversize pots. A short corridor leading toward the north side of the building ended in a T junc-tion. To the left was Spears's office. To the right, a massive metal door with a cipher lock mounted on the center. As Sam reached the turn, a large man with acne-scarred skin was just coming out from behind the steel door. Sam recognized him as Spears's special assis-tant, John Weeder.

There was a sizeable group of men with an unmistakable mili-tary bearing who worked behind that particular door and who seemed to have no particular responsibilities. The analysts referred to them as the "Morlocks." Sam had not been read into the pro-gram, but he had a pretty good idea of what they were doing behind the door. Argus's contract with the Agency was for the collection and analysis of intelligence information on South Asia. Sam's team handled the analysis. The Morlocks, he suspected, were responsi-ble for collection. And Weeder, he believed, was the king of the Morlocks.

Weeder did not so much as register Sam's existence as he walked past him toward the elevator. His hair was not quite long enough to reach his collar, and Sam could see the tattoo on his neck, a small frog holding a trident. There was something unsettling about the man. Sam felt a slight chill as Weeder passed him, almost as if he moved inside an envelope of cold air. Sam turned left toward the office of the CEO.

Spears's secretary, Patty Delaney, was a no-nonsense Washington veteran who was unquestionably loyal to the CEO. They had been together a long time, going back to Spears's years in the navy. She kept Sam waiting for five minutes while the CEO finished up a phone call. Patty was not a big believer in idle chitchat, and she spent the time managing e-mails while Sam leafed through a copy of the salmon pink *Financial Times* from the side table and mentally rehearsed his apology. Argus had not been mentioned in Kamen's column, but the people in town who mattered would know.

"Okay," Patty said. "He's off. You can go in."

"Good morning, Sam," Garret Spears said, rising from his desk to shake hands after Patty had ushered Sam into the room.

"Morning, Garret. Welcome back." Spears had been away for the better part of the last two weeks on a business trip to Europe and the Middle East. It was a reminder for Sam that South Asia was only a small part of what Argus Systems did on behalf of the American government.

They sat in stylish black leather chairs that were paired with a matching couch and clustered around a sleek glass-and-bronze coffee table. The only sign that this was not the office of a Wall Street executive was the two-foot-square stainless-steel sliding door inset into one wall. This was a burn chute. At the end of the workday, Spears could toss his classified papers down the chute where industrial-strength shredders would chew them up before feeding the material into a smokeless furnace that reached temperatures well above the famed minimum of Fahrenheit 451. Every unit in the building had one. Spears had his own.

Without being asked, Patty brought in a silver tray with a carafe of coffee and a pair of mugs emblazoned with the Argus pyramid and the company's motto: *semper vigilans*, ever vigilant. Sam thought the motto, and the Latin, was a little pretentious. Spears considered it good business.

"This is the good stuff," Spears said, pouring the coffee. "Jamaican Blue Mountain. I did some counternarcotics work with the Jamaican services a few years back and they've kept me supplied with my drug of choice ever since."

Spears's smile was that of a politician, easy, practiced, and plastic. It was not quite enough to overcome the cruel set to his mouth. He was in his late forties and had founded Argus Systems after a twenty-year career in the navy, much of it with the Special Forces community. The Argus CEO kept his sandy blond hair shorter than the Washington norm. Sam had always suspected that this was to remind people of his professional past as a SEAL. He also kept in shape with the help of a private gym that was part of the executive suite. Even under his suit jacket, you could see that Spears had the arms and shoulders of a serious bodybuilder.

There were creases around Spears's icy blue eyes that seemed to speak of years squinting against the sun, either out to sea or in some inhospitable desert clime. Sam knew better. Before accepting the job at Argus, he had called in a few markers at DIA and reviewed Spears's classified military personnel file. Spears was a former SEAL, and he had done a few operational deployments, but he had spent the vast bulk of his navy career in the Pentagon and at the headquarters of the Joint Special Operations Command in North Carolina. He had also done a stint at the National Security Council as an advisor on counterterrorism. It was the connections Spears had developed as a "political" SEAL that had helped Argus stand out in a sea of government-contracting outfits.

The coffee was good.

"I'm sorry about the Kamen column this morning," Sam said. "I let things get a little heated with Newton. It was my mistake. I should have known better. I hope this doesn't make too much trouble for you or Argus."

"Trouble?" Spears replied. "You have it backwards. I'm glad you stuck it to Newton. He and I had it out once over some security work that we did for the Agency for International Development in Iraq and he doesn't play nice in the sandbox. I would have been happy to have Argus's name associated with anything that puts Richard Newton in his place. Maybe next time you could wear a company tie when you demolish him in public. It was well done."

This was hardly what Sam had been expecting to hear. It certainly would not have been the reaction of anyone at the State Department if he were still an active FSO. Maybe this was just one more advantage of life in the private sector.

"Thanks, Garret. I appreciate that. I'm still enough of a diplomat to want to keep my name out of the papers."

"And I'm enough of a businessman to believe that there's no such thing as bad publicity, as long as it doesn't involve a prison sentence, or at least a long prison sentence. Sam, I know it's been a while since you and I have had a chance to talk. I suppose we could go over the latest news from the region, but I'm sure you and your team are on top of all that. I don't believe in micromanaging. I would, though, like to get your take on a couple of hypotheticals."

"Sure. Shoot."

"You'll have to bear with me. The questions seem a little odd.

Understand, please. There are no right answers to any of this. This is more like the Myers-Briggs personality test. It isn't pass-fail."

"Okay." Sam was a little nonplussed at this, but it was certainly preferable to having to defend his ill-considered remarks at the CFR meeting.

"I want you to imagine that you're the sheriff in a small town in the Old West. There's been a horrible crime and a group of towns-folk are rioting, demanding justice. They have five hostages they're threatening to kill if you don't find the man responsible. You have no idea who committed the crime, but you could frame a man, and let's say for purposes of this story that he's what they used to call a no-account drifter, and hang him for the crime. That would save the hostages, all of whom are productive citizens of your town. Would you do it?"

"No," Sam replied without hesitation.

"What if you were the driver of a runaway trolley and you were going to run over a group of five workmen on the track? You could switch the car to a side track on which there was a single worker, killing only the one instead of the five. Would you do it?"

Sam actually recognized this question. It was one of a series of moral dilemmas loosely clustered together as an ethical thought experiment. It was sometimes called "trolleyology" and Sam vaguely remembered reading about it in a moral philosophy class in college. The question Spears had just posed was the most basic variant.

"Yes."

"What's the difference between the two scenarios? Don't both involve sacrificing one to save five?"

"Maybe at their most utilitarian, if the only thing you're trying to do is count. But the first seems to me to be deliberative and the second reactive."

"So it's a question of how much time you have to make a decision?"

"In part. But it also seems to me that the second scenario is binary. You only have two tracks. The first scenario includes a world of possibilities that you left out. Maybe there was a better answer to the problem than judicial murder."

Spears nodded his head and seemed to be considering his next question.

"What if the single worker on the track was a friend or a relative? Your brother, perhaps, or your son or daughter. Would you make the same choice?"

"No," Sam admitted. "Probably not."

"Is that ethical?"

"No. But I'd do it anyway."

"What if the balance was ten to one? Or ten thousand to one? What would you do?"

"I hope I never have to find out."

"One more variation," Spears said. "The last one, I promise. You're standing on a bridge watching the runaway trolley bear down on a group of workmen. You could stop the trolley by pushing a heavy weight onto the tracks. Coincidently, you are standing next to a fat man. A complete stranger who weighs three hundred pounds. Pushing him off the bridge would save the five men working on the line. Do you do it?"

"No."

"What's the difference between pushing the fat man off the bridge and switching the train onto the side track to kill the one instead of the five?"

"People are not entries on a balance sheet. We all have an internal moral compass, an inner voice in our heads and our hearts that tells us the difference between right and wrong. You need to listen to that voice even if you don't always understand why it has reached the conclusions that it has."

Spears seemed oddly disappointed by Sam's answer.

"I think that's all that I need. Thanks for bearing with me. I know this can seem a little odd, but I find this line of reasoning very helpful in what we do."

"But not helpful enough to ask the questions in the initial interview?"

"No," Spears admitted. "This isn't for everyone. I want to get to know the person first. And I only run through this exercise with a select few."

Sam knew he should leave it at that, but he also knew that he would not.

"You wouldn't hesitate, would you?" he asked.

"About what?"

"About switching tracks, framing the drifter, even pushing the fat guy off the bridge. You'd do it in a heartbeat, wouldn't you?" Sam tried not to make the question sound accusatory. He was not entirely successful.

Spears paused for maybe half a beat as he considered his response.

"Yes," he acknowledged. "Yes, I would."

LAHORE, PAKISTAN
MARCH 18

00:04

Kamran Khan was devoted to the mission. It was the single most important thing in his life after his love of Allah. He had sacrificed so much already and he was prepared, he knew in his heart, to sacrifice so much more. There were days, however, that tried his patience. Since giving himself over to jihad, Khan had spent most of his time in menial and uninspiring duties: cooking, cleaning, keeping watch, delivering the occasional package or letter to a particular person at a particular address. E-mail, cell phones, radio. All of these were dangerous. The Indians or the Americans with their computers the size of houses would find you and take for themselves that which you had hoped to keep hidden. That was why the Pakistani leadership of Haath-e-Mohammed, for all of their ambitions to liberate Kashmir from the Hindu yoke, communicated almost exclusively by courier. The couriers themselves knew nothing of what they carried. That was not their concern.

Haath-e-Mohammed meant the Hand of the Prophet. HeM, as it was called in the newspapers, or the Hand, as they called themselves, was not as well known as Lashkar-e-Taiba or some of the other top-tier jihadi groups. But the fighters as well as the leaders in HeM were righteous and committed. They would make their mark.

Kamran Khan played his part, and so far he had played it patiently. He was, however, running out of patience.

He had once asked his friend Ali, the one real friend he had made in his first five months in the Hand, why his role in the organization was so circumscribed. Ali had already been sent for training to one of the camps in Afghanistan. He had been gone for more than a month, and when he returned, he was stronger and more confident. He had already been on three missions inside occupied Kashmir. Khan was envious of his friend's success and embarrassed by that envy.

"It is simple," Ali had told him. "They don't trust you."

"Who doesn't trust me?"

"Masood Dar and the people around him." Dar was the number two person in the Hand, operations commander, and deputy to the organization's spiritual leader, Hafiz Muhammad Said.

"Why would they distrust me?" Khan asked.

"You have been to school," Ali explained. "You speak languages. You are not the usual quality of recruit we see straight out of the madras whose passion for jihad burns in the veins. Your relationship with jihad is more a matter of the head than the heart. You are smart, Khan, maybe too smart. The HeM leaders prefer their foot soldiers to be a little on the slow side. That is why I am successful."

Khan had bowed his head at that, for he knew that Masood Dar was not wrong. He was guilty of the sin of pride, like Iblis, the devil, who had refused to prostrate himself before Adam as Allah had ordered because, as a jinn, he had been made by Allah from smokeless fire while Adam was a mere creature of clay. Iblis had been cast out for his arrogance. Masood had been merciful in letting Khan remain, even if only to sweep the floors. In the three months since that conversation, Khan had endeavored to be humble in all that he did. His time would come.

Khan was working in the garden of the villa in the city of Lahore that the Hand used as a kind of informal headquarters. He was on his hands and knees, weeding around the grapevines, when Masood's secretary tapped him on the back.

"You have been summoned," he announced.

"Can I at least wash my hands?"

The secretary looked with some distaste at Khan's dirt-stained clothes.

"I think that would be a good idea."

Masood received Khan in his library. Khan looked with wonder at the walls of books with their spines labeled in Urdu and Arabic. There were even a couple of books in Russian. For a moment, Khan was struck by how much he missed books. Here, the Quran was the only book he read. It was the most important book in the world, he knew, but he was not among those who believed it to be the only book worth reading. Neither, evidently, was Masood.

The mullah was a heavyset man with a long and somewhat unkempt black beard. Oversize tortoiseshell glasses gave him something of an owlish appearance. He wore a white skullcap and a tunic with a vest. His feet were bare.

"As-salamu alaykum," Khan said, with a slight bow.

"Sit," Masood commanded.

There were chairs in the library, but Masood was sitting on the floor, which was where Khan sat. He rested one arm on an overstuffed pillow and accepted a cup of green tea that the secretary served from a copper tray. The tea, called *kahwah*, was boiled with saffron, cinnamon, and cardamom.

Khan sipped his tea somewhat uncomfortably as Masood looked him over as though he were inspecting vegetables in the marketplace.

"How long have you been with us?" he asked.

"Almost eight months, Janab," Khan said, using the formal title that was the closest approximation to "sir."

"And in those eight months, what have you done for us?"

"I have kept house, Janab. I have delivered messages. I have done what has been asked of me."

"And does that satisfy you?"

"No, it does not."

"You would like to do more for the organization, would you? More for jihad? For Kashmir?"

"I would, Janab."

"You will have your opportunity."

Khan said nothing, but he felt his heart quicken slightly.

"You speak languages," Masood said. It was not a question.

Khan nodded agreement.

"How is your English?"

"It is excellent." Khan spoke in English and was rewarded with a slight smile from Masood.

"I need a translator," the mullah explained. "For a meeting that must remain secret. My regular interpreter is too ill to travel. Everything you do with respect to this event you will carry with you to the grave. If you do anything that causes me to question your loyalty and obedience, you will find yourself explaining your choices to Allah somewhat earlier than you otherwise might."

"I understand, Janab."

"Do you? Do you really?"

Masood did not tell Khan where they were going. But only an idiot would have failed to understand at the early stage of the journey that they were crossing into India. They traveled at night, on mountain roads that the Hand used as infiltration routes. Masood's face was well known in India, and Hindu extremist groups would have paid significant sums to see his head mounted on a pike.

HeM operatives took them as far as Amritsar. For most of the trip, Khan and Masood were wedged into a smuggling compartment in the back of a truck. They traveled largely in silence. Near Amritsar, they were allowed out of the truck to stretch and relieve themselves. It was dark and cool, and the place they had stopped seemed far from any lights. Their Pakistani guides left them here and three Indians took their place. Their new guides were beardless and their hair was cut short in military style. Khan said nothing to them, but he observed everything around him carefully.

Their new guides drove through the night until they reached their destination. Khan was not certain where they were, but when he got out of the truck, they were parked in front of a dimly lit warehouse building. Inside, a cluster of four wooden chairs stood in a pool of light cast by a single bare bulb dangling from the ceiling. Two of the chairs were occupied. One man had dark skin and was wearing a Western-style suit with no tie. He was short and wiry and almost completely bald. He looked to be in his midfifties. Khan assumed he was an Indian Muslim. Although India was a Hindu country, it was so vast that its Muslim minority numbered in the hundreds of millions. There were nearly as many Muslims in India as there were in Pakistan, many of them no doubt sympathetic to the HeM and Islamabad's claim to Kashmir. The second man was younger and looked Middle Eastern with an olive complexion and a carefully trimmed mustache. He was dressed in a white Arab-style *thawb*, or dishdasha.

Without asking permission, one of the Indian escorts frisked both Khan and Masood quickly and expertly.

The older Indian-looking man rose and offered Masood a traditional greeting. *"As-salamu alaykuma."* Peace be upon you. As he said it, he placed his right hand over his heart. The use of *alaykuma* meant that Khan was included in the sentiment.

"Wa alaykumu s-salam wa rahmatullahi wa barakatuh." Masood replied with the most elaborate and polite of the available formal responses. May peace, mercy, and the blessings of Allah be upon you too.

"We will speak English," the Indian said. "We will use no names."

Khan translated into Urdu for Masood, who nodded.

"That is most sensible," he agreed. Khan translated back into English. His English was good, with only the slightest trace of an accent. He also spoke passable French and decent Russian.

"Our mutual friends have made it known to me that you are interested in acquiring a certain package. I have the information necessary to facilitate this. It is not, however, a simple matter."

"There is nothing about this that is simple for any other than Allah," Masood replied. "But the cause is righteous and He is with us."

The Indian nodded. The man dressed as an Arab produced a black briefcase from beside his chair and handed it to Masood.

"Inside is the information you will need," the Indian said. "It includes timetables and maps regarding the transport of the package and precise information about its location. You will also find special instructions regarding the handling of the package. The contents are . . . sensitive."

"I understand." Masood did not open the case.

"You have considered the consequences of this?" the man asked.

"Very carefully."

"There have been certain . . . expenses . . . associated with procuring this information." The Indian addressed this to the Arab, if that was, in fact, what he was.

"I understand," the Arab replied with equanimity. His English was smooth and cultured, the accent more British than American. "My organization strongly supports this project. The agreed sum will be deposited in the account in the Caymans as you requested. A second deposit will follow upon successful conclusion of the operation."

The Indian turned back to Masood.

"You understand that the time frame for this operation is very precise. It is not open-ended. There will be only this single opportunity. If you miss the window, we will not try again at a later date. There are no second chances."

"That has been made clear to us," Masood replied. "We will be ready. God is great."

"Yes," the man agreed. "But He is also extremely busy. You will have to do most of the work yourself."

Masood smiled enigmatically.

"We will be ready," he repeated.

Masood and Khan left the warehouse by a side door. Khan carried the briefcase with the mysterious instructions. The young Indian who led them was wearing a dark suit, but it was not much of a disguise. With his square shoulders and straight back, he looked like what he was, a soldier out of uniform. Khan was glad for the guide. The streets were dark and unfamiliar. The Indian soldier led them to a guest house on the edge of the industrial zone where the warehouse was located. There was a reception area on the ground floor, but no one else was there, and there was no sign on the building announcing its identity as a hostel. It did not have the feel of a business. Khan suspected that this was a safe house operated by Indian military intelligence.

"Is this place secure?" Khan asked their guide in the Hindi he had learned from watching Bollywood movies and Indian television.

"It should be. We have been careful." For such a large man, the soldier had a surprisingly soft, almost feminine voice. "I will keep watch outside your door. You may sleep if you wish. Your ride will be here before dawn. I will wake you."

The room was spartan. The wood floor was splotched with betel-nut stains where previous occupants had spit gummy wads of the noxious leaf mixed with tobacco or areca nuts. The thin breeze coming through the slats of the windows carried the intermingled smells of sewage and curry. Khan felt his stomach turn slightly, and he was glad that he and Masood had not eaten that day. There were two single beds with low wooden frames and mattresses stuffed with lumpy rice straw. Khan had slept on worse. The moment he saw the beds, Khan realized that he was bone-crushingly tired. Masood insisted that they pray before sleep and Khan complied. They removed their shoes and spread the thin prayer rugs they had carried with them on the floor, giving thanks to Allah for bringing the tools of victory so close. When they had finished, Khan settled onto the bed fully clothed. Within a minute of laying his head on the rough rice-husk pillow, he was asleep.

A sharp cough woke him. He thought at first that it was Masood, but in the dim light he could see that the portly mullah was lying asleep on the next bed, snoring softly. There was a second cough, followed by a dull thud from the other side of the door. Now Khan recognized the sound. A silenced pistol. Their Indian protector was dead. The night was warm enough that there was no need for blankets. Khan only had to roll to his left and he was on his feet, crouched next to the bed frame. He needed a weapon. There was a lamp on the bedside table. He pulled the cord from the wall and stripped off the cheap paper shade. The lamp felt solid in his hands and he tested the base against his palm. Through the door, he could hear the sound of the dead guard being dragged awkwardly to one side.

Moving on the balls of his bare feet, Khan glided soundlessly over to the door and stood with his back pressed up against the wall. The doorknob turned slowly and silently. There was only the slightest click as the latch disengaged. The door swung inward on its hinges. A black-clad arm extended a pistol carefully into the room, sweeping the gun from left to right. A long sound suppressor was screwed onto the front of the barrel.

Khan did not wait for the intruder to finish his reconnaissance. He grabbed the gunman's forearm with his right hand and pulled. The intruder lunged forward, off balance, and Khan brought the base of the lamp down hard against the back of his skull. In a single motion, he wrapped the cord around the man's neck and twisted him so that the gunman's body was between him and the door. He was limp in Khan's grasp. Whether he was stunned, unconscious, or dead Khan was not certain.

As he had anticipated, a second man appeared in the doorway, firing a suppressed automatic. Three rounds slammed into the body of the gunman Khan was using as a shield. The intruders were using subsonic ammunition to dampen the noise of the shots, and as Khan had gambled, the body of the first shooter absorbed the bullets with no through-and-throughs. He thrust the body of the dead gunman into the path of the second shooter as he tried to rush into the room. Khan leaped forward at the same moment, swinging the lamp in a wide arc that connected with the assassin's gun hand. The wrist broke with a satisfying crack of bone. Khan reversed his swing and brought the lamp back up quickly, catching the killer on the chin and snapping his head back into the doorjamb. Without hesitation, Khan retrieved the first man's gun from where he had dropped it on the floor and methodically shot both of the intruders twice in the head.

When Khan turned around, Masood was sitting up in the bed, squinting somewhat to compensate for the glasses he was not wearing. Calmly, Masood took in the scene before him.

"Where did you say you went to school?" the deputy Hand of the Prophet asked.

00:05

Sam could not escape the feeling that he and Garret Spears had been having two completely different conversations. Spears had been testing him about something. And Sam had, he suspected, failed that test. Washington was a town where management fads came and went with dizzying speed. Reinventing government, matrix management, total quality management, and Six Sigma had all had their day. Some senior leaders swore by the Myers-Briggs Type Indicator, a kind of personality test based on the theories of Carl Jung. Others were devotees of the balanced scorecard or contingency theory. Spears was the first executive Sam had encountered who relied on moral philosopher Philippa Foot's somewhat arcane trolleyology thought experiments as a management tool.

As an undergrad, Sam remembered being irritated by Foot's elaborate hypotheticals predicated on a set of circumstances so bizarrely particular as to be impossible to reconcile with the complexities and subtleties of the real world. There was a legal aphorism that difficult cases made for bad law. The same, Sam believed, was true of morality. The trolleyology dilemmas were attractive both to ethicists and neuroscientists who liked to pose the questions to subjects in the lab while imaging their brains with PET scanners to see which areas would light up. The trolley scenarios were appealing because the fundamental decision point was so simple. Do you hit the switch or not? That's why Foot relied on trolley cars rather than buses or trucks for her scenarios. Hitting a switch was a binary choice. There was no third option, no middle ground in which to steer. The real world was rarely that neat and clean. There was, Sam supposed, a good argument to be made for simple mathematics. The greatest good for the greatest number. But people were more than numbers. If Lena was the one, it wouldn't matter to Sam if the whole world was on the other side of the equation.

The unit was busy. All of his analysts had assignments and they were working on deadline. The U.S. intelligence machine was an insatiable beast with an ever-expansive appetite for information, data, and analysis. There was an eager audience for everything the unit could produce. Sam sat at his computer reviewing the most recent intel reports. Reading intelligence was a tricky business. Individual reports could be wildly misleading. It was important to put things in context, to read skeptically and critically. HUMINT sources could be wrong or deliberately seeking to mislead. SIGINT intercepts could well have recorded two people lying to each other for reasons unknown. There was nothing as dangerous as raw intel in the hands of senior policy makers. It made them feel smart even if they did not know how to read them with a critical eye.

Sam paged quickly through the afternoon's take, using subject lines to sort the small number of interesting reports from the ocean of marginal data. He was scanning reports from the CIA, the Defense Intelligence Agency, the NSA, and the National Geospatial-Intelligence Agency on his Top Secret computer system when he saw something that made him freeze. A name in a report.

Vanalika Chandra.

He clicked on the link to call up the complete report. It was an NSA product, an intercept of a telephone conversation picked up by the omnivorous ECHELON collection system. ECHELON gathered electronic data from all over the world and transmitted it to giant computer farms warehoused in suburban Maryland. Artificial intelligence programs constructed around complex algorithms searched massive databases of intercepted communications looking for key words. Certain combinations of words or phrases—*bomb, New York,* and *jihad,* for example—would flag the message for secondary review by a human analyst. Most of those were discarded as immaterial or obscure. A few, a tiny percentage of all of the messages sucked into the maw of ECHELON, were disseminated to the intelligence community as raw product. Sam's team took the raw reports and used them, along with diplomatic reporting out of the embassies in South Asia and open-source reporting from foreign newspapers and media outlets, to prepare finished intelligence products for policy makers that represented, at least in theory, the collective wisdom of the expert analysts.

The piece on the screen in front of him was a single raw report. By itself it would have been of little significance were it not for the name.

Vanalika Chandra.

Sam thought briefly about deleting the report unread, but he knew he could not.

ORCON, GAMMA, FIVE EYES, NOFORN, PANOPTES, ECHELON

DTG: 03292014Z1030

ASSOCIATED NUMBERS: +1 (202) 645-1970; +91 (11) 7789-5492

Participants: Vanalika Chandra; political counselor; Indian Embassy; Washington, D.C.

Panchavaktra Guhathakurta, director of the Pakistan Desk; Indian Ministry of Foreign Affairs; New Delhi

1. Chandra pressed Guhathakurta for a status report on the program (NFI). She complained that time was running short and the group (NFI) was in danger of letting an opportunity slip through its fingers. (Prime Minister) Rangarajan was determined to restore equilibrium to the relationship with Pakistan. The group could not allow that. The mullahs needed to be put in their place, and if that required another war with Pakistan, then so be it.

2. Guhathakurta urged patience. The group was reluctant to contemplate any changes to the plan. The others would

come around, but in the meantime, it was important to drive
a wedge between the United States and Pakistan so that when
the inevitable conflict came Delhi would not find itself under
intolerable pressure to cease hostilities before finishing the job
and bringing an end to the Pakistani threat once and for all.

3. Chandra agreed that separating Pakistan from its U.S.
protector was essential. She assured Guhathakurta that she and
her associates (NFI) had a workable plan and they were executing
it. They had allies in the CIA and the Pentagon. Under President
Lord, the White House was less sympathetic to India's concerns
about Pakistan than it had been in previous administrations.
The Department of State was also a problem, but ultimately the
diplomats did not have an especially loud voice on South Asia
policy. At the end of the day, the diplomats would salute and
follow their instructions.

4. Guhathakurta thanked Chandra for the work she had done
to date and the services she would continue to provide in the
weeks ahead.

The piece in front of him was shocking on multiple levels. It was
damning in terms of what it said about Vanalika and her politics. It
undermined the integrity of her relationship with Sam. It implied
that there was a cabal of highly placed actors in Delhi pushing for
war. And it was almost certainly a fake. For one, it did not sound
like Vanalika. Sam could not reconcile the hard-edged and cynical
worldview of the character from the intercept with the warm,
sophisticated, witty woman he knew and, he admitted to himself
although they had never said it, loved.

More significant, the date-time group on the report indicated that the conversation had taken place last Saturday while Sam and Vanalika had been at the cabin in the Shenandoah with no land-line and no cell reception. Vanalika could not have made the call when she was supposed to have done so. The intercept was a fabrication.

It was a good fake, Sam had to admit. It looked real. The cell number associated with the call was hers. He knew it by heart. To those who did not know Vanalika, it would sound credible. Only her friends would know it was out of character. Only Sam would know that the timing was impossible.

He picked up the phone and dialed another number he had committed to memory.

"Krittenbrink."

"Hi, Andy. It's Sam."

"Hey. It was great to see you the other night even if being seen talking to you was not the best career move for me. Not after the blistering you gave Newton the Golden. Nice piece in the *Post*, by the way."

"Do you think they got my best side?"

"Thin-skinned, easily riled, and smarter than the guest of honor? Yeah, I'd say so. To what do I owe the pleasure of this call?"

"I need a favor."

"Tell me."

"Can we meet this afternoon?"

Sam had not been back to the State Department since the day he had retired nearly six months ago. The process of joining the Foreign Service was full of pomp and circumstance. There was a swearing-in ceremony and reception in the ornate Benjamin Franklin room on the eighth floor. Often, the secretary of state or some suitably senior stand-in muckety-muck delivered the oath. Newly minted officers received commissions signed by the president and embossed with the Great Seal of the United States. At this point in their careers, officers were unlikely to know that the physical Great Seal was actually kept in a giant Lucite box on the first floor near the cafeteria, knowledge that tended to strip some of the majesty from the proceedings. Clerical staff occasionally entered the box to stamp stacks of commissions or treaties on the one-hundred-year-old press, looking like nothing so much as figures in a life-size diorama at a low-budget museum. There were more ceremonies tied to graduating from A-100, the diplomatic equivalent of basic training, and receiving your first assignment.

The process of leaving the Foreign Service, in contrast, was something of an anticlimax. Sam had turned over his badge and his BlackBerry to some bureaucrat in the personnel office he had never met before and signed a few forms. That was it.

He stood in the art moderne C Street lobby looking up at the row of flags from the some hundred and ninety nations with which the United States had diplomatic relations. He was an outsider now. He had a new badge that allowed him access to the building, but it was marked with a red "C" for contractor. It might as well have been a scarlet "A."

The uniformed guard looked at his badge with what seemed to Sam like mild contempt but was almost certainly nothing more than bored indifference. *I'm projecting,* he thought to himself.

On the walls of the lobby, names and dates were carved into green malachite panels and highlighted in gold. This was a list of American diplomats who had given their lives in the line of duty. It was a long list, stretching back to William Palfrey, 1780. The older names listed the cause of death. Going backward in time, gunshots and bombs became less frequent with more disease and natural disasters accounting for the grim toll. There were even a few who had been killed by "volcanoes." Next to Palfrey's name was the inscription "Lost at Sea." Palfrey had been aide-de-camp to George Washington in the Continental Army. After the war, the Congress named him consul-general to France. His ship had vanished without a trace.

Sam had some friends on one of the newer panels on the east side of the lobby. He had lost two friends when al-Qaeda bombed the U.S. Embassy in Kenya. One had been his closest friend from A-100. Another colleague, a vivacious woman who had worked with Sam on the visa line in Islamabad, died in a plane crash in Bolivia. He stopped to read their names and offer them a silent moment of remembrance.

INR was accessible by a single bank of elevators that served the subbasement. Besides the analysts, the only other State Department personnel to ride that particular set of elevators were members of the maintenance crew responsible for the boilers. The INR office space made the South Asia suite at Argus headquarters look like a sultan's palace. There was a definite cut-rate flair to the bureau and something of a 1970s vibe to the decor. On one wall was a framed and faded poster inviting travelers to FLY PAN AM TO YUGO-SLAVIA. Both had ceased to exist about the last time the office was redecorated.

As a junior analyst, Andy Krittenbrink occupied one of the less desirable cubicles near the copy machine. The copier should have been retired two secretaries of state ago, but there never seemed to be enough money in the ever-shrinking budget. Something had come loose in the machine years earlier and it rattled around inside like loose change in a dryer.

Andy had three computer monitors on his desk alongside a pile of unread Indian newspapers and magazines.

"Hi, Andy."

Andy jumped. He had clearly been so engrossed in whatever was on the monitor that he had not seen Sam approaching.

"Jesus, you scared me. How'd you get in here?"

Sam showed him the department ID card hanging around his neck.

"Part of the contract with Argus. I get passes to State, the Agency, and the Pentagon. NSA is a little more labor-intensive."

"Sweet. I'd spend most of my time at the Agency. The cafeteria is way better and the girls are prettier." It was an old line about the intelligence world: The CIA hired for beauty; the NSA hired for brains; and the Pentagon's Defense Intelligence Agency hired the rest.

"Nothing beats coming back home."

"True 'nuff. Pull up a chair and let me know what I can do for you."

Sam sat in the one guest chair that Andy could fit inside his cube.

"I want to ask you about a particular NSA piece. Here's the reference number." He handed Andy a slip of paper on which he had scribbled the intercept's catalogue number. It took only a few minutes for Andy to retrieve it from the system. He read it and whistled softly.

"Dynamite stuff. I didn't think the lovely and charming Mrs. Chandra had quite so much kick to her curry."

"She doesn't," Sam replied. "That piece is a fake. That conversation never took place. I want to know how it got into the system and why."

Andy looked skeptical.

"What makes you so sure?"

"Because the time frame is wrong. She could not have made that call when the DTG says she did."

Andy looked at it quickly.

"Saturday night? Where was she?" He paused for a minute while the gears in his brain turned. Andy's brain worked extremely fast and he was well trained in the art of connecting data points into a coherent story.

"She was with you, wasn't she? You were making the beast with two backs with the Indian political counselor." He looked around quickly and lowered his voice to a conspiratorial whisper. "The married Indian political counselor. Married to a guy who could have you killed and leave your body for the crows, by the way. Jesus H. Christ, what a stupid thing to do. If DS finds out . . ."

"Yeah. If. This has to stay just between me and you, Andy. Okay?"

"Sure, Chief. No worries. You absolutely sure she didn't sneak in a quick call when you were in the can?"

"There was no phone and no cell reception. No way to make a call from where we were."

"Or to be tracked," Andy suggested. "So what do you want me to do?"

"Analysis."

"Of what?"

"Do you remember what I taught you about cockroaches?"

"That if you see one on the kitchen floor there are a thousand hiding in the walls."

"Which means that if this report is fabricated it's almost certainly not the only one. There are probably a thousand like it hiding in the system, and I want to know which ones and whether there is any kind of pattern to the information."

"Good God. Do you have any idea how hard that will be to do, even with the whole office working on it?"

"Not the whole office. If I wanted to put a big team on it, I'd have my guys do it. I want to keep this very quiet until I know what's going on. I want you to do this on your own."

"Why me?" Andy asked, perplexed.

"Because I trust you. And because I think you can do it."

Despite himself, Andy smiled at the compliment. Sam knew Andy looked up to him. It was an obvious button to push, even if it made him feel sort of scummy to manipulate the young analyst like that.

"What's the time frame on this?" Andy asked.

"Right away."

"Give me a week."

HAVANA HARBOR
FEBRUARY 15, 1898

00:06

*S*ound carried near water, and the music from the chamber orchestra playing at one of Havana's waterfront clubs was so clear that it could have been coming from the foredeck. The parties seemed to go on all night in this town. Havana was the capital of Spain's most important overseas possession, the jewel in the Spanish crown. But Spain was a fading power, its glory days were long past, and the empire was rotten and sclerotic. As surely as day follows night, the Old World empires would be shunted aside by the muscular young power of the United States. It was only a matter of time.

Machinist's Mate Second Class Nathan Oliver stood listening to the music on the main deck in the shadow of the port-side gun turret as though the shade would somehow help cut the steamy tropical heat. The orchestra was passable. Not up to the standards of London or even New York but passable. Oliver hummed along softly to Johann Strauss's Kaiser-Walzer. There were not many grease monkeys in the U.S. Navy who would have recognized that piece of music, but Nathan Oliver *was not really a machinist's mate. For that matter, neither was he really Nathan Oliver.*

For the last two months, however, he had lived on this ship, learning its routines and its quirks, getting to know its crew of 355 men and boys, and being careful to think of himself as Nathan Oliver, machinist's mate.

He had bided his time, waiting for the moment he knew would come.

Oliver had been chewing on an unlit cigar. He would have liked nothing more than to light it up, but fire discipline was something that Captain Sigsbee took seriously and Oliver could not afford a run-in with one of the petty officers. Not tonight. He had a schedule to keep.

With a small twinge of regret, he tossed the unlit cigar stub over the rail into the inky black waters of Havana Harbor.

It was time.

He slipped quietly through the hatch and down the ladder to the second deck. From a utility closet, he retrieved a small wooden box that was stashed away discreetly in the corner of the top shelf. With the box tucked under his left arm, Machinist's Mate Nathan Oliver walked calmly and purposefully to Coal Bunker Number One. The room inside reeked of coal dust and sweat. When the ship was under way, as many as a dozen men would be crammed into this room shoveling coal into the chutes that led to the boiler room. There, other men stripped to the waist against the heat would feed the coal into the insatiable furnaces that produced enough power to propel the great white ship at speeds of up to sixteen knots.

With the ship at anchor in the harbor, however, the bunker would be empty. Or at least it should have been.

When Oliver stepped through the hatch, he saw the broad back of a sailor bent over a broken pipe in the far corner of the bunker.

"Hey there, Nathan," the sailor said, when he looked over his shoulder and saw who it was. "Did they send you to help me out?"

"They sure did, Chester," Oliver replied to his fellow machinist's mate, Chester Ott. "How does it look?"

"The pipe is pretty mangled. I think we'll need to replace the whole section. Pass me the wrench, would you?"

"Sure thing."

Oliver set the box down on top of a pile of bags stuffed with coal and picked up the heavy pipe wrench that was leaning against the wall. It was easily as long as his arm.

He walked over to stand behind Ott.

Chester had turned his attention back to the broken pipe, and he did not see Oliver raise the wrench over his head with two hands as though he were holding a baseball bat.

"What's in the box?" Chester asked.

"A surprise."

The wrench contacted the back of Ott's skull with a dull, wet thud. The sailor sprawled forward, his face slamming into the bulkhead. He fell over on his side, probably dead. If not, he would be soon enough.

Oliver pulled the device out of the box. Carefully. He was used to working with explosives, but this was like no bomb he had ever seen. A dozen sticks of dynamite were wrapped around a conical sphere of metal. The shape was supposed to concentrate and magnify the blast wave. It was the latest thing. Built to pierce armor. He pressed the open end of the cone against the forward bulkhead and wedged the device firmly in place with heavy bags of coal, being careful to leave room for the fuse to breathe. The fuse had been precut and measured to exactly ten minutes. On the other side of the bulkhead was the locked magazine where the battleship's six-inch shells were stored. He lit the fuse with a match and hurried out of the bunker and up the ladder to the *main deck. Without hesitating, he vaulted over the rail and fell feet-first into the harbor, keeping his legs straight and his arms at his sides to minimize the splash.*

The water was blood warm. Within moments, he was swimming as hard as he could to put as much distance between himself and the ship as possible. He was a strong swimmer and fast. Even so, the blast was powerful enough to set his ears ringing. Looking over his shoulder, he could see the ship leap out of the water and come down with her back broken. Almost immediately, she began to settle to the bottom.

Oliver felt only slightly more regret for the death of the ship and its crew than he had for tossing a perfectly good cigar into the harbor. It was just a job. He did not know why it had to be done, only that it was part of a larger design that was not his concern. That sort of planning was for the Governing Council. He was just an operative. He contin-ued swimming. A launch would be waiting for him at the harbor mouth to pick him up. Mr. Smith had made the arrangements.

A few short weeks later, the United States declared war on the King-dom of Spain as the emperor of the yellow press, William Randolph Hearst, incessantly urged the American public to "Remember the Maine."

THE PENTAGON
APRIL 2

00:07

It was a shame, Garret Spears thought to himself. He had had such high hopes for Sam Trainor. He was smart and tough and unafraid to challenge established positions and butcher sacred cows. His public put-down of that blowhard Newton was proof enough of that. Sam would have been a solid contributor to the team. Spears needed a deputy, someone to help manage the workload of the operation. There was Weeder, of course, and there was no denying that the Commander had a certain valuable skill set, but he was hardly a great thinker. No, Spears needed an intellectual equal, someone who would push him in private and who could represent him effectively to others in the group. Sam had the right capabilities, just not, it seemed, the right mind-set.

They called themselves the Stoics. They had not chosen that name, they had inherited it. The group was old . . . very old . . . with roots that stretched back to the time when the American elite had felt themselves to be the direct successors to the Greeks of Periclean Athens. The Stoics believed in the power of remorseless logic.

Sentiment was the enemy of reason. Only clear, crystalline logic could ensure the security of a great nation like the United States. Even the Shining City upon a Hill had an engine room that was by nature of its responsibilities dank and fetid. Someone, Spears reasoned, had to keep the lights on.

They did not meet often. They were all busy senior officials with complex lives and tight schedules. Finding time to meet was never easy. Moreover, every meeting was a calculated risk. What they were doing was important. But it must remain secret. The candy asses in Emily Lord's White House would not understand the importance of their work or the role the group had played throughout the history of the Republic. The general public, of course, needed to be kept in the dark about the actions of those entrusted with their security. They wanted to be kept in the dark if you really thought about it. Let them stay fat and happy and ignorant, secure in the protection provided for them by men like him.

Still, they did need to meet face-to-face periodically, particularly as their current operation was perhaps the most audacious and far-reaching in the group's long and storied history. It would have been much easier if they could communicate by phone or e-mail, but the members of the group knew better than most how insecure electronic communication was, and the immortal footprints that e-mail inevitably left behind.

The Stoics did keep records. They were bureaucrats, after all. There was a book, a black leather-bound ledger in which the decisions of the Governing Council were recorded and the outcome of the group's operations assessed. The Librarian was responsible for the book. His name on the Council was more than an honorary title. He was an actual librarian. For more than two hundred years, the Librarian of Congress had been the keeper of the records.

New members of the Council were invited to the library for an afternoon reading the records and learning from the Librarian about the group's history. It was important for newcomers to understand, to see how the Stoics had defended the Republic in its darkest hours and sought creative ways to advance the nation's noble mission. Garret Spears had been read into the program five years ago. He had been in awe of what their predecessors had done.

Some operations had been wildly successful. The destruction of the USS *Maine* at its mooring in the port of Havana had justified the war with Spain and secured America its first overseas colonies. There had also been mistakes and failures, of course, even tragic failures. And at times the group had fallen short of its own ideals. The assassination of Lincoln, for one, had been a consequence of divisions on the Governing Council of the Stoics that had mirrored those plaguing the United States. Passion had trumped logic. After the fact, the Stoics had clawed back some of the ground they had lost, turning Lincoln into a national martyr and symbol of unity. Even so, it had not been the Council's finest hour.

Now the Governing Council was executing an operation that would stand among the most important the Stoics had ever undertaken. It would reshape the world and secure the future of the United States and the American people for decades to come.

During his time in the navy, Spears had done a number of tours in the Pentagon, including as a staff aide to a vice admiral. But he was now in a part of the building that he had never seen before. In truth, he had not been aware that the *floor* existed, a subbasement level excavated in secret in a fit of 1960s Cold War paranoia. Water dripped from exposed pipes overhead, making small puddles on the bare concrete floor. Exposed wiring on the wall seemed to make for an uncertain pairing with the leaky pipes. It was a good thing, Spears decided, that there was nothing organic on this level, nothing that would burn.

The conference room was dated. It was outfitted with the kind of electronics and communication equipment that would have been used to fight World War III in the Johnson administration. The hard metal folding chairs around the table were spotted with rust. Still, it was secure and the Stoics most certainly valued security above comfort.

Spears was five minutes early, but he was still the last to arrive. The Chairman looked at him with unconcealed irritation. He was famous, at least in Washington policy circles, for a militant insistence on starting meetings on time. *Bite me,* Spears thought. *It was easy enough for you to be on time for this meeting; you work in this building.*

Spears locked the door behind him and took his seat at the table.

There were eight of them. There were always eight on the Governing Council. Each had a role and a mission. When they moved on from the positions that made them useful to the organization, they were replaced. They were six men and two women. All were white. This was not deliberate, but neither did it disturb anyone at the table. The Stoics considered both racism and affirmative action to be the height of illogic. One of the men wore an army uniform with the three stars of a lieutenant general on his shoulders. The rest were in business attire appropriate for Washington's formal-but-not-flashy ethos. Spears was the only member of the Council not drawing a government paycheck. Two of the members were rich beyond counting from family money, but their positions on the Council were due to their government jobs rather than to their wealth. Spears was the only denizen of the private sector, and his appointment was a sign that even the Stoics were not immune from the push for outsourcing government responsibilities.

Another eight people sat in a row of chairs lined up along the back wall. Each Council member was entitled to one assistant, who could—in extremis—take the principal's place at the table until a permanent replacement could be found. There was a little more color in the back row, an African American woman who was an up-and-comer in the Treasury Department and two Hispanics. The Chairman's assistant was the colorless but capable James Smith. By long tradition, the individual in that position always used the name Smith, although the records were somewhat fuzzy as to the origins of that custom. Spears's backbencher was Commander John Weeder.

"Now that we're all here," the Chairman began, with only a quick glance in Spears's direction to indicate that he meant it as a rebuke. "Let's get started. Reports, can I ask you to begin with an update on South Asia?"

Real names were never spoken aloud in meetings. This was more than just another layer of OPSEC, it connected the current members of the Council to their predecessors. It tied them to those who had come before.

"Reports," a career professional with three decades of experience at the CIA, was the twenty-fourth person and the third woman to carry that name on the Council. She was responsible for intelligence and had perhaps the most analytical mind among the eight.

"Thank you, Mr. Chairman," Reports said. Her face was long and thin, and reminded Spears of a greyhound. "The rise of the Islamists in Pakistan is accelerating. Talwar is effectively captured by the clerics, and the traditional role of the military as a bulwark against Islamist influence is eroding. The army has sponsored Islamist groups for decades and used them as proxies against India.

What's changed is that the military establishment can no longer control the extremists in the way they used to. Tensions between Pakistan and India are as high as they have been since the midseventies, but Rangarajan is doing everything he can to defuse them. He doesn't want the war that Pakistan is offering."

"We need the war as the trigger for Cold Harbor," Plans commented. He may have been a brilliant academic, but Spears thought that the man responsible for strategic planning on the Governing Council had an annoying habit of stating the obvious.

"Yes," Reports replied calmly. "That is why we have developed the intel-sharing program. It is also the reasoning behind our current delicate undertaking." She put a slight emphasis on the word *reasoning*. For the Stoics, reason was both their touchstone and their shibboleth. Plans's intervention had been laced with frustration and anxiety, emotions that had no place in the Council's deliberations. It was an artful put-down.

For Spears, the rest of the brief on developments in the region tracked pretty closely with what he had already read in the assessments that Sam's South Asia Unit had prepared for Argus. Reports's analysis may, in fact, have been drawn directly from those same products. The world of intelligence could be unwittingly circular, and there was always something of an echo-chamber effect in analytical judgments. Irrespective of the sourcing, it was clear that Pakistan was a basket case, a failed state in all but name that was slipping inexorably under the control of the Islamists.

When Reports had finished with the brief, the Chairman looked at Spears. "Operations, can you update us on the progress your team is making?" Spears was Operations, or "Ops," responsible for translating the Council's decisions into action. It was a position he shared with some of the most exalted, if controversial, figures in American history. Allan Pinkerton had held the job during the Civil War. Colonel House had served as Operations during the Wilson administration. Harry Hopkins held the title during the Second World War, even as he had been living in one of the upstairs bedrooms at the White House. Spears was conscious that the history books would never group him together with these lions of the American experience. He was anonymous. A gray eminence. But, the operation he was spearheading would—he knew—be greater than anything that they had accomplished in his position. It was elegant. Visionary. And it was a shame that the world must never know.

"The wheels are turning, Mr. Chairman," Spears said. "Everything is in train." Spears smiled at this private joke. There was a level of granular operational detail that the Council did not need to know.

"But this is a complex op," he continued, "and it will take time to come together. We have identified a number of possible time slots for the final stage, with the earliest opportunity approximately a month out. The initial meeting between our Indian and Pakistani assets was successful. The Indians have set it up as a false flag. Masood and the HeM think that they're dealing with Middle Easterners who have purchased access to the . . . material. There will be no direct transfer. The Hand of the Prophet will have to make the next move on its own timeline. This obviously limits our ability to dictate the pace of events, but it significantly reduces our risk profile. The information we have made available to HeM, however, is time-sensitive. They will have to move quickly if they are going to move at all."

"They had better move pretty damn quickly," Plans said vehemently. "We've all seen the Cassandra projections."

Spears nodded. It had been almost a year since the oddly mismatched pair of academics from Agilent Industries had presented their preliminary findings to the Council. It was only a matter of time, they had predicated with high confidence, until a nuclear bomb exploded in an American city as an act of terror. The massively powerful computer system and clever algorithms that Agilent had funded had been equally clear about the origin of the weapon itself. The bomb that would destroy an American city and kill hundreds of thousands of American citizens would come from Pakistan. Agilent was, in reality, a front company registered in the Bahamas and controlled by the Council. So, for that matter, was Argus Systems. The Council made use of the tools it had and made the tools it needed.

"There is precious little time," the Chairman agreed. "But we are moving as quickly as is possible under the circumstances. We all approved of the plan and the schedule that Operations outlined for us. Now is not the time to second-guess. It is the time to look for loose ends, anything we may have missed that could jeopardize the success of the operation. Does anyone at the table have a useful contribution to make in this regard?"

"I believe that I might," the Vice Chair remarked.

The Vice Chair had been Spears's predecessor as Ops, moving up in the group's hierarchy to the number two spot on the Council when the previous Vice had left government service and returned to his walnut farm in California. She was young, both for this job and the senior management position she occupied at the State Department. She was also telegenic, something that had not hurt her rapid rise to the top.

"What do you have?"

"We have a new problem with the White House."

"What is our dear friend Emily up to now?"

"It's not Lord personally. It's her chief of staff, Solomon Braithwaite. Our op has too many moving parts to fly completely below radar. The White House has picked up enough data to suspect that something is going on in South Asia that does not have official sanction. I have a source in the NSC who told me that Braithwaite has put together his own team of experienced operatives who report directly to him and, through him, to President Lord. I don't have any information on numbers or the nature of their assignment, just that they are out looking for us. I know Braithwaite. He's a pit bull. Once he gets his teeth into a problem, he's not going to let go easily."

"What about co-opting Braithwaite?" the Chairman asked. "What are his weaknesses?"

"He's a bit of a prig," Reports offered. "But he's squeaky clean. Nothing exploitable."

"Do you think he could be persuaded? Made to see reason? Would he understand the underlying logic of what we're doing?"

"I'd be surprised," Legal said, shaking his head with an air of sorrowful resignation. The group's lawyer, a graying D.C. native from the Justice Department, was the longest-serving member of the Council. Twice over the last ten years he had turned down offers to assume the Chairman's role, a lack of ambition that Spears found hard to understand. "Braithwaite and Lord go back a long way. They were allies in New Jersey when she was governor and he was majority leader in the state senate. I don't see him doing any-thing he would interpret as betraying her."

"Legal's correct," Finance chimed in. Although a banker by both training and disposition, Finance had a keen political mind as well as close connections to the Lord administration. In his civilian life, Finance had been a partner at Goldman Sachs and a leading fund-raiser for Emily Lord before joining her administration as an under-

secretary at the Treasury Department. He had quickly grown dis-
enchanted, however, with what he saw as the softhearted naivete of
the Lord White House. The current Vice Chair had recognized his
discontent and recruited him to the Stoics. It had been a real coup
on her part and even the Chairman respected Finance's views on
Lord and her inner circle.

"Braithwaite is even more obtuse than Lord when it comes to
the Islamist threat," Finance continued. "They're essentially apolo-
gists for the extremists. As though it were somehow the fault of the
United States that lunatics in thrall to a violent ideology would seek
to do us harm. Braithwaite would not understand. And he is a dangerous opponent. It would be an error to underestimate him."

"We are at an extremely delicate moment in both the operation
and the history of our country," the Chairman said. "We cannot
afford the risk that Braithwaite might be successful in interfering
with the plan. If he cannot be suborned or reasoned with, he must
be removed from the equation. But I would put that decision to a
vote of Council members to be recorded in the records. It is not one
to be made lightly."

"Seconded," Spears said.

"All in favor?"

Seven hands rose in the air. Only the Librarian did not vote.
He kept the records and the history, but by tradition, he did not
have voting rights. Spears could hear the thin scratching sound of
the Librarian's Waterman pen recording the results of the vote in
the black ledger.

The hands were lowered. There was a pause. Spears recognized
it for what it was. A moment of silence.

The Chairman looked over at John Weeder, who nodded his
understanding.

00:08

Kamran Khan's days of sweeping the floors at the villa in Lahore were over. He had not yet, however, been assigned to an operational unit. Instead, he waited. He prayed. And he practiced patience. Shortly after he and the HeM leader had returned from India, the villa's steward had moved him from the communal bunkhouse to his own room on the second floor of the main building. It was a mark of Masood's favor. But Khan had not seen the leader since their return from India, and he did not know what Masood had planned for him.

He had hoped that the physical prowess he had displayed in India would open the door to jihad. Khan could feel the weight of his mission pressing on his heart, and that mission had nothing to do with a broom and a dustpan. It seemed, however, that there were still tests to pass. One afternoon, a battle-scarred veteran of the Kashmir wars had taken Khan into the mountains to see if he could handle a weapon. Khan could shoot, and he proved himself to be a more than adequate marksman with both rifle and pistol.

Most of the tests were pen and paper. Some of it was religious exegesis exploring his depth of knowledge in the study of the Quran and the Hadith. Much of it, however, seemed to be standardized intelligence testing with logic puzzles and analogies. He was also asked to write a number of essays, including one on the history of Kashmir and another on the meaning of jihad. Khan breezed through the tests. He was smart and he knew it.

Ten days after the fight in the guest house in India, the steward told him that he had been summoned to lunch with Masood Dar. Khan changed into clean clothes and combed his hair, but he left his beard untrimmed as a mark of his piety. He knew Masood would be pleased by that.

The HeM leader typically ate in his study on the third floor, the same room where he had interviewed Khan before agreeing to take him on the trip to India. Masood was wearing a white *shalwar kameez*, the national dress of Pakistan with the pajama-like trousers and a long tunic slit at the sides. He sat cross-legged on the floor in bare feet. Khan removed his sandals and left them on a rack by the door. He sat on a cushion across from Masood and bowed slightly.

"*As-salamu alaykuma.*"

"*Wa alaykumu s-salam.*"

The steward served the meal, small plates of traditional Punjabi dishes. Masood was a strict vegetarian so there was no tandoori. Instead, the meal featured *sarson da saag* made with green mustard leaves and eaten with corn-flour roti, *dal makhani*—a dish of lentils with cream—and a thick stew of red beans and rice called *rajma*.

Khan ate sparingly and drank weak tea, while Masood consumed impressive quantities of the excellent food and drank yogurt spiked with mint and salt. Khan would have eaten more, but he felt self-conscious as Masood seemed to be examining him as he would a bug under a magnifying glass, an impression heightened by the HeM leader's oversize spectacles.

"You will be pleased to know that we have identified the viper who betrayed us to Indian intelligence. A low-level member of our group working on the logistics of our little trip. It seems he had a rather serious gambling problem of which we were unaware and which made him vulnerable to temptation. It is not a mistake that we shall soon repeat."

"I trust that you interrogated him before you had him killed," Khan said emotionlessly. This was business.

"Of course. But he knew nothing, not even the name of his contact in RAW." The Research and Analysis Wing was the branch of Indian intelligence responsible for overseas collection and counterterrorism. RAW had been playing cat-and-mouse with the Hand of the Prophet and other Pakistani groups for years. The Indian service was small, nothing like the massive American, Russian, or Chinese services, but it was competent and, as Khan himself had seen, ruthless.

"Trust me," Masood continued. "Had he known anything of value he would have given it up. There are some people in our organization who can be most persuasive."

Khan did not doubt the truth of that statement. He said nothing.

"I have not thanked you," Masood said, "for saving my life. Had the Indian assassins succeeded, our movement would have been most seriously damaged. Which is not to say that I am irreplaceable. I am a mere instrument of Allah's will. But even so, there are certain things I know that would be lost if I were to die prematurely."

"All death is according to the will of Allah," Khan replied dutifully.

"Of course."

Masood lapsed into silence, and Khan was again cognizant of the intensity of the mullah's gaze.

"Tell me about your family," Masood commanded.

"My family is from Quetta. We are Baluchs. My parents spoke Saraiki at home."

"I thought I recognized the accent. Brothers and sisters?"

"I have a brother. He is a dentist."

"In Quetta."

"No." Khan paused, considering whether there was a way to avoid the inevitable. There was not. "In New Jersey," he admitted.

Masood did not seem surprised by this. Khan suspected that the HeM leader already knew about his family history. Their experience in India had no doubt piqued his interest in Khan's past.

"You also have spent considerable time in America?"

"Yes."

"And you hid this fact from us?"

"No, Janab. I did not hide. Nobody asked me where I was from and I did not feel it was necessary to offer this particular piece of information."

"Because you felt we would reject you if we knew?"

"The thought had crossed my mind."

"Maybe we would have been right to do so."

"In which case, Janab, you would be dead."

Masood smiled at that.

"There are Americans in al-Qaeda," Khan continued. "There are Americans in the Taliban. I am Pakistani first by birth and choice, and I choose to defend Islam against the Hindus rather than the crusaders, but I believe that I have proven my loyalty to you and my commitment to jihad."

"Tell me about your time in America."

"My family moved there when I was ten and my brother was eight. It's been eighteen years. My uncle was a mechanic in Newark and he got a visa for us to immigrate. My father went to work for him at the garage."

"Did you like America?"

"At first," Khan said. "We had a television and I learned English by watching cartoons. I did well in school, but it wasn't easy to fit in. We didn't fall in with any of the established groups. Too dark for the white kids. Too Asian for the black kids. Too Muslim for the Asian kids. There were only a handful of Pakistanis in the school and we were the only Baluchs."

"Were you pious?"

"Not especially. My family was not devout. But living among the godless Americans taught me the value of submission to the will of Allah."

"How did your family react to the awakening of your Islamic identity?"

"Not well," Khan answered truthfully. If anything, this was something of an understatement.

"You went to college in the United States," Masood said. It was not a question.

"Yes. I studied math and computer science for two years at the New Jersey Institute of Technology."

"Why didn't you finish?"

"I heard the call for jihad."

"What happened?"

Khan hesitated. His awakening to jihad predated his time at NJIT by several years. The decision to drop out of school had developed slowly rather than overnight. Like many who had followed a similar path, Khan had made a decision born of anger and pride. It was a story he had told to very few people.

Inwardly, Khan burned at the memory. He was sixteen. She was a pretty blond girl named Kathleen. Never Kathy. She insisted on Kathleen. They were lab partners in chemistry. She liked Khan, she was drawn to him, but she did not want her Irish Catholic friends to know that she was seeing a dark-skinned immigrant kid.

They thought they were alone in her house that afternoon. Kathleen's shirt was off and Khan was fumbling with the unfamiliar bra strap when her father burst through the door of her bedroom with a look of anger and contempt on his face that Khan could easily recapture even though more than a dozen years had passed. Kathleen's father had hit him with an open hand, but hard enough to give him a black eye.

"Get away from my daughter, you filthy raghead!" the beefy trucker had shouted, as Khan fled the house. Kathleen had never spoken to him again.

It was uncomfortable to think that the roots of something as pure as jihad could be grounded in the muck of teenage sexual humiliation. Khan had no desire to share this with Masood. It was, in any event, too American a story for him to really understand.

"There was a teacher in Newark, Janab," Khan offered instead. "He opened my eyes and my heart to jihad. All the rest has been according to the will of Allah."

Masood seemed satisfied with that answer and it was true, after a fashion.

"In India, I saw you fight in a manner I would not have expected from a student of math. How did you come by those skills?"

"The imam in Newark encouraged a few of us to study martial arts. He said it would sharpen our minds and would one day help us with jihad."

This also was not entirely true. Khan had begun training in Brazilian jujitsu the day after Kathleen Halloran's father had humiliated him. His teacher had been a Mexican immigrant with a run-down dojo in a strip mall in a low-rent part of a low-rent city, but he was an experienced semipro fighter and as quick as a bat. He had taught Khan well.

"And what did you do after you left school?" the mullah asked. "Did you work? At your uncle's garage perhaps?"

"No, Janab. I joined the army."

"The American army?"

"Yes."

"The army of the infidel?"

"Yes."

"Why did you do this?"

"Because they had much to teach me and I had much to learn."

"What did the infidel teach you in their army?"

"Explosives, Janab. I was trained to dispose of unexploded ordnance. To do this, they must teach you about explosives."

"And where did you apply these skills in the service of the army of infidels?"

"In Afghanistan."

"And what did you learn there?"

"I learned how to hate, Janab." In his mind's eye, Khan could see the bodies and the pieces of bodies at the wedding party in Herat, the bride and groom and scores of guests blown apart by the powerful bomb. He could smell the stench of burned flesh and singed hair. He could feel anew the anger that flowed so freely through his veins, the source of his dedication to the mission. His call to jihad.

"And so now you have joined the army of the righteous?" Masood asked.

"Yes."

They ate in silence for some time as Masood seemed to be weighing what Khan had said.

"Your name is auspicious," the HeM leader offered, after perhaps ten minutes of contemplation.

This was somewhat cryptic and Khan was not sure that he had understood properly.

"Khan? How so?"

"Kamran Khan. You have three vowels in your name, all 'a's. The numerical values of the consonants total nineteen according to the system that I recently developed on the basis of revealed knowledge. It is the same as the numerical value for the word *wahid*, which is Arabic for one and representative of the oneness of God. The word *wahid* is used to describe Allah in the Quran exactly nineteen times."

Khan nodded at this as though he understood what Masood was saying. In truth, he had no idea.

"The sum of the digits in the number nineteen is ten as there are ten digits in Kamran Khan and the sum of those digits—one and zero—is one, completing the circle. The Quran itself elevates the number nineteen. Sura 74.30 explains that 'over it are nineteen. And we have set none but angels as the guardians of the hellfire.' God has ninety-nine names, but he himself is one and loves odd numbers. There are markers in the physical world as well. The ecliptic cycle of the earth and moon is exactly nineteen years. The word *year* occurs seven times in the Quran and the word *years* twelve. Together they are a perfect nineteen."

It was now clear to Khan what Masood was saying and why. He was a mystic. Numerology was a vehicle for the direct experience of the divine. This was Sufi stuff . . . and it was dangerous. It was a belief system that Salafist fundamentalists such as the Taliban would have considered heretical. And there was only one acceptable punishment for heretics. The Hand of the Prophet, however, was less dogmatic.

Masood wasn't finished.

"Nineteen is an extraordinary number. It is matched only by the Basmala. In fact, 786 is the most sublimely beautiful of numbers. I have written many books and scholarly articles, but I never write the name of God. The number 786 preserves the purity of our prayers."

This reference Khan understood. The Basmala was a kind of shorthand for one of the most common and yet most sacred phrases in Islam: *Bismillah ir-Rahman ir-Rahim*. In the name of God, the most gracious, the most merciful. It was the first verse of the first sura in the Quran. Believers recited the phrase at prayers, before meals, and before performing any important tasks. When the letters of the Arabic alphabet were arranged in their traditional abjad order, the assigned values of the letters in the Basmala totaled 786. Many Muslims in South Asia used the number as a substitute for Allah when writing on ordinary paper that might come into contact with unclean things. The name of God could not be used to wrap fish or line a parakeet's cage.

"The Basmala is connected to the number nineteen, of course. There are nineteen letters in the Basmala. The root words appear in the Quran as exact multiples of nineteen. *Isim* is repeated nineteen times; *Allah* two thousand six hundred and ninety-eight times, which is nineteen times one hundred and forty-two. *Rahman* is repeated fifty-seven times, or nineteen times three, and *Rahim* appears one hundred and fourteen times, which is the same as nineteen times six. But it is the Basmala in its totality—786—that represents the divine. *Bismillah awwalahu wa akhirahu.* I begin with the name of God at the beginning and at the end. Never forget this."

They finished their meal. The steward collected the plates and then served coffee in the Pakistani style, a frothy mix of milk, sweet cardamom, and cinnamon.

"I do not believe that your presence in the guest house that night in India was an accident," Masood said.

"No, Janab. You chose me."

"Allah chose you," Masood insisted. "It would be foolish for us to ignore this sign. We've been watching you, Khan. You are different than our other recruits. Most, I'm afraid, are village boys only recently moved to the big city. They come to us for reasons of clan honor. This is entirely legitimate. But you come to jihad as the culmination of a personal journey. You are educated. You have an American passport. And you feel jihad in your beating heart."

"That is true, Janab." And Khan knew that it was.

"You traveled a road similar to my own in coming to jihad. Men like us, we see more clearly, feel more deeply. We have tested you. You are, it would seem, extremely intelligent. That is good."

"I am whatever Allah made me."

"I have plans for you."

"I am grateful."

"What would you say if I told you that you could do something special, something spectacular in the service of Allah? Would you wish to do this thing?"

"I would."

"What if I told you it was dangerous?"

"I would still want to do it, Janab."

"What if I told you that it was more than dangerous, that you would surely die?"

"If it is Allah's will, then, yes, I would do it." And Khan knew that he would. His life was a relatively small price to pay. All men died. Not all could do so for a noble cause.

"You may well get the chance," Masood said.

MUMBAI, INDIA
APRIL 2

00:09

Lena Trainor was cooling her heels. At least one part of her body would be cool, she reasoned, as the wait in the outer office of the commissioner's deputy subassistant for something or other entered its second hour. It was well over a hundred degrees in the building, or at least it was in the waiting room. Lena suspected that the commissioner and his senior staff had air-conditioning in their offices. It was the hoi polloi and lower castes who came to pay obeisance to what remained of the License Raj who were made to wait in the sweltering heat.

If it was true that the Eskimos had seventeen words for snow, then the denizens of Mumbai surely should have at least as many words for heat. Lena killed another ten minutes coming up with an imaginary list of words to describe the different shades of hot that afflicted the city. She had just reached *wet-and-steamy-hot-stinking-of-seagull-droppings-at-low-tide* when the door opened and a thoroughly bored-looking clerk announced that the assistant to the acting deputy commissioner—or something like that—would deign to see her.

In truth, Lena did not have high hopes for this meeting. It was just one in a series of conversations with midlevel bureaucrats in the Mumbai city government who inhabited a world of process, stamps, and triplicate forms that she found maddening. At times, she felt as if she were drowning, held under the surface of a murky sea by thick strands of red tape wrapped like kelp around her arms and legs. She could see the sunlight above, but she was immobilized by the famously inefficient Indian bureaucracy.

The secretary—or maybe he was the secretary to the secretary, it could be hard to tell—showed her into Deputy Assistant Commissioner Sayyap Vamsam's office. It was refreshingly cool in comparison to the waiting room, but it was still probably somewhere in the eighties. A single window air conditioner wheezed and gasped like an old man as it fought its endless losing battle against the tropical heat.

Vamsam was wearing a lightweight Western-style suit. Lena had learned early on in her battle with the city administration not to be fooled. A Western suit was not necessarily a sign of Western thinking. Indian political culture had its own rules and its own logic, and it had to be understood on its own terms. Vamsam did not rise to shake hands. In fact, he barely seemed to register her presence.

Automatically, Lena assessed her adversary; for whether he knew it or not, that was certainly what he was. Vamsam was a small man, which in her experience was rarely a good thing. That may have been why he did not stand up from the desk, so as not to draw attention to his size. He was middle-aged and might once have been handsome, but the comfortable life of a city official had softened him and given him something of a swollen appearance as though he were about to shed his skin. He would be cautious and defensive, Lena reasoned, concerned primarily with preserving his position of privilege rather than using it to advance some goal or even to pursue higher office. He had "risen to the middle" of Mumbai's faceless bureaucratic hierarchy and that was quite enough, thank you very much.

She looked quickly around the office. Awards and decorations hung on the walls alongside pictures of Vamsam with various Indian dignitaries. A vain man, then. Maybe something of a weakness. She filed this data point away.

The name Sayyap Vamsam was also a marker of caste status. He was a Kshatriya, one of the four *varnas* in the Hindu social order. Traditionally, the Kshatriya had been warriors in periods of conflict and administrators in peacetime. Those traditions had long faded, but Lena had an intuitive sense that they would still matter to Sayyap Vamsam.

"What can I do for you, Ms. Trainor?" the bureaucrat finally asked, with an edge of impatience in his voice. Another weakness, perhaps?

"I'm here to talk to you about the Gummadi brothers' development plans in Dharavi."

"Yes." He was suddenly wary. Everyone knew the Gummadi brothers, and their Five Star development was one of the largest projects on the city's balance sheets. Vamsam sensed a threat, and Lena could almost see him pulling back into a defensive crouch.

"The Five Star plan would flatten six blocks in Dharavi. There are nearly fifty thousand people living there now who will lose their names if the development moves ahead. Instead, you'll have housing for maybe a hundred wealthy families. The tens of thousands the project will displace will have nowhere to go."

Lena was confident that she knew what Vamsam was thinking. *What's another fifty thousand low-caste homeless in Mumbai? Who will ever notice?*

"What would you have me do, madam?" he asked instead. "All of the permits are surely in order."

And therein was the problem. The Gummadi brothers were entirely devoid of scruples, but they were also careful and smart. They had spread their money liberally through the city administration to procure the necessary permits and licenses. Bundles of thousand-rupee notes were the only knife blade sharp enough to cut through the red tape of local government. It was all legal and it was utterly corrupt.

"No doubt they are. But the citizens who live there have a right to a public hearing before the final permits are approved. Any development plan should include compensation for the people who will be displaced. I want that hearing scheduled, and I want it open to the press."

"And just what is your interest in this case, Ms. Trainor?" He elongated her name to emphasize its foreignness. *Just who are you to be interfering in Indian business?* he seemed to be saying.

"I am an Indian citizen. Dharavi was my mother's home. My godfather still lives there. I run a school in the district with students whose futures matter to me. And you, Mr. Vamsam, are threatening their futures. I'd say that that's a pretty significant equity stake, wouldn't you?"

Lena was not at all uncertain about who she was. She was not half American and half Dalit. She was 100 percent American and 100 percent Dalit. They were not separable. At the same time, she recognized that the Indian elements of her identity and experiences were far more fragile than her Americanness, and she took care to nurture her connections to her Dalit self and her ties to Dharavi.

"We are only a few weeks away from the beginning of construction. It hardly seems useful to reopen debate and discussion on a foregone conclusion. In fact, it seems somewhat cruel, does it not? You run the risk of engendering false hope."

"We are not weeks away from construction," Lena shot back. "We are weeks away from *de*struction. The destruction of thousands of people's homes and livelihoods."

"Well, if you wish to request a hearing, there are procedures to follow; you will need to fill out the proper forms and submit them through the registrar's office at the BMC."

The Brihanmumbai Municipal Corporation was the real power in the city. The mayor was a largely ceremonial position. The commissioner of the BMC was a civil servant appointed by the Indian Administrative Service who was surrounded by other civil servants like Vamsam and charged with keeping the wheels of the country's largest city turning smoothly. Vamsam's reply was a classic bureaucratic brush-off. He was just a local ward boss. Lena should take her problems to the big boss in the BMC's gothic-style headquarters in the city center. He seemed exceptionally pleased with that answer, as though it were something that would never have occurred to someone like Lena.

"I did that months ago," she said flatly.

"Well, it seems like it's all taken care of, then. Good day, Ms. Trainor."

Lena protested, of course, but the audience was, for all intents and purposes, over. It had ended as the others had, with the buck passed to some other part of the system. Not infrequently, two offices would point directly at each other to assign responsibility for Lena's request.

Frustrated and angry, Lena decided not to go back to the office. SysNet would survive an afternoon without her. Lena was on the long-range planning end of the telecom company's operations. The work was important and challenging, but rarely urgent or short-fuse. Lena's expertise was in hardware rather than software. She knew how to code, of course, but she preferred to make physical things, to hold the product of her labor in her hands as though she were a craftsman or a farmer rather than an engineer.

Outside the office, Lena flagged down a three-wheeled auto rickshaw. She negotiated a rate with the driver who did not seem to find it at all strange that a woman in a tailored suit wanted to go to Dharavi. The sprawling slum was nestled between the Western and Central rail lines. To the north, Dharavi bordered a mangrove swamp, and to the south, it butted up against the fashionable sub-urb of Bandra. The rickshaw driver dropped her off in front of her building, which was located on 60 Feet Road just across the street from one of the western entrances to the Dharavi district.

A block from her apartment building, a flat lot had been fenced off. A dozen pieces of heavy machinery stood idle. The bulldozers, front-end loaders, and backhoes were waiting for the go-ahead to begin leveling the portion of the district right across from Lena's apartment that was slated for demolition. The cheery canary yellow paint jobs seemed somewhat incongruous, like a muscled mob enforcer with a KISS ME, I'M ITALIAN button on his lapel. The machines were the face of the enemy in a war for the control of the fabulously valuable land on which nearly a million poor and out-caste squatted with few rights and little security.

On impulse, Lena decided to forgo the pleasures of a hot shower in favor of an impromptu visit to Uncle Ramananda. She did not have to worry about whether he would be home. Her godfather was agoraphobic to the point of being a virtual shut-in. He rarely, if ever, left his house.

The entrance to Dharavi was less than inviting. A rickety wooden bridge spanned a canal that seemed to contain more bottles and plastic bags than it did water. A few dense mats of foul-smelling weeds floated on the surface. Sometimes, the Dharavi boys swam in the canal, a sight that always caused Lena's stomach to turn slightly. The plastic was doubtless the least objectionable thing in the canal.

On the far side of the bridge, a young boy in dirty red shorts and a white T-shirt sat on a thin reed mat with a wooden bowl set on the ground in front of him. He had no legs below the knees. A growth on his neck the size of a golf ball added to his misshapen look. Begging was his profession. The boy sat there at the end of the bridge all day, every day. At night, he slept under the bridge like a troll in a children's fairy tale.

Lena fished a ten-rupee coin out of her purse and dropped it in the boy's bowl.

"Here's the bridge toll, Tahir."

"Thank you, madam."

Lena and the boy had something of an understanding. He did not beg from her and she did not provide charity. He was performing a service, collecting the ten-rupee toll for crossing the bridge. That Lena was the only one asked to pay the toll was immaterial. She paid him every time she crossed. For Tahir, it was the difference between hunger and starvation.

There were no real streets in Dharavi, just narrow twisting alleys lined with businesses, homes, and workshops. There were no street signs or maps either. You had to know your way around. For those who had been born here, it was second nature. Lena was still learning, and it was easy for her to get lost if she wandered too far from any of her established routes.

The slum had a vibrant if unregulated economy. Some businesses actually relocated to Dharavi to take advantage of the relative freedom from red tape. Pottery and textiles were the biggest businesses, but on the short walk to her godfather's home, Lena passed a noodle shop; two beauty salons; a bar that she suspected doubled as a brothel; half a dozen kiosks selling magazines, cigarettes, and warm Coca-Cola; and a small factory that turned out cheap plastic toys for the domestic market. There were jobs to be had in Dharavi if you were willing to work hard. They just did not pay especially well.

Even in the hothouse of the slums, a few exceptional individuals thrived. Ramananda was one. He was a rogue, and her father was right that she should be skeptical of his motives, but she enjoyed his company and she could use a little cheering up right now. Her godfather was wealthy by Dharavi standards. He occupied an entire three-story building that in an American city might have been considered a modest townhouse, but in Dharavi it could have housed fifty people.

Lena knocked on the door frame and ducked her head as she stepped inside. At five-ten, Lena was tall for an Indian. Her lanky height was a constant reminder that there would always be something foreign about her here. It was good never to forget that. Ramananda was sitting on a cushion on an elevated dais.

It looked like Ramananda was cleaning up from a party, or at least having it done. Ramananda never exerted himself more than he absolutely had to, and a young boy wearing a T-shirt with the swirling saw blade logo of the Mumbai Indians cricket squad was collecting plastic cups and discarded napkins from the floor. When he saw Lena, however, he dropped his trash bag and came close to her, smiling shyly but expectantly.

"Hello, Nandi," she said. "Don't worry. I have something for you."

Lena fished through her purse for a moment before producing a Halloween-size pack of Twizzlers red licorice. The kids in Dharavi loved American candy and her father sent care packages that she could parcel out to the children. Red licorice and Starbursts were the most popular and the easiest to keep close at hand. Chocolate had an unfortunate tendency to turn to soup in the Mumbai heat.

Nandi was one of her favorites. His family was poor even by the standards the residents of the slum used to judge poor, but he had a spark about him that made those around him want to smile. Even his name, Nandi, meant "one who pleases others." Nandi was one of the regular students in Lena's school, and one of the best. He was a quick study in math. He had already learned to code in Python, and he could repair just about any of the dated pieces of technology that kept the Dharavi economy stumbling forward. Lena used copious bribes of candy to keep Nandi and the other kids coming back for their lessons. But Ramananda too had seen something special in the boy, and his plans and hers had little overlap.

Ramananda's business model was a conglomerate, like an underworld version of General Electric. A number of independent divisions within the firm ensured a consistent revenue stream even when times were tough in any one particular area. Some of the divisions were relatively respectable: recycling trash, begging, and gambling. Others were manifestly on the wrong side of the law. He did not like to talk about it, but Lena knew that Ramananda had a piece of the action in extortion, bid rigging, fencing stolen goods, and petty larceny. Her godfather "the Godfather," as her father had put it. A group of street toughs called the Hard Men served as enforcers. Nandi was currently apprenticing in petty theft, but Ramananda—who had no children of his own—had told her that he hoped to train Nandi to serve as his number two and ultimately, perhaps, to inherit the business.

Ramananda had long ago earned enough money to move on from Dharavi. But he stayed. He liked it here, he had told Lena once. His criminal activities were all outside the ward. He offered Dharavi businesses his "protection" on a pro bono basis and the loans he made to the residents of the slum were closer to the bank rate than to the usurious interest he charged in his more traditional loan-sharking operation. Dharavi was his home. Ramananda was a gangster and a mob boss, Lena knew, but he had a softer side as well.

It was in his capacity as an advocate for the ward and the underclass who lived there that he had first crossed paths with Lena's father. He had been perhaps less hardened back then, not quite so captured by the criminal net that he would ultimately weave around himself. Still, the compassion he felt for the poor and downtrodden of the slums was, Lena believed, genuine, both then and now.

Ramananda had once explained to Lena that he saw himself as a kind of Robin Hood, redistributing India's newfound wealth to ensure that the lower castes were not left permanently on the lowest rung. Robin Hood, Lena had observed, had not kept 80 percent of his Merry Men's take for himself. Ramananda had laughed at that.

Lena herself had visited Dharavi often as a child. Sometimes with her mother when she came to teach art classes or visit friends who had stayed behind. Sometimes with her father when he came to meet with Ramananda or other Dalit activists in the slum. She had grown up playing in these narrow, twisted alleys. It was why she had chosen to live if not in Dharavi then at least alongside it and do what she could to improve conditions for even a few of the hundreds of thousands living there in grinding poverty. Dharavi was her home too.

Ramananda had not moved. He sat cross-legged on the dais, a thin sheen of sweat on his face as though the simple act of breathing were enough to exhaust him. Lena walked over to him and bent to kiss his cheek. He smelled of cardamom and cheap aftershave.

"It looks like you've been entertaining."

"That makes it sound as though I was enjoying myself, and I assure you that I was not. I was receiving petitions."

The social contract in Dharavi demanded that Ramananda, as a man of power and wealth, listen to the problems and concerns of the residents of the slum and do what he could to improve their lot in life. Many asked for a loan to start a business or feed their families, and Ramananda was typically happy to oblige. Others needed help navigating the Indian bureaucracy. Ramananda was well connected and with a phone call could often make minor disputes with the BMC and its various service branches disappear. Unfortunately, the Gummadi brothers were even better connected, and Ramananda had not been able to stop the Five Star development's approval.

"How did it go with Vamsam?" Ramananda asked.

"Not well," Lena admitted.

"I'm not surprised."

Ramananda's relationship with Vamsam, the ward administrator responsible for implementing BMC policies in Dharavi, was not an easy one. Twenty years of development planning—some well meaning and naive and some grasping and greedy—had foundered on the rocks of entrenched local interests. No interests were more local, or more entrenched, than those of Ramananda. Lena knew that no development plan for Dharavi could succeed unless the developers were willing to work with the residents rather than seeing them as obstacles, stones they needed to remove before plowing the soil.

"Vamsam is a snake," Ramananda continued. "And there is only one way to deal with a snake." He slammed his open hand on the floor beside him with enough force to make the raised platform jump.

"So what do you think we should do?" Lena asked.

"Fight back."

"Against the BMC? That's taking a pretty big bite, don't you think?"

"Not more than I can chew, I assure you," Ramananda said, baring his teeth in a mock scowl.

"Why, Uncle, what sharp teeth you have."

"The better to chew Sayyap Vamsam a new orifice with."

"Don't do anything foolish," Lena pleaded. "The last thing the neighborhood needs is more trouble with the authorities. You too. Prison wouldn't suit you."

"I'm too pretty, aren't I?"

"That's one way of looking at it."

"Okay, not Vamsam. He's not the weak link, in any event. How about the Gummadi brothers?"

"As the weak link?"

"Yes."

"That's an even more ridiculous idea."

Ramananda did not make idle talk. He always had an agenda, an angle. If he said the Gummadi brothers were somehow vulnerable, there was a reason for it.

"I don't mean head-on. No muscle."

"So what do you have in mind?"

Ramananda stood up. This in itself was worthy of note. It was not something that Lena had seen often.

"Nandi," he called. "Bring me the bag you picked up for me earlier today."

The boy brought over a blue paper sack that looked like the kind that held sugar or flour in the supermarket.

"The Gummadi brothers are tough customers. But the machines they have positioned to assault our homes are not quite so invulnerable."

Lena thought about the earthmoving equipment parked in the lot across the entrance to the slum. There had been a fence, but no guard.

"Uncle, are you going monkey-wrenching?"

Ramananda sat back down, puffing at the exertion, the blue sack balanced precariously on one knee.

"I'm unfamiliar with the term, but if it means what I think it means, then, yes, I am."

"What's in the bag? Are you planning to put sugar in the gas tanks?"

"Alas, that doesn't really work. It's an urban myth, like the old story about the crocodiles in the Kolkata sewer system. The sugar just clogs the fuel filters. Put in a replacement and the engine's as good as new."

Ramananda pulled a small folding knife out of his pocket and sliced open the top of the bag, pouring a small pile of white powder out onto the floor next to him.

"This, on the other hand, is another story altogether. I have a cousin in Jaipur in the gem-polishing business. He sent me a few bags of silicon carbide. They use it to polish diamonds. Mix it in with the oil in the crankcase and it will shut down the engines permanently. It will take weeks to get replacement parts."

"And just who's going to get that assignment? I have trouble seeing you squeezing under the fence, Uncle."

Ramananda laughed. "Me? Never. That kind of work is for the Hard Men . . . and the young and nimble." He looked over her shoulder, and Lena turned to see Nandi sitting at a small table in the corner with an empty Twizzlers wrapper in front of him and a small pile of Starbursts that he had doubtless pilfered from her purse while she was talking to Ramananda. Nandi had demonstrated a remarkable natural aptitude for picking pockets.

"Nandi," she scolded him gently. "No more taking candy without permission. If you do it again, you're cut off. No more Tootsie Pops, no more licorice, no nothing."

"I'm sorry, Ms. Lena," he replied in his Bengali lilt. "It was really just for practice. Here, you can have them back." He pushed the small pile of Starbursts toward her on the table.

"You keep them this time. But no more stealing."

"No more stealing," Nandi lied solemnly.

00:10

I t was his favorite painting, the one that reminded him most powerfully of her. Sam had set up the living room in their Capitol Hill townhouse in such a way that it occupied the spot where a normal family might have put a television. Sitting on the couch, with his feet up on the coffee table, NPR's *JazzSet* on the radio, and a tumbler full of sixteen-year-old Lagavulin in his hand, he was looking right at the picture.

It was not a self-portrait, or if it was, it was not a literal representation of what Janani had looked like. There were enough photographs scattered throughout the house to serve that purpose. The woman in the painting had sharp, angular features. His wife's face had been rounder and softer. But the woman in the diaphanous sari floating above the city like a figure in a Chagall painting captured something about her that was simultaneously ineffable but essential. Sam never tired of looking at the painting with its dark, somber colors and suggestions of impending mortality.

Janani had already been diagnosed when she started the painting and was suffering through the first round of the chemotherapy that would ultimately leave her too weak to hold a brush. The painting had depth to it, a pathos that was well beyond anything that she had done previously. The certainty of dying had elicited in Janani something that transcended her talents as a serious amateur, as though that knowledge had allowed her to tap into a well of artistic sensibility that had been buried somewhere deep and safe. Lena hated the painting for the same reason that Sam loved it. It was more reliable than their memories. More real than the truth.

Vanalika was right, Sam decided. He was living with a ghost. He should move on with his life. Lena said the same thing, and she had loved her mother at least as much as Sam had. But he did not want to. He did not want to meet somebody new. He wanted to look at the painting. If Vanalika would leave Rajiv, maybe the two of them would have a future. But even though Sam had proposed that very thing to her, his reaction to Vanalika's gentle rebuff had been closer to relief than disappointment.

He thought about the intercept he had read of Vanalika's purported conversation with Guhathakurta. He tried to think as an analyst: clearly, objectively, and dispassionately. He had been gone for maybe half an hour, and he had taken their one car. It was possible, he supposed, that Vanalika had arranged for another car to be parked somewhere nearby. She could have gotten dressed after Sam left, followed him to town, and made the call before driving back, ditching the car, getting naked—and here Sam momentarily lost his hold on professional dispassion—and getting into bed before Sam made it back from town. It was possible, he supposed, but somewhat far-fetched. On top of that, it was impossible to reconcile the contents of the message with what he knew Vanalika believed about Kashmir and the Indo-Pak dynamic. Sure, she was a patriot. But she had a sophisticated worldview that was not consistent with the paranoid fearmongering from the alleged intercept.

Occam's razor—the principle that the simplest explanation was the correct explanation—argued in favor of the message being a fabrication. Why and how were secondary questions, and for the moment, Sam would have to put them aside until he could learn more.

He worked the issue over in his mind as though he were prodding a loose tooth with his tongue. He finished the glass of Lagavulin and poured himself another two fingers.

JazzSet was followed by the news program *All Things Considered*. The lead story was the death in the early-morning hours of White House Chief of Staff Solomon Braithwaite. It had been the talk of Washington all day, and the parade of journalists and "experts" on NPR had little new information to offer. Preliminary reports from the D.C. police indicated that the single-car accident on Rock Creek Parkway was a result of alcohol and excessive speed. The usual conspiracy nuts and talk-radio loonies were already calling it a government cover-up.

President Lord was going to miss Braithwaite. Her administration had proven difficult to control. This was not unusual. Sam remembered reading something that Truman had said when Eisenhower had won the 1952 election. "Poor Ike. He's used to giving orders . . . and having them obeyed." But the Lord cabinet was especially fractious, and Braithwaite had been Emily Lord's most important ally and confidant. It would be more difficult for her to control the hardliners in her own cabinet without Braithwaite to hold the whip in hand. Sam liked Lord. He had voted for her, but you did not need to be an experienced analyst to see that internal divisions within her administration could undo everything that she had accomplished.

The phone rang. Sam glanced at the caller ID screen. It read FEDERAL GOVERNMENT. He used the remote to turn down the radio.

"Trainor," Sam said, when he picked it up, taking care not to slur.

"Sam. It's Andy."

"Hah. I was just thinking about our little project. Are you still in the office? It's late."

"Yeah, I kinda lost track of time. You'll understand why when you see what I have."

"What is it?"

"Not for the phone is what it is. Can we meet tomorrow? Early . . . like, six a.m. I'd rather have this conversation when there's no one else around."

"Sure." Sam felt a rush of adrenaline burn through the light fog of alcohol at the implication in Andy's comment that he had uncovered something significant. "I can be at State at six. Your office?"

"No," he replied. "Let's meet in the Fish Tank. That early, we'll have the place all to ourselves."

The products that INR dealt with could only be handled in secure rooms. Most of the bureaus in the State Department maintained a SCIF where senior officials would do a weekly read of the "traffic" and hold particularly sensitive conversations. INR was the keeper of the department's SCIF network and had given internal nicknames to most of them. The Fish Tank was the secure conference room in the Bureau of Oceans and International Environmental and Scientific Affairs. It was one of the more obscure SCIFs in the building, and the civil-service scientists who made up the bulk of the bureau's personnel rarely dealt in the kind of highly classified information that was INR's stock-in-trade. At six in the morning, the OES bureau would be a tomb. It was a strictly nine-to-five operation.

"The Fish Tank at six," Sam agreed. "I'll see you there."

"Good."

"Andy, is this big?"

"It's bigger than that."

When Andy got excited, his left eyebrow twitched. It was an obvious tell, the kind Sam had seized on when he had been subsidizing his college costs at Northwestern by playing poker against barely numerate liberal arts majors. At six in the morning, Andy's eyebrow was jumping up and down like he had made an inside straight on the final pot.

The Fish Tank was one of the smaller SCIFs. There was room for maybe eight to sit around the table. They had the room all to themselves. Sam set his cardboard cup of Starbucks on the polished conference table and took the seat opposite Andy.

"You look like you've already had your coffee," Sam said.

"Three cups. The guys in INR got one of those espresso machines a couple of weeks ago. I didn't used to drink the stuff, but I'm starting to like it a lot."

Sam could see Andy's hands shaking slightly from the caffeine overload.

"You might want to think about cutting back on the hard stuff," Sam commented, "or you'll have a hell of a time sitting at your workstation."

"There's no time to sit. We've found something . . . Hell, I've found something . . . that'll blow the doors off the intel community. We're going to be famous."

Sam was not entirely persuaded this should be considered a good thing.

"Go on. Tell me what you've got."

There was a dark blue briefcase on the table made of ballistic cloth. An industrial-strength zipper at the top was closed with a chunky key lock. It was the kind of bag used to move intel products from one secure location to another. This one was emblazoned with the State Department's Great Seal and the words BUREAU OF INTELLIGENCE AND RESEARCH.

Andy pulled a key out of his pocket and opened the lock. Unzipping the bag, he pulled out a brown folder sealed with tape. *Andy was always one for following the rules,* Sam thought.

The young analyst used a pair of scissors to slit the thick envelope open and slid a sheaf of papers onto the table.

"I've got somebody by the balls is what I've got."

It was a bit melodramatic, and Sam had to bite the inside of his cheek to keep from smiling at Eagle Scout Andy Krittenbrink's best effort at cursing like a sailor.

"Who?"

Andy suddenly seemed less triumphant.

"I'm not sure," he admitted, before adding somewhat defiantly, "yet."

"Show me. Walk me through what you've put together."

"Okay. I started from the assumption that the Vanalika intercept was fraudulent. As you know, I wasn't entirely sold on that idea, but I was willing to test it out. It makes no sense as a lone plant, so I went looking for similar products, things that we could cross-check. I found almost thirty pieces that don't check out, both

HUMINT and SIGINT. Conversations that allegedly took place when the participants were known to be in different countries. Telephone intercepts that aren't backed up by the raw logs of calls made and received. That sort of thing."

"Let me see some of them."

"Sure."

Andy riffled through the papers in front of him like an experienced Texas Hold'em dealer in Vegas.

"Let's start with this one." He slid a single report across the table to Sam.

"It's purportedly an intercept of a conversation between General Qalat from the Pakistani Army's Third Missile Corps and Hasfan Darzada from President Talwar's office. Most of the conversation was focused on nuclear triggers tied to specific Indian provocations. It's a fairly complex topic, and they agreed to meet for lunch the next day to continue the conversation. Only that's impossible. Qalat was in Brussels for a meeting with NATO on Afghanistan and would be there for another four days. I have cables from the U.S. Mission to NATO that report on Qalat's interventions at the meetings. Darzada was in Islamabad. There's a newspaper account of his meeting with clerics at the Presidency on the same day he and Qalat were allegedly lunching together."

Sam had skimmed quickly through the report as Andy was describing it. It was exactly what he said it was, but there was something else about it as well. It was too perfect. It provided a crystalline snapshot of high-level Pakistani thinking about nuclear doctrine. It was the kind of thing that Indian strategic planners would have been salivating over. But it was *too* neat. The intel world, in Sam's experience, was muddy, murky, and uncertain. Significant information rarely came gift-wrapped with ribbons and bows. It had to be painstakingly assembled from data that often pointed in different directions. The piece in front of Sam just did not feel real.

"Show me a few more."

"Okay. This one is a HUMINT piece. The Indian source provides details of an analysis of a reported incursion across the Line of Control by elements of the Second Artillery Division's Third Brigade. That division doesn't have three brigades. Maybe the source was wrong, that's always a possibility with HUMINT. But this one is harder to explain." He passed another report to Sam. It was formatted as an NSA product, meaning it was signals intelligence.

"This is an intercept of a call by Rangarajan's national security advisor to the number two person in the Indian intel service outlining hypotheticals for an assassination attempt on President Talwar in the event of an imminent nuclear launch. This stuff is absolute dynamite. But we also happen to have access to the complete call log of one of the phones associated with the conversation. There's no record of the call having taken place. In fact, the date-time group overlaps with another call to a different number. There was no report of that conversation, meaning that NSA didn't consider it interesting or important enough to circulate. I got a friend at Fort Meade to dig up the original tape of the call. The guy was just making plans with a friend to go to the symphony with their wives. A far cry from planning to murder a head of state."

Andy offered up a few more. All were damning and all had that too-perfect quality that Sam had sensed in the first report.

"Is there any pattern to the reports? Anything that ties them together?" Sam asked.

"You mean other than being super scary and threatening to start World War III?"

"Yes. Other than that."

"There are a couple of things. Nearly all of the products have been marked for inclusion in the intel-sharing program."

"These were being given to the services in Islamabad and Delhi?"

"Yes."

Jesus, Sam thought. *This must be what Sara and Shoe were seeing when they talked about the intel program driving relations between the two giants of South Asia off a cliff. These pieces were confirming the two sides' most paranoid fears about each other.*

"The one thing I can't understand is who benefits from this," Andy added. "Cui bono is one of the standard analytical frames and on this one I have no idea. It's like someone wants a war in South Asia, but who in their right mind would want that? Guys who make body bags, maybe?"

"Is there anything else about the reports that stands out?" Sam asked. "Any clues that might help answer that question."

"Well." Andy sounded a little hesitant, as though there were parts of the story that he had not yet puzzled out. "There is an origin code on nearly every one of the products that I haven't seen before. It's not one of the standard programs like Five Eyes or Hardcore. I'm not sure what it means."

"What's the program name?"

"Panoptes."

Sam remembered seeing this code on the report of Vanalika's conversation with Guhathakurta. He had not recognized it either, but it had not seemed important at the time. Now, Sam realized, it was crucial.

"I don't know what it refers to," Andy continued, "but I have a friend over in DNI and I was going to ask him when he gets to work this morning."

"Don't do that," Sam said just a little too quickly.

"Why not?"

"Let me handle that one, okay? I think I know where to look for that answer."

"All right, Sam. You're the boss."

Even though that was technically no longer true, Sam was grateful that Andy was not fighting him on this point. A few pieces had clicked into place for Sam, and he understood that the ice they were standing on had grown thin and brittle.

"Who else have you talked to about these reports?"

"No one."

"I need you to do me a favor. Keep it that way for a while."

"I don't understand. This is a big deal. I think some pretty serious laws are being broken here . . . procedures and protocols for sure. Whoever's doing this should at least lose their jobs, maybe even go to jail. We'd be the ones to break this thing. Think about what that could mean. I know it's selfish, but there's a GS-14 job coming open at the CIA next month, and something like this would make me a lock for the position."

Sam understood full well the pull of ambition in the Washington universe. The idea of holding back on something like this was hard for Andy to wrap his mind around. Mentally, he was already picking out what he would wear to the Rose Garden medal ceremony. Sam was confident that even in his narcissist fantasy Andy's suit would be too big. There was more at stake here, however, than the young analyst could know. Sam would have to rein him in.

"I'm not sure the system would reward you for blowing the whistle on this thing just yet. Let's make sure all of the ducks are lined up before we start shooting. There are some angles on this that I want to check out first."

"Sam, you gotta understand something. These reports are almost certainly fake, but they are beautiful fakes. Someone here really knew what they were doing. The mistakes are small, and if I hadn't gone looking for them, I never would have found them. There's something big at the heart of this. I can feel it."

"I can too, Andy. That's exactly why I want to make sure that we have covered all the bases. I need you to trust me on this. We will do the right thing, and the bad guys will be punished appropriately. But there are some things I need to do first. This is important. Okay?"

"All right." Andy did not sound convinced. "But I think it's a mistake. I think we need to move fast or we'll lose the leads."

Sam was less concerned about that. The prime suspect was not going anywhere.

I should have keyed in on it earlier, he thought angrily. Not that figuring it out made it any easier to know what to do. *Panoptes* was Greek for "all-seeing." In mythology, it was also the epithet for Hera's faithful guardian, the monster who could sleep with half of its hundred eyes open and watchful. Hera had sent her servant to watch over the white heifer, Io, and protect her from Zeus.

Hera's servant was Argus.

Panoptes was Argus Systems.

THE TOBA KAKAR RANGE
APRIL 6

00:11

It was a brazen daylight assault. The six men advanced toward
the objective in pairs, with two teams providing cover for the
third and trading off as they leapfrogged forward. Khan could
see the silhouette of a man in one window, but no one raised an
alarm. The metal pistol grip of the Zastava M92 carbine he carried
was smooth and just slightly slick from gun oil. The stock was
extended, and he pressed the butt firmly against his shoulder to
ensure maximum control.

When they reached the single door of the building, Khan shifted
the carbine to hang over one shoulder. He was no longer a shooter.
He reached back and his partner, a hulking Pashtun tribesman
named Saad Ahmedani, slapped an explosive charge into his hand,
a white-gray block of Semtex plastic explosives with an electrical
detonator.

Something about the charge in his hand did not feel quite right,
but the team was in position and primed for entry. There was no
time to consider the nagging uncertainty that pulsed from some-

where deep in the recesses of Khan's brain. He slapped the charge along the door frame just over the lock and pressed his body up against the wall.

"Clear," he hissed, before triggering the charge. The other members of the assault team lowered their chins to their chests.

The moment the charge went off, he realized why it had felt wrong in his hand. It was much too big. A spray of rocks and dirt and wood debris covered the team. A piece of the door frame whipped past Khan's head, traveling almost too quickly to see. Although they had been braced for the blast, two of the six commandos had been knocked off their feet. Khan could feel a hot line stretched across one cheek where a flying splinter had cut him almost down to the bone.

Khan knew what had gone wrong. Ahmedani was carrying two charges, a small one for the door and a substantially larger one that Khan would have used to blow a hole through the back wall if the team needed an emergency exit. His partner had handed him the wrong charge.

It was a good thing that this was just practice, or they would all be dead.

One of the jihadis who had remained on his feet, a man with a wild black beard and wild eyes, stepped toward Khan and slapped him in the face.

"You'll blow us all to Allah, you son of a whore, if you aren't more careful with the fucking explosives!"

"I'm sorry, Jadoon," Khan said evenly.

He was quite confident that Ahmedani's "mix-up" with the charges had not been an accident. He was the outsider here. The others on the team never missed an opportunity to let him know in no uncertain terms that he was not welcome. Moreover, there was no chance that Ahmedani had come up with that idea on his own. The tribesman may have been devoted to freeing Kashmir from the Indian yoke, and he was most certainly as strong as an ox, but he was as clumsy as one as well and maybe not as bright.

Team leader Sangar Jadoon was not finished.

"That hunk of lumber could have taken someone's head off," Jadoon growled. "It might as well have been yours, because you don't seem to be using it."

"Yes, Jadoon." Khan did not try to defend himself. There was no point.

Jadoon hit him again.

The team leader was quick and strong, but the open-handed slap he employed so liberally that it was almost a leadership style was intended more to shame and dominate than to inflict pain. For Khan, the slap was evocative of Kathleen Halloran's father and the "filthy raghead" slur that the meaty trucker had thrown in his face after striking it. He bore it as he knew he must. Jadoon, he understood, was hoping to provoke a response that would let him send Khan back to Lahore. He bore it. But it was not easy.

"You are here because you are Masood's lucky number," Jadoon continued, and Khan could hear the anger and contempt in his voice. "I don't believe in any of that mystical magic-number shit. You're an amateur and a liability. Allah does not play games. He favors those who fight in His name and those who fight well above all others. *Allahu Akbar.*"

The last was shouted as a challenge to the entire group. Jadoon stalked off in disgust.

The team leader's frustration was understandable. This was their third "assault" on the objective, a single-story building made of pressed board and cheap framing timber and defended by department store mannequins wearing Indian army uniforms. Each of the assaults had quickly degenerated into farce. *If this was all that the HeM could muster,* Khan thought sardonically, *then neither India nor the mighty West had anything to fear. They would have to do better.*

Individually, the team members had résumés that should have made them perfect for the job. Khan was far and away the least experienced. The others were hardened jihadis with multiple missions across the Line of Control into India. Jadoon alone had crossed into Indian-occupied Kashmir at least twenty times and had a dozen or so notches carved into the stock of his Kalashnikov. After a week's training, however, the group had yet to jell into a coherent fighting force.

Khan was on the team at Masood's insistence because the value of the letters in his name was an "auspicious number." Jadoon was a believer and a jihadi, but he was a practical man with no time for the abstractions of Masood's somewhat idiosyncratic theories. Jadoon was a warrior and a Kashmiri patriot. He wanted to express his love of Allah by killing Hindus and returning all of Kashmir to the *ummah,* the wider Islamic community.

Masood had tried to reassure Jadoon that Khan could handle himself, but the commando refused to credit the HeM spiritual leader's report of what Khan had done to the Indian security forces at the guest house near Amritsar.

The men collected their gear. It would take time to rebuild the section of the Indian "outpost" that Khan's explosive charge had demolished. There would be other training sessions. The HeM camp up here in the rugged Toba Kakar Mountains was well equipped. The Hand had money. The weapons were good. Whatever equipment they needed Jadoon could secure. And there was cash to buy influence and access in Islamabad and abroad. The organization had not always been this flush. No one Khan had spoken to could explain where the money came from, and few expressed much curiosity. Allah provided for the faithful.

They humped their heavy packs down the hill to the main camp.

The camp had a bunkhouse, dining hall, and classroom space as well as workshops and a fully equipped garage. There was an obstacle course as good as any that Khan had used in the American army, rifle and pistol ranges with their own armories, and an expansive area backing a cliff face set aside for practice with explosives. A sandy pit in the heart of the camp was intended for training in martial arts. There was also, of course, a mosque. The camp was built to house many more people, but now it was just the six of them. Jadoon had not explained why, but Khan knew the answer. Security.

Jadoon was waiting for them. He seemed calmer, but he had not completely lost his look of irritation and disappointment.

"Prayers first," Jadoon said. "Then food."

Outside the small wooden mosque was a platform with benches and faucets that the men used for *wudu*, the ritual ablution that was an essential component of prayer. They removed their boots and lined them up on a shelf that was there for that purpose. Khan washed his hands up to the elbows and his feet and legs almost up to his knees. The baggy *shalwar kameez* made this easy to do. The water from the faucet was cold and bracing as Khan washed first his face and then the back of his neck. He ran his wet fingers through his hair for a cleaning that was more symbolic than effective.

The team laid out their prayer rugs inside the small mosque, facing west toward Mecca. Khan's rug was an antique Baluch design, abstract symbols and a representation of the Tree of Life. Some of the jihadis had Afghan-style rugs bearing images of Kalashnikovs and attack helicopters.

It was time for *zuhr*, the noon prayer. The men recited the prayers in unison, in this if in nothing else working in a spirit of cooperation. As it always did when he prayed, a feeling of peace descended on Khan. He felt the universe in harmony and the warm love of Allah embracing him. He knew there was nothing that he would not sacrifice in defense of the will of Allah. He knew that the others praying beside him felt the same, and for a brief moment, they were a team, united in their vision of an Islamic world. The *ummah*.

Then the prayers concluded and the divisions on the team returned.

After the *zuhr* prayers, Jadoon announced that it was time for lunch. The stove in the cookhouse was wood-fired. The sniper, Atal Mashwanis, used small lumps of Semtex to help coax a fire from a pile of damp sticks before adding enough kindling to boil the water. Khan did the cooking. It seemed that even though he had traded in his broom for a submachine gun, he was still regarded as little more than a jumped-up houseboy. The other men laughed and joked as their rice and lentils cooked. Khan was not included.

They ate with their hands, using only the right hand to touch the food as Islam prescribed. The rice was gluey and the lentils were bland. This was fuel rather than a meal. They ate quickly, conscious of how little time they had to drill before the action would be for real.

When Khan finished, he collected the plates and brought them to the sink. Doing the dishes was another of the duties that Jadoon had assigned him as punishment for his temerity in being Masood's pet. Khan bore this minor indignity too without complaint.

After lunch, Jadoon led them on a double-time march straight up the hill wearing heavy packs and carrying weapons. It was understood by all that this was a form of punishment. The team leader was running out of patience. A forty-five-minute hike brought them to a relatively flat area at the top of the hill.

"I want you to low-crawl your way to that rock," Jadoon announced, pointing to a distinctive white boulder pointing to the sky like a bony finger.

"Any man sticks his head up for any reason and I'm going to shoot him with this." Jadoon held up his rifle, an Italian Beretta M501 Sniper. "Full packs," the team leader added.

Khan estimated that it was maybe half a kilometer across scrub and stony soil. With the weight of their packs pressing on their forearms, it was going to hurt.

The five jihadis crawled on their bellies across the rough ground. Khan's bare arms were soon scraped and bleeding, and they stung fiercely every time he pushed off to claim another half meter of ground.

Periodically, Jadoon fired rounds into the ground near their heads or in between their legs. One bullet struck a rock maybe a foot and a half from Khan's face. *Thank Allah, he's a good shot.*

With only fifty meters or so to go, Khan looked to his right and saw something that made him forget the pain in his forearms. A scorpion. It was about four inches long and black. Its chitin was smooth and gleamed in the sun like a piece of polished jet. The broad weaponized tail was distinctive. Khan recognized it immediately. The fat-tailed scorpion was the world's deadliest. From the genus *Androctonus*. Greek for "man killer." The powerful neurotoxin in its sting was nearly always fatal.

This one was inches from the outstretched hand of Atal Mashwanis. The stinger was raised, poised to strike the fingers that looked to the arthropod like either a meal or a threat.

There was a gap of some two meters between Khan and Mashwanis.

In one smooth movement, Khan pulled the five-inch knife strapped to his boot and rose to his knees. Pushing off with his legs and left hand, Khan leaped for the scorpion shouting, "Atal, roll right!"

As he brought the knife down toward the scorpion, his aim was nearly spoiled by a sudden sharp pain in his right thigh. Jadoon had shot him. Ignoring the pain, Khan drove the blade through the carapace, pinning the scorpion to the ground. Mashwanis rolled to his right and sat up before abruptly falling back to the ground. Jadoon had shot him too.

Khan looked at his leg. There was no blood and it did not hurt enough to be a real bullet wound. Jadoon must have been using rubber riot-control rounds. Mashwanis was in much worse shape. Jadoon's second shot had hit him right in the head, and the sniper was clearly struggling to remain conscious.

Jadoon quickly closed the gap with Khan and the other jihadis. He had abandoned the Italian rifle and was marching forward with a grim determination.

Khan rose and spread his hands in an effort to placate the HeM leader.

"Listen, Jadoon," he tried to explain. "There was a scorpion."

Jadoon was not listening.

He stepped in close with the clear intention to slap Khan.

Enough of this shit, Khan thought, as Jadoon started to swing his arm. Khan shifted his weight back just a little in rhythm with Jadoon's attack. The HeM commander struck nothing but air. His hand whistled harmlessly past Khan's face. Jadoon grunted in surprise and anger. His fingers closed into a fist and he shot a short jab at Khan's solar plexus. It was a good punch. Khan could see that he had had some training. But Jadoon had done his killing in Kashmir with guns and bombs. It had doubtlessly been a long time since he used his fists against someone other than his subordinates, his wives, and their children. Khan bent his left knee and twisted his torso sharply to the right. Jadoon's punch grazed the fabric of his tunic but did no damage. Khan counterpunched with his left hand, striking Jadoon with the base of his palm at the intersection of his jaw and right ear. Jadoon's head snapped back and the HeM commando fell to one knee with a slightly dazed look on his face.

It was not a killing blow. Khan had held back. Jadoon stood and shook off the effects, snorting like a bull preparing to charge the matador. That usually ended badly for the bull.

"Do you really want to do this, Jadoon?" Khan asked.

"You don't belong here," Jadoon replied. "You haven't earned it."

"I would earn it now if you like."

"I don't think so, lucky number."

Jadoon's second attack was more cautious. He had underestimated Khan and was not about to repeat the mistake. The two men circled each other warily, hands extended. Khan was not yet sure if this was going to be a boxing match or a wrestling match, but he had trained in Brazilian jujitsu and either was acceptable to him.

The other jihadis stood to one side, watching. All but Mashwanis, who was now able to sit up but was still visibly disoriented. The others would not interfere with the fight. This was a test of both manhood and Allah's favor.

Jadoon was considerably bigger than Khan and had maybe six

inches of reach on him. Size did matter. A good big man would beat a good little man every time. Jadoon was good. Khan would have to be better than good. As Khan had expected, Jadoon went for the head. Khan saw the opening to step in and go for the take-down. Within twenty seconds, it would be over. But he didn't. Instead, he let Jadoon's punch through, twisting his head slightly to take the blow on his skull rather than his jaw. He did not want to humiliate the HeM commander. He wanted acceptance.

For the next thirty seconds, he stood toe-to-toe with Jadoon, trading blows like bare-knuckled boxers from another century. Khan went for the body shots, short, sharp jabs that would sap the strength from the big man's arms. Jadoon tried to lay a knockout blow on Khan's jaw. Khan ducked and moved his head enough to keep Jadoon's punches soft. One left hook caught him on the cheek that was still bleeding from the splinter wound, and for a moment the pain was so intense that Khan saw white. Time to end it.

Khan stepped inside Jadoon's next punch and stood chest-to-chest with the bigger man as though they were dance partners. Grabbing both of his opponent's arms by the triceps and lifting with all of his strength, Khan effectively froze Jadoon in place. The next series of moves were too quick for the onlookers to follow. A leg sweep dropped the HeM leader onto his back like a sack of rice. Khan never let go, transitioning from the clinch into a control position called a *kimura* after the Japanese judo champion who had patented it. Jadoon's arm was bent at an angle behind his back and there was no direction the larger man could move that would not result in a dislocated elbow. Khan gently increased the torque on the elbow until Jadoon grunted and ceased struggling.

"Tap the ground," Khan commanded.

Jadoon tried again to wriggle out of the hold. Khan clamped

down even harder on the elbow, trying not to snap it but not caring especially if he did. Jadoon seemed to sense this. His body went limp to take the pressure off the arm and he tapped the hard dirt with his free hand.

"You win," Jadoon said loudly enough for the whole team to hear.

Khan released the hold and Jadoon stood, shaking his arm to get feeling back into it. He glared at Khan with his typical intensity, but this time without the contempt that had routinely accompanied it. Khan saw him look over at Mashwanis and at the scorpion that was pinned on Khan's boot knife. He grinned.

"Can you teach the boys to do that?" he asked.

"I can."

"Good. Give them a training session after dinner tonight. No broken bones. You're our new hand-to-hand-fighting instructor."

The HeM commander abruptly embraced Khan, wrapping his arms around him in a bear hug and kissing him violently on both cheeks.

"You may be our lucky number after all."

00:12

On some days, Lena felt like a nineteenth-century Kansas schoolmarm in a one-room schoolhouse. Except for the robots. On any given day, there were a dozen or more children ranging in ages from eight to sixteen working on various engineering and technical projects or sitting at one of the low-slung tables working on math problems. Lena recycled most of her Sys-Net salary into material for the school, which was operating out of a converted toy factory in the center of Dharavi that Ramananda had helped her find.

The facilities in the slum were basic, and the power supply was spotty at best, albeit without cost to the end user. In Dharavi, municipal services such as electricity were largely pilfered. Running water came and went on a cycle known only to the gods, and trash pickup was more an aspiration than an expectation. A backup generator at the school that Lena had purchased herself helped with the inevitable black- and brownouts. Most important, Lena had made damn certain that her Internet connection was on a par with any in the city. Ramananda's workers—the more legitimate kind—had run a fiber-optic cable from the school to the edge of Dharavi where she could splice it into the Mahanagar Telephone Nigam network.

Lena made sure the kids were supplied with computers, electronics labs, and even robots as part of their education. Although artistic talent had been her mother's ticket out of the slum, Lena believed that STEM—science, technology, engineering, and math—was the surest path to a better future for the lower-caste kids of Dharavi.

The expensive equipment Lena had procured for the school would ordinarily have been a magnet for thieves except that Ramananda had put the word out that the school was sacrosanct. It would have taken an especially brave or desperate thief to ignore that instruction and cross Ramananda. Just in case, however, the unsmiling Hard Man by the front door kept the computers and electronics inside as safe as they would have been in a suburban high school in the United States.

Lena surveyed the controlled chaos that was entirely typical of the two-hour evening sessions she more or less led and was largely satisfied with what she saw. One group of young children was gathered around a laptop coding a basic video game in Python. A couple of older kids had disassembled a television and were painstakingly fitting the parts back together.

Nandi and a twelve-year-old girl named Pia were racing Roombas. With only minimal help from Lena, they had hacked the robotic vacuum cleaners and linked them to Microsoft Kinect controllers. Waving their arms up over their heads propelled the Roombas forward and wild arm motions to either side would turn the robots left or right. A few plastic cones on the wooden floor marked out the racecourse.

Pia laughed riotously as her Roomba cut in front of Nandi's, forcing him to slow down as he sought to maneuver around one of the cones. He laughed with her. It was all in good fun, and Lena's spirits lifted at their infectious enthusiasm.

Nandi had a knack for electronics and Pia was developing into a first-rate programmer. They both had bright futures, as long as Nandi stayed out of jail and off the streets and as long as Pia dodged the all-too-common trap of a bad marriage at a young age. Her parents did not know that she was a regular at the school. They were traditional people from the country. Lena did not know what kind of lies Pia had had to tell her parents to keep coming to the school, and she had no intention of asking. In Dharavi, everyone did what they had to do to get by, get ahead, and—if at all possible—get out.

Lena spent the next half hour helping a group of the oldest children with their math problems. Two of them would soon be taking the entrance exams to a prestigious state-sponsored science high school, and they would need to ace the calculus part of the test. At eight-thirty, Lena had the kids pack all of the equipment away neatly into lockers that were padlocked and bolted to the floors.

"That's it for tonight, kids," she announced.

The children all stopped to thank her individually before heading off into the steamy tropical night toward the overcrowded shacks and shanties that passed for homes in the slum.

Feeling somewhat guilty as she did every night, Lena locked the doors and windows, and headed off to her considerably more comfortable apartment outside of the Dharavi district.

Maybe I should live here, she thought, as she wandered the familiar alleyways that led back to the canal. *It wouldn't be so bad, really. I could ask the older kids to help me build a solar water heater so that I could at least have a real shower now and then.*

Lena knew in her heart that this was both unrealistic and unnecessary, the equivalent of wearing a hair shirt. The kids she mentored would be no better off for her discomfort. They would be considerably worse off, in fact, if she got sick. She could give more to the poor kids of Dharavi through the school than she could as a resident. Besides, she wasn't cut out to be Mother Teresa. Lena had once met Mother Teresa at a hospice in Kolkata run by the Missionaries of Charity when her father had been involved in a project to provide care to the city's HIV-positive poor. She had been a little girl, no more than seven, but Lena remembered Mother Teresa as a figure of almost saintly calm. The contrast with her own roiling emotional life could not have been starker.

She stopped at the bridge to pay the ten-rupee "toll" to Tahir.

"How were the lessons this evening, madam?" he asked politely.

"Just fine, thank you. Why don't you come one night and see for yourself?"

"No thank you, madam. My place is here, guarding the entrance to the district. It is an honorable profession."

"Yes, Tahir. Yes, it is."

She dropped the coin in his bowl.

There was nothing fancy about Lena's small apartment. She made a good salary and she could have afforded a larger place in a nicer part of the city, but most of her pay went to buy books and equipment for the school. She dropped her purse on the end table by the door and slipped her shoes off. It had been a long day, and she wanted nothing more than a quick meal, a shower, and bed. But she had promised her father that she would call him this evening and she did not want to disappoint him.

Lena was worried about her father. It seemed to her that he was spending too much time alone, too much time thinking about the past. Lena was afraid that her move back to Mumbai, to her mother's old neighborhood, might have been too much for her father to handle. But she knew he was strong. He had proven that over the years, caring for her mother when she got sick, dealing with Lena's rebellious teenage persona as a single parent, and trying to do some good in South Asia even as he was forced to advocate for policies he frequently did not believe in. It had not been an easy road for him. But he had done well, and he was a good man.

She hoped he could find some way to be happy. A girlfriend might help. There had been one or two over the years, but they had not lasted long.

She was one to talk. Her father was the top entry on her Skype favorites bar. Someday, maybe, he would be bumped out of the top spot by a boyfriend who might become a husband. But that opening remained vacant, and Lena was in no rush to fill the position.

Lena sat down at the desk in the living room and called up the Skype application on her computer. She clicked the button next to his picture.

Her father picked up after half a dozen rings. The picture was a little jumpy, and Lena guessed that he was using his iPad rather than the desktop. The resolution was still good enough for her to see that Sam did not look well.

"Hi, Dad."

"Hi, baby."

"Are you okay?"

"What do you mean?"

"You don't look so hot."

"That's too bad. You look great. What have you been up to?"

It did not take a rocket scientist to recognize the brush-off.

Okay. No frontal assaults. She would have to find a back door in the conversation.

"I'm a little tired of wrestling with the accursed BMC. I'd swear there's no bureaucracy quite like the Indian bureaucracy."

"They've had thousands of years of practice," her father agreed. "Any luck moving the ball?"

"None," Lena admitted. "It feels like I'm just spinning my wheels. And I'm afraid that Uncle Ramananda is planning to take things in . . . a different direction."

"Violence?"

"More like destruction of property. But still the kind of thing likely to attract the attention of the BMC in an altogether different way than I had in mind."

"Don't let Ramananda drag you into anything. I know he's your godfather and my friend, and I know I've told you this already, but he is totally unworthy of trust."

"I know, Dad. Don't worry. But I'm torn. Uncle Ramananda is doing something that I think is basically right. He's going to go all Edward Albee on the Gummadi brothers, and I'm going to sit on the sidelines too scared of the consequences to pull my weight."

"You can contribute in different ways. The school for one. Ramananda has lots of guys who can put sugar in a gas tank, but not one who can design a microchip or go toe-to-toe with a BMC lawyer and come out on top."

"Actually, I don't know the first thing about chip design and the sugar-in-the-gas-tank thing doesn't work. I thought so too, but Ramananda says . . ."

"Okay. Okay. But the point's the same. I know this is important to you. But it's his fight."

"It's mine too."

"Is it?"

"I'm an Indian citizen and I'm from Dharavi . . . sort of," she acknowledged.

"Sort of." He was gentle, but Lena could hear the emphasis in his response. "Remember that the defining feature of life in a place like Dharavi is the inability to leave. You're there by choice, but you and Ramananda are among only a handful who are. Your mother got out the first chance she had and she never looked back."

"But she never forgot."

"No," Sam agreed. "She didn't. She couldn't."

"And she fought for what she believed in. She fought against caste prejudice, for one."

"In her art, yes. In her words. By her actions. Not in the streets battling the police."

"Don't worry. I'm not going to start channeling Patty Hearst."

"That's a relief. Did you know that the Symbionese Liberation Army's seven-headed cobra was originally a Sri Lankan symbol? It was a guardian *naga* that would watch over the irrigation network and the rice fields."

"Actually, that's kind of cool." One of the things that Lena loved about talking to her father was the way his mind worked. He jumped quickly and easily from subject to subject, making linkages that were not always obvious but invariably interesting. Like many FSOs, he was also dynamite at Trivial Pursuit.

"Still," she continued, "I don't want to man the barricade. But I do want to do what's right."

"So do we all, sugar."

Lena could see that her father was distracted. Something heavy was weighing on him. She knew that look. After her mother had died, her father had tried to shield her from so much, tried to protect her from the world. She had rebelled against it and perhaps she still was. Maybe that was part of the reason she had come back to Mumbai.

"Dad, what's bothering you?" she asked. "Don't deny it. I can read you. Something's wrong. Tell me."

"It's nothing. Just some trouble at work."

"I thought your new job was supposed to be low-stress."

"I thought so too, but it's more . . . complicated than I thought it would be."

"Are you eating okay?" Lena knew that her father had a tendency to rely on Indian and Chinese takeout as his primary source of nutrition.

"More than okay. I could stand to lose a few pounds. I need to get back on the bike."

"I miss riding when I'm out here." Lena shared her father's love of the D.C. area's extensive network of bike trails. The C&O Canal offered mile after mile of shaded trails and the W&OD Trail ran some forty miles out toward the beautiful Shenandoah Mountains. Riding a bike through the chaotic Mumbai traffic and sucking on diesel fumes while dodging overloaded trucks on potholed streets wasn't quite the same.

"Come home, then. Even just for a visit. We'll go riding out by Chincoteague."

"Maybe this summer," Lena offered.

"Listen." Her father's face was suddenly quite serious. "Things are really starting to heat up in Kashmir. Another war with Pakistan is absolutely not out of the question. And this time, they'd both have nuclear weapons. There's no way of knowing just how far they'd go. Maybe it's time to think about coming home."

This was not the first time they had covered this ground, and Lena knew that it would not be the last.

"It's not going to happen, Dad. Rangarajan is totally reasonable, and he'll find a way to compromise with Talwar."

"Hey, which one of us is the political analyst? It takes two to compromise, and Talwar's increasingly boxed in at home."

"I know. I know. We've talked about this. But I have a good job out here and I feel perfectly safe."

"Okay for now. But I want you to promise me that you'll get out immediately if I tell you that things are moving closer to a fight."

"We'll see," Lena equivocated.

It was a good thing, Sam thought after he broke the connection with Lena, that he had stopped playing in high-stakes card games. His poker face was clearly not what it once was. Or maybe it was only Lena. Maybe she understood him in ways that no one else could. No one except her mother, at any rate.

Sam took a look around the townhouse. His housekeeper, Carmen, had been by that day, and the place was in reasonable shape. He had a date with Vanalika in just a few hours, and if the planets aligned, there was a chance she would be able to come home with him. Of course, that depended in part on how well things went with the difficult conversation that Sam knew they had to have. He took a quick shower and changed into a pair of dark slacks and a blazer. Vanalika, he knew, would be dressy. She always was.

It was a forty-five-minute drive to Rockville, Maryland. Rockville was actually considered a close-in suburb of D.C. It was not far from Capitol Hill as the proverbial crow flies, but there was no easy way to get there. Rather than cut north through the city, it actually made sense to drive south and get on 395. This soon put Sam on the George Washington Memorial Parkway, one of his favorite drives in D.C. There was a Coltrane disc in the CD player and he let *Giant Steps* wash over and through him as he sped down the rain-slicked parkway.

Rockville was a soulless suburb that seemed to be made up entirely of car dealerships and tae kwon do studios with grubby windows, but it had at least one redeeming quality: spectacular ethnic food. A few minutes before eight, Sam pulled up in front of Goa, an Indian restaurant that was nothing special to look at from the outside. Inside, however, Goa was intimate and charming, decorated by someone with good taste and the budget to make good use of it. The decor was midcentury modern rather than Indian kitsch, and the artwork on the walls was more than a cut above what one would have expected from a strip-mall restaurant.

The reservation—somewhat unimaginatively, Sam thought—was under the name of Johnson. Vanalika claimed to like the cloak-and-dagger aspects of their illicit relationship, but she was not especially good at it.

The maître d', a young Indian woman in an elegant emerald green sari, seated Sam at a table in the corner under a Keith Haring lithograph.

He ordered a Kingfisher.

Vanalika walked in and bypassed the maître d' and came straight over to Sam. They did not kiss their hellos. Avoiding PDA was part of what Vanalika in mock seriousness called their OPSEC protocol.

"Hello, handsome," she said, taking the seat across from him.

"Good evening, beautiful."

Under the table, Vanalika slipped one foot out of her pump and rubbed it against Sam's calf. Secret PDA was part of another equally important protocol.

"You look . . ." Sam paused, looking for the right words. "Like a goddess."

"Is it my elephant head?" She giggled.

"If only. I have a thing for girls with substantial noses. But I was thinking more of the one with eight arms."

"Careful. That's Durga the Inaccessible. She hurls thunderbolts and rides a lion. You sure you want to go there?"

"I like my chances."

"Play your cards right and you'll believe I have eight arms before the night is done."

The waiter came by to take their orders. Goa specialized in South Indian food, which was generally spicier than its northern cousin, and Vanalika chose a vegetarian *biryani* made with saffron and nutmeg, and a yogurt chutney. Unconstrained by Vanalika's vegetarianism, Sam ordered lamb with coconut curry, roti, and a cucumber and mint *pachadi* to help cut the heat of the curry.

While they waited for the food, they chatted about largely inconsequential things: a conference of South Asia academics that Vanalika was helping to organize in Chicago in a month's time, a new biography of Nehru that Sam was reading, and the upcoming India-Australia cricket test match.

The waiter arrived with a large tray balancing half a dozen dishes. Steam from the dishes wafted across the table redolent of curry and tamarind. The food at Goa was worth the drive up from Capitol Hill. Sam had eaten here before, but it was Vanalika's first time.

"I'm impressed," she said, after sampling the food. "This is the real deal."

Sam had to nod his agreement, his mouth full of lamb.

After the food had been cleared away, they ordered coffee and cognac. It was the perfect counterpoint to the spicy Indian meal.

"Vee, there's something I want to talk to you about," Sam said.

"I'm still not moving in with you, Sam," Vanalika replied light-heartedly.

"Not that. Or at least not only that. No. It's something else."

"Okay. Shoot."

Sam hesitated. This was uncertain ground for him. No matter how general he was, he was about to discuss highly classified information. It was a breach of not only his professional obligations but also the law. He could, in theory, go to jail for what he was about to say. Choosing his words carefully seemed the least he could do.

"You're familiar with the intel-sharing setup that we have with you and Islamabad?"

"Sure. You share stuff on Pakistan with us and stuff on us with Pakistan, something of a confidence-building arrangement."

"Yes. And it's been a successful program up to now."

"Up to now?"

"Yes. I have reason to believe that there is information being passed through that channel that is . . . not accurate."

"How inaccurate?"

"Try 100 percent. Like fiction, only considerably more dangerous."

"How do you know?"

"Because you're a part of the story, Vee. When was the last time you talked to Guhathakurta?"

"Panchavaktra? It's been a couple of weeks. Maybe even a month or so."

"Well, I saw an intel piece last week in which you supposedly called Guhathakurta in Delhi to complain about the prime minister coddling the Pakistanis. It was pretty aggressive stuff, but Guhathakurta is known as a hardliner, and people who don't know you would find it pretty credible."

"Panchavaktra's a knuckle-dragging Neanderthal. He and I disagree on many things, politics not least among them."

"People see what they want to see or what they expect to see. Guhathakurta sets the frame for this piece. People expect him to be like this. They could have picked any of a dozen people senior enough to be the foil in the conversation, but they picked you. On top of that, you supposedly made the call on the evening of March 29."

"That Saturday? The day we went to the mountains?"

"Yeah."

"With no phone lines and no cell reception?"

"Yeah."

"Kind of poor planning on their part."

"Or good planning on ours."

"Except that we can't tell anybody where we were that night. It would cost us both our jobs."

"There is that."

"And this work of fiction has been shared with Pakistan's intelligence services?"

Sam thought Vanalika looked worried. She had reason to be.

"I think so."

"That's not good."

It was an enormous understatement.

"No. It's not."

They were silent for a moment as Vanalika seemed to mull over what Sam had told her.

"It's not the only one, is it?" she asked. "There would be no real point to it if it was the only one."

Vanalika, Sam thought to himself again, *was extremely smart.*

"No," he acknowledged. "It's not."

"How bad are the other messages?"

"Pretty bad."

"And they go in both directions? Some for Islamabad and some for us."

"Yes."

"What are you going to do about it? Besides telling me, I mean."

"I don't know yet."

"Who's behind it?"

"I don't know that either."

"Why? What's the purpose? Who benefits?"

Sam shrugged.

"Sam . . ."

"Yes?"

"Whoever is in a position to do something like that is in a position to do an awful lot of other things too."

"The thought had crossed my mind."

"Be careful," she urged.

"I will."

"Don't do anything stupid."

"We'll see."

00:13

Andy is dead."

Sam felt like he had been punched in the gut. He did not need to ask which Andy Sara meant.

"How?"

He could see that Sara had been crying. Her eyes were red, and there was a dark smudge on one cheek where she had tried to wipe off a line of mascara that had blackened her tears.

"He was murdered. Maureen in INR told me that the police are calling it a mugging gone bad. You know that he moved into that apartment up by the Mount Vernon metro stop a few months ago. It's kind of a rough neighborhood that's starting to turn around. 'Pioneering,' he called it."

Sara started to cry again, and what was left of her eye makeup dripped onto her cheeks. Sam pulled a pack of Kleenex out of his desk drawer and offered it to her. As Sara wiped her eyes, Sam walked around the desk. With a stifled sob, she turned toward him and buried her face against his chest, clinging tightly to his arms with both hands.

They stood that way for a minute or more before Sam broke the clinch and steered Sara to one of the two chairs in his office. He sat across from her. His shirt felt hot and wet where she had cried against his chest.

Sam wanted desperately to close his eyes, put his head on the desk, give himself over to the crushing sadness that came with the knowledge of his friend's death.

"What can I do?" he asked instead.

"You can't do a damn thing, Sam. Andy's dead."

"I meant for you, Sara."

Sam was glad to see Sara demonstrating the kind of combative moxie she was famous for. It would help her through this. Sara and Andy had been friends for years. It was going to be hard for all of them. She shook her head.

"Not now."

"Do you know anything more about what happened?" Sam asked.

"Just that he was found early this morning on Ridge Street, about three blocks from the metro station. He'd been shot. His wallet and watch were gone, and the police think it was an addict looking for a quick score. The neighborhood fits the profile. There are no suspects."

Even under emotional duress, Sara Zehri could give a briefing.

"His watch was gone?" Sam asked.

"Yes. Why?"

"Andy wore one of the cheapest digital watches I have ever seen. It looked like something you would find in a box of cereal. It couldn't have cost him more than a couple of bucks. Who'd want to steal it?"

"I doubt the guy thought it through. He's probably got a mental checklist: wallet, rings, watch. That kind of thing. Addicts aren't the most logical sort."

If it was an addict, Sam thought to himself. As an analyst, he did not believe in coincidences. On Tuesday, Andy Krittenbrink identified a data set that linked a secretive government contractor to what was potentially a massive intelligence fraud. On Thursday, he was dead. Correlation is not causality. But it was still suspicious as hell. The first creeping tendrils of guilt began to claw at Sam's conscience.

Sam did not want to jump to conclusions without evidence. It was most likely that Andy's death was just what it was purported to be, tragic and utterly explicable. A bad neighborhood. Bad luck. And a bad day. Unless Andy had done the one thing Sam had asked him not to do and had talked to someone about the Panoptes messages. They had not spoken about it on the phone, at least not in a specific way. But Sam was not willing to write Andy's death off as a random act of violence. Not yet. Could he have inadvertently put Andy in danger by asking him to dig into the intel records? It was possible. Maybe the search that Andy had performed in the database had triggered a warning. Sophisticated algorithms stood guard over the nation's secrets, looking for the kind of search queries that were hallmarks of espionage. Edward Snowden's exposure of the full range of NSA activities had prodded the intelligence community into reinforcing that kind of passive surveillance. Andy's search terms may have tripped an alarm of some sort. If so, was Sam ultimately accountable for his death? It was painful to even consider the question.

"What about the funeral arrangements?" he asked.

"The Parklawn cemetery in Rockville on Saturday morning.

Andy's parents have suggested a donation to the Red Cross instead of flowers. Andy was never a big flowers guy."

She started to cry again, softly this time.

Sam closed his eyes. There would be time later for questions and recriminations. For now, he had a friend to mourn.

Mother Nature offered up a suitably gloomy backdrop to the funeral. It wasn't raining, but it wasn't not raining either. The sky was an iron gray, and the mist that clung to the ground ensured that the mourners were damp and miserable despite the black umbrellas that many of them carried.

There was a good turnout, somewhere around fifty or sixty people. Sam hoped that he did as well when his time came. He knew some of them, mostly South Asia policy people and a few other State Department types. Most of the mourners, however, were strangers, family and friends from other parts of Andy's life.

An attractive blond woman in a tailored black suit had been introduced to him as Andy's fiancée. She looked to be totally out of Krittenbrink's league. *Well done, young grasshopper,* Sam thought. *I'm so terribly sorry about the life you're going to miss out on: love, family, a house in one of the D.C. suburbs with good schools for the kids. It's not fair.*

Andy's parents were stolid Midwesterners who were staggering under the weight of a burden that no parent should have to bear. To Sam's surprise, Andy's mother had asked him to be a pallbearer.

"He looked up to you," she had explained. "He talked about you all the time and said that he admired your integrity. I would like it if you would help carry him to his final rest and maybe say a few words."

Sam had been struck by her composure, and now he stood waiting for the hearse to arrive alongside the eclectic group that would carry Andy's body the short distance to the gravesite: a brother, a cousin, a friend from Andy's hometown in Minnesota, a college roommate, and a Sri Lanka specialist from Brookings with whom Andy had been working on a book.

The hearse pulled up as close to the grave as possible, and Sam helped pull the heavy maple coffin out of the back. It felt like an out-of-body experience. When he closed his eyes, he was looking down on the scene, hovering some twenty feet overhead like the figure in Janani's final painting. His feet moved over the slippery grass, and he carried his share of the weight, but it was all autopilot. Muscle memory.

The funeral home had laid a green carpet around the grave as a kind of border lined with flowers in white and yellow. It was a poor disguise. Like garish makeup on a corpse. Gussied up, it was still a naked gash in the earth in which Sam would have to place the body of a friend. The pallbearers laid the coffin on the thick nylon webbing that stretched over the grave itself. The coffin was suspended in space, lying on the cusp of the underworld.

Folding chairs stood in ragged rows under a broad white awning. Sam sat between Sara and Shoe. It was raining for real now and the light staccato of the rain beating against the canvas was oddly soothing.

Andy hadn't exactly been the churchgoing type. The Unitarian minister who had agreed to lead the services had never actually met Andy. He had met with the family and a number of friends so that he would have some material to work with, but it was still pretty threadbare. Sam paid minimal attention to the minister's words. Inevitably, the man quoted Ben Jonson's line—"in short measures, life may perfect be"—which was actually about fleeting moments of happiness rather than death and certainly not about dying too damn young. Andy would have known that, and it would have rankled just a little. As an analyst, he had been nothing if not precise.

But what did it matter? What did it matter to Andy?

While the minister spoke, Sam's mind wandered back and forth across the problem set. Was Andy's death a tragic accident, to the extent that murder can ever be an accident? Or was it somehow connected to the mysterious Panoptes program. How was Panoptes tied to Argus Systems? And—he approached this one tentatively, ashamed of its inherent selfishness—if whoever was behind Panoptes knew about Andy, did they know about Sam too? Underlying all of this was the $64,000 question: What the hell was Panoptes?

He felt a sudden sharp pain on his right instep. Sara had driven one six-inch heel down hard on his foot. He realized that the minister had stopped speaking. People were looking at him. It was his turn to speak.

Sam stood and made his way to the front. There was a lectern decorated with the outlines of doves. Sam stood beside the lectern rather than behind it, leaning one hand on the top for support.

"Hello," he began. "My name is Sam Trainor and Andy Krittenbrink was both my colleague and my friend. We worked together in the State Department's Bureau of Intelligence and Research. INR they call it. I was just passing through, but it was Andy's professional home for most of his adult life. We shared a passion for South Asia: the people, the cultures, the history, and the complex politics of the place. Nothing made Andy happier than solving a puzzle.

"Not long after I joined INR, one of the youngest analysts we had, heck one of the youngest analysts I'd ever seen . . . he looked to me to be all of sixteen or seventeen . . . gave me a report to review. It was a piece of leadership analysis, essentially a bio of the new chief of the Bangladeshi military who was coming to Washington for a round of introductory calls. We were under pressure to keep everything we wrote short and tight, and there was a paragraph in the report about the general's lepidopterist leanings. He was evidently an avid butterfly collector, a point that this young analyst had expanded into some four sentences of our one-page report. When I told him to cut the butterflies and replace them with something more military-sounding, Andy pushed back. Firmly and persuasively. The butterflies were what he called the telling detail, the small point that illuminated the larger whole. The general, he explained, was acquisitive and almost pathological in his need for order and structure. He liked small things. He was more a tactician than a strategist. That was the point. It wasn't about the butterflies.

"In the end, the butterflies survived and we got the report back from the secretary of state with a hand-scribbled note about how much she had enjoyed reading the bio and how helpful it had been. I learned something pretty important that day.

"With that in mind, I would offer you a brief story about Andy that I consider a telling detail.

"Two years ago, Andy and I were part of a fact-finding team traveling through India and Sri Lanka assessing the progress in the fight against human trafficking. Slavery is not a thing of the past. Tens of thousands of people still live in bondage in South Asia.

"As part of our research, we met with the director of a shelter and halfway house in Lucknow who was working with victims of trafficking to help them start new lives. It was a noble mission, but an expensive one, and the director told us that the center would likely have to close its doors sometime in the next couple of months unless he could find a consistent source of funding. The twenty-odd families living there would be out on the streets.

"This was not an uncommon tale of woe in what we jaded diplomats often dismissively refer to as the do-gooder sector. Listening with empathy, or at least apparent empathy, is part of the job. We had all heard stories like this many times before, however, and five minutes after leaving the meeting it was gone, like water off a duck's back. For me that is. Not for Andy.

"Andy showed up for breakfast in the hotel the next morning looking like he'd slept in his clothes—like he hadn't slept at all, in fact. The rest of us teased him mercilessly, I'm embarrassed to admit, about a young man's night on the town in Lucknow.

"On our way to the first meeting of the morning, Andy asked to stop by the shelter we had visited the day before. There, he handed the director a memory stick with a well-researched and carefully constructed grant application along with the names and e-mail addresses of a dozen relevant foundations. Andy had stayed up all night to write it.

"The shelter got the grant and it is still in operation today, helping some of humanity's least fortunate to build new and better lives.

"Andy was a superb analyst, but he was an even better human being. He was not content simply to observe the world. He wanted to change it. And he did."

And it may have killed him, Sam added silently.

"The world is a poorer place without Andy Krittenbrink in it," he concluded, looking at Andy's mother as he said the final words. From the brightness in her tearstained eyes, Sam could tell that he had hit the right note. He hoped that he had brought her some small measure of comfort in her hour of grief.

At the end of the ceremony, cemetery workers lowered the casket into the grave. Sam joined a line of mourners who waited to throw a shovel full of dirt on top of the casket. Afterward, he stood alone under the shelter of a beech tree as Andy's family gathered by the gravesite for a private moment.

Someone touched his arm from behind. He turned to see a familiar face. "That was a nice speech."

"Thanks, Quick. I can barely remember what I said."

"You diplomats are all so damn glib."

Edward "Quick" Sands was the head of the CIA's South Asia analysis unit. Sam had not noticed Quick among the mourners. That was one of his talents. Blending in. No one ever seemed to notice Quick. With his long face, gray hair and dark suit, he looked like an undertaker, just part of the backdrop at the Parklawn cemetery.

"Can we talk?" Quick asked.

"Sure."

Quick led Sam away from the gravesite to a relatively dry spot under the eaves of a massive marble mausoleum.

"How have you been?" Sam asked. "I haven't seen you since I moved over to Argus."

"I know. The siren song of the private sector. I've heard it too. The Beltway Bandits have been gobbling up so many of my best people that I decided it was time to make the move myself. I've been in talks with Xenos about taking a job with them and being seconded back to the Agency. It'd be a 50 percent bump in salary and I'd be drawing my pension on top." Quick looked almost apologetic.

"Xenos is an Argus subsidiary."

"It is. Which explains what I did . . . maybe a little bit. Even if it can't justify it."

"What are you talking about?"

"Andy came to Langley three days ago to see me," Quick said carefully.

"Oh, shit."

Quick looked at him appraisingly.

"You know about this?" he asked.

"Panoptes?"

"Yes."

"I told him not to talk to anyone."

"I can understand why."

"What did he tell you?"

"He showed me a copy of the analysis he'd done. It was good work, remarkably good work. I think that was one of the reasons he came to me. Andy knew it was good and it killed him to sit on it." Quick winced at his own poor choice of words. "Stupid pride."

"I told him I needed some time," Sam said miserably.

"Maybe he had doubts. You being with Argus and all."

"Wait. Did Andy tell you that Argus was the source of the Panoptes material?"

"He did. He told me it wasn't clear to him at first, but he'd figured it out."

Sam should have thought of that. Krittenbrink was smart as hell and a trained analyst. The connection between Panoptes and Argus was not especially hard to draw once you knew to look for it.

"Andy didn't mention to you that we'd worked on this together?"

"No."

Sam's stomach turned over, and for a moment, he thought he

was going to be sick. Maybe Andy had gone around him to the CIA because he was trying to protect Sam from any possible retribution from his employer. Or maybe he was uncertain about Sam's ultimate loyalties. Whatever his reason, the results were the same. His friend was dead. And he was dead at least in part because Sam had not trusted him with the full truth. It had been a stupid decision on Sam's part, and another data point to add to the guilt set. He swallowed hard and tasted bile in the back of his throat.

"Now, here's the thing." Quick paused as though searching for the right words.

"Yes?"

"Andy clearly wanted me to do something with the report. Push a button under my desk and summon some secret CIA SWAT team to assault Argus headquarters in Arlington. I'm not sure what he wanted. Probably he wasn't either."

"So what'd you do?"

"I called Garret Spears and I asked him what was going on. Spears was absolutely accommodating. He denied any knowledge of Panoptes but said he'd look into it. If it was an act, it was one hell of a convincing one."

"You called Spears?"

Quick looked at the ground between them.

"Yeah. I did. And I wish like hell that I could take that back. So, maybe twenty-four hours after my conversation with Spears, Andy is shot in a crime that is never going to be solved. Doesn't that set off your coincidence alarms?"

"Mine were ringing even before you told me that Andy had talked to you," Sam admitted.

"I called a friend on the D.C. police force to get some background on the case. Andy was shot twice in the head with a 9mm.

What kind of addict does a double-tap to the head? That's more like a professional hit than a fucked-up drug deal. Believe me, Spears knows people who do that kind of thing for a living."

"I don't doubt it," Sam said, thinking of John Weeder's cold, dead eyes. "I think he may even employ some of them."

"I have thirty years in the intel community," Quick said. "And this is the first time I've ever been afraid, the first time I've known something I wish I didn't know. If Argus is really behind what happened to Andy, what's to stop them from coming after me? Spears seems to trust me for now. But how long will it last?"

"So what are you going to do?"

"I have four months of leave saved up. I'm using a chunk of it starting tomorrow. At this point, my primary career objective is not to die. I'm going somewhere I can lie low for a while and see if I can escape notice."

"I'm confident you'll succeed in that," Sam said, without a hint of irony in his voice. "Let me ask you, Quick. What the hell is Panoptes?"

"I have no idea."

"Who would?"

Quick shrugged.

"Watch yourself, Sam. I think Spears may be a little unbalanced."

"What makes you say so?"

"After I told him about Andy's report, all he wanted to do was ask me a bunch of questions about fucking trolley cars."

SKYLINE DRIVE, VIRGINIA
APRIL 11

`00:14`

It should have been a seven-hour drive from D.C. to Linville, North Carolina. When Sam reached Front Royal, however, he made a spur-of-the-moment decision to take Skyline Drive rather than follow I-81 South, which was put-a-brick-on-the-accelerator flat and straight. Skyline was a beautiful meandering route along the ridge of the Shenandoahs.

In the summer, Skyline Drive was a virtual parking lot. But this early in the season, he had the road to himself even on a Sunday. Driving helped him think, and as he zipped through the park Sam wrestled with the unanswerable questions that had kept him up at night since seeing Vanalika's name in the NSA intercept. His thoughts kept drifting back to Andy. There was no getting around the fact that the young analyst would still be alive if Sam hadn't asked him to start turning over rocks. It was his fault that Andy was dead. That would be with him forever. Overlaying this sense of responsibility was a burning shame at the relief he had felt when Quick had told him that Spears did not know he and Andy had been working together. It was instinctual, something at the animal level. Self-preservation.

He stopped at the Ivy Creek overlook to stretch his legs and clear his head. The trees were just coming into bloom at the higher elevations, and Sam had an unobstructed view down the length of the Blue Ridge to Stony Man Mountain. To the west, he could see the Alleghenies outlined against a sky that was a perfect cerulean blue. Off to the east, however, Sam could see a dark band of clouds on the horizon like a portent of a gathering storm.

It seemed appropriate. Powerful pieces were being moved around the global chessboard, but Sam could not see whose hands were moving which pieces. Not from the perspective of a pawn.

He had an idea, however, about someone who might, an interesting friend who himself had interesting friends.

Skyline Drive fed into I-64 not too far from the mountain cabin where Sam and Vanalika had so recently spent an idyllic weekend. I-64 took him to I-81 and for some two hundred miles it was all straight and flat.

At Glade Spring, Virginia, he got off the interstate onto a rural highway that took him into North Carolina. The single-lane road crossed in and out of a national forest before reaching Linville. From there, he followed the GPS program in his phone to an unmarked dirt track that Google assured him was called Dry Gulch Road.

Sam pulled into a dirt-and-gravel driveway and parked next to a black mailbox that had a number 9 on it hand-lettered in white paint. The farmhouse at number 9 was ramshackle, with a swayback roofline and peeling red paint. Sam got out and walked up to the front porch. At one end of the porch, two telescopes were propped up on tripods. One was fat and stubby, and the other long and graceful. They were not toys, and they did not look cheap.

At the other end, a heavyset man in jeans and a blue work shirt was dozing in an overstuffed chair with his head tipped back and his mouth open. He snored softly. There was a half-full bottle of bourbon on the coffee table in front of him and a glass tumbler in which melting ice cubes had lightened the liquor by several shades. Sam sat down on one of the other chairs arranged loosely around the table. He took off his sunglasses and set them next to the bottle.

"Why don't you go into the kitchen and get yourself a glass. Bring some more ice while you're at it." The man's eyes did not open and the snoring only scaled back a decibel or two rather than stopping, but he was clearly awake.

"Afternoon, Earl."

"Afternoon, Sam."

Sam went to the kitchen, which looked like it could have been a model from the Sears catalog of 1935. He found glasses in one of the cabinets and a bowl that he filled with ice from a Frigidaire that was old enough to have rust spots.

On the porch, he poured two healthy slugs of bourbon over ice. It was good stuff, a small-batch Kentucky bourbon called Knob Creek.

Sam placed one of the glasses in front of his host, who was now wide-awake and attentive. He looked largely as Sam had remembered him, with a head of thick white hair that was all but untamable and icy blue eyes that sparkled with a kind of fierce intelligence. There was an ugly scar under his right eye, white and purple and about two inches long. Sam had heard half a dozen different stories about that scar. All of them, he suspected, were wrong.

"Thank you kindly," his host said, raising his glass briefly before taking a sip.

"You're more than welcome. It's your whiskey."

"That it is. How long has it been, Sam?"

"Almost five years."

Sam had known Earl Holly since his first post in the Foreign Service. In Islamabad almost twenty-five years ago, Sam had been the junior guy in the political section and Earl had been the CIA station chief. Holly had taken a shine to Sam and he had brought him in on meetings that had given Sam a new and richer understanding of how things in Pakistan actually worked. Through Holly's patronage, Sam had developed a network of contacts and connections well beyond what a junior officer could ordinarily expect to achieve. As a result, Sam had started to build a reputation as an up-and-comer, a potential that he had manifestly failed to fulfill.

The Islamabad assignment had led to stints in New Delhi, Mumbai, and Karachi. Often, his career path had intercepted with Holly's. Earl had bounced back and forth between South Asia and Washington. But while Sam's responsibilities were open and straightforward, Earl had been part of the secretive puzzle palace of Cold War espionage. He had cut his teeth on the 1965 war between India and Pakistan that had threatened to embroil the United States and the Soviet Union in a potentially catastrophic proxy conflict. Later, he had played a key role in arming the mujahideen in Afghanistan, precipitating a humiliating Soviet withdrawal from South Asia and contributing to the eventual collapse of the USSR. In D.C., Earl had occupied a succession of senior intelligence positions, eventually rising to deputy director of the clandestine service before age and a power play on the part of a rival in the DNI's office had forced him into retirement.

"The fish will never see me coming," he had promised at his retirement party.

Sam had lost touch with Earl when he left D.C. and the South Asia policy universe. A North Carolina native and a proud Tarheel, Earl had once told him that he did not want to be one of those D.C. lifers who never realize when it's time to move on.

"When I'm gone, I'm gone," he had explained.

Sam had had to call in a few favors to get Earl's current contact information. Earl liked his privacy. Even so, the word was that he had not broken completely with his former life. A CIA contact told Sam that Earl had kept his own private network active. The same contact had warned him that Earl was more interested in the bourbon bottle than the dusty fishing rod Sam had spotted propped up against the wall in the kitchen.

Half-soused and living like a mad hermit in the woods, Earl Holly still knew more about South Asia and, more important, about South Asia specialists in the intelligence community in Washington than any man alive. He knew where most of the bodies were buried, if only because he had interred so many of them himself. If anyone could help Sam tease apart the mystery of Panoptes, it was Earl.

"So what motivated you to make the long drive down here? To say nothing of finding me in the first place. You in trouble? I'll bet it's about a girl. It's always a girl."

"It's partly about a girl," Sam agreed with a grin.

"You need romantic advice? Well, you've come to the right place." Earl took another snort of bourbon and set the glass to rest at the apex of his substantial belly.

Yeah, what woman could resist?

"I need your help with a puzzle," Sam said instead.

"I'm good at puzzles."

"You're the best."

Sam laid out for Earl everything that he knew, from his discovery of the suspect NSA intercept to his conversation with Quick Sands at Krittenbrink's funeral.

"I'm sorry about Andy," Earl said, when Sam had finished. "I didn't know him. He came in after I was already out. But I heard good things from some of my old friends, and I know that you and he were close."

"Thanks. We were. And what happened to him was my fault. I never should have gotten him involved in this. Andy's death was a tragedy. But if Quick was right, it was more than that. It was premeditated murder."

Earl closed his eyes for a moment as though deep in thought. Without opening his eyes, he reached sure-handed for the tumbler he had set back on the coffee table and took another generous sip of the Knob Creek.

"Tell me more about Argus Systems."

"What do you want to know?"

"Who owns it. Who runs it. How profitable is it. What kind of ties does the management have to the government. And whatever else you think might be of value."

"Argus is privately held and the owner of record is a shell company in Bermuda. I did a little digging around before I took the job, and word was that the initial financing for Argus came from a VC firm called Perseus Capital."

"Argus. Perseus. Panoptes. Someone really likes their Greeks."

"That's modern Washington. Romans who think they're Greeks."

Earl chuckled and poured himself another two fingers of bourbon.

"What about management?"

"The CEO is a guy named Garret Spears. Ex-military. Former

Special Forces. Spent some time in North Africa but more time in South Arlington. He's been with Argus from the beginning. Very smooth and very, very well connected."

"To whom?"

"I'm not sure," Sam admitted. "At least I don't know who his primary patron is inside the Lord administration. He had the connections to get a very lucrative contract to provide intel and analysis on South Asia. That's why they brought me on."

"The contract is for both collection and analysis?"

"That's right."

"So who's doing the collection part?"

"There's a group within Argus that operates in their own private universe. They sure don't look like analysts. Or talk like analysts, for that matter."

"Former Agency?"

"Military, I think. Maybe some PSYOPs types and certainly some guys who were former Special Forces. The head of the unit is a guy named Weeder."

"John Weeder?"

"Yeah."

"Ex-navy?"

"Former SEAL, I believe. Same as Spears."

"Maybe at one point. After that, he worked for a . . . darker . . . part of the SpecOps world."

"Do you know him?"

"I met him once. It was like being introduced to Death at a cocktail party. He has a reputation, and I'm familiar with at least some of the accomplishments on his résumé. He is not a nice man."

"No," Sam agreed. "He is not."

Earl sat silently for a minute, and Sam could almost see the gears turning in his head. Earl Holly had a class-A brain. Alcohol may have dulled the edge a bit, but he was still plenty sharp.

"Let's look at Panoptes for a moment," Earl said, when the critical components seemed finally to have meshed. "The program seems aimed at driving India and Pakistan closer to war, maybe even right over the edge into nuclear Armageddon. Who in their right mind would want to do such a thing?"

It seemed to be a rhetorical question, as though he already knew the answer and he was just walking Sam forward to the same conclusion.

"In their right mind? No one I can think of."

"Commander Weeder's involvement leads me to a conclusion that I don't especially like."

"Which is?"

"Tell me. Have you ever heard of a group called the Stoics?"

"More Greeks? It was a school of philosophy in Athens. Wasn't it Zeno who founded it?"

"Ah, the value of a liberal arts education. Yes, it was Zeno. But those aren't the Stoics I mean. There's an American group of the same name that has been on the fringes of policy making in Washington since long before you and I were around."

"Like a club?"

"Of sorts. The membership is limited. They are people of influence who believe they have a special duty to lead the Republic through hard times, to make difficult choices on the basis of rational calculus and then take action."

"How come I've never heard of them?"

"They prefer it that way. They do most of their work through cutouts and front companies. They do as little as possible directly."

"And how come you *have* heard of them?"

"I have run into this group a number of times over the years. They had certain interests in Afghanistan, for example, that were not aligned with mine. They wanted to include the hardline Wahhabi elements in our train-and-equip program. I thought we could do the job without them and warned my superiors that we needed to look ten or twenty years down the road before bringing the crazies in on what we were doing. It wasn't even close. I lost. There's three thousand American dead from 9/11 who can attest to that."

"So you know who the Stoics are?"

"No."

Sam looked quizzical.

"Do you know why I moved out here to the middle of nowhere?"

"Fishing?" Sam offered, on the theory that this answer was more polite than "bourbon."

"Nah. I don't really like fishing. That's just what you're supposed to say at your retirement party. No, I moved out here for the skies." Earl nodded toward the twin telescopes at the far end of the porch. "I didn't like to talk about this back in the world. It's a little too sissy for someone who was in my line of work. But I've been a sky watcher since I was a kid. The night skies out here are fantastic. There's no light pollution and we're up pretty high so you get a clear view of the stars. I'm hoping maybe someday to get my name on a comet, even if 'Holly's Comet' comes dangerously close to copyright infringement."

Sam nodded encouragingly, confident that Earl would eventually get around to the point.

"Do you know how astronomers—real astronomers, I mean—not us amateurs. Do you know how they find black holes?"

"With a very big telescope?"

"Well, yes. But not really. At least not directly. You can't see a black hole. The gravity is so strong it sucks in everything around it, including light. But massive gravity like that affects other things that are nearby, things like stars and planets. The black hole affects their movements ever so slightly. But with the right instruments, you can capture the change. Measure it. And from those measurements, you can tell that there's a black hole in a particular part of space."

"So you don't have to see it to know it's there," Sam suggested.

"That's right. Did you know that there's a supermassive black hole at the center of our galaxy that just sits there eating solar systems like popcorn?"

"I'll confess that I did not."

"Well, no one's seen it, but the astronomers are pretty sure it's there. You can see how it influences the stars around it, and it's the only explanation that fits the data. Now here's the thing. As important as that black hole is, you wouldn't want to get too close to it. It'd suck you in and scatter your particles across the eighth dimension or whatever. It would be decidedly unhealthy."

The corner of Sam's mouth turned up just slightly at the Buckaroo Banzai reference. Earl Holly, legendary CIA case officer, was a closet science-fiction geek. *Who knew?*

"And the Stoics are like that?" he asked. "You can't see them, but you can see what they do?"

"Pretty much. You can see its outlines because it's the part of what you're looking at that you can't see. You can see its shadow and you can see its effects. But don't get too close."

"Weeder is a part of this?"

"I don't think he's a member. At least not a member of the senior leadership. He's a killer. An assassin. I think he does the wet work for the Stoics, or at least he used to. If he's with Argus Systems now, there's a good chance that the company is somehow linked to the Stoics. It'd be consistent with past practice."

"So why would a group like that want a war on the subcontinent? Arms sales?"

"I don't think so. That would be a little too venal for the Stoics. They aren't salesmen and they aren't interested in money."

"What does interest them?"

"Cassandra."

"Another Greek?"

"The last one for now . . . I hope. Cassandra is a computer, an extremely powerful computer that some very smart people were using to model nuclear terrorism. Where a weapon might come from. Who would use it. How they would get it into the United States. Whether they might simply explode it or try to blackmail the government into pulling out of the Middle East, for example."

"Let me guess. Cassandra decided that Pakistan was the most likely source of the bomb."

"That's what my . . . friends . . . tell me."

"I wonder how many millions of dollars the government spent to reach that blindingly obvious conclusion."

"Not 'M,' my boy, 'B.' Billions."

"And your friends the Stoics decided that a nuclear war was the way to solve the problem? Have India turn the country into a smoking pile of glass?"

"I don't think that's it."

"Then what?"

Earl hesitated. For just a moment, Sam had the impression that he was about to say something important, to fill in a piece of the puzzle. But the moment passed quickly, and it was possible that Sam had simply imagined it. Hope, he knew, could do that.

"I'm not sure," Earl said finally, although his answer was not quite—for Sam at least—believable.

They sat there in silence, listening to the sounds of the insects and birds from the woods.

"What are you going to do?" Earl asked after a while.

"I need answers."

"Do you even know the questions?"

"Maybe not. But I think I know where to start looking for both."

"And where's that?"

"On the other side of a big metal door on the fourth floor."

"What's behind it?"

"Morlocks."

SOMEWHERE NEAR RISHIKESH, INDIA
APRIL 12

00:15

The training was over. They were as ready as they were ever going to be, Khan thought. It was possible to overtrain. Too much rote practice dulled the reflexes, stripped a unit of its edge. The men on the assault team were all experienced. They knew how to fight. The training had been important to forge the group into a team. For the first time since joining the Hand of the Prophet, Khan felt that he was a part of that team. Jadoon's acceptance had opened the door. Khan had walked through it, building a rapport with the others through daily practice in unarmed combat. They were all good at hand-to-hand, but Khan was a cut above. He was exceptional.

The team sat together in the back of the truck, an ancient American-surplus "deuce and a half," as it jounced over the Indian back roads that led from Chandigarh to Rishikesh. The men sat on wooden boxes. More boxes were piled up against the wall of the cab and strapped in place with nylon webbing. The driver was a local with HeM sympathies who knew these roads as well as he knew the faces of his wives and children. He had introduced himself as Ali.

They had been traveling for two days. Khan was road-weary and his clothes were stained by dust that he could no longer be bothered to brush away.

At an unmarked junction, Ali turned off the macadam onto a rutted service road. He maneuvered the big truck skillfully as the road snaked up and over a series of steep hills. After nearly half an hour of nausea-inducing switchbacks, Ali pulled the truck onto a broad flat area looking out over a valley. He parked behind a boulder that was approximately the same size as the truck. This was a remote part of India. It was rough country with rocky and infertile soil. The vegetation was mostly scrub, with only a few windblown trees for shade.

Khan and Mashwanis retrieved a camouflage net patterned in gray and brown tiger stripes from one of the boxes and stretched it across the top of the truck. For what they had come to do, it was important to remain unseen and undisturbed, especially as the other boxes held Kalashnikovs, RPGs, and plastic explosives. These would be hard to explain away. Khan was acutely conscious of being part of a very small team operating in the heart of an enemy nation of one billion people. Their truck was like a raft floating on a hostile sea a three-day sail from the nearest shore.

Like the others, Khan was carrying false papers, an Indian ID card that identified him as Baahir Daoud. It might stand up to cursory scrutiny by a local cop looking for a bribe, but that was about it. India, like Pakistan and America, had secret prisons where enemy combatants could be disappeared. Conditions in these prisons were rumored to be inhuman, and the jailers did not shy away from torture as a tool of interrogation. None of the team would let themselves be taken alive.

When the netting was secure, Khan took a moment to survey the tactical situation. They were on the lip of a valley with sides steep enough that it might have qualified as a gorge. The valley floor was some seventy-five meters below where a double set of train tracks paralleled a dry streambed. At the far end of the valley, the train tracks and streambed diverged, with the tracks leading into a tunnel that cut through a mountain. The tunnel was the reason that they were there. He glanced at his watch. Eleven forty-five a.m. They had three hours.

Working quickly, they unloaded the truck. Ahmedani opened the boxes with a crowbar and Jadoon supervised the distribution of the equipment. Khan slipped a heavy bulletproof vest on over his shoulders and cinched it tight. He strapped a tactical holster holding an Indian copy of a Browning 9mm to his thigh and checked that the combat knife in his boot would draw smoothly and easily. Although the sun was strong, he wrapped a pair of low-end night-vision goggles around his neck. It would be dark in the tunnel. Ahmedani handed Khan a Kalashnikov. Khan popped the magazine off and reinserted it after checking the load.

Mashwanis had armed himself with an imposing-looking Dragunov sniper rifle that he leaned against the truck so that he could help Khan and Ahmedani finish unpacking the boxes. They had nearly finished when they heard something that made them freeze. The tinkling of a bell; a man-made sound coming from just around the curve in the road. They were not alone.

Responding to Jadoon's hand signals, the entire team went to ground, looking for whatever cover they could find. The truck itself was largely shielded from casual observation by the boulder and netting, but the vegetation here was sparse and the risk of detection was high.

Khan was sheltered behind a large rock and further screened by a clump of high grass. He had pulled the Kalashnikov from his shoulder on the way down to the ground, and he thumbed the safety off as he trained the weapon at the bend in the road. The others, he was confident, were doing the same.

The bell chimed again, closer this time.

Khan's grip tightened on the trigger. He sighted down the barrel, lining up with the likely kill zone.

With a pathetic bleat, a brown goat wearing a bell on a rope around its neck stepped into Khan's narrow field of view. He was so surprised that he almost pulled the trigger.

One by one, more goats rounded the corner, stopping here and there to pull at the dry grass by the side of the road. A moment later, the goatherd came into view. The boy could not have been more than ten. He wore loose cotton pants and a T-shirt. His hair was tied up in a Sikh-style turban secured with a dirty white cloth, and he carried a stick across his shoulders that seemed to be more of a toy than a tool. Swinging the stick off his shoulders, the boy used it to poke and prod some of the slower goats down the trail.

Khan kept his sights fixed on the goatherd, hoping that the boy would not turn in their direction.

Khan's rifle was aimed at center mass, or what there was of it on a boy nearly as thin as the stick he carried. His palms felt cold and clammy, and there was an almost unbearable tension in his back and shoulders.

He prayed silently to Allah. *Please don't let the boy turn around. Don't let him see us. Spare his life.*

Jihad was struggle and Khan had accepted that he would have to kill if he was to fulfill his mission. He had no compunctions about killing armed men, soldiers who took on their roles willingly. This was part of jihad, and he had made his peace with it. Killing women. Killing children. That was something different. He had never killed a child and he had no desire to start now.

Unbidden, a vision of dead children from the wedding party in Afghanistan floated across his vision. Was this different? He was just a boy, but he was a danger to them. He could summon help.

The goatherd bent down and picked up a small stone. He threw it at one of his charges that had started to wander off the road. Chastened, the goat rejoined the herd. They were moving, but slowly. Agonizingly slowly.

The boy started to whistle a tuneless song that nevertheless had an air of carefree joy about it. Khan knew at that moment that he could not pull the trigger. The tension in his shoulders eased, and he slipped his finger onto the outside of the trigger guard. He could not kill this child. But the others on the team would not share his reservations. If the boy spotted them, he was as good as dead. It would not matter whether Khan squeezed his trigger or not.

One goat broke off from the herd and rambled toward the spot where Ahmedani was sheltered behind a rock that looked to Khan much too small to conceal his ample girth.

Don't follow the goat, Khan pleaded silently.

The boy glanced quickly at the wayward animal, clearly bored by his formal responsibilities. He did nothing to indicate that he had seen Ahmedani pressed flat against the earth behind the boulder with his Kalashnikov trained at the goatherd's head.

Don't follow. Don't.

The goat seemed to lock eyes with Ahmedani. It cocked its head to one side as if curious about why a man would be lying on the ground just there.

Don't.

The boy threw a stone.

The goat retreated slowly back to the group, the bell around his neck clanking disconsolately.

The goatherd turned his back on the HeM jihadis and led his small flock down the road. Moments later, he had rounded the next curve and was lost from sight. The sound of the bells grew fainter and then disappeared altogether.

The boy would live.

Now it was time to kill.

There was one last box in the back of the truck. It was square and approximately a meter in length along each dimension. Khan helped Ahmedani wrestle it out onto the ground. The box was steel, painted dark green, and covered with numbers and cryptic symbols. The most unusual thing about the box, however, was the lock, a sophisticated-looking LED keypad rather than a combination or key lock. It was heavy. Ahmedani grunted with effort as they manhandled it out of the truck, and Khan felt his back muscles strain from the unexpected weight.

They loaded the now-empty wooden boxes that had held weapons, armor, and tools back into the truck. Mashwanis prepared a sniper's nest that gave him a clear field of fire in the direction of the railroad tracks.

Khan and Ahmedani packed explosive charges in a backpack and half walked, half slid down a scree field to the track. They followed the tracks into the tunnel. Khan slipped on his night-vision gear. It was an older model, but more than adequate for the conditions in the tunnel, which were closer to low light than to darkness.

The tunnel was maybe a kilometer long, and it cut right through the heart of the Mohand mountain range. On the far side, the microclimate was different. Just one valley over, the countryside was lusher, with tropical vegetation taking over from rock and arid scrub. Thick stands of rhododendron covered the slopes.

It took nearly twenty minutes to find what they were after. Some thirty feet up the southern slope, Khan saw a large boulder set firmly into the soil. Ahmedani used a trenching tool to dig a hole at the base of the rock. Khan placed one of the charges in the hole and set the timer for sixty seconds. The earth muffled the sound of the explosion, but it was a powerful charge and Khan had set it well. The blast knocked the stone free and sent it rolling downhill, slowly at first but gathering speed.

When it reached the bottom, the stone was moving so fast that it bounced completely over the train tracks and started up the reverse slope. Khan cursed under his breath. But the rock rolled back, this time stopping right on top of the rail line.

"Bull's-eye," Khan said in English.

Ahmedani looked at him quizzically.

"Nice shot," Khan offered in Urdu by way of explanation.

The train crew would be able to move the rock eventually and repair any damage to the rails. It would take time, however. And it would make noise.

They walked back through the tunnel to rejoin their comrades. Jadoon and one of the other jihadis, a rat-faced Punjabi named Umar who had more than twenty HeM operations under his belt, had brought the heavy box down to the railbed and stashed it in the culvert that ran alongside the tracks. The last of their number, a taciturn Pashtun tribesman who called himself Amir Kror, was cutting brush to screen it from view. Amir Kror was the name of a famous eighth-century warrior poet and Khan considered this nom de guerre something of a boastful affectation. The original Amir Kror had written poetry of timeless beauty. This Amir Kror was barely literate.

Khan looked up the slope toward the truck, trying to see it from the vantage of the train engineer. If you knew what to look for, it was possible to make out the shape of the truck behind the camouflage netting, but only if you knew what to look for. Moreover, the train would be moving at least forty miles an hour and the engineer would be thinking about the approaching tunnel rather than gawking at the unremarkable scenery. He would not see the truck. Atal Mashwanis was even harder to spot. Khan had to squint and concentrate to pick out the telltale shape of the Dragunov barrel peeking shyly through the firing gap in the sniper's nest. Atal was insurance. If he fired his weapon, it meant that something had gone wrong. But if something went wrong, they would be glad he was there.

The preparation was complete. Now they had only to wait. As always, the waiting was agony. From his time in Afghanistan, Khan knew that each soldier developed his own strategies for managing this period, the limen between peace and violence, between the quotidian world of the everyday and the insane, upside-down, bizarro world of combat. Some of the soldiers in the highly trained irregular unit he served with in Afghanistan would spend the time obsessively caring for their weapons, the tools of their chosen profession. They cleaned gun barrels that had already been scrubbed raw and smooth, and sharpened combat knives that could slit a throat as easily as they opened a letter. Others stole furtive glances at pictures of loved ones or pored over tactical maps that they had long ago committed to memory. Khan prayed.

"*Subhana rabbiyal a'la wa bihamdihi,*" he murmured softly as he, Jadoon, and the others crouched down low in the culvert. *Glory to my God the most magnificent.*

Allah, guide me. Give me wisdom and strength to serve you. Help me to see the right. Bring me victory, though I am surrounded by enemies.

The train was late. This they had anticipated. But it was hot in the sun, and soon they were all sweating profusely under the heavy gear.

Khan felt the train before he heard it, a rhythmic vibration that seemed to come from deep in the earth. A few minutes later, he heard the clacking of wheels and a single whistle blast.

At four-fifteen p.m., more than an hour after the train was scheduled to reach the tunnel, the locomotive rounded the curve. It did not look like an ordinary engine. It was squat and black and practically screamed "military." The cars it pulled were similarly distinctive. A flatbed immediately behind the locomotive held three armored personnel carriers secured by enormous nylon straps. The boxcars looked as if they had been reinforced with metal plates for added security.

Khan counted cars. Mentally, he tagged the sixth car back from the locomotive and counted an additional five cars between the target and the caboose. Dead center.

Khan did not know what or who the car carried. He knew only that this was their target. Since they had not opened the heavy box that he and Ahmedani had taken from the truck, it seemed reasonable to assume they were supposed to load it on the train. Maybe it was a bomb. No one had told that to Khan, however. It was simply an assumption.

Jadoon spoke.

"There will be men in the car," he reminded the team. "Do not shoot them. I would prefer that you not stab them either. Nor should you allow yourselves to be shot. It's not that I cannot replace you. I can. But we want no blood, no sign of a struggle. Even so, the men inside the car must die. We cannot take prisoners. Is this clear?"

He looked at Khan expectantly.

"Yes, Jadoon," Khan replied. "It is clear."

A sharp squeal of brakes came from inside the tunnel. The engineer had spotted the rockfall. Whether the train hit the boulder or not was immaterial to the objective, although an actual derailment would have presented the team with significant complications. Khan did not, however, hear anything that would have indicated a crash. It seemed that the train had stopped in time.

Jadoon led the team of jihadis into the tunnel. Through his night-vision goggles, Khan saw the cars outlined in eerie green light. It looked like a ghost train carrying freight for delivery to the devil himself.

They moved quickly and silently. Khan counted off the cars. They stopped alongside the target car, which was located at about the midpoint of the tunnel. While some of the cars seemed to have been up-armored in postproduction, this car looked like it had been purposely built as a vault on rails. The door was solid steel and set into a reinforced frame that seemed to extend as a kind of cage around the bed of the entire car.

A running board ran around the edge of the car, and Khan and Ahmedani climbed up and positioned themselves on either side of the door, holding on to metal handgrips that had been welded onto the frame. They both stripped off their night-vision goggles and left them dangling around their necks. Jadoon stood directly in front of the door. From memory, he typed a long series of numbers into the LED cryptolock.

"Ready," he whispered, just loud enough for Khan and Ahmedani to hear.

Jadoon hit enter and jumped back. The door hissed open.

A burst of light from inside the car would have blinded Khan if he were still wearing his goggles. He swung around the door frame into the boxcar and did a rapid scan of the interior.

There were two soldiers inside sitting on a bench set into the back wall to the left of the door. They were wearing light combat armor and carrying Heckler & Koch MP5 submachine guns. Not regular army, then. The MP5s marked them as Indian Special Forces. Neither was as big as Ahmedani, but they both outweighed Khan by at least ten kilos. The one farther to the left had the three stripes of a *havildar* on his sleeve, the Indian equivalent of a sergeant. The other was a sepoy, a private.

Khan processed all of this information instinctively and immediately.

The sergeant would be more experienced, more dangerous. Khan did not hesitate. He closed the distance rapidly. To reach his target, however, he had to vault over a large steel box strapped to the floor. A tiny piece of Khan's brain registered that the box was an exact duplicate of the one he and Ahmedani had unloaded from the truck.

The Indian was good. Before Khan could reach him, he was up off the bench swinging the MP5 high enough so he could take a shot. Khan saw him thumb the safety off with a smooth, practiced movement. It was a race and it was close, but even with the box as an additional obstacle, Khan had too much of a head start. He stepped inside the arc of the gun and grabbed the sergeant's wrist with one hand. He pulled hard and twisted the wrist to get the Indian off balance. Khan was hoping the move would also dislodge the man's finger from the trigger. As he pulled with his right hand, Khan shoved his left elbow up into the sergeant's now-exposed throat. He missed crushing the windpipe, but the blow was nearly incapacitating.

Khan shifted his grip to the gun and used it as a lever to force the *havildar's* arms up until the weapon was pointed at the ceiling. His left arm wrapped around the sergeant's neck even as his right leg swept the Indian soldier backward. Khan kept his grip on the gun until he was able to lever it out of his opponent's hands.

He had the Indian soldier bent backward in a bridge. Khan was in a half crouch. His left knee was pressed in between the sergeant's shoulder blades. Releasing the gun, he wrapped his right arm over his left around the Indian's neck. *"Allahu Akbar,"* he grunted, as he rose from the crouch, simultaneously pulling his opponent's head backward with a quick jerking motion.

Back in New Jersey, his jujitsu instructor had warned him never to do this either in training or in the ring. You could snap a man's neck, he had explained.

He was right. The neck broke with a dull crunching sound. The Indian sergeant went limp.

Khan looked over in time to see Ahmedani finish up his adversary. There was no finesse to the big jihadi. He had his powerful hands wrapped around the sepoy's neck and was simply choking the life out of him.

The sepoy was little more than a kid. If he was older than twenty, it was by a matter of months rather than years. Still, Khan put him in a different category than he had the goatherd. This was an enemy soldier, armed and trained. He was fair game, and if he was less skilled or less lucky than Ahmedani, that was the will of Allah.

The sepoy clawed at Ahmedani's wrists and hands, but his movements were panicky rather than purposeful. In truth, he was already dead. Khan watched the light in his eyes go out. Ahmedani laid the dead sepoy gently, almost tenderly, on the floor of the car.

No more than two minutes had passed since Jadoon had opened the door.

The team leader stepped inside the car. He pulled two black rubbery bags from his backpack. Body bags.

"Bag 'em," he ordered.

Khan helped Ahmedani with the sepoy first.

"We can remove the bodies," Khan said to Jadoon. "But won't these two be missed on the other end?"

"There will be no record of guards on this train," Jadoon replied confidently. "These two were dead before you killed them. They died this morning when their helicopter crashed in the Indian Ocean. Their names are on the flight manifest, but their bodies could not be recovered. There are sharks in that sea."

Jadoon's smile made him look like a shark himself. Khan considered the kind of juice it had taken with the Indian military establishment to make those arrangements. He thought about the bald man he and Masood had met with in India. He must be high up in the military hierarchy.

As Khan and Ahmedani were dealing with the bodies, Umar and Amir Kror were wrestling the heavy box from the truck into the train car. They loosened the straps holding the duplicate box in place and made the requisite switch, being careful to reattach all of the straps and to cinch them as tight as a bowstring.

Twenty minutes later, they had both the bodies and the mysterious box in the back of the truck. Atal had dismantled his sniper's nest and all of their gear was locked down. A whistle and the harsh sound of metal striking metal indicated that the engineers had succeeded in clearing the track and the train was moving out.

Umar and Ahmedani pulled the camouflage net off the truck and added it to the stack of equipment piled up against the cab wall.

Ali began maneuvering the clumsy deuce and a half back down the access road.

From a soft-sided bag wedged into one corner, Jadoon pulled out a tool that Khan recognized. It completed the picture of the operation.

The instrument was about the size and shape of a book with a screen and a handful of buttons. Something that looked like a microphone was attached to it by a cord. It was not a microphone.

Jadoon held the instrument up to the big steel box they had taken from the train car and pushed one of the buttons.

Click, click, click, sounded the Geiger counter as it measured the radiation from the nuclear warhead that Khan knew was inside the box.

00:16

The Morlocks, whose formal name was Argus Systems Security Operations Unit, kept to themselves. They did not socialize with other Argus employees. They did not participate in the regular senior staff meetings. They were a company within the company, a piece of Argus but not a part of it. The Morlocks worked behind their iron gate, which marked them as a thing apart as surely as their regulation haircuts and straight-backed military bearing. But like all such gates, it had a keeper.

The keeper, Sam realized, was the gate's weak point. His name was Neil Linnehan and his world was as subterranean as that of the original Morlocks in the H. G. Wells novel. He was the head of IT and his office was in the subbasement, where the racks of servers could be easily cooled and the secure connections with Langley and Fort Meade could be protected.

Sam had briefly considered stealing a passkey from one of the Morlocks and then somehow figuring out the unique cipher lock code that went with that key. All of the various scenarios he played out in his head, however, ended with a jarhead's beefy hands wrapped around his throat. The Security Operations Unit was staffed by professionals. None of them was going to leave a passkey lying around unattended, and the idea of taking one by force or theft was just unrealistic.

If he could not steal a key, Sam decided, the next best thing would be to make one. Neil Linnehan made the keys, and Neil had a weakness of his own. Her name was Sara Zehri.

Sam had thought through the plan from every angle, trying out different variables. The timing was tricky. Sara would have to play her part to perfection.

As an additional complication, Sam could not explain to Sara why he needed her help. It was safer for her that she not know what he intended to do and why. Certainly, he could not share his suspicions that Weeder and his cohorts were somehow complicit in Andy's death. Sara would likely have marched down the hall to bang on the iron door with the heel of one of her Manolo Blahniks and demand Weeder surrender himself to her justice. Sam had been cryptic in his explanation. He had simply told her that he needed a favor and it was important. Sara did not press him for an explanation. She even seemed to enjoy the secretive nature of the request.

"Don't worry," she had assured him. "I can handle Neil."

It was good to have friends.

Sam was not certain exactly what he expected to find behind the steel door on the fourth floor. Maybe there were no answers there to be found. Maybe Weeder and his team had nothing to do with Andy's death. The evidence, such as it was, was all circumstantial. But Sam believed at a gut level that there was something important on the far side of that door. Something important and wrong and dangerous. Something worth killing to keep secret.

. . .

There was nothing dark or dingy about the basement levels at Argus. B2 was just another floor, no different really from the floor where Sam and his team worked. The lack of natural light did not matter. None of the rooms in the secure parts of the building had windows. The one thing that set the subbasement apart from the other floors was a constant low-level hum. The massive banks of computers and servers that Argus needed to maintain its thousand-eyed reach out into the world produced a kind of white noise that was easier to feel than hear. The slight vibrations under the soles of his feet seemed to whisper to Sam of power and secrets.

Linnehan was in the office, which—while not unusual—was something of a lucky break. Sam had not wanted to give the IT head any advance warning of his request, so he was popping in unannounced. Linnehan's was a small kingdom. He had only two technicians who worked under him. But his word in this narrow world was absolute law.

Sam knocked on the door as a courtesy before opening it. The IT space at Argus had seemingly been designed for a different era when teams of people might have been needed to staff the operation. Now Argus, itself a beneficiary of government outsourcing, had outsourced much of its IT needs to other, smaller firms that chased after subcontracts like pilot fish feeding on the leavings from a great white's meal.

The IT space was big and echoing, and Linnehan sat alone at his desk behind a long counter that in a busier office would no doubt have been where staff members came for customer service. Linnehan was short, balding, and overweight, the middle-aged trifecta, and his sartorial choices provided nearly irrefutable evidence of his bachelor status. His sweater was stained and fraying at the collar, and his corduroy pants were a color that was not found in nature.

"How you doing, Neil?" Sam asked.

Linnehan looked up from the monitor, seemingly perturbed at the interruption.

"What? There are no phones on the third floor?"

"Yeah, I probably should have called."

"It's like your lot thinks that I have nothing to do all day but sit here and wait for you to need something."

"I'm sure it feels that way. Do you need me to come back another time?"

"No." Linnehan seemed mollified by Sam's offer. "What do you need?"

"I'm having some trouble in the office," Sam said, striving for a tone that suggested he was bringing Neil into his confidence. "We've gotten dinged for a couple of security violations in the last few weeks. Safes left unsecured. Classified left on the printer. That sort of thing. Shoe and Ken are accusing each other of being the last out of the office on the nights in question. I'd like to look at the logs to see when they swiped in and out of the office. That should give me a sense as to which one of them is in the right."

"Sara's not a suspect, is she?" Linnehan asked with evident concern.

Sorry, Neil. She is way out of your league.

"No. It's got to be either Shoe or Ken. Nothing else fits."

"Okay. Let me call up the records."

Linnehan turned back to his monitor and began furiously pounding keys. Sam walked around the counter and pulled up a chair to sit next to him. As best he could, he tried to follow what Linnehan was doing and where the key cards were stored in the database. It looked like the cards were grouped by unit and each card had a series of columns associated with it that identified the date of issuance, the holder's clearance levels, and authorized areas of access. A subfolder contained a complete history of where and when the cards had been swiped and the codes punched in. It was neat and orderly. Maybe even a little obsessive. Just like Neil.

"Let's begin with Mr. Balusibramanijan," Neil suggested, with just a hint of pleasure in his voice. Sam suspected that the IT head considered Shoe a rival for Sara's imagined affections. *Love is blind, but did it have to be stupid too? Probably.*

"Sounds good."

"What dates did you want to check out?"

Sam made a show of looking through his notebook. He took his time.

"Let's start with the twenty-fourth."

"Okay. It looks like Shushantu swiped into the suite at seven forty-seven a.m. He swiped out again at ten-twelve and back in at ten-twenty."

"Candy machine," Sam explained.

Neil read through the details of Shoe's comings and goings for the day. Abstractly, Sam understood that this was what the ID cards were for, but to see the monitoring of a friend laid out on the screen as raw data was still somewhat disconcerting. Orwell would have understood twenty-first-century America and he would have been amazed at its subtlety. Big Brother had nothing on Big Data. People had gradually become accustomed to their loss of privacy and anonymity, first in the name of security and then in the name of convenience and commerce. The technology had evolved to the point where the surveillance was all but invisible. It was also all but constant. There was no place to hide.

Near the end of Neil's recitation of Shoe's movements for March

24, the door opened with an attention-demanding bang. Sara Zehri was standing there with a laptop tucked under one arm.

"Sorry to interrupt your fantasy football league or whatever it is you boys are working on down here in the basement, but I need a favor from Neil." The smile she gave Linnehan should have made a statistically significant contribution to global warming.

Sam noticed that Sara had undone both the top buttons of her blouse and the madam-librarian bun she typically favored. She had also ditched the headscarf and the reading glasses. With her hair loose around her shoulders, she looked several years younger and several degrees less intimidating. To Neil, Sam was quite certain, Sara's new look was like catnip, utterly irresistible.

"What do you need, Sara?" Neil asked, already rising from his workstation.

"What are you offering?"

Linnehan's Adam's apple jumped up and down as he swallowed.

"For you? Anything."

"Good to know. Let's start with this laptop."

As Sam had hoped, Linnehan had left him alone with the workstation logged on as administrator. He did not have much time, but if Sara could just keep Linnehan busy for a few minutes . . .

He clicked out of Shoe's history and into his own card file. Clicking on the access column produced a drop-down menu that allowed him to drag and drop parts of the building into a box marked AUTHORIZATIONS. Most of the locations on the menu were familiar to Sam, but he could not find anything that looked like the Security Operations Unit.

With a part of his attention, he listened in on the conversation between Sara and Neil, trying to gauge how much time he had to work with.

"Have you tried rebooting the system?" he heard Neil ask. It was the standard IT department first-line answer to every computer problem and it fixed 80 percent of them.

"No. I didn't even think to do that," Sara replied in an embarrassed voice that was Academy Award–level acting. How someone as smart and blunt as Sara Zehri could play the coquette was beyond Sam, but she seemed to be enjoying herself.

Sam considered simply pushing all of the available choices into the authorized box and hoping that one of them controlled access to the Morlocks' lair. This would be the fastest method and the odds seemed good, but Sam wanted to be sure. Realistically, he would have only one shot at this.

Instead, he navigated back several screens until he found the badge entries for Weeder and his team. He clicked on Weeder's name and looked to see what parts of the building the Commander was authorized to access. There was one entry he did not understand. It didn't have a name, just a number code, H6576-89.

"Let me get the manual out of my desk drawer," he heard Neil say. The hairs on the back of Sam's neck stood up and he was about to hit the red X in the upper right corner to exit the program when Sara stepped in to save him.

"Oh, I'm sure you don't need the book to tell you what to do, Neil. Let me come over there with you and we can look at this together."

Sam glanced quickly over his shoulder as Sara glided around the edge of the counter and sidled up so close to Linnehan that their hips were pressed together. She spun the balky laptop around to face them and pointed at something on the screen.

"What does this mean?" she asked innocently. "It wasn't there before."

Oh, Neil, you poor dumb bastard.

Sara had bought him a little extra time.

Sam quickly noted down the mysterious authorization code and navigated back to his own card file. Rather than drop and drag, he input the code manually into the appropriate field and hit SAVE.

A dialogue box popped open. SYNCHRONIZING DATA SYSTEMS. THIS MAY TAKE A FEW MINUTES. PLEASE DO NOT TURN OFF YOUR COMPUTER.

Fuck.

A bar at the bottom of the dialogue box tracked the progress in completing the operation. The bar filled up with a reassuring digital blue as the system processed the upgrade to Sam's access authorities. But slowly. Too slowly.

We're so close. Just give me a minute or two, Sara.

"Your antivirus software is out-of-date," Neil warned. "You'll need to reinstall the new company security program."

"Sure," Sara said breezily. "How do you do that?"

To Sam, Sara's helpless female act was wearing thin. It was so counter to her nature that it was hard to maintain the fiction of incompetence. But Neil was smitten, and he seemed incapable of seeing past whatever Sara put forward on the surface.

After an agonizing wait that felt to Sam like an hour but according to the clock on the computer screen was closer to two minutes, the bar filled to the end and a new dialogue box opened to announce CHANGES ACCEPTED.

As quickly as he could, Sam navigated back to the page listing Shoe's movements through the building.

"I really need to check one thing," Neil said, and Sam could feel him turning around even as he clicked on the last icon to return to the screen that had been up on the monitor just before Sara had appeared at the door.

"You okay there, Sam?" Linnehan asked.

"Never better." Sam minimized the window and looked quickly at Sara before turning his attention back to Neil. Even for the socially obtuse IT head, the message was unmistakable. Sara shouldn't know what they were doing.

"I think I have everything I need," Sam added. "I'll leave you two kids to sort out the laptop."

Late at night, the Argus building was deserted. The operations centers at Langley and the State Department were staffed twenty-four hours a day. Argus was strictly nine-to-five, which in Washington-speak typically meant eight-to-seven, or at least to six-thirty. In a town where what you did largely defined who you were, working long hours was fundamental to one's self-respect.

The clock on Sam's office wall read eleven p.m., however, and the building was quiet. It was time to test out whether his manipulation of the Argus computer system had been successful.

Even for a steel door, the entrance to the Morlocks' lair was ugly. The surface was rough and pitted, and it more closely resembled a hatch from a World War II–era submarine than a shiny bank vault.

Sam slid his card through the reader next to the door frame and typed his personal code into the keypad. From somewhere deep inside the door, there came a soft click and the light on the cipher lock changed from red to green. Belying its bulk, the door opened easily. With the door open, the lights in the office came on automatically. This reaffirmed that the Security Operations Unit was, in fact, shut down for the night. Sam stepped over the six-inch-high threshold and closed the door behind him. The whirr of titanium locking rods reengaging gave him pause. He was relieved to see the green button just to the right of the door that read OPEN.

Whatever Sam might have expected to find, he was disappointed. There were no racks of weapons on the wall, no maps of either Washington or Islamabad marked with secret drop sites. There were no shelves piled with spy gear. It was an office. A cubicle farm. It may have been tidier than most, but beyond that there was little on the surface to distinguish it from thousands of similar office suites in the D.C. region.

Sam walked through the office looking for something that would give him a better sense of what the Security Operations Unit did for a living. There was remarkably little paper in the unit. The Morlocks, it seemed, either burned everything on a routine basis or locked up their work in one of the half-dozen Mosler safes lined up along one wall. In frustration, Sam pulled on the levers of the safes to see if maybe one had been left unlocked. No luck. He looked through the drawers in a couple of the cubicles. There were pens and pencils, but no paper. There were also numerous tins of Skoal and Copenhagen dipping tobacco. U.S. Special Forces soldiers were disproportionately white and Southern. And there were few women in the Joint Special Operations Command. Dip was JSOC's universal lubricant.

There was only one private office in the suite. Sam searched it thoroughly, being careful to replace every object exactly where he had found it. The desk was neat and orderly with even the pencils arranged by size on the desktop. A brass nameplate on the desk engraved with the SEAL trident read CDR. JOHN S. WEEDER. The

Commander was a Skoal man. That was about the sum total of what Sam learned from the contents of his desk.

The computer screen was dark. Without Weeder's log-on, there was no way of knowing what the chief Morlock had been working on.

Weeder had a small "I love me" wall, a Washington staple, of awards and citations, kitschy unit souvenirs of overseas deployments, and autographed beauty shots of lesser officials standing next to the powerful and important. There were pictures of a much younger John Weeder with top brass that Sam recognized. On one picture, a former chairman of the Joint Chiefs had scribbled "to Lieutenant John Weeder. Your country owes you more than it can ever know." That, Sam knew, was the nature of life in the black ops world.

Sam wrestled back the sense of frustration at having penetrated the Morlocks' lair only to find it empty. Whatever there was to know was doubtlessly locked up in one of the safes or secured on a password-protected hard drive. It looked more and more like the Security Operations suite was a dry hole.

If it hadn't been so quiet in the office, he would not have noticed the sound, a distinctive sound that commanded his attention. On the other side of the door, someone was typing a code into the keypad. He could hear the soft beeps of each number being keyed in and the whirr of the locking rods as they disengaged.

Crouching down behind the desk in Weeder's office, Sam willed his heart to stop its jackhammer beating.

"I tell you, the Bulls looked great. They held LeBron to fifteen and shot the lights out from behind the arc. I like 'em this year."

"So they had a good night. That doesn't mean they've solved

their problem at center. Live by the three-point shot and die when the hot hands cool off. They can beat anyone on a good night, just not every night. Maybe not even most nights."

Sam recognized the voices. The Bulls fan was Aaron Stafford, a Chicago native who was deliberately vague about what exactly he had done in the army. The skeptic was Commander John Weeder, USN.

Sam was suddenly quite certain that if Weeder discovered him in his office he would kill him right there. Stafford would doubtlessly help him dispose of Sam's body, and there was a high-temperature incinerator in the basement of the building. If either had noticed that the lights were already on when they opened the door, he was in serious trouble.

"Let me get the file out of the safe," Stafford said, "and we can make a copy that you can bring out to Spears. I don't know why the hell he needs it tonight."

"And you don't need to know," Weeder said forcefully. "Stay in your lane, Captain."

"Yes, sir. It's just that we're working the guys flat out and I'm not sure how much longer they can keep it up."

"They're tough."

"I'm not worried about burnout. I'm worried about mistakes."

"We can't afford any of those."

"I know. That's why it would be good to throttle back a bit so we can ramp up later. We have another three weeks before Cold Harbor."

"Don't say that name out loud," Weeder commanded. There was a sharp, almost nervous edge to his voice.

"Not even in here?"

"Not anywhere."

From the shadow of Weeder's desk, Sam heard the sound of Stafford spinning the safe dial and the clunk of the drawer opening up.

"Here it is. I'll make a copy. You mind grabbing an envelope?"

"No worries. I have a stack in my desk drawer."

The drawer in question was no more than six inches from Sam's face. There was nowhere for him to go. He was trapped like a rat. Sam pressed his back up against the wall and his right hand brushed against something cold and metallic. It was the door to the burn chute in Weeder's office. The chute led straight down to the mouth of the weight-activated industrial shredder in the basement. The gears were powerful and the shredder blades were razor-sharp. They could handle stacks of paper as thick as phone books with ease. They almost never jammed. Sam could imagine what one would do to flesh and bone, but it was even easier to imagine what John Weeder might do. The shredder, at least, was not sadistic.

The door to the chute opened smoothly and soundlessly on oiled tracks.

Sam got on his hands and knees, and slid feetfirst into the chute. It was a straight drop into the basement, maybe forty or fifty feet. It was certainly enough to kill him. If he somehow survived the fall, the shredder blades that ripped so easily into the bulky burn bags would grab on to his clothes and pull him down into one of the most grisly ends he could conceive of.

The chute was tight and narrow, and Sam had to push hard to get his body oriented the right way. He could not afford to make any sound. He pressed his feet along the walls to find some kind of purchase. About four feet down, he found a seam where two sections of the chute had been welded together. It wasn't much, but it was better than nothing.

As quietly as he could, Sam ducked his head inside the chute and pulled the door closed behind him. It was black as pitch in the chute, and Sam's muscles strained to hold him in place. He pressed his back up against one wall and crouched with his feet pushing against the opposite side. The strain on his quads reminded him of the one time he had completed a century ride of one hundred miles on the back roads of Virginia.

Through the thin metal of the burn-chute door, Sam could hear Weeder open the desk drawer and rummage through it for an envelope. He wanted desperately to shift his position and take some of the stress off his legs, but he did not dare move.

"Got it," Weeder shouted to Stafford. "Let's move out."

"Copy that."

Sam stayed in the chute suspended four stories over the blades of the shredder listening to the sounds of Weeder and Stafford closing the office. *What the hell was Cold Harbor that it could scare a man like John Weeder?*

WASHINGTON, D.C.
APRIL 13

00:17

When the alarm went off at six-fifteen, Sam was already awake. He had not really slept at all. A toxic combination of frustration and impatience had kept him up for most of the night. He had penetrated the Morlocks' inner sanctum only to find its secrets locked up inches out of reach. It was maddening.

As he pulled himself out of bed, his muscles screamed in protest at the abuse he had subjected them to the night before. It was hard to believe that it had only been a few hours since he had crawled slowly and painfully out of the burn chute. His hands still stung. The walls of the chute had been coated in soot from the incinerator. Standing under a hot shower, Sam had washed off as much of the black dust as he could. Some particles, however, were lodged deep in the raw patches of skin on his palms and knuckles, and stubbornly resisted even the most aggressive scrubbing.

By seven, Sam was on his bike riding toward Argus headquarters. His brain felt fuzzy from the lack of sleep, and the half a pot of coffee and 800 milligrams of Advil he had for breakfast had made him jittery rather than alert. His legs ached, but Sam wanted the ride to help clear his head. The commute by bicycle from Capitol Hill to Arlington was spectacular. His route took him past the imposing Capitol Building and down onto the wide gravel paths of the National Mall. He rode past the Lincoln Memorial onto the bridge with the gilded bronze equestrian statues guarding the approach.

The crisp morning air and exercise were clearing the cobwebs and helping Sam to focus his thinking. By the time he arrived at the Argus building in Ballston, he felt as refreshed as if he had had a good night's sleep.

At the front gate, he bumped into Garret Spears. A nervous part of Sam's psyche wondered if Spears somehow knew about last night. There was at least a chance that Sam had left something out of place that had raised suspicions. If Weeder had Neil check the logs to see who had swiped in and out of the suite, he would have seen Sam's ID card as one of the last in, and it would have triggered all kinds of alarm bells. Spears's expression gave no indication of anything out of the ordinary, but Sam was increasingly of the view that the CEO of Argus was a sociopath and that there was no way to connect the face he showed the world with what was behind the mask.

"Good morning, Sam. I didn't know you were a climber."

"A climber?" Sam was now absolutely convinced that Spears knew about the burn chute and was toying with him.

"Yeah. I see the friction burns on your hands. I've gotten more than a few of those raspberries myself climbing out in Great Falls. I still have a scar on my elbow from a bad scrape I got last fall at Juliet's Balcony."

"Nothing so dramatic happened to me, I'm afraid. I just fell off my bike the other day."

"Really?"

To Sam, it sounded accusatory.

Argus had a gym in the basement and Sam was able to take a quick shower before changing into one of the suits he kept in his office. The ever-efficient Dorothy Cornett had already opened Sam's safe and set his in-box on the desktop and his burn bag on the floor next to his chair. All Sam had to do was log on to the two computer systems. On his desk, he had both a "low-side" system for Internet access and unclassified e-mail communications with the outside world and a "high-side" system that included everything from State Department diplomatic reporting classified at the lowest Confidential level to Top Secret NSA intercepts.

For as much information as there was on these electronic systems, Argus still generated a remarkable amount of paper. Sam's in-box was full of unread reports and drafts of various products that were easier to edit in paper form. Still distracted by his suspicions of Weeder and the operations run out of his fourth-floor empire, Sam picked a report off the top of the pile in his in-box. It was a Defense Intelligence Agency analysis of the resurgent al-Qaeda presence in Pakistan's tribal belt. Sam didn't really care what it was about. His focus was elsewhere.

He remained convinced that the answers he was looking for were somewhere in the room upstairs. Maybe he could find some way to get the combinations to the safes and try it again. Even as he formulated the thought, however, he knew it was a pipe dream. He would not even know where to begin looking for that information. It was entirely possible that the numbers were stored exclusively in the heads of the Morlocks themselves. He would need to think of something else.

Sam realized that he had read over the same paragraph in the report three times without absorbing any of it. In truth, it was a pretty uninteresting analysis, with little in the way of new information and nothing in the way of original insights. Sam tossed the half-read classified report into the burn bag. The bag was full almost to overflowing. He pushed the mass of classified paper down into the bag far enough to roll the top down and tape it shut. Sliding the door to the burn chute open, Sam picked the bag up, intending to drop it down the shaft to the shredder and incinerator. Abruptly, he stopped. The germ of an idea had sprouted and was cautiously taking root.

Back at his desk, Sam worked through the problem set, considering the idea from various angles. The chance of success, he had to admit to himself, was not especially high. The plan had several moving pieces and an unavoidable element of luck. Moreover, he would need Sara's help again if he was going to carry it off. In its favor, the plan was relatively low-risk, especially in comparison with his foray into the Morlocks' lair. Most of what he would need to do could be explained away as a part of his job or an unfortunate oversight. All but one part. The important part.

Before he even realized that he had made a decision, Sam was looking around the office for the tools he would need. On the bookshelf, he found a stiff three-ring binder with a metal spine and thick steel rings to hold papers prepared with a three-hole punch. In his desk drawer, he found a handful of large steel clips that he attached to a thick stack of classified paper. All of this material went into a fresh burn bag along with a mix of classified material to fill it out. Sam included only widely available material that could have come from almost any office in the building. When he was satisfied that the bag was as anonymous as he could make it, Sam dropped it into the chute. It clanged off the walls three times as it fell to the subbasement where the shredder gorged on its strictly vegetarian diet of paper products.

"Sara," Sam said, sticking his head out of his office. "I need a favor."

At eleven-thirty, an admin notice appeared in Sam's e-mail queue. The first paragraph announced that the shredder was down for repairs and the burn chutes should not be used to dispose of classified material until it was back online.

The second paragraph was a pointed reminder to all employees to remove all metal fastenings from classified material before placing it in the burn bags.

The third paragraph noted that until the shredder was repaired the IT department would be coming around from office to office at the end of the workday to collect any classified material for destruction. There was also a handy schedule and a reminder that all materials handled in this way would need to be logged in and accounted for.

That afternoon at twenty minutes to five, Neil Linnehan arrived at the South Asia suite pushing a metal cart loaded down with burn bags. The bags themselves were made of thick brown paper like a grocery bag and printed with a distinctive pattern of red and white stripes that anyone in the U.S. government with a clearance would recognize instantly. Each bag was tagged with a suite number, the name of the person accountable for the bag, and the highest level of classified material inside. A clipboard hung from the side of the cart with a complete record of all of the transactions.

"Anyone order room service?" Shoe asked. He and Sara were the only other people in the suite. Ken was at a meeting at the Pentagon and Dorothy had gone home early.

Neil gave Shoe a look that he no doubt hoped conveyed the world-weary air of a serious professional required to do a menial task far beneath his station, but, in fact, it came across as piteous.

"That's funny, Shushantu. Funny enough maybe to crash your system."

Shoe held up his hands in a gesture of surrender.

"My bad, Neil." Schlub though Neil was, no one wanted to get on the bad side of IT.

"Neil, could I see you for a minute?" Sara's voice was softer than the all-business tone she usually employed in the office. Neil would have had to have a heart of stone to refuse.

"Of course."

The IT director walked over to Sara's cubicle and leaned over to look at something on her monitor. Sam could not hear what she asked him, but he hoped it would occupy 100 percent of Neil's attention for the next few minutes.

Sam carried two burn bags from his office to Neil's cart. He dropped one bag onto the pile and picked up the clipboard to fill in the requisite information. As he did so, he quickly scanned the list looking for what he was after. He found the entry: Fourth Floor, Aaron Stafford, Top Secret, Bag No. 14.

Sam glanced over in the direction of Sara's cubicle. Neil was bent over far enough that only the top of his head poked above the divider. It took just a few seconds for Sam to find bag number 14.

With a black Sharpie, he hurriedly copied the identifying information from that bag onto the second bag he had brought from his office. With one more furtive glance over his shoulder, Sam switched the bags. He walked deliberately back to his office with the Morlocks' daily burn bag and stuffed it under his desk.

By the time he emerged, Neil was standing upright again, Sara's computer "crisis" apparently resolved.

"Thanks, Neil," Sam heard her say in a light, flirtatious tone. "You're an absolute lifesaver."

"Anytime."

Neil seemed as puffed up as a peacock.

"Did you log your bag in, Sam?" he asked, returning to business.

"Sure thing."

Neil picked up the clipboard and scanned it briefly. Then he set it back on the hook and steered the overloaded cart out into the hall.

When Sam turned around, Sara and Shoe were standing shoulder to shoulder glaring at him as though he were a wayward child.

"Sam, what are you doing?" Shoe asked.

"Something I have to."

"Does this have anything to do with Andy's death?" Sara asked.

"I'm not sure," Sam admitted. "Maybe. I think so."

"The Morlocks?"

"Yes."

Sara seemed to consider this information for a moment.

"Do me a favor?" Sara asked.

"Name it. I owe you."

"If they had anything to do with what happened to Andy . . ."

"Yes."

"Make them pay."

"You know I will."

00:18

Taking classified information home was a cardinal sin in the intelligence world, right up there with cohabitating with a North Korean. For the thousandth time, doubts about what he was doing crept to the surface. Sam brushed them aside. He was faced with a series of open questions, and he had to hope that the answers were in the bag.

He set the burn bag down on top of the coffee table in his living room. He had smuggled it out of Argus in his gym bag. And while there was no reason to believe that anyone other than Shoe and Sara knew what he had done, he did not want to leave the bag in his home for longer than was absolutely necessary.

Sam piled kindling and a few split logs in the fireplace and lit a small block of fire starter. Within a few minutes, the logs had caught and the kindling was crackling. He dumped the contents of the bag onto the coffee table and shaped the pile into a semblance of order. The paper on the top was marked CONFIDENTIAL. It was an assessment from the National Intelligence Office about the ways in which climate change would increase the risk of conflict in Central Asia over the next decade. It was perfectly ordinary. Sam tossed it in the fire.

One by one, he read through the thick stack of papers. Most were uninteresting. A few were from special access programs that Sam did not know existed. These he read carefully. They were far from uninteresting. One in particular that identified possible candidates in Yemen and Somalia for targeted assassination was fascinating, if appalling. When other governments did this sort of thing, it was extrajudicial killing. When the United States did it, on the other hand, it was policy. None of the documents from the burn bag offered any insights into Panoptes, the Stoics, or Andy Krittenbrink's death. Murder, Sam reminded himself.

After two hours of reading, near the bottom of the pile, he found something different.

Unlike the other papers in the burn bag, this one had no classification markers on it. In fact, it had no markings of any kind. It was just a block of text. A single page. The draft of a speech or at least the fragment of a speech. The first sentence was enough to grab Sam's attention.

"My fellow Americans," it began.

There was only one person who would deliver a speech that began with those words. This was intended for Emily Lord. Someone had been working on the speech with a red pen, striking out words and phrases, and scribbling notes in the margin. It was a work in progress.

Sam read quickly through the draft with a growing sense of disbelief. The outline of what the Stoics were planning was becoming clearer, and it both angered and terrified him. It was monstrous. And it made no sense. *Why would they do this?* Sam's mind whirled in confusion as he read through to the end. *How could he stop it?*

He poured himself a drink. Three fingers of Talisker. Neat.

My fellow Americans, he read again.

Today, we have witnessed the world's first act of nuclear terrorism, the nightmare we have long feared. Although the target was not an American city, make no mistake that this was an attack directed against all of human civilization. It was an act of barbarism that has no equal.

An untold number of people, but certainly many tens of thousands, lost their lives. And with the death of Indian Prime Minister Rangarajan, the world has lost a great friend of peace.

Although no one has stepped forward to take responsibility for this cowardly and callous act of mass murder, I promise you that my administration will not rest until those behind this attack have been identified. Whether the perpetrator of this crime is a state or a nonstate actor, the terrible swift sword of justice will be unsheathed.

Today, we are all Indians. Today, we are all citizens of . . .

There was a blank space where the name of the target city should be. It was an Indian city and the prime minister was clearly among the victims, but that did not necessarily mean it was New Delhi. Rangarajan traveled widely throughout India. The city could just as easily be Kolkata or Varanasi . . . or Mumbai.

Mumbai.

Lena.

If this speech was more than a creative-writing exercise. If it was part of an actual operation—and Sam felt at an instinctive level that it was—then Lena might be in terrible danger. Not incidentally, so was a major world city.

This speech and the falsified intelligence that Andy had uncovered were linked somehow. They were part of a plan, an operation that Sam sensed was ambitious to the point of audacity. Sam and Andy had uncovered a small part of the operation, but like an iceberg, the vast bulk was still hidden underwater and out of sight. Whatever it involved, it was enough to unnerve a cold-blooded killer like Weeder.

He looked at his watch. It was eight-thirty. In Mumbai, it would be six in the morning. He picked up the phone and dialed from memory.

"Hi, Dad," Lena answered. She sounded surprised to hear from Sam.

"Hi, sweetie. I hope it's not too early."

"Not at all. I was just getting ready to leave for the school."

"I'm glad I caught you."

"How's everything in D.C.?"

"Not so good, Lena. Listen, baby, I need you to come home."

"What's wrong? Are you sick?"

"No. It's nothing like that. It's just that I've come into some information that makes me think that Mumbai is not safe."

Lena laughed.

"Of course it's not safe, Dad. It's a city of twenty million people, 98 percent of whom don't have two rupees to rub together. It's dirty and dangerous and there's sewage in the street and I love it wildly."

"That's not what I'm talking about. That stuff is all background. I'm talking about a specific threat to the city. A bomb."

"I spend most of my time in Dharavi. A bomb would be redundant. Don't worry. I'll stay away from the Taj and any other place that would make a likely target. It's not really my scene anyway."

"The kind of bomb I'm talking about won't care that you're not standing right next to it."

"What do you mean? Like, a nuclear bomb?"

"Yes."

"I don't think India and Pakistan are going to start lobbing nukes at each other, Dad. Or at least there's no more risk of that than there was a week ago."

"What about terrorists?"

"And nukes? Where are they going to get them?"

"I'm not sure yet," Sam admitted.

"Okay then. Let me know when you are sure."

"Lena. I'm serious. I don't have all the evidence, but I feel in my bones that something very bad is about to happen. I think there's a very real risk of a city in India being attacked with a nuclear bomb, maybe by Pakistan, maybe by one of the terrorist groups. I don't know. I just know that I want you out of there."

"I know you do, Dad. But I'm not ready to leave. The risks you've described are always there. I knew that when I decided to move here. You knew that when you made the same choice, and if you hadn't, then I wouldn't be here today. Listen, I'll be back for Christmas, okay?"

Sam fought on gamely, but it was a losing battle. He didn't have the evidence he needed to persuade his daughter, and Lena was like her mother: stubborn, independent, and self-assured. He thought about getting on a plane and flying to Mumbai and somehow physically carrying her back to Washington. That was not going to end well. Sam wasn't ready to give up. But he knew he was not going to win this round. He would need to pull back, marshal his arguments, and try again. He'd need something compelling and concrete to bring Lena around, to get her to leave that city. Sam knew he would never sleep well as long as his daughter was on the subcontinent.

. . .

The draft speech alone, Sam realized, was a terribly thin reed on which to build a case against Argus. It was just a Word document. It could have been written by anyone for any purpose. It was not a part of the system. It lacked agency. There were no origin codes, no information about the drafter, no clearance page, no routing information, nothing that gave life to the information in the context of the government, nothing that would leave electronic footprints. It was a dead block of text that could have been drafted on any computer.

The falsified intelligence reports, on the other hand, were something altogether different. These were official records. They had agency and accountability. Together with the speech, Sam believed, he could use these to make a credible argument that would get traction with people in the system he thought he could trust.

Andy was gone, but Sam should be able to re-create the file of falsified reports that the young analyst had put together.

At the office the next morning, Sam logged on to his high-side system where he could access NSA products and typed a few key words into the search function. He chose *Vanalika Chandra* and *Panchavaktra Guhathakurta* as the easiest route to find the original piece that had triggered his approach to Andy.

The search took only seconds, but the response was frightening in its implication.

NO RECORD FOUND.

Sam tried again, using the original date-time group that he still remembered.

NO RECORD FOUND.

He tried searching for *Panoptes* as a program function and drew a blank.

He tried other key words and got the same response. Quickly, he tried to search for the other intel pieces that Andy had shown to him. Sometimes, his search produced results but not the relevant product he was looking for. More often, the search algorithm repeated the NO RECORD FOUND mantra.

Someone had gone through the database and stripped out all of the suspect products linked to the Panoptes program. Sam was pretty sure he knew who had done that. He was also confident that Weeder and his team had covered their tracks carefully.

The draft speech was now the only real "evidence" he had that Argus Systems was up to no good. The odds were that it would not be enough.

That assessment turned out to be distressingly accurate. Sam went to see an old friend at the State Department. J. Winston Tennyck, who went by the almost unbearably preppy nickname "Tenny," was a deputy assistant secretary in the South Asia Bureau. He was third-generation Foreign Service and had grown up bouncing around the Indian subcontinent and the Middle East back in the days when India had been part of the Near Eastern Bureau. Even so, there was a substantial piece of Tenny that was forever Connecticut, from his penny loafers with no socks to his Brooks Brothers linen driving cap. He was more Groton than Goa.

Sam had cashed in a couple of favors to get on Tenny's calendar that afternoon. He had hesitated before making the call, but he needed to go to someone in a position to make a difference and

Tenny was an unlikely candidate for membership in the Stoics. His attitude toward South Asia had always seemed to border on noblesse oblige. He was a classic on-the-one-hand-on-the-other-hand-let's-split-the-difference State Department deal maker, the kind of person who saw the world in shades of gray rather than the stark black-and-white of the Stoics. Moreover, if you could get past the preppy exterior, Tenny had a sharp and incisive mind that would allow him to recognize the significance of what Sam had uncovered . . . if only he could summon the necessary imagination. Sam showed Tennyck the draft presidential speech, asking him to keep their conversation strictly in confidence and being somewhat vague about exactly how he had acquired a copy.

Tennyck was a few years older than Sam and he needed reading glasses. There were at least half a dozen pairs scattered around the office that Sam could see. Doubtless there were even more stuffed into the desk drawers and the pockets of the spare blazers Tenny kept in the office closet.

When he had finished reading the speech, the DAS removed his glasses and wiped them idly on the skinny back half of his club tie before setting them down next to the bone china cup that held his tea.

"It's really not a terribly good speech," he observed. "A bit windy, maybe even a tad pompous for the occasion. The 'terrible swift sword' thing in particular struck me as a bit over the top."

"That's not really the point, Tenny. I didn't write this. It was drafted by someone who knows what's coming because he's part of the group that's planning to make it so."

"Yes. The Stoics, was it?"

"That's right."

"And you had other material evidence, but it's mysteriously disappeared from the servers of the intelligence community. Do I have that right?"

"Yes," Sam said helplessly. He knew how ridiculous the whole thing sounded.

"Do you want to know what I think this is?" Tenny asked.

"Tell me."

"I think this is part of a war-game exercise. Argus does that sort of thing, doesn't it?"

"On occasion."

"So this is almost certainly one of the pieces the game designer has put together to include for color. You know, the kind of thing they need to make the otherwise terribly dull at least palatable. That's probably why they left the name of the city out of the draft, so that they could have some flexibility in the scenario. Some people like it, I suppose, but I find war gaming so tedious, like talking about food and wine rather than sitting down to dinner."

Deputy Assistant Secretary Tennyck had missed his calling. He should have been a colonial official in India during the British Raj. Give him a pith helmet and he would blend right in.

"I understand how this sounds," Sam said. "I know that the evidence is weak. But look at what's happening on the ground. Tensions between Delhi and Islamabad are spiking for no real reason. I believe someone is cooking the intelligence that we are sharing with the services there and that the data being fed into the system is designed to push the two sides closer to conflict."

"But why?" Tennyck asked. "*Cui bono?* as they say. Who benefits?"

"I think the Stoics would tell you that we do . . . in the end."

"Well, it's all right then, isn't it?"

Sam knew that it was time to cut his losses.

"This has to remain strictly between us," he said.

"Don't worry, Sam. I'm not taking this up with anyone. I'm quite certain no one would believe me if I did."

Garret Spears hated Washington parties. Boring, plastic people eating boring, plastic food and trolling for gossip. Whoever you spoke to would keep looking over your shoulder with at least one eye hoping to spot someone more important in the crowd so they could trade up. As much as Spears hated going to the parties, however, he would have hated not being invited considerably more. He wanted to be A-list, a confidant to presidents and prime ministers.

Argus was just a starting place for a journey that he was sure had limitless upside potential. Secretary of defense, perhaps. Senator Spears. Maybe even one day an office with no corners and its own rose garden. Why think small? Ambition was not a sin.

For now, however, it sometimes meant putting in appearances, which is why he was here at the Mandarin Oriental hotel in downtown D.C., where Raytheon was hosting a reception for the president of Kazakhstan. No doubt the corporate titans at Raytheon assessed that Nursultan Nazarbayev could be persuaded to purchase multiple billions of dollars of Raytheon missiles in exchange for little plates of cheese and crackers and tumblers of icy vodka.

Spears helped himself to a glass of sparkling water with lime from the tray of one of the gloved waiters circulating the room.

The third-tier congressman that Spears was technically talking to, if not really listening to, was prattling on about something, maybe ethanol. Spears didn't really care. He was from some Podunk district in the Midwest with more hogs than constituents . . . unless you counted the hogs as constituents and maybe he did. He was also, however, on the House Permanent Select Committee on Intelligence, so Spears was ready to stand there and smile while he blathered.

That the congressman had sought him out was a good sign. People were talking about him. His membership in the Stoics was putting him on the Washington map. Not the one of gala dinners and congressional hearings. The one that mattered. The Washington of back rooms and secret deals. Real power.

The next few weeks would be critical. Spears and Argus were on point for perhaps the most complex and far-reaching operation in the Stoics' long history. If he pulled it off, he would be able to move up in the organization's rigid hierarchy, assuming, of course, that the operation came off as planned.

It was a shame about the kid . . . Krittenbrink. But when Quick had told him about the analysis he had done, Spears knew that there was no other choice. There had not been time to summon the Council. Spears had made the call as head of Operations and Weeder had done the work. It was not as elegant as how he had handled Braithwaite, but he hadn't had much time to work with and Krittenbrink's death would go largely unnoticed, except by his family, of course.

Quick was another potential complication. With any luck, however, it would be weeks before anyone noticed he was missing. The CIA man had been something of a loner. Now he was rotting in a jungle grave in Brazil. Weeder had subcontracted the job out to a local network he had done business with before. They were professional, discreet, and expensive. Spears was confident that problem at least had been contained.

He thought of Krittenbrink and Quick much as he had of the

soldiers he had ordered into combat. It was a dangerous business and sometimes you had to lose a pawn to get to the king. The trick was to remember that other people were playing the same game, and while you were pushing your pawns around the board, some other player was looking at you with the same idea in mind. You never wanted to be someone else's piece, or at least not a pawn. Pawns were for sacrifice.

The congressman finished his pitch on ethanol and shook Spears's hand with the consummate skill of a practiced politician. Firm grip. Two pumps. Left hand on the upper arm. "Stay in touch. Don't forget to vote." Spears flashed the ingratiating smile that had been instrumental in his climb up the slippery pole in the Pentagon.

He sipped his mineral water and looked over the crowd as he mentally reviewed the state of play with the operation. The security leak surrounding the Krittenbrink analysis had been a real scare. He believed the leak had been plugged, but there was no way to be sure. Panoptes had done its work and it was time to deactivate the program. They had moved past that point.

Krittenbrink's putting the pieces together the way he had had been a neat piece of work. Spears was not, by nature, introspective. His few short forays into quiet reflection had led him to conclude that he was not particularly good at it nor especially interested in what was there to be found. It was the competitive world around him that engaged Spears. He was smart enough, however, to know that he needed people who could do the kind of thing that Krittenbrink had done. Sam Trainor, for one, would have been a real asset. He may have failed the trolleyology test, but, hell, no test was perfect. It was just broad-brush. Interesting, but not necessarily dispositive. Maybe he should give Sam another shot?

Spears felt a hand on his shoulder and turned to find a man he knew vaguely standing there with a gin and tonic. He was wearing a blue blazer and gray flannel pants and one of those school ties with little emblems all over them that the East Coast elite seemed so fond of. He was State Department. What was his name? Tennyson? Tannenbaum?

"Garret, how are you?"

Tennyck. That was it. J. Winston Tennyck. He was the South Asia DAS who had helped steer the Panoptes contract to Argus.

"Just fine, Tenny. Thanks."

"So your man came by to see me today," Tenny said.

"My man?"

"Sam Trainor."

"What about?"

"Well, that's the thing. He had the strangest damn story to tell. I didn't follow the whole thing, but frankly I'm worried about Sam. He didn't sound entirely rational, and after the Snowden mess, we need to be careful about contractors with clearances."

All of Spears's internal threat warnings lit up, but he kept his expression neutral. He needed more information.

"To tell you the truth, I've been a little concerned about him myself. Sam hasn't seemed quite right for a while now, and the death of that young analyst in INR hit him really hard."

"Do you think it would be a good idea for him to be evaluated?" Tennyck asked, with evident concern. "By a mental health professional, I mean."

"This may well require the services of a professional," Spears replied flatly.

He leaned in closer to Tenny as though taking him into his confidence.

"Now, tell me exactly what he told you."

. . .

There was nothing about his demeanor that would have betrayed any hint of alarm to J. Winston Tennyck as the South Asia DAS summarized his conversation with Sam. But behind the mask that he controlled with such care, Garret Spears felt a brief stab of fear and anger.

Krittenbrink had had a partner.

00:19

Do you mind if I join you?"

Lieutenant Commander Arthur H. McCollum, Office of Naval Intelligence, looked up from his beer and assayed the man who had interrupted his circular train of thought. A civilian in a dark suit and a fedora. He was thin and of average height. In his right hand, he held a black briefcase. The eyes behind the silver wire-rimmed glasses he wore were so blue they were almost clear and they reminded McCollum of the sea. It was a maudlin thought. He was on his fourth beer of the afternoon.

"It's a free country," he said.

"For now."

The civilian doffed his hat and sat across from McCollum at the small table near the back of the bar at the Cosmos Club. He set his hat on the table and his briefcase next to his chair.

"I haven't seen you here before. Are you a member?"

"No," the man replied. "But I have certain privileges. My name is

Smith and there is a particular issue that I would like to discuss
with you."

"What is it?"

"This." From the briefcase, Smith retrieved a manila folder and
placed it on the table. McCollum opened it and the shock of adrenaline
he felt at the contents cut through the fog of alcohol like a hot knife.
McCollum did not need to read the Top Secret memo inside the folder.
He knew what it said. He had written it.

"How did you get this?" he asked.

"It came to me in the normal course of my duties," Smith explained
unhelpfully.

"Am I under investigation?" Smith looked like a G-man and McCollum had been keenly aware when he sent the memo that it was the
kind of thing that could be used to hang a man.

"Perhaps. But not by me."

"Are you Naval Intelligence?"

"No."

"What then? FBI?"

Smith smiled, exposing his teeth. "Something else."

"What do you want from me?"

"You have it backwards, Commander. The question is not what I
want; the question is what am I offering."

McCollum looked at Smith suspiciously.

"Your reasoning in this memo is quite compelling. It so happens that
there are others in positions of influence in this government who share
your views and appreciate your logic."

Some months ago, McCollum had drafted a memo to his superiors
in Naval Intelligence detailing eight actions the United States might
take to provoke Japan into an attack. War was sweeping the globe. The

democracies were losing. The American people, however, having burned their fingers in the Great War and having just begun to pull themselves out of the Great Depression had no interest in foreign entanglements. By the time they awoke to the dangers, it would be too late. The United States could not remain neutral in this global conflict, but it would require some shock to the system to rouse the sleeping American giant. Pushing Japan into an overt act of war, McCollum had argued in his memo, would do just that. His superiors had warned him off this line of argument. It was dangerous, maybe even treasonous. McCollum had been shunted off into a series of lesser assignments, but he had not lost faith in the fundamental rightness of his views. It was this logic loop that had been occupying his thoughts when Mr. Smith arrived to interrupt his beery reverie.

McCollum closed the folder and pushed it back toward Smith.

"So what do you propose to do about it?" he asked.

"Those of us of like minds have been working to put in place policies quite similar to those that you describe in this memo. We believe that we have been successful in bringing the Empire of Japan around to the view that it has no choice but to attack the United States preemptively, although the when and where are for the time being uncertain. Personally, I think the Philippines is the most likely target. More important, there are reasons to believe this attack will trigger war not only with Japan, but also with Germany—a much more dangerous opponent."

"What sort of reasons?"

"Magic."

McCollum did not deign to respond.

"We have broken the Japanese codes," Smith explained. "Naval and diplomatic. The program is called Magic."

McCollum worked in intelligence and he had heard rumors from those in a position to know that the U.S. government was reading the emperor's mail, but this was the first solid confirmation he had that the program was real.

"And what do you want from me?"

"It is important that when the blow finally falls it is strong enough to force the United States into a war it does not yet want. If the military knows through intercepted Japanese traffic that the attack is coming, the navy might respond to preempt it or at least soften the attack to the point where it is no longer a compelling casus belli."

McCollum understood this.

"In my memo, I made the same point, that when the Japanese were ready to attack we should let them hit us hard enough to hurt."

"We know. And we appreciate the clarity of your arguments."

"I need to ask you again. What's my role in all this?"

"Magic is a priceless asset, but it is poorly understood by the navy's senior leadership and it is underfunded. There are a limited number of translators and analysts. All are overworked. There is a single position responsible for taking the raw intelligence and directing it to the analysts. They only have the time and resources to examine the pieces marked high priority. Routine reports are rarely, if ever, looked at. Those deemed nonsubstantive are simply destroyed. We want you to take that position and use it to ensure that any Magic traffic related to an attack on the United States is kept out of the system."

"Who would I be working for?"

"Nominally, you would be under Admiral Croft, the head of the Magic project. In reality, you would be working for me."

There were risks to this, McCollum knew. But they were manageable. The naval bureaucracy was slow and cumbersome. Once war came, all of the antecedents would be lost in the flood of new information. No one was likely to go back to review old reports, at least not until the war was over. He was a patriot. He couldn't say no.

"When do I start?" he asked.

"Would tomorrow be soon enough?"

"I think that will do. Where do I report?"

"That's the best part. One of the sweetest and safest assignments the United States Navy has to offer, right in the belly of the beast. Magic operates out of the headquarters of the Pacific Fleet . . . Pearl Harbor."

DEPARTMENT OF HOMELAND SECURITY
APRIL 15

00:20

S pears had little respect for the Department of Homeland
Security. The agency had been cobbled together like some
kind of Frankenstein's monster from various cast-off pieces of
the federal government in the frantic and panic-stricken atmo-
sphere following the 9/11 attacks. When the Bush administration
ran the proverbial twenty thousand volts through the hybrid beast,
however, it did not come to life. Quite the opposite. There was no
plan in place to merge the cultures of such disparate agencies as the
Secret Service and the Animal and Plant Health Inspection Service. Bodyguards and botanists, it turned out, had very different
corporate cultures. DHS was a misshapen mishmash of goals and
missions typically presided over by a second-tier, swing-state politician who had just lost an election. Little wonder it routinely came
in dead last in every federal government survey on the quality of
life and work.

The physical plant of the DHS's sprawling Nebraska Avenue
Complex reflected its organizational entropy. The NAC had begun

its life as a World War II–era U.S. Navy facility where mathematicians had worked on cracking Nazi codes. It had all been downhill from there. Since then, the NAC had been—among other things—a seminary and an all-girls school. Now it was in a sorry state of disrepair, with peeling paint, moldy carpets, and exposed asbestos insulation. The government did not want to put any money into the place because it was planning to build DHS a shiny new headquarters facility in southeast D.C., fittingly on the grounds of a former psychiatric hospital.

Building 19 was a tired-looking, five-story brick structure that was as ugly as it was dysfunctional. But it had a SCIF and it was Homeland Security's turn to host the meeting of the Governing Council. The Stoics had to keep moving. Routine risked exposure and exposure would ruin them. The country was not yet ready for the kind of higher thinking that the group represented. Someday, maybe. But not today.

The SCIF on the second floor had mustard-colored drapes covering a window that had been bricked in. The conference table was vintage seventies Formica.

God, Spears thought with some distaste, *DHS really is the bottom feeder in the national security establishment.*

He was early. He had made a point of it.

One by one, the other members of the Governing Council arrived for what was nominally a routine review of the intelligence collection priorities for the next calendar year. It was the kind of agenda that would explain a senior-level interagency gathering while simultaneously eliciting exactly zero curiosity or interest in the proceedings. In D.C., there were hundreds of meetings a day that looked like this.

Weeder arrived separately from Spears and took his customary seat in a chair alongside the wall rather than at the table. Ordinarily, the outer ring in a Washington meeting was for staffers and less important participants in the conversation. Weeder, Spears knew, was neither of these.

Spears looked around the room and marveled at what this group could do. These were largely anonymous men and women whose names would be all but unknown to ordinary people in outside-the-Beltway America. But from within the bureaucracy, the people on the Council could move mountains . . . or crush them into gravel if that was more convenient.

The current Vice Chair commanded no more than a desk and a phone, but with a single call, she could deploy aircraft carriers across oceans on the far side of the globe. Finance could make you rich or break you as a single carefully worded statement sent stock prices climbing or wheat futures crashing. Cross him and Legal could turn your life inside out with a federal investigation so overwhelming in its intensity that it hardly mattered whether you were ultimately found guilty.

This was real power, the power to change the world. Change it for the better, Spears was confident, even if that meant that some had to be sacrificed for the greater good.

The Chairman brought the meeting to order.

"Thank you for coming on short notice," he began. "This is an extraordinary session of the Governing Council, which itself is a rare event. It will be so noted in the records. We are approaching the culmination of one of the most ambitious and complex operations in the history of our organization, and it may behoove us to scale back the meeting schedule once our plans have come to fruition. For now, however, there are decisions to be made. Operations requested this session and I turn the floor over to him for his report."

Spears took a sip from the glass of water in front of him. He was uncharacteristically nervous. The Council, he knew, would not be pleased with what he had to say. He would have to shape his message with care.

"Thank you, Mr. Chairman. I'd like to begin by emphasizing that Cold Harbor remains very much on track. There is no change in the timeline, and the operation on the ground has been making better-than-expected progress."

"It sure sounds like there's a sizeable 'but' attached to the end of that sentence," Reports interjected.

"There have been some challenges," Spears said, "and some setbacks requiring . . . creative solutions."

"Like murder?" Plans asked icily.

"Yes," Spears replied with equanimity. "Something very much like that. The greatest good and all . . ."

"So what . . . setbacks . . . haven't you told us about, yet?"

"You are all aware of the Krittenbrink situation." Heads around the room nodded. "We had to act urgently and before obtaining the full authorization of the Council. Krittenbrink had drafted a paper describing in remarkable detail the outlines of the Panoptes program. Even if he did not yet understand the purpose of the program, a document like that in the hands of our opponents in the Lord administration would almost certainly have forced the cancellation of Cold Harbor. That outcome was not acceptable. We needed to move quickly. I authorized the Commander to eliminate the threat."

This was not entirely accurate. Weeder did not really take orders from Spears. He took his cues directly from the Chairman, and it had been the Commander who had recommended taking Krittenbrink out before he could share the document more widely.

"In addition to dealing directly with Krittenbrink, we eliminated any trace of the Panoptes material from the databases. The DTG numbers linked to the products produced as part of the Panoptes program now link to innocuous material unrelated to Cold Harbor. That program had largely run its course in any event, and we would soon have moved to strip those products from the system, so it is no real loss."

"I assume, though, that your efforts to contain the threat were not successful," Reports said. "Otherwise, why summon the Council to an extraordinary session? What is the current complication?"

"Krittenbrink was not operating alone. I now have reason to believe that he had a partner, Samuel Trainor. He is an Argus employee hired to head up the South Asia unit and he previously worked with Krittenbrink at State/INR. Trainor has somehow obtained a copy of some of the material that our operations team has been preparing for Phase II of Cold Harbor. It is not on the face of it incriminating material, and we are prepared to dismiss it as war-gaming activity. But Trainor has been shopping some theories to at least one senior official that are distressingly accurate. This is not as urgent as the Krittenbrink situation since Trainor does not seem to have a copy of the Panoptes file, but it is important and I am bringing this issue to you to seek guidance from the Council."

There was silence. It was not the silence of assent. It was the silence of mounting anger.

"Jesus Christ." The Vice Chairman was the first to speak in response. "How do you know that Krittenbrink and Trainor were a duo? How do you know that there aren't three or four or a hundred and fifty more who know about Panoptes and Cold Harbor, or at least enough about the programs to make them dangerous? How can you assume anything at all at this point?"

"Yes," Plans added. "You haven't given us enough information to formulate an effective response."

"I appreciate the difficulties of the position we are in," Spears said. "That is why I asked for this session. We are on the cusp of something great. We have options. And we must not lose heart. We must not give in to our fears."

"That is easy to say," Plans replied. "But that does not absolve you from the responsibility for the security breach. How did a junior analyst like Krittenbrink get access to the Panoptes messages to begin with?"

"Panoptes was integrated into the mainstream intelligence reporting. That was a decision we made to reinforce the credibility of the product. It was the only way we could ensure that Panoptes material would be included as part of the regular intelligence-sharing program with Islamabad and New Delhi. Krittenbrink had access to all of this information as a matter of course. So did Sam Trainor. One of them must have identified a pattern in the Panoptes material that triggered concerns. We are looking into this."

"You are assuming again that it was either Trainor or Krittenbrink who realized something was out of place. Couldn't it just as easily have been a third party? Someone you have yet to identify."

"It is possible, yes," Spears acknowledged reluctantly.

"The level of incompetence demonstrated here is frankly stunning," Plans said. "I think that merits further review. We need to understand what the hell happened."

"There will be time enough for a postmortem later," the Chairman interjected. "There is no percentage in seeking to assign blame at this point. That can wait. For now, our task is to identify a way forward that protects the operation."

"How many people do we know Trainor's talked to?" Finance asked.

"Just one," Spears said. "A DAS at State who dismissed him as a loon. As I said, Trainor doesn't have any evidence, and without that, the story he has to tell is quite literally incredible."

"If he doesn't have anything solid to offer, maybe we should just leave it alone. That may be the least risky course of action." Unsurprisingly, this was Legal. Washington lawyers, in Spears's experience, were all alike. They never wanted to do anything. In contrast, Spears himself had always believed in the credo embodied in the slogan of the SEALs' British counterparts, the SAS: Who Dares Wins.

"I don't think we can afford to take the chance," Vice said. "If the subject is aggressively pushing a story line that, in fact, comes to pass, it would add ex post facto credibility to the allegations that the outcome in the Indo-Pak conflict was manipulated. No, I think we need to engage."

Spears noted the way the Vice Chairman used "subject" instead of Sam's name. It was clinical. Dehumanizing. The prelude to what in the SEALs they used to refer to as "direct action." Spears knew which column he could put her in.

"I'm inclined to agree," Reports said. Others around the table nodded their heads.

"Commander," the Chairman asked. "Could you take care of Mr. Trainor in such a way that it would not arouse suspicions? An accident or even a suicide. A second random homicide of a friend of Krittenbrink's would be an extraordinary coincidence. It would attract too much attention and perhaps raise some awkward questions."

There was a pause while Weeder considered the answer.

"It can be done. But it will take some time to arrange."

"Weeks?"

"Days."

"Wait a moment," Plans interjected. "Shouldn't we be thinking about interrogating him first? We don't know if there are any others. I would suggest that we need an opportunity to discuss this with Mr. Trainor in a manner conducive to complete honesty."

Torture, Spears thought. *That was the word you didn't want to use, you prig. Language was the last refuge of the moral coward.*

Like all SEALs, Spears had been through SERE training: Survival, Evasion, Resistance, and Escape. As part of the training, the young SEALs had been waterboarded until they revealed a secret that they had been instructed to keep. They all broke. Torture was effective as long as the subject had the information you were after. If not, he or she would make up anything you might desire if it promised to stop the pain.

"Commander?" the Chairman asked.

"That will take a little more time. But it can be done."

"Very well. Make the necessary preparations."

"Is there anything else we should be doing?" Vice asked. "Are there other sources of leverage against the subject that we could potentially employ as part of a backup or contingency plan?"

"He has a daughter," Weeder replied.

"Here in Washington?"

"No. In India. In Mumbai, in fact."

A few eyebrows were raised at that.

"That's not of much help then," Finance commented.

"We have a team on the ground in India that could potentially pick her up. She would be leverage against him."

"That would seem an appropriate precaution."

"Again, the preparations would take some time."

"How much time?"

"Days."

"At a minimum," the Chairman suggested, "I believe we should put the daughter under surveillance and develop the option to take her if necessary. The authority to take that step can be invested in the Commander here. Is that agreed?"

It was.

"And the father?" the Chairman continued. "Should we authorize the Commander to use all necessary means to determine whether there are any others who may know about Cold Harbor and Panoptes, and to take any other action that he deems appropriate to protect the integrity of the operation?"

"I believe we should," Reports said quickly. "I'll make the motion. Trainor is a legit threat."

"I agree," said Finance. "Seconded."

It was unanimous.

MUMBAI, INDIA
APRIL 14

00:21

I t sat in the center of the room as though it were some kind of conversation piece. But they did not talk about it. As much as they could, the men tried to ignore its existence. They had not opened it. No one had told them what was inside. It was not necessary. They knew. They were living with a bomb.

Although the sealed box was a grim reminder of death, Khan was almost exultant. Now he understood. This was his mission. This was why he had abandoned everything he had known in America and pledged himself to the Hand of the Prophet. This was jihad.

Jadoon had set them up in an abandoned movie studio in Navi Mumbai, a depressed industrial zone separated from the city center by the Thane Creek estuary. Hill Station Productions had specialized in cheap, low-end musicals that typically went straight to video. The studio had tried to go more up-market, but a few big bets on bad movies had sent Hill Station Productions into bankruptcy. It was perfect for their needs, isolated but still close to downtown. Toward the end of its life, and in what Khan suspected had been a desperate attempt to stave off the creditors, the studio had started pirating basic services such as electricity and water. These still worked because there was no record of Hill Station Productions being connected to the grid.

Jadoon had implied that there was another reason he had chosen the abandoned studio as their base, but he had been secretive as to exactly why.

The set for the last movie the studio had pinned its hopes on was still standing in the spacious soundstage, and if you ignored the film of grit and dust that covered every exposed surface, the cameras looked ready to roll at the call to "action." It must have been a period piece, because the set was an old Hindu temple made of fiberglass and Styrofoam. There doubtlessly would have been a barbarian princess, sword fights, and—it was Bollywood, after all—song-and-dance numbers. To Khan, the set looked terribly cheesy. Maybe it would have shown up better on film, or maybe there was a good reason that Hill Station Productions was out of business.

On the second day, a new member of the team arrived. Adnan was no fighter. He was small and thin to the point of emaciation. He could not even grow a proper beard. It grew in uneven patches like the fur on a mangy dog. He wore a white *taqiyah* prayer cap. Khan suspected it was more a mark of vanity than piety since it covered his substantial bald spot. Jadoon had told him that Adnan was a professor of physics and high up in the Pakistani nuclear bureaucracy. The jihadis agreed that he looked like a toad.

Adnan seemed afraid of the guns the HeM jihadis carried, but he had no fear of the box. He set a small wooden stool and a box of tools alongside it. Khan helped him lift the lid gently. Inside was a perfectly ordinary-looking bomb, with tail fins and a bulbous nose.

A small hemisphere protruded from the tip and Khan wondered if something as sophisticated as a nuclear bomb could be triggered by something as primitive and basic as a contact fuse.

"Masood told me that you know explosives," Adnan said.

"Yes. I was trained to be part of a bomb squad."

"For the Americans, no?"

"Yes."

Adnan looked at him appraisingly.

"I need an assistant for what I am about to do. Someone with steady hands and no fear of death."

"I will do my best."

"Yes. You will. And you will not fail me."

"Insha'Allah."

Adnan handed him a plastic badge on a metal chain. A small manila envelope was slotted neatly into the badge. Khan could see that Adnan was already wearing one around his own neck.

"You will want one of these," Adnan said.

"What is it?" Khan asked.

"Something I can use to measure our exposure to radiation."

"What's in the envelope?"

Adnan laughed and gestured toward the soundstage.

"Movie film."

With a small screwdriver from the toolbox, Adnan removed the screws securing a large convex plate to the side of the bomb. The casing had been painted army green and the panel was glued in place by the dried paint. Adnan needed to scrape the paint clean to remove the panel. Khan did not know what he had expected, but the inside of an atomic bomb was disappointingly ordinary, a sphere of what looked like pretty standard explosives with electronic triggers embedded in the material. Adnan seemed to sense what Khan was thinking.

"It's an implosion-style warhead, with high explosives surrounding a hollow core of uranium-235. The explosives have to go off at precisely the same time to collapse the core fast enough for the uranium to reach critical mass. If the timing is off, you get a nuclear fizzle rather than an explosive chain reaction. Really quite embarrassing if you're trying to blow up a city."

"What was in the box that we put on the train?" Khan asked. "A different bomb?"

"A dummy," Adnan explained. "It will pass a simple visual inspection and weighs exactly the same as the real thing, but there is no warhead inside. No fissile material. For most purposes, nuclear weapons don't need to work as long as the enemy believes they will. For most purposes. Not ours."

"You know how this thing works?"

"I designed it. Indian intelligence stole the blueprints for one of our warheads and the Indian defense establishment adapted the plans to their own purposes. It was my design. It will produce a ten-kiloton yield consistent to within plus or minus 5 percent." The pride in his voice was plain, as though he were describing the accomplishments of his children.

"What now?"

"Now we teach a bomb trained to go off at a certain altitude to go off at a certain time."

Adnan pulled a set of metal rods from the box and built a rectangular frame alongside the bomb. For the next three hours, he worked meticulously to extend the electronic controls of the weapon out of the bomb casing and onto the external frame. Khan held the light for him and assisted with the wiring when Adnan asked him to. The circuitry was complex, much more so, Khan thought, than it needed to be. It looked almost as though the bomb had been hooked up to a life-support system.

"Why all of the redundant loops?" he asked.

Adnan stopped what he was doing and turned to him with a look that somehow straddled impressed and irritated.

"Some of the complexity stems from my need to circumvent the PAL, the permissive action link. Essentially, it's a code that lets the warhead know that it's okay to fire. Some of the complexity is about setting up the timing mechanism and introducing the connections for our own PAL. And then some"—Adnan paused as if considering what he should say—"some of the loops are traps meant to prevent tampering. If someone cuts random wires or otherwise tries to disable the weapon without knowing the proper sequence, it will explode. The timing may not be optimal in those circumstances, but it would be a shame to waste a perfectly good fissile core and at the very least it would take the saboteur with it to Hell."

"Are you expecting trouble from any of us?" Khan asked, shocked.

"Of course not. We are all servants of Allah. But we are in the middle of an enemy city and the Indian services are far from amateur. It is a precaution is all. And now for the final piece."

The physicist pulled two thin rectangular objects made of glass and steel from the toolbox. Each one had a screen and there was a row of buttons along the bottom edge. Adnan looked at his watch and pressed a series of buttons on one of the boxes. A row of numbers appeared on the screen glowing in blood red and upside down to Khan. He tried to read them, but it was hard to get a good look.

The last four numbers were 2-5-0-0. The preceding number might have been a 7 or a 9. The physicist's thumb partly obscured that number and the 3 in front of it.

Adnan set the second box on top of the first and pushed at the corners until they snapped together with a metallic click. The blank screen on the upper device lit up with a sequence of numbers. Now Adnan was holding the object in such a way that Khan could read the screen easily. He saw two things. The sequence of numbers was 20072500.

And it was counting down.

It was a timer.

20:07:24:59

20:07:24:58

There was no need for Adnan to explain what would happen when the counter reached 0. At 0, Mumbai would burn.

"We're almost there," Adnan said. "I just need to lock it."

He touched a larger button on the side of the device and the screen toggled to present a row of nine dashes.

Adnan entered the code, but his body blocked Khan's view and he could not see the numbers.

"Now we control the weapon," Adnan explained. "It will respond only to our PAL. Masood himself gave me the code. He was quite insistent on the sequence of numbers. It was all mumbo jumbo, mystical nonsense to me. But any string of numbers is as good as any other as long as you remember what it is."

"What is it?" Khan asked.

Adnan smiled.

"Something that only Masood and I are empowered to know," he answered.

. . .

Adnan's modifications may have been essential to the operation, but they left the bomb leaky. He instructed Khan to cover the box with lead blankets like the kind that a dentist might drape over a patient before taking an X-ray, in New Jersey, at least, if not necessarily in Lahore. As an added precaution, he distributed film badges to each of the jihadis. Khan and the other foot soldiers took turns guarding the box.

They passed the time with prayer and exercise. When Khan had been in the army, the soldiers had whiled away the hours of boredom with card games. But gambling was *haram*, sinful. The only book they had was the Quran. It was enough. Khan took his turns standing guard over the box. They waited. Once a day, the physicist would develop the film to check their levels of exposure to radiation. So far, the level of exposure was within acceptable limits, at least according to Adnan.

Khan had just finished his morning shift on guard duty five days after the HeM team had set up camp at Hill Station Productions when Jadoon summoned him.

"I have a new assignment for you." He did not seem happy about it.

"What is it?"

"I want you to follow someone."

"Follow him where?"

"Her. And wherever she goes. I want you to watch this woman, track her movements, learn as much as you can about her habits."

"Am I going to kill her?"

"I don't know. At least not yet. As it stands, our instructions are just to follow her. We will learn more when we need to know."

"Who is this woman?"

"Her name is Lena Trainor." Jadoon put a thin manila envelope on the desk of the office where they were meeting. The walls were decorated with posters from Hill Station movies, mostly crime dramas, it looked like.

"Why is she important?" Khan asked. "What does she have to do with our mission?"

Jadoon shook his head impatiently.

"You ask too many questions."

"The answers might be important."

"They might," Jadoon conceded. "But not as important as obedience to orders."

"I understand. When do I start?"

"Right now."

"Why me, Jadoon? Why not one of the others?" Khan was genuinely curious about why the team leader had chosen him.

"Because you are not a robot," Jadoon replied. "The others on the team will do as I command, but they cannot think for themselves. I do not know what will happen with this girl, but I suspect that it will require a man of judgment to know what to do when the time for action comes."

"And you think that I am this man?"

"I do."

Khan wished that he could be so certain.

The file had not been especially informative or useful. There were a few headshots of the woman he was supposed to follow. One looked like a driver's license or passport picture, and the other may have been a college yearbook photo. There was a name and address for her employer, a high-tech company called SysNet on Hari Mandi Road. There was some biographical information about the subject, her work history, and a summary of her impressive academic credentials. There were a few interesting tidbits. She had both American and Indian citizenship. Her father had been a minor-league bureaucrat in the State Department and was now a government contractor of some kind. Her mother was from Mumbai, a designer or artist who had died some ten years ago. Her father was an American, an Anglo judging by Lena's photographs. The mother's last known address in India was included. It was in Dharavi.

She was beautiful. That was the first thing Khan thought when he saw the subject walk out the front door of SysNet Technology. He was sitting in a café with a cup of tea and a small plate of cookies. He had a magazine that he pretended to read as he kept watch on the entrance to SysNet. Tucked discreetly into the magazine was one of the headshots from her file that he had brought in case he needed a reference. The photograph had not done her justice. She was tall for an Indian, half Indian he reminded himself, and she moved with an enviable grace and self-assuredness that the two dimensions of film had been unable to convey.

He did not yet know how the subject moved around town. Whether she had a car and a driver or took taxis or public transportation or even walked. A Kawasaki two-stroke motorbike parked nearby would help Khan navigate the dense Mumbai traffic without calling undue attention to him. But it looked at least for now as though she was moving on foot. He would do the same.

Khan dropped a hundred-rupee note with its picture of Gandhi on the table and slipped the photograph of the subject back into his wallet before stepping out from under the umbrella that had shaded him from the intense afternoon sun. He could feel a thin sheen of

sweat on his forehead. His sensitivity to the heat was something of
an embarrassment to him. He felt it marked him as an outsider. A
citizen of New Jersey rather than Pakistan.

He took a position on the street opposite the subject, where he
could keep her in sight without looking like he was following her.
Even on the crowded streets of Mumbai, she stood out. The subject
was wearing Western clothes, a white blouse with mother-of-pearl
buttons, and a skirt that was somewhere in between blue and green.
Her shoes were flats, sensible, made for walking through the con-
gested streets of a sprawling, chaotic megacity. Khan had thought
that Islamabad had prepared him for Mumbai, but it was not even
close. Nothing could prepare you for Mumbai except perhaps
another Indian city. They were in a class of their own.

Mumbai was a shadow's paradise. It was nonstop sensory overload with so much coming at you in the form of sounds, smells,
crowds, and spectacle that it was hard to focus on any one thing.
Certainly not on one man who did not wish to be noticed trailing
at a discreet distance.

Indian street life was a mass of contrast and contradiction. Cows
wandered freely through the streets, their ribs sticking out promi-
nently in testament to the travails of city life for a grazing animal.
The cows brushed up alongside the cars and trucks that jammed
Mumbai's streets. Everything from Bentleys to rickshaws were
packed in nose to tail. On the sidewalks, crippled boys begged for
spare change and girls as young as seven or eight hawked fresh sug-
arcane juice or street food from carts piled high with fried chapati
and green coconuts.

The air smelled of manure and urine and fried food. It was an
unfortunate combination.

She walked with purpose and Khan suspected that this was her regular evening commute. If he followed her, she would show him where she was living. It was the kind of information that he was expected to gather. Her home address had not been in the file, which Khan understood to mean two things: The information on the subject had been assembled quickly and it was unlikely that she either owned her own apartment or lived in one of the higher-end rental buildings that catered to expats and kept electronic records of their tenants. If the subject was living on the cash economy, it was on Khan to find out where.

They walked past a Hindu temple covered in ornate and intricate carvings of gods that Khan could not identify. Monkeys lounged insouciantly on the temple steps, waiting out the worst of the afternoon heat. Next to the Hindu temple was a mosque with whitewashed walls and green shutters on the windows. The minaret was squat with a dome on top that was almost a Russian-style onion.

Khan followed the subject to the edge of the great Dharavi slum. Walking up to the entrance of an unprepossessing apartment building on 60 Feet Road, she pulled a set of keys out of her purse, the universal signal for "I'm home." That she needed keys also signaled that there was no doorman. That bit of information might prove to be important at some point and Khan filed it away. He watched from the other side of the street and was rewarded by a light that came on in a window on the third floor on the far right side of the building. The subject's apartment.

He waited alongside the foul-smelling canal that delineated the border of the Dharavi slum. Some thirty minutes after she had gone inside, the subject reemerged dressed considerably more casually in khaki pants and a short-sleeved blouse.

She waited for the light to change and crossed over 60 Feet Road, walking almost directly toward Khan. He turned away from her, hoping to blend into the crowd on the sidewalk without losing track of which direction she took. She surprised him by turning neither left nor right, but proceeding across the wooden bridge that spanned the canal. The entrance to the slum.

It seemed an odd destination for a Mumbai yuppie.

A legless boy with a hideous growth on his neck sat on the ground at one end of the bridge begging passersby for a few rupees. Khan watched as she leaned over the boy. She spoke a few words and pressed something into his hand. The boy nodded his head to acknowledge the gift.

Khan followed at a distance. There was nothing about the subject's behavior that indicated she was aware that she had grown a tail. She was all but oblivious to what was happening behind her. But the legless beggar boy watched him suspiciously. Khan was a stranger, an outsider to Dharavi. That could be a problem if he needed to make a return visit. The bridge was a chokepoint. Moreover, he suspected that this was the boy's permanent home. There was a sleeping mat under the bridge and a few small boxes that doubtlessly contained his worldly possessions.

The narrow, twisting alleys of Dharavi were like a maze, and Khan was careful to identify landmarks on the route so he could find his way back. The slum was surprisingly vibrant. There was more industry here than he would have thought. Massive trays of bread were piled up on the street in front of bakeries waiting to be delivered, he supposed, to restaurants and hotels across the city. Small-scale factories turned out cheap cookware and plastic washtubs. The entire district smelled of sweat and decay and desperation.

Khan hoped that the subject's stop in Dharavi was a onetime thing. He was soon disabused of that. She led him to a single-story warehouse-style building that looked to be in a slightly better state of repair than the buildings around it. There were screens on the windows and doors. Metal shutters could be rolled down to cover the windows, and Khan saw that they could be secured with substantial padlocks. There was something inside worth protecting. For those undeterred by mechanical obstacles, there was a man sitting on an overturned bucket by the door. He was not especially large or otherwise physically imposing, but something about him said "don't mess with me."

A hand-lettered wooden sign next to the front door identified the building as THE DHARAVI ACADEMY OF MATH AND ENGINEERING. Khan did not slow down as he walked past the school. The guard looked alert, and like the boy on the bridge, he would recognize and remember an outsider. Khan would need to find a place off 60 Feet Road from where he could keep an eye on both the bridge and the subject's apartment, at least until he had learned her routine. He did not yet know what he would be tasked to do with that information, and he was not sure that he wanted to know.

The next morning, Khan waited for Lena on the canal side of 60 Feet Road. He was amused to find himself thinking of her as "Lena" rather than the "subject." He told himself that it was because he was trying to get inside her head, to learn everything that he could about her. But he knew that wasn't the full truth of it. Lena Trainor was an attractive woman, and it had been a long time for Khan since he had been with a woman. Following her like this was the nearest thing he had had to a date since starting down the all-consuming path of jihad.

He squatted on the back of his heels in the South Asian style, sucking idly on a clove cigarette. A few old magazines were spread out on the sidewalk in front of him as though he were just one of the thousands of small-time peddlers working the streets of Mumbai. He had changed his clothes and his hairstyle from the day before, but the legless beggar seemed to look at him from time to time with keen interest. Khan sensed that he was a bright kid. He would need to be to survive for long on the streets given his handicap. That was one thing that India and Pakistan had in common, the extraordinary amount of human talent they wasted by tossing young minds into the crushing jaws of poverty.

He did not yet know Lena's morning routine, so he had been up early. It would be easier with a team of watchers, but Jadoon could not spare any of the others to join him. Khan alone had been given the assignment.

It was close to eight before Lena appeared at the front entrance to her building dressed for work. She waved at the boy on the far end of the bridge and he waved back.

Khan abandoned the magazines, sweeping them up into a pile and leaving them in the shadow of a palm tree. He imagined the boy on the bridge marking his sudden departure. He would need to find a new vantage point tomorrow.

Khan had thought Lena would retrace her route to SysNet, but instead she flagged down an auto rickshaw that headed off through the crowded streets of South Mumbai in the opposite direction. Khan was prepared for this eventuality too. The Kawasaki was parked nearby. Trailing the rickshaw was even easier than following Lena on the street. She led him on a twenty-minute drive through the smog-cloaked streets of the city, dodging potholes and sacred cows. The rickshaw stopped in front of a run-down concrete building with a sign over the door that read GUMMADI BROTHERS REAL ESTATE DEVELOPMENT.

Khan drove past without slowing down and pulled his bike over to the side of the road on the next block. He pulled his phone out of his pocket and quickly Googled the Gummadi brothers. It did not take long to make the connection. There were numerous articles in the local press about the Gummadis' plans to develop a swath of the Dharavi slum into a gated community. Maybe Lena was working with the Gummadis. Even as he formulated the thought, however, Khan knew that he had it backwards. The boy on the bridge was hardly on the lookout for a new home with central air-conditioning and a shared pool, and her work at the Dharavi "academy" did not match the profile of a grasping land speculator. Lena, he was quite sure, was on the opposite side of that fight.

He waited.

As camouflage, Khan bought a *vada pav* from a street vendor for ten rupees. Mumbai was world famous for its street food and the *vada pav* was the apotheosis of working-class cuisine. Two deep-fried balls of mashed potatoes were sandwiched in a bun with a chutney made from coconut meat, tamarind pulp, and garlic. It was incredibly good and, more important, eating it gave Khan a reason to be standing on the street in front of the Gummadi brothers' building.

Less than thirty minutes later, Lena emerged from the building looking downcast. Yes, she was on the other side, and she was losing. Instinctively, Khan empathized with her position. She was representing the downtrodden against the powerful. Khan could relate to that.

He thought of the box that sat at the abandoned studio under the watchful gaze of Adnan and the jihadis. Lena Trainor had her mission, but its significance paled in comparison with his own.

Khan followed Lena's auto rickshaw through the backstreets,

but he saw quickly that she was headed to SysNet. When he was certain that she had gone into the shiny headquarters building, Khan rode his bike back to Lena's apartment.

The lock on the front door to the building was not difficult to bypass, but it took nearly thirty seconds and Khan was concerned that he was drawing further unwelcome attention from the boy on the far side of the bridge. Khan slipped inside quickly and closed the door firmly behind him. In the bare concrete entryway, a sleek rat sat up on its hind legs staring insolently at Khan as though he too recognized an outsider when he saw one.

This building was a far cry from the kind of high-end apartment that someone with a job like Lena's should have been able to afford. The stairs were dark and narrow. There were four apartments on the third floor, but it was easy to identify the door that was associated with the windows Khan had marked earlier. This door was even easier for Khan to jimmy open than the entrance door on the ground floor had been. Inside, the apartment was more comfortable than the austere common areas indicated. Lena had clearly put some thought into making it livable and a little bit of money into furnishing it. The dining table and living room set were worn but perfectly serviceable. A television in one corner had neither aerials nor a cable connection, but an Indian-brand DVD player and a pile of American movies offered some indication of how it was used. Cheery yellow curtains framed the windows and the kitchen area was clean and well stocked with fresh fruits and vegetables.

The most striking thing about the apartment was the art on the wall. There were five or six paintings that appeared to be the work of the same artist. One painting seemed to be of the rape of Europa with an Indian twist. A distinctive humped Brahman bull was straddling a woman with dark blue skin and four arms that Khan recognized as an incarnation of the goddess Kali. It was a powerful image, and disturbing. Khan wondered why Lena would want it hanging over her couch. It said in her file that her mother had been an artist. Maybe the paintings were hers.

The bedroom was separate from the living area, and it was there that Khan found what he was looking for, Lena's desk. There was an Apple PowerBook on the desktop and an accordion file with papers. The computer was password-protected. With the right equipment, Khan knew, he would be able to circumvent that protection, but now was not the time.

The papers in the file were mostly related to Lena's efforts to stymie the Gummadi brothers' plans to develop Dharavi. There were copies of letters to the BMC and the *Times of India* as well as blueprints outlining the extent of the developer's ambitions. It was a big project that would no doubt generate considerable money for well-placed city officials and create a large number of newly homeless who would simply be swallowed up by the streets.

Within forty-five minutes, Khan had learned everything about Lena that he could from her apartment. He was building a mental picture of her and a database of her habits and preferences that he could draw from when the order came from Jadoon to do what must be done.

He did not yet know what that would be. But he found himself already hoping that he would not be ordered to harm her.

That realization came as something of a surprise. It was a weakness. It was exploitable. He would have to be careful. He was expendable. So was Lena Trainor.

The mission must come first.

WASHINGTON, D.C.
APRIL 20

00:22

I t was, perhaps, the ultimate Washington cliché, but the city's monumental core was beautiful at night. The National Park Service used enough electricity along the Mall to power a small town, and the effect was to isolate the individual monuments and memorials in islands of light. Stripped down to their basic geometric forms, they looked like enormous translucent blocks of glass that seemed to glow from within rather than from reflected external light. On a warm spring night, it was all but magical, and Sam and Vanalika were just one pair of lovers among many who strolled hand in hand along the Tidal Basin. It was one of the few times and places where they could be both public and anonymous.

"I think maybe you are making too much of this," Vanalika suggested gently. "I mean, what are you basing all of this on? Some obscure intelligence reports that seem to have gone missing and a rough draft of a speech that may or may not be part of an exercise of some sort."

"And a dead friend," Sam observed grimly. "Let's not forget about Andy so quickly."

"You know that I haven't. I liked him too, and I am terribly sad about what happened to him. But he lived in kind of a sketchy neighborhood. D.C. has gotten much safer over the years, but it isn't Disneyland. Is it possible that you're hearing hoofbeats and seeing zebras where there should be horses?"

Sam shrugged.

"I don't think so. What Andy and I found, the Panoptes material, was pretty exotic for horses."

"You know that I asked a friend in our service to dig up the piece about me, the one you told me about."

"Yes."

"There was nothing there, Sam. There is no such piece anywhere in the records. Is it possible, is it conceivable, that what you and Andy tapped into was all part of a gaming exercise of some sort and there was some break in the firewalls that made it look, even for a time, like these were real products? They may have been using the names of actual players to give it a veneer of reality. That would explain how come these Panoptes products were close to true but somehow just a little bit off."

"That's an awful lot of trouble to go through for no apparent purpose."

"But hardly the strangest thing that your government has ever done, no?"

"No."

"I'm worried about you."

"Don't worry about me. I'm fine. I'm worried about Lena."

"Of course you are. You're her father. That's your job. But she's a big girl now. She can take care of herself."

"And then some."

"Living on the subcontinent is always something of a risk. But is it really that much riskier now than when you took her there as a child? Or is it just that you're not there to look after her in person?"

"It's not the same. The tensions between India and Pakistan are so much higher than they were back then. Couple that with nuclear weapons and the growing reach of the Islamists in Pakistan and it's hard to be optimistic."

"Who can be? But that's pretty much true anywhere on the planet. Even in India, Lena is more at risk from typhus and traffic accidents than she is from nuclear bombs. It's normal for a parent to jump to the far end of the bell curve of possibilities, the nightmare scenario. You're hardly the first to do so. Children have to find their own way in the world. Lena will come home when she's ready. Or she won't. But it will be her choice."

Sam could hear a note of bitterness in Vanalika's words. He suspected she was thinking of her own structured upbringing and the choices that had been made for her at least as much as she was thinking of Lena. Sam could not fault her for it. For all of its privileges, Vanalika's life had been something of a golden cage.

As if reading his thoughts, Vanalika squeezed his hand.

"You must think I'm a selfish little bitch projecting my own frustrations onto Lena's situation," she said.

"Not at all," Sam said, but he laughed. Vanalika Chandra was very, very perceptive. He felt a brief flash of pity for her husband, Rajiv. There was no way he would be able to keep up. "All right, maybe a little," he confessed.

Vanalika stopped. She put her arm around Sam's waist and turned toward him, tilting her head back slightly.

"Kiss me," she commanded.

Sam was only too happy to comply.

Later, he drove Vanalika home to the bucolic estate in Potomac, Maryland, that had been the home of the Indian Embassy's political counselor for at least the last two decades. The neighbors were "horse people" who looked somewhat askance at the parade of dark-skinned men and women in saris who came and went from No. 97 Hickory Lane.

Vanalika made him park two blocks away to minimize the risk that anyone she knew would see them together. There was little chance of that. The houses here were far apart and there were only a few streetlights to do battle with the inky suburban darkness.

"It's not too late to change your mind and come home with me," he said.

"Yes, it is."

"Can I see you next week?"

"We'll see. The assistant minister is coming to town and he will want to be feted in the style that he feels is appropriate to his station. It could be busy. If it is at all possible, then, yes. I would like to see you."

She kissed him softly. Her lips tasted of dark cherries and chocolate.

He ran his hand over her black silky hair and along the curve of her neck.

"I love you, Vanalika."

"No, you don't. You just think you do. You're a sweet man, Sam Trainor."

She kissed him again and she was gone.

. . .

Was she right? Sam wondered. Maybe he was confusing love with a lack of loneliness. This was the first time he had said "I love you" to a woman since Janani had died. He had not thought about it. He had just said it. Did that make it more true or less true? Did it even matter? Vanalika Chandra was complex. There were depths to her that Sam knew he could never plumb, mysteries and secrets that she would never reveal. How much did he really know about her? How much could anyone ever really know about someone else's inner life?

In any event, Vanalika had made it clear to Sam that what they had together was enough for her. It would have to be enough for him too. Maybe she was right. Maybe he didn't love her. But he sure did enjoy her. Vanalika was something else.

He turned off the Capital Beltway onto the George Washington Parkway. During rush hour, both the beltway and the parkway came to a virtual standstill. This late at night, there was little traffic on the roads and Howlin' Wolf was singing the blues on the CD player.

"I am a backdoor man," the Wolf sang in his unmistakable gravelly voice. *"When everybody trying to sleep, I'm somewhere makin' my midnight creep."*

"I can relate, Chester," Sam said sardonically. When the lyrics to classic blues songs started to feel relevant, you knew you were in trouble.

Just south of Potomac Overlook Park, he saw flashing blue lights in his rearview mirror. The single squawk of the siren was universal police talk for "pull over."

Shit.

How fast had he been going?

Sam pulled over to the side of the road, grateful that there was so little traffic. He fumbled in the glove box for the registration. It had been years since he had been pulled over for anything.

A man wearing the blue uniform of the park police tapped lightly on the glass. Sam lowered the window.

"Sorry, officer. Was I speeding?"

"License and registration, please."

Sam handed over the documents.

There was something familiar about the officer, but he could not quite place what it was. Maybe he had seen him on patrol downtown at some point. The man was tall and had dark hair that was mostly covered by his cap. He was unsmiling and had a prominent lantern jaw with a cleft chin. It was a distinctive feature and there was something about it that made Sam uneasy.

In the rearview mirror, he could see a second cop get out of the vehicle, which was an unmarked Ford. The flashing blue lights had been set into the grille. They had been turned off in favor of the Ford's regular blinking hazards. Was it normal for uniformed officers to ride in unmarked cars? That would seem to defeat the purpose.

"Sir, I need to ask you to step out of the vehicle, please."

"What's the problem, officer?"

"Just step out of the car, please." Sam saw the cop's right hand drift down toward the gun on his hip. Something did not feel right.

An image of the cop flashed into his mind, dressed not in the blue of the park police but in U.S. Army green. Sam remembered where he had seen this man before. He had been with John Weeder coming out from behind the steel door that led to the Morlocks' lair. Sam wondered if this was the last man to see Andy Kritten-brink alive.

Without conscious thought, he slammed the shift lever into drive and smashed his foot on the accelerator. The Prius jumped forward and the "cop" stepped back, fumbling for his gun.

Sam had a head start, but he was driving a 134-horsepower Prius and the big Ford was soon on his tail. That they were not using the lights and siren only reinforced for Sam that this was not the police. The Ford slammed into his rear with a crunch of metal. Sam took a curve at high speed and felt the rear wheels slip on the slick pavement. He fought for control and kept the car from fishtailing. But the Ford used the opportunity to get in between Sam and the sheer rock wall on the right. His pursuers slammed into the rear quarter panel of the Prius and nearly spun Sam into the wall.

Before his first Islamabad assignment, the State Department had required Sam to take a defensive-driving course outside of Richmond. The course, which was known informally as Crash-and-Bang, was widely considered something of a lark among the diplomats. It was a fun field trip, but few of them could envision ever being in a situation where they would be required to employ the somewhat esoteric skills the course was designed to impart. Sam remembered that the best way to drive a car off the road was not to slam it full-on but rather to nudge either the front or rear quarter panel exactly as the Ford was trying to do. Maybe the driver of that car had graduated from the same course.

The instructors at Crash-and-Bang had been the particular mix of ex-military and "security professionals" that had begun to accrete, barnacle-like, to every exposed surface of the federal government after 9/11. At graduation, the lead instructor—a former DEA agent named Dwight with an immense beer belly and a Southern drawl—had passed out hats that featured the logo of TacTrain, the company that ran the program on behalf of the State Department.

"Here you go," he had said. "With our compliments. If you are ever attacked by terrorists and survive the experience, we'd like you to wear this hat to the press conference. If you fuck up and get yourselves killed, with your last dying breath I want you to take your hat and toss it far enough away so that it'll be out of the frame when the good people from CNN show up."

They had all laughed at that. It had been funny . . . at the time.

Sam remembered another element from his time on the track. The bootlegger turn. He pulled up hard on the emergency brake with his right hand while simultaneously jerking the steering wheel to the left in a controlled movement of something less than a quarter turn. The Prius swung into a sharp 180-degree spin in front of a pickup truck that swerved to avoid him with a loud honk. Sam jammed down the accelerator as the Ford sped past, caught by surprise.

It was a temporary reprieve. Even going as fast as he dared, it was only a few minutes before his pursuers were again on his tailpipe. Sam was hoping to make it to the exit in McLean for the CIA. There were real cops in abundance to be found on the access road to Agency headquarters.

It was not to be.

The Ford again nosed up to the Prius's right rear quarter panel and locked bumpers. The Taurus outweighed the Prius by at least five hundred pounds and put out at least twice the horsepower. Ever so gently, the Ford pushed against the rear panel and Sam could only watch helplessly as his car spun out of control. He did a complete 360-degree turn before plunging off the edge of the parkway and down the steep embankment that led to the Potomac River.

The Prius smashed through a stand of saplings and ripped thick bushes out of the ground by their roots. About halfway down the hill, the right front corner slammed into a thicker oak tree, spinning the car sideways and causing the air bag to deploy.

Sam lost his orientation as the car rolled at least twice before finally coming to a halt propped up against the side of a maple tree. It was at least upright.

The air bag deflated. The windshield of the Prius was smashed and a thick tree branch had penetrated the glass on the passenger side. It was sticking into the seat like a spear and would have impaled anyone who had been sitting there.

Bizarrely, Howlin' Wolf was still playing on the stereo.

"Something just ain't right. That's evil. Evil is goin' on wrong."

Sam unbuckled the seat belt. His body felt sore and bruised. The door would not open. He kicked it and it popped loose.

He looked up toward the road. It was dark, but he could hear the sounds of two men clambering down the slope.

"You go for the car," he heard one of them say. "I'll head to the river."

The river.

Sam shook his head in a vain attempt to clear it. There was a ringing in his ears and he felt oddly distant from what was happening. He was in shock. But if he did not move, that wouldn't matter because he would soon enough be dead.

He turned and ran as quickly as he could downhill. He misjudged a leap over a log and went sprawling into a bank of soft mud at the edge of the mighty Potomac River. It might have saved his life. He looked up and saw the lantern-jawed soldier dressed up as a park police officer. A wolf in sheepdog's clothing. His gun was drawn and he was scanning the riverbank. As quietly as he could,

Sam slithered into the cold, dark waters of the Potomac. The icy current grabbed him and threatened to pull him deep under the surface, but a few quick, strong strokes underwater brought Sam into deeper water where the flow was not quite as fast. He stayed under for as long as he could, swimming out toward the middle of the river and letting the current carry him away from the crash site.

When he could no longer hold his breath, Sam stuck his face out of the water long enough to quickly exchange the carbon dioxide in his lungs for a gulp of life-giving oxygen. His limbs were already heavy with cold. In April, the river was still running high with snowmelt.

He did not dare return to the Virginia side, however, and he swam the breaststroke on the surface toward the Maryland shore, trying not to think about the stories of the six-eyed fish and eight-legged frogs that had come out of the polluted Potomac. Eventually, he made landfall by the point near Fletcher's Boat House. He was shivering and he had to beat his arms and legs to get some feeling back into them.

Oddly, the dominant emotion he felt was vindication. Two of Vanalika's zebras had just tried to kill him.

"At least I'm not crazy," he said out loud to no one in particular.

00:23

The taste of defeat wasn't so much bitter as it was sour. Even more interesting, Lena thought, was that it had texture as well as flavor. It was like trying to eat a mouthful of ash. You could chew it, but you could never swallow it.

The Gummadi brothers were coming. Ramananda's little monkey-wrenching trick had bought Dharavi a little time, maybe two weeks but no more. Her last meeting with the brothers had ended badly. In truth, she did not know what she had expected. The land the slum was built on was worth too much and the people who lived there were worth too little for the outcome to be in doubt.

She had stayed late at the school, ostensibly to organize the tools and equipment but really to organize her thoughts. She was just about out of ideas. One of the lawyers she had hired had told her that day that he would keep taking her money if she insisted on it, but there was nothing more that he could do. The legal battles were over. The PR campaign had never really taken off. And there was no political white knight ready to ride in on his trusty charger to save the day. Lena was on her own, and she had failed.

It was so late when she reached the little bridge across the fetid canal that Tahir had already crawled onto his sleeping mat under the stairs.

"Madam," he called out, as Lena crossed the bridge. "Madam, I must speak to you."

"Good evening, Tahir. I hope you weren't waiting up for me."

"No, madam . . . well, not entirely." The boy stammered as he pulled himself up onto the bridge by his hands. Lena wanted desperately to help him, but she knew that she could not. It would have been an insult. Instead, she reached into her pocket for a ten-rupee coin.

"No, madam. No toll tonight. There is something I must tell you."

"What is it?"

"Do you know that you are being followed by a man?"

"Is it Brad Pitt? Or maybe Shahid Kapoor?"

"No, madam. A much less handsome man with a beard."

"Do you see him now?"

"No," Tahir admitted. "He comes and goes. I think he knows that I see him. But he watches for you, and when you leave, he follows you."

"How long has this been happening?"

"Just a couple of days, madam. I do not know what he wants with you, but I am afraid."

"Don't worry, Tahir. I'm not. It will be fine."

"But . . ."

"It's okay. Really."

"Of course, madam."

And the young legless Indian boy who so tugged at her heart-strings dragged himself back under the bridge.

As she picked her way carefully across the trash-strewn bridge, Lena found herself scanning 60 Feet Road looking for the man Tahir had described. He was just a boy, with a boy's imagination, but Lena had no trouble believing that the Gummadi brothers had sent someone to keep an eye on her. Not that they really stood to gain much from it. For all intents and purposes, they had already won. At this point, her campaign against the Five Star development amounted to little more than tilting at windmills.

Maybe they thought that she was responsible for the vandalism of their heavy machinery. Even a few weeks' delay in the schedule would have been costly, and an old-fashioned gumshoe tracking her movements would be a cheap countermeasure. It would be in character for the Gummadis to assume that Lena would look for some last-ditch way to hurt them, even if the effort was fruitless. It is what they would have done.

Lena saw nothing out of the ordinary as she crossed the street to her building. There was no mysterious bearded figure lying in wait in the entryway. Everything seemed perfectly normal.

By the time she reached her small apartment, Lena felt ready to surrender to her exhaustion. It had been a long and emotionally trying day.

Once through the door, she kicked off her shoes and wiggled her toes, enjoying the feeling of release and freedom that came with bare feet. Nandi and the other boys went barefoot all the time and Lena might have envied them if she had not known that it was only because their families could not afford shoes.

There was a bottle of cold Bisleri mineral water in the refrigerator and a clean glass in the dish rack. She sat down on the couch and thought idly about putting the next episode of *Mad Men* on the DVD. She was about halfway through the third season and seriously addicted to the travails of Don and Betty.

There was a knock at the door. Soft. Almost tentative.

Nandi was there, carrying a bright blue plastic bag.

"Oh my. Is it Wednesday already?"

Every Wednesday, Nandi delivered a small bag of groceries to Lena's apartment. She really did not need him to, but she wanted him to have the experience of doing honest work and making honest money. The temptations of the criminal life for the boys of Dharavi were hard to resist, particularly for a kid with Nandi's natural talents.

"It is, Miss Lena. I have your dal and some rice and some chilies and a bit of chicken."

"Are you sure it's chicken?"

"Well, it had feathers on it."

"That's a relief."

Nandi smiled and it went a long way toward brightening her mood.

"Go ahead and put it in the kitchen, please," she said. "Do you want a glass of water?"

"No thank you. I have to meet my friends."

"What are you boys going to do?"

Nandi smiled again, but this time it darkened her mood.

"No stealing. You promised."

"And you would trust the word of a thief?"

"I would trust the word of a friend."

The boy had the good grace to look sheepish.

"No stealing, Miss Lena. I promise. We are playing *kabaddi*."

Lena remembered playing the same game on the streets of Dharavi when she was a girl waiting for her father to finish his meeting with Ramananda or some other political figure in the slum. It was a cross between tag and capture the flag with simple rules. Lena could see her nine-year-old self darting into enemy territory, calling *"Kabaddi kabaddi kabaddi"* the whole time to show that she was not breathing when she was across the line. If you took a breath, you were captured.

Lena was not certain that she believed Nandi's alibi. But she chose to. She was too tired to fight with him.

After the boy left, Lena cooked dinner. While the rice soaked, she heated oil and a few tablespoons of ghee in a deep dish and blended in garam masala, a mix of spices that she kept in a plastic container. She chopped a small onion and a few of the chilies that Nandi had brought and simmered them in the mix. There were thousands of recipes for chicken *biryani*, but this was the one that her mother had taught her. It called for tomato and coriander, mint leaves and coconut water. Like most Indian dishes, it involved a multitude of ingredients and numerous steps. Lena had made it so many times, however, that she could have done it blindfolded. It was a shame, really, to go through all of this effort to make dinner for one. She needed some more friends, Lena realized, women her own age. Maybe even a boyfriend. Her best friends were an eleven-year-old thief and a ten-year-old beggar. The only family she had within eight thousand miles was a geriatric mob boss. This was not much of a social life.

She ate in front of the television and caught herself tearing up at the graceless way the beautiful but self-centered Betty Draper responds to the death of her father. Lena was worried about her own father. Their last conversation had been so strained. His ramblings about terrorist conspiracies had sounded so off-the-wall that

Lena wondered whether he might be suffering some kind of break-down. Maybe she should go back to Washington, at least for a few days. She could see her father, judge for herself whether he was okay. Maybe they could go hiking together in the Shenandoah, like they had when she was young. It would be nice to get out of Mumbai for a while, she admitted to herself. She loved this city, but it was hard living. It could wear you down.

At least some of this, she understood, was self-inflicted. She had a good job and a perfectly respectable salary, and she insisted on living on the margins of South Asia's most notorious slum. Maybe she had done enough. Or maybe it was all just a self-aggrandizing fantasy. When the Gummadi brothers' bulldozers knocked down her school, maybe she should take that as a sign to move on. She could rent a nice apartment in a part of town where there were young educated people she could be friends with. She could accept the offer from Parnaa in accounting who wanted to fix Lena up with her neurosurgeon brother. Maybe it was time to grow up.

On *Mad Men*, Sally fell asleep clutching her deceased grandfather's copy of *The Decline and Fall of the Roman Empire*.

We all deal with grief in our own way, Lena thought. She was self-aware enough to know that the penance she was paying in Dharavi was on some level part of the grieving process for her mother's death. Her father was dealing with it in his way. Slowly. Haltingly. She wished that there was something more she could do to help him.

Lena turned off the TV, consigning the troubled employees of Sterling Cooper to suspended animation where they would be forced to await her pleasure.

She did not dare leave the dishes unwashed. The battle with roaches was hard enough as it was.

As soon as the dishes were done, however, she dressed for bed in an oversize Stanford T-shirt and turned in. It had been a hell of a day.

Everything seemed a little brighter in the morning light. Lena had no better idea about what the future would hold, but she was more confident of her ability to handle it. After a good night's sleep, Tahir's dark warnings about shadowy figures trailing her across the city seemed even more fantastical, the product of a young boy's active imagination.

She fixed a mug of masala chai, boiling water and milk with a mix of cardamom, cinnamon, cloves, and other aromatic spices. She spooned in some black tea and let it steep for a few minutes before pouring it through a strainer into a chipped celadon mug. Lena did not eat much for breakfast. To go with the tea that she sweetened with brown sugar, she boiled an egg and sliced it over a piece of flatbread. That would see her through to lunch.

While she sipped her tea, Lena skimmed the morning papers on her iPad, first the *Mumbai Mirror* and then the *New York Times*. She wished she had time to do the crossword puzzle. Maybe over her lunch break.

Lena dressed for work in an aggressively cheery outfit, as though she were pushing back against the black cloud that had threatened to envelop her the day before.

She slipped sandals into her shoulder bag and put on a pair of sneakers. She needed to stop by the school before work. Two of the older kids had entrance exams for a state-run science academy next week and she had promised them an extra tutoring session in trigonometry.

By eight-thirty, Lena had finished up at the school and was on her way to the office. She enjoyed the work at SysNet. It was challenging and her colleagues were top-notch professionals. Even so, it did not come close to providing the emotional satisfaction she got from her work at the school. Lena did not suffer from false modesty when it came to her engineering talents. She was good. But at this point in her life, engineering paid the bills so that she could teach the lower-caste kids of Dharavi. That was why she had come back to Mumbai.

At the bridge, she leaned over to drop the ten-rupee "toll" into Tahir's bowl. The boy handed it back to her.

"Madam. You must not cross this morning."

"And why not, Tahir?"

"The man is back."

"Really? Where is he?" Even this early in the day, the streets were crowded. In truth, they were never empty. Mumbai was a city of twenty million, more people than lived in the entire state of Florida, and the sidewalks were home to tens of thousands who had no place else to go.

"I cannot see him now," the boy admitted. "But I am certain he is there. Watching. You should not cross here."

Lena was already running late and she did not have the time to humor the boy.

"Don't worry, Tahir. I'm not walking into a dark alley. I will be careful. It's the middle of the day and there are thousands of people around us. Nothing is going to happen to me." She forced herself to smile, acknowledging that his advice was well intentioned. Even so, he did not look happy.

"If I had legs, I would walk with you to work," he said miserably. "Then I could keep you safe."

Lena thought her heart might break. She squatted as low as she could in a skirt and took his hand.

"You already do that, my friend. You don't need legs to look out for me."

Lena crossed the bridge.

She waited for the light and crossed to the far side of 60 Feet Road, skirting around the back of a beat-up panel van that was parked halfway up on the sidewalk.

She turned right on 60 Feet Road.

The van followed her.

Lena looked over her shoulder. *It's a coincidence. He was making a delivery and now he's moving on to his next stop.*

She turned onto a side street that led toward Jasmine Mill Road.

The van turned with her.

Lena quickened her pace. The driver of the van matched it. She could see his face now. Dark skin. A beard.

Her heart began to beat faster and there was a tightness in her chest that Lena recognized as the first stirrings of fear. A delivery van was not the kind of vehicle you would choose to follow someone in the streets of a crowded city like Mumbai. It was the kind of vehicle you might choose for a kidnapping.

She bumped into an older woman who was selling betel nut wrapped in paper tubes.

"Murkha," the woman cursed her, using the local Marathi word for idiot. Her teeth and gums were stained black from years of chewing betel and her breath was foul.

"I'm sorry," Lena muttered, without breaking stride.

The van was closer now. She could feel the driver's eyes on her. Looking over her shoulder, she saw that the van was no more than twenty feet behind her. The intense look on the man's face kicked her heart rate into an even higher gear. She started to run down the crowded sidewalk. The van accelerated, pulling closer. Although there were hundreds of people on the street, none paid any attention to either Lena or the van. It was merely a single vignette in the vast, sweeping tapestry of the Mumbai cityscape.

Up ahead, just before the intersection with Jasmine Mill Road, Lena saw one of the most beautiful things that she had ever seen. A traffic jam. An auto rickshaw had hit a cow, knocking both the animal and the three-wheeled scooter onto their sides. A crowd of onlookers had gathered around the accident site shouting out their version of events. The drivers in the cars and trucks backed up behind them were already honking their horns as they searched unsuccessfully for a way to maneuver past the tangled knot of sacred cows and profane vehicles that blocked the road.

Moving now at a dead run, Lena shot past the intersection onto Mahim Station Road. Behind her, she could see the gray van turn off into a narrow alleyway lined with carpet shops and stalls trading in low-end merchandise. It was exactly the kind of place where a beat-up panel van would be making a delivery.

Lena slowed to a walk. Had the van really been following her, she wondered, or was the paranoia of Tahir and her father making her jump at shadows?

Tahir greeted her that evening with a joy typically reserved for the return of a long-lost relative.

"Madam, I thought you were dead," he said, and Lena could see that there were tears in his eyes. "When the van started after you, I was certain."

"It was nothing," Lena said, more than half convinced that this was true. "I don't think he was looking for me at all."

She put ten rupees in the bowl.

After school, Lena went straight back to her apartment.

She had left the blinds open and there was enough light coming into the apartment from the outside that she did not bother to flip on the lights. Dropping her bag on the chair by the door, she walked straight to the kitchen and retrieved a bottle of cold water from the fridge. The heat and grit of Mumbai always left her feeling dehydrated and run-down by the end of the day. She stood in the kitchen drinking straight from the bottle and looking out the window onto the corrugated tin roofs of the slum on the far side of 60 Feet Road.

The lights came on.

Lena froze.

"Good evening, Ms. Trainor."

She turned around slowly.

There was a man standing by the door to the hall with one hand on the light switch and the other resting easily on the handle of a pistol tucked into his waistband.

He was the driver of the van that had followed her that morning.

The intruder had chestnut-colored skin and a neatly trimmed beard. His hawkish nose was framed by piercing eyes that were so brown they were almost black. There was an intensity to his gaze that Lena remembered from her single glimpse of him behind the wheel.

She thought about screaming. But this was the outer edge of Dharavi. Screams in Dharavi were like car alarms in an American suburb. If you ignored them long enough, they would stop. The police were almost completely uninterested in what happened in the slum. The people there were just Dalits after all.

Lena set the bottle of water down on the countertop behind a stack of cookbooks next to a paring knife with a sharp six-inch blade. Her right hand crept slowly toward the handle even as she maintained eye contact with the intruder.

"Who are you and what are you doing in my apartment?" she asked calmly.

"I need to talk to you, Ms. Trainor." His English was perfect. If he had an accent, it was not subcontinent. If anything, it sounded New York or New Jersey to Lena. Definitely tristate.

"Just talk?"

"No."

"What do you want?"

As they talked, her fingers closed around the handle of the knife. The cookbooks, she hoped, would conceal what she was doing. She slipped the blade up inside the sleeve of her shirt with her wrist angled to keep it in place and the handle balanced lightly in the crook of her palm.

"Please," the man said, gesturing to the table. "Let's sit and I will explain."

Lena crossed over to the dining table, casting a furtive glance at the front door as she considered whether to make a run for it. The intruder seemed to sense what she was thinking.

"Don't," he said. "Sit. Please."

Although the man looked relaxed, she could see that he was anything but. He was a coiled spring. If she ran, he would catch her.

Lena sat down, uncertain.

"What do the Gummadi brothers want from me? They're winning. They're going to get everything they're after."

"I do not work for the developers," the man said.

Now Lena was afraid.

"What do you want, then?" she repeated, trying to keep the sharp edge of anxiety out of her voice. "Who are you?"

"Would you like a glass of water? It's quite warm in here."

"Who are you?" she insisted.

"You can call me Khan."

"Okay, Khan. I'm listening."

Under the table, Lena let the knife slip free of her sleeve. Her palms were damp with sweat and the handle was slick to the touch. She grasped it tightly as though the knife were as much a talisman as a weapon.

"I mean you no harm," Khan said.

"Well, I'm glad we've cleared that up."

To her surprise, Khan smiled and it softened his features. He seemed less fanatical, less intense. He didn't look like a serial killer, or what Hollywood had taught her to believe they should look like. Even discarding the superficial, Lena was certain that this was something different. Whatever was happening to her was extremely dangerous, but she did not believe it was a random act of violence. The intruder was in her apartment for a reason.

"I'm going to have to ask you to come with me," he said.

"Why? Where?"

"You will find out when we get there."

"Am I being kidnapped?"

"Yes. You are."

"But not by the Gummadis?"

"No."

"Who do you work for?"

"That I cannot tell you."

Lena felt strangely calm.

"What if I refuse to cooperate? Will you hurt me?"

"No."

"So why should I come with you?"

"Because of the boy sleeping under the bridge."

Tahir. Oh my God, had they taken him too?

Lena forced herself to show the man who called himself Khan neither fear nor anger. Either would be a sign of weakness.

"What have you done to him? If you have hurt one hair on that boy's head, I swear to God . . ."

"He is fine. And he will remain fine . . . if you cooperate."

"And if not, you will hurt him. Is that what you are telling me?"

"No. I will not. He is a boy with no legs. I would not hurt him. But I am not alone. There are other men I work with who are not above this. So, while I assure you that I will not hurt the boy, that does not mean he is not in danger. It would be better for you and for him if you come with me."

"What do you want from me?"

"I do not know," Khan said, and Lena sensed that he was being truthful. "I only know what I have been instructed to do."

"I think I'll have that glass of water," Lena said, rising from her seat and pressing the blade of the paring knife against her thigh to keep it hidden. As she stepped past Khan, she swung the knife up toward his throat, unsure even as she did so whether she intended to kill the intruder.

It didn't matter.

With an alarming nonchalance, Khan caught her wrist and twisted it in such a way that the knife popped out of her hand and clattered onto the floor. Whatever he had done, it did not hurt, but her fingers tingled and she could not close them into a fist.

"Don't worry," Khan explained. "The numbness will pass in a few minutes. Don't do anything like that again."

He let go of her wrist and Lena flexed her hand open and closed as much as she could in an effort to restore feeling.

"I will ask you once more, please, to come with me."

She considered her options. None were especially appealing.

"Give me time to pack a few things," she said.

ASHEVILLE, NORTH CAROLINA
APRIL 21

00:24

I t had been a long time, maybe thirty years, since Sam had taken the bus. The Greyhound that crossed back and forth between Richmond and Asheville looked like it was at least that old. The passengers were the same eclectic mix of people that Sam remembered. Some kids on the way home to see the family. Retirees. And a few weirdos. One old man in a raincoat sitting all the way in the back spent the better part of three hours talking to himself.

What the bus offered, and what Sam needed at that point more than speed or convenience, was privacy. No one batted an eye if you paid cash for a bus ticket. No one checked IDs. Except for the psychotic in the rear, nobody tried to make conversation. No one even really looked at Sam once he had settled into his seat. He had dried his clothes as best he could under the hand drier in the bus station bathroom, but his jeans still felt clammy and cold.

Sam had four hundred and eighty-six dollars in his damp wallet. After walking from the boathouse to Georgetown, he had taken as much as he could out of a gas station ATM. The bus ticket to

Richmond had set him back forty-three dollars and the connection to Asheville was another one hundred and twenty-four dollars. He did not know when he might be able to risk another try at an ATM. There were few more effective ways of broadcasting a "here I am" message to Weeder and his hired assassins.

For now, he needed to find a place to hide and think. He'd need to stretch his money out for as long as he could. And he would need allies. The men who were after him were not amateurs, and Sam was dispiritingly aware that he was now playing out of his league. He was not kidding himself about what had happened on the parkway. He had gotten lucky.

The only one he could think to turn to was Earl Holly. There was no guarantee that Earl would be willing to help, but Sam did not have any better ideas.

His phone had been ruined by the swim across the river. He had briefly thought about buying a prepaid phone in Georgetown. The idea of carrying around anything electronic was unsettling enough that he had decided to leave that for later. Nothing mattered now but space and time. And Lena. Sam was worried about her. He had wanted Lena to get out of Mumbai and come back to Washington, but maybe that was only trading one kind of danger for another.

It started to rain, and Sam watched the fat drops splash against the window. His head hurt and various parts of his body ached dully from the crash. He tried to sleep, but he was too keyed up. His hands shook slightly as though from too much coffee. He wished that he could talk to Vanalika.

By the time they reached Asheville, it was almost noon. Sam realized he was famished and wolfed down a club sandwich and french fries at a diner across the street from the bus station. That set him back another eight dollars. There was a local bus leaving for Linville in just over an hour. Sam bought a couple of newspapers and found a Starbucks nearby where he could sit. He caught himself staring at the door and out of the plate-glass windows expecting to see a team of Morlocks that had somehow tracked him down. It would be easy to grow paranoid, he realized.

The bus to Linville was slow. It made half a dozen stops and waited for at least twenty minutes at each one. Sam had no idea why and he did not want to ask. He did not want to do anything that might attract attention, something that might lead people to remember his face.

Linville did not have a bus station. The driver let him off in front of the IHOP in what passed for a downtown. It had been even longer since Sam had hitchhiked than it had been since he had been on a Greyhound. It was not that hard to get a ride. After about fifteen minutes, a man with a bushy red beard and a flannel shirt coming out of the pancake house offered him a ride to the end of Dry Gulch Road. From there, he walked the mile and a half or so to No. 9.

Earl was sitting on the front porch right where Sam had left him. It was late afternoon. There was a bottle of Knob Creek and a half-full glass on the coffee table next to a copy of Tyler Grigorievich's book on the history of India's Congress Party. Earl's eyes were closed.

"That book put me to sleep too," Sam said.

"Are you sure it's not the bourbon?" Earl asked. His eyes did not open.

"Pretty sure. I know Tyler."

"So what brings you back so soon?"

"Somebody tried to kill me."

Earl opened his eyes.

"Thought that might happen. Go on and sit."

Sam sat in one of the raggedy easy chairs that did not really belong on a porch.

"Was it Weeder's people?" Earl asked.

"I think so."

"So how is it that you ain't dead?"

Sam told him about being pulled over by the fake park police, the desperate chase down the GW Parkway and his midnight swim across the Potomac. Earl listened intently but did not interrupt. When Sam had finished, he stood and waddled into the kitchen, returning with a second glass and a few ice cubes. He poured a stiff shot of the Knob Creek and set it in front of Sam.

"Serves you right for not driving American," he said. "That little Japanese piece of crap could get run off the road by a tricycle."

Earl raised his glass and offered a toast.

"To not being dead."

They drank.

"Why were they after you?"

"I found something I wasn't supposed to. And then I tried to get other people interested in it. People who were in a position to do something about it." Sam told him about the speech he had found in the Morlocks' burn bag and his unsuccessful efforts to get Tennyck to pay attention to it.

"Fuck me," Earl said, when Sam had finished. "I didn't think they would really do it. Not even them."

"Tenny was convinced that it was just part of some war-game exercise."

"Tennyck is an asshole. John Weeder doesn't play games. Leastwise, nothing that you or I would recognize as a game."

"You agree it's real? The speech, I mean."

"I do."

"Earl, there's something you're not telling me. Something important. I think you almost told me the last time, but you didn't. What is it? I know you have secrets to keep. But not this one. Not now. I need to know what you know. I overheard Weeder talk about something called Cold Harbor when I was stuck in that damn burn chute. It seemed to scare him. Do you know anything about it?"

Earl was quiet. He sipped the bourbon and set the glass down on the table. Then he looked down at the floorboards between his feet. This pause in the conversation was considerably longer than the others. Sam could hear the thrum of insects in the woods girdling the farmhouse. A black-headed Carolina chickadee landed on the railing by his elbow. The bird bobbed his head twice as though in greeting and flew off.

Earl finally looked up. His face graver than it had been.

"Sam, there's a program you haven't been read into that you should probably know about."

Earl was talking about Sensitive Compartmented Information. All SCI material was "need to know." A Top Secret clearance was just the baseline. Just because you had a clearance did not mean that you had access to any and all classified information. There were a significant number of information streams that were restricted to people who had an operational need for the knowledge. They were called programs. Each one had its own rules and "being read in" meant first being briefed on what they were and then signing away your firstborn as the penalty for violating them.

Sam waited.

"Cold Harbor is part of a larger set of protocols," Earl said, after another thirty-second pause that he had, no doubt, used to consider the question of whether he should go further. Earl was out of government service, but he was still bound by the rules of secrecy that had governed his professional life. "Nuclear protocols. The various scenarios are named after Civil War battles. I don't know the history behind that, but the program is highly classified. Even the name 'Cold Harbor' is considered SCI."

"If I remember right, Grant got his ass handed to him by Lee at Cold Harbor. Seems like odd nomenclature for an Agency program."

"It's military. Cold Harbor is a contingency plan for United States Special Forces to seize control of Pakistan's existing nuclear weapons and for the air force and navy to destroy every last nuclear site on Pakistani soil."

"Couldn't Pakistan just rebuild the weapons after a few years?" Sam asked.

"Not if all their nuclear scientists and engineers are dead. There's a kill list. Drones and SpecOps. That's another part of the protocol."

"The Lord administration would never do that. This president would never give that kind of order."

"No," Earl agreed. "She wouldn't."

"So how does Cold Harbor tie into Panoptes?"

"Cold Harbor has prearranged triggers. A major war between India and Pakistan is supposed to set Cold Harbor in motion before Pakistan either uses a nuke or loses control of a weapon to the extremists. The actual use of a weapon is an automatic trigger. The president could stop it, but the hardline elements in her own administration could make that very, very hard to do both politically and strategically. She'd likely have to go along with the recommendation from her own SECDEF. Otherwise, the Republicans on the Hill would tear her apart."

Sam knew that this was true. The presidency was a bully pulpit, but presidents had considerably less freedom in decision making than many people assumed. Time and again, presidents had been maneuvered by the people around them into making decisions that they would come to regret, often recognizing the trap well in advance but feeling powerless to stop it. Like Kennedy at the Bay of Pigs. The outlines of the Panoptes program now seemed clear—and terrifying.

"You're telling me that the Stoics are prepared to kill two hundred thousand people, give or take, to force president Lord to authorize the Cold Harbor operation."

"They'd be prepared to do a lot more than that. But I'm guessing they figure that that'll do the trick. The Cassandra projections scared people, Sam. Powerful people. They see Pakistan's nuclear capability as an unacceptable threat to U.S. interests, and they would happily sacrifice a million Indians to defend ten thousand Americans."

"Is there any paper trail for Cold Harbor?" Sam asked. "Is this written down anywhere?"

"Somewhere, I'm sure. But I couldn't tell you where and I don't think you'll have any luck getting access, not if you aren't read in. And that's not even counting the highly capable killers who would just as soon see you dead right now."

"We can't let them get away with this."

"We? Sam, I'm just an old drunk living in the woods with an expensive telescope. Look, you can stay with me for a while until you figure out what to do, but I don't have much left in me to help."

Sam looked at Earl more carefully than he had. His old friend did not look well. The skin on his neck was loose and sallow. His white hair was brittle and thinning.

"What's wrong, Earl?"

"I'm dying. Cancer."

"How much time?"

"Not a lot. A couple of months, maybe. I feel all right. I'm just tired is all."

"I'm sorry."

"Don't be. My ex told me that the bourbon would kill me. It's worth dying of cancer just to prove her wrong."

They sat in silence for some time.

"So what are you gonna do now?" Earl finally asked.

"I don't know. I need some time to think that over, and if you have any brilliant ideas, I'm all ears. I want to get in touch with Lena, make sure she's okay. I'd like to take another run at getting her out of India."

"If that speech you read talked about Rangarajan's death, then Delhi is the most likely target, no?"

"I suppose so . . . but the blank space bothers me. It's like the bomb is an instrument of assassination and the tens of thousands of other casualties are collateral. If they're going after the prime minister personally rather than the capital, they could attack anywhere, and at least some of the extremist groups from Pakistan have already demonstrated an ability to operate in Mumbai."

"They may have had a little extra help on this one," Earl said carefully.

"What do you mean?"

"The Stoics are hardly unique. There are homologues in other countries, particularly in the democracies where the elites sometimes feel they need to shield their irrational publics from some of the more unsavory necessities of governing. The one-party dictatorships usually have security services that can operate pretty much as they see fit. They don't need a man behind the curtain."

"So there's an Indian equivalent of the Stoics?"

"We think so. They call themselves the Sons of Ashoka after the Maurya emperor who conquered pretty much the entire subcontinent in the third century BC."

"But why would they cooperate in a plot to destroy an Indian city? It's kind of counterintuitive."

"Losing one city in exchange for a guarantee that your sworn enemy will be stripped of his nuclear weapons, the program burned to the ground, and the earth salted? Seems like a pretty fair exchange, particularly if your stock-in-trade is strategic thought. Herman Kahn and the boys at RAND came up with way wackier shit in the sixties. About the time I left the Agency, there were reports that Ashoka and the Stoics were making common cause on Pakistan, but it was all pretty hazy and nonspecific. We didn't know the players or the programs. It was just shadows. Black holes where there should be stars."

"It still seems to me like a huge risk, even for a big payoff."

"They may be using a cutout. One of the militant groups active in Kashmir. Something deniable."

"That seals it. I need to get my daughter out of there."

"Well, if the mountain will not come to Muhammad . . ."

"Yeah, I've thought about that. First, I need to see if I can get ahold of Lena. I need to talk to her. I don't want to use your phone. It would be too easy for Argus to trace it back here."

"Yeah. I wouldn't use the phone. But you can use my car. The keys are in the kitchen."

Earl drove an ancient Chevy Blazer. Jouncing down Dry Gulch Road, Sam could feel every bruise and muscle kink in his body complaining about the shocks. On Earl's advice, he drove into Tennessee. Knoxville was the closest big city, but Sam drove right through it and kept going another two hours to Chattanooga. Argus had direct access to the NSA database and it would be easy enough to trace a call to Lena's number back to the point of origin. Earl was pretty sure that Weeder's team was already working up a "known associates" matrix, a kind of wire diagram of Sam's connections built from Facebook and other social media sites, phone and e-mail records, and the address book on his Argus computer. Earl was somewhere on that list, and Knoxville was close enough to Linville that it would not be too difficult for the analysts to zero in on No. 9 Dry Gulch Road as Sam's most likely hiding place. Chattanooga was far enough away to fall outside the immediate search zone, and it would look like Sam was on his way to Atlanta or even Mexico.

For the foreseeable future, Sam knew that he was going to have to think this way about all of his movements. It was not natural to him and he did not like it. Neither did he especially like the Beretta M9 pistol tucked under the driver's seat. *It's like an umbrella,* Earl had explained. *You probably don't need it, but if you don't have one, it's sure as shit gonna rain.*

Earl had also given him two thousand dollars in cash.

"Who keeps two grand lying around a house in the woods?" Sam had asked.

"Ex-spies."

It was almost ten-thirty at night when he reached Chattanooga. At a Walmart on the outskirts of town, Sam bought a prepaid cell phone. He picked up an international phone card from a pharmacy in a nearby Latino neighborhood. He paid cash and he did not park the Blazer close to either of the stores. If Weeder and his team succeeded in tracking the call back to the phone's purchase, he did not want any security-camera footage that might show the license plate. It would not take fifteen minutes for the Morlocks to trace the plate back to Earl. There was no answer when Sam dialed Lena's cell. After half a dozen rings it rolled over into voice mail. Sam did not leave a message. Lena did not have a landline in her apartment and there were any number of harmless explanations as to why she might not have her cell phone with her. Still, it made him nervous. He wanted desperately to speak to her.

In line with the plan that he and Earl had hashed out, Sam was supposed to check his e-mail in Chattanooga as well. Then, he would drive south for two hours before trying Lena again and logging on to his Gmail account. Assuming Weeder was tracking his personal e-mail, Argus would eventually get the location of the computer he used to access his account from the service provider. It might take time, but they would get it in the end. Sam was laying a trail of electronic breadcrumbs that was supposed to make it look like he was heading toward Atlanta. Then he would turn around and drive back north to Linville.

"Does this stuff work?" Sam had asked Earl, looking for reassurance when they had mapped out this strategy.

Earl had shrugged.

"Sometimes."

Internet cafés were not as easy to find as they were even five years ago. Smartphones had undermined the business model. There were still a few places, however, and Sam found a café with a view of the Tennessee River that brewed decent coffee and had computers available for rent.

He checked the *Washington Post* first, looking for anything about a single-car accident on the GW Parkway. There was nothing. Sam wondered whether the Morlocks had hauled his Prius back up the hill or if they had just pushed it into the river. His next car, he decided, would be a Chrysler 300 with a V-8 or some similar iron monster. Screw the gas mileage.

Sam logged on to Gmail, hoping that there was something from Lena.

A part of him expected to find access to his account blocked, but it opened normally and he skimmed briefly through the twenty or so unread messages in his in-box. Most were trash, "special offers" from various businesses and putative Nigerian princes that had managed to get ahold of his e-mail address. As much as possible, Sam used a separate account, biteme99@hotmail, that he had set up for when websites demanded his e-mail address. Over the years, however, his real account had bled over enough that his box was starting to get clogged with junk. There were also a few notes from friends and one from an address that Sam did not know but immediately recognized: Zeno of Citium.

That was the only identifying information. There was no ISP provider and no generic or country-specific top-level domain. Just the name and birthplace of the Greek philosopher from the third century BC, the father of all Stoics. The subject line was no more informative. READ THIS was all it said.

He opened it.

There was an audio file attached to the message. Under the link were words that sent a chill down the back of Sam's spine. *No evil is honorable; but death is honorable. Therefore, death is not evil.* It was a famous syllogism, one of the few surviving quotes attributed directly to Zeno.

The café did not have headphones to rent, but they had them for sale. Sam bought a pair and plugged them into the computer. He hesitated before clicking the link. Maybe it was a trap of some kind that would immediately broadcast his location to the Morlocks. Maybe he should talk this over with Earl first. Sam knew he could not wait. He opened the link.

A marble bust of a bearded man that Sam assumed was Zeno appeared on the screen.

"Mr. Trainor. Listen carefully. The reason we have two ears and only one mouth is that we may hear more and speak less.

"We congratulate you on your survival. You are a resourceful individual. This is a character trait that we respect and admire. You are also, however, something of a problem for us. Your understanding of morality is immature. It is micro rather than macro. You do not see the big picture and you do not appreciate that our society is made safe by those who make the difficult choices. This is a trait that we neither respect nor admire."

The voice was computer-generated or electronically distorted in some way. If it was Spears or Weeder or one of the other Morlocks, Sam could not recognize the voice. Even so, he recognized the sentiment. These were the same principles as those behind the trolleyology questions Spears had posed to him in a conversation that seemed a lifetime in the past.

"You have seen a piece of a complex picture," the voice continued. "We understand how this can be disorienting. We bear you no ill will. To do so would be at odds with the logic of the current situation. Neither, however, can we trust you with the fragment of information that you have uncovered. This would be equally foolish. You are a distraction from our purpose. We will not hesitate to eliminate this distraction, but will not focus disproportionate resources on managing it. We believe that we have found an acceptable balance of risk."

It was hard for Sam to fully appreciate that he was the abstract "distraction" the voice was discussing so dispassionately. The car crash on the parkway that nearly killed him was, to the Stoics, merely an attempt to remove a minor irritant.

"We have secured an insurance policy. Your daughter, Lena, is currently in our custody. Please be assured that we are treating her well and courteously. She is healthy and unharmed, and she will remain so as long as you do nothing that we would consider threatening in any way. We do not think that you will be at all confused as to what sort of actions might constitute a threat. If in doubt, we recommend that you err on the side of caution.

"Once our objectives have been achieved, we will turn attention to the issue of our future relationship.

"We understand that you will want proof of life. That is not unreasonable." The head of Zeno morphed into Lena. There was no background, just a still shot of Lena's head and shoulders against a black background.

"Papa Bear." It was her voice and Sam felt his throat constrict. His girl was in danger and it was his fault.

"I'm okay," she continued. "They won't let me tell you anything more than that, but they haven't hurt me. I love you, Papa Bear."

The marble Zeno replaced the image of his daughter.

"Good-bye, Mr. Trainor," the voice said. "And remember these words from Zeno of Citium. 'Love is a god, who cooperates in securing the safety of the city.'"

The bust of Zeno disappeared from the screen.

Sam wanted to explode. He wanted to rip the computer from its mount on the desktop and throw it across the room. If Spears or Weeder walked into the café at that moment, he knew that he would launch himself at the ex-SEALs with murderous intent.

They had his daughter. They would pay for this. There would be an accounting.

Despite the blithe reassurances from the voice that if he did nothing Lena would be released unharmed, Sam knew in his bones that they would kill her. Then they would kill him. For the Stoics, for Argus, this was the tidiest solution. Why not kill them? It was safer that way.

Sam would not sit and wait. He would go after them, even if he did not yet know how.

To start with, he wanted to listen to the message again to see if there was anything he had missed. But when he went to click on the link, he saw that the e-mail had disappeared. It had erased itself from the screen, and Sam knew that there would be no record anywhere of the message ever having been sent.

"Hang in there, baby," he whispered to himself. "I'm coming for you."

Sam felt a complex mix of emotions. Fear and anger were the top notes, but they overlaid a deep reservoir of love for his only child and something else. Parental pride. His little girl had been captured by killers and she had already got the better of them. She had told Sam where she was.

DALLAS, TEXAS
NOVEMBER 22, 1963

00:25

The kill zone was smaller than he would have liked. There was no getting around that. He did not want the tip of the rifle to be visible from the street. Neither could he risk the muzzle flash, so he was set up almost ten feet back from the open window. The weapon was not ideal either. It was an older-model rifle and foreign, a balky bolt-action Italian design. But he had zeroed it carefully at an isolated spot in the hill scrub outside of town. For the distance at issue, it would serve.

He had been waiting for more than four hours in the small, stifling room. The target was behind schedule. In the enervating heat, it was hard to stay alert and focused. Looking through the sights of his rifle, he scanned the narrow kill zone one more time. An American flag hanging from a lamppost made for a suitable wind gauge. There was a light breeze from the northwest. Not enough to affect the trajectory of the bullet. A sizeable crowd had gathered along the parade route to welcome the target. He was a politician running for reelection. He would want to be seen. The target would be riding in an open-top vehicle.

There would be security, of course, the best in the world. But there was little enough that even the best bodyguards could do against a skilled man and a high-velocity rifle.

He was not worried about the shot itself. He was an expert marksman who had learned the basics of his trade in the U.S. Marine Corps. Of greater concern was the reaction of the security detail after the shot. Getting away was at least as important to the mission as getting the kill.

It was the crowd that alerted him to the imminent arrival of the target. The civilians lining both sides of Elm Street cheered and small children were waving miniature American flags.

He pulled a small pair of binoculars out of a leather case and focused in on one particular man standing on the grassy knoll that overlooked Dealey Plaza. His spotter. The man held three fingers up in front of his chest. Three hundred yards. Two fingers. Two hundred yards.

The sniper turned his attention back to the rifle and sighted on the kill zone. The open-topped limousine traveled at a slow and constant pace. It was not an especially difficult shot. He lined the sights up on the back of the target's head and squeezed the trigger. His first shot was a little low, hitting the target in the neck. He ejected the empty shell case and fed another bullet into the breech, working the bolt carefully to minimize the risk of a jam. His second shot was dead-on, blowing out the top of President Kennedy's head and spraying his brains over his wife and the other passengers in the car.

Mission accomplished.

The passenger in the front seat of the Lincoln Continental was down as well. It looked like Governor Connally. That was not his shot. The sniper had heard the distinctive crack of a high-velocity round in between his two shots. There was a second gunman. That hadn't been a part of the plan briefed to him, but Smith kept his cards close and it

was possible that taking down the governor was part of a parallel oper-
ation that was piggybacking on his. It was a little irritating that Smith
hadn't told him about the second gunman, but it was not a real
problem.

He laid the rifle on the floor near the window and stripped off the
surgical gloves he had worn every time he had handled it. The gloves
were likely the reason his first shot had been a little low. They made it
hard to establish a connection with the rifle, to make it part of his body.
But they also meant that the only fingerprints on the gun would be
those of its owner—one Lee Harvey Oswald.

The nut job Oswald would take the blame for the death of the pres-
ident . . . and the credit for what had been a fine piece of shooting.
Such was life in the shadows.

Oswald himself would need to be eliminated, of course, but that
was not his responsibility. That was Smith's assignment. Whether
Oswald's life was measured in hours or days, he was not long for this
world. And unlike Kennedy, he would die unmourned.

The president's killer took the stairs two at a time down six flights
and did not look back as he left the Texas School Book Depository
behind him.

ARLINGTON, VIRGINIA
APRIL 24

```
00:26
```

Officially, it was NFATC, or the George P. Shultz National Foreign Affairs Training Center. But nobody ever called it that. It was FSI. This was the older acronym for the Foreign Service Institute, the training center for America's diplomats.

FSI was like a little college campus of yellow- and redbrick buildings set just off Route 50 in Arlington, Virginia, no more than three miles from the main State Department building in Foggy Bottom. It was crowded. As with many government projects, the population of FSI had outgrown the facilities even before they opened.

This was where America's newly minted diplomats came for training and indoctrination in a six-week program that had a long bureaucratic name but was colloquially known as A-100. The "100" was a reference to the room in the old State, War, and Navy Building at Seventeenth and G Street where the first class of diplomats selected by competitive examination had met for orientation in 1926. The "A" was added sometime in the 1940s to indicate that it was part of the school's "advanced" program of studies. Courses in the "basic" program began with a "B." That distinction had disappeared over the decades, but A-100 remained A-100 and Foreign Service officers kept track of their classmates over the years as a kind of informal yardstick for measuring their own progress in the long, slow climb up the rigid and unforgiving State Department hierarchy.

A-100 was still the beating heart of FSI, but language training was the school's primary mission. The vast majority of students were at FSI to learn the language of their next assignment. Sam had done his A-100 orientation before NFATC had opened up, but he had spent ten months as a student here learning Urdu before his assignment to Lahore.

The school taught nearly every major language on the planet. Students were given five or six months to learn a relatively "easy" language such as Spanish or Italian and ten months to learn more difficult languages such as Vietnamese or Hungarian. A handful of "super hard" languages—Chinese, Japanese, and Arabic—were two-year programs with the second year spent overseas as a full-time student. Language skills, particularly for more obscure languages such as Georgian or Khmer, set the U.S. Foreign Service apart from most other diplomatic services.

The other big training program at FSI was consular tradecraft, or ConGen. This was where new consular officers learned the ins and outs of visa processing and immigration law. They also practiced interviewing visa applicants, role-played various scenarios involving Americans in distress overseas, and learned everything they needed to know about U.S. passports.

It was this last responsibility that interested Sam. It was the reason he had risked coming back to Arlington, to a facility that was no more than a mile and a half from the headquarters of Argus Systems.

If he was going to get to India, he would need a passport. He had two of them, a standard blue tourist passport and a black diplomatic passport. Both were in the desk drawer in the second-floor study of his Capitol Hill townhouse. It was all too likely that the Morlocks were watching his house. Even if he was somehow able to get his passports, it would have been easy for Spears or Weeder to either cancel his travel documents or flag them in the system to trigger an alert if he bought a ticket for international travel. Since 9/11, all of the various databases had been linked together, which made the country safer but also made the system easier to manipulate. Compared to what Argus had already done, keeping tabs on Sam's passports was child's play.

He needed a new passport, and Earl Holly had told him that this was something he could not help him with. Earl knew document forgers, of course, but the introduction of biometric passports with digital chips linked to the government's various security databases had complicated the business. Sam would have had to start over, creating a new identity, beginning with a forged or stolen birth certificate, and then applying for a new passport in his new name. It could be done, but it would take time. Time that Sam could not afford.

If Sam could not use his own passport and he could not get a new one, then, he reasoned, he would have to make one.

"How can I help you?" The woman sitting behind the reception desk at the front entrance to FSI was black and somewhat heavyset. She was wearing a Diplomatic Security uniform, a white shirt, and a police-style peaked cap with the DS eagle-and-shield logo on the band. And although he could not see it, Sam knew that she was also wearing a wide leather belt holding a 9mm pistol and a pair of handcuffs.

"I'm a new student in ConGen," Sam explained, "and I'm afraid that I left my badge at home."

"Can I see some ID, please."

"Sure." Sam handed her a Tennessee driver's license issued in the name of William J. Christiansen. Earl Holly knew a guy in Nashville who had gotten Sam the license in a couple of hours. "It'll work as picture ID," the man had told him, "but I wouldn't recommend using it if you get stopped by the cops. It won't pass that kind of test. There'd be no record in the DMV database."

Fortunately, FSI was considered a low-risk facility. ID checks were cursory. The DS officer typed the name and date of birth from the driver's license into the computer. There was a record for a Foreign Service officer named William J. Christiansen with that DOB in the system. He was Sam's classmate from A-100, currently serving as deputy chief of mission in Vientiane, Laos, which was about as far off the beaten track as you could get. Sam remembered Bill's birthday. It was exactly two days and two years earlier than Sam's. During training, they had organized a joint birthday party that had resulted in a memorable hangover. He had borrowed Bill's identity for the express purpose of gaining entry to FSI.

The logbook was still pen-and-paper. The guard wrote his name and license number in the book and asked Sam to sign it. She handed him a blue temporary badge that identified him as a student.

FSI was so open that it posted its course calendar online. ConGen was offering a course on passports for new consular officers at ten o'clock. It was now nine forty-five. The guard at the main door just to the left of the reception desk looked at his badge and waved him through.

ConGen was in C Building on the other side of an open expanse called the Quad. Every year, flocks of migrating Canada geese adopted the grassy Quad as a temporary refuge on their long flights north and south, forcing urbanized diplomats to learn the origins of the rural expression "like shit through a goose." Their substantial droppings littered the Quad and the geese were unimpressed by the cardboard cutouts of foxes and coyotes that the grounds crew had set up in a desperate attempt to protect their carefully manicured lawn.

They were losing more than that battle. The pathways were designed to force students to walk around the edge of the Quad to get from building to building. But generations of otherwise law-abiding diplomats had carved an informal path of hard-packed dirt that led directly from the front entrance to C Building. Sam had used this rogue path on his way to Urdu lessons. It was a minor—and completely satisfying—act of defiance.

"Sam!"

Fuck.

This was one of the risks he took in coming here. The Service was small and the odds of running into someone he knew were high. It was why he had tried to time his arrival closely to the start of the passport class.

He turned around.

"Hi, Roger. How's tricks?" Roger Browley was never going to set the world on fire. He had been the supervisory general services officer in New Delhi when Sam had been posted to the embassy almost twelve years ago. The GSO ran the motor pool, paid the bills, and kept the embassy's physical plant running. It was not terribly exciting, but then neither was Browley.

"Keeping busy. We're off to Kenya in July. I'll be the head of budget and fiscal for all of East Africa."

"Congratulations. That's a great gig." Sam forced himself to smile in feigned enthusiasm.

"Hey, what are you doing back here? I heard you'd retired."

"Lecturing the South Asia Area Studies students about India and Pakistan. I'm running late actually. My class starts in five. Give my best to the family."

"Will do, Sam. And my best to . . ." He paused somewhat awkwardly. "Lena. I heard about Janani. I'm sorry."

"Thanks. I appreciate it."

Roger Browley headed off across the Quad, stepping gingerly around piles of goose shit, while Sam continued toward C Building uncomfortably aware that he had just dodged a bullet.

A woman who looked to be about Sam's age with graying hair and overly large glasses sat at a registration desk in front of room C-247 with a printed list and a matrix of name tags spread out on the tabletop. Knots of eager students stood deep in conversation, many clutching cups of the execrable coffee served in the FSI cafeteria.

"Your name, please," the woman asked, when Sam approached the desk.

"Bill Christiansen," he replied, making a show of looking for his name tag.

"I'm sorry, I don't have you on the list," she said, after thumbing through a number of pages. "Are you sure you're registered for the course?"

"My CDO signed me up," Sam said, using the acronym for career development officer, the State Department's equivalent of Human Resources. "It's kind of last-minute. I'm supposed to be the backup consular officer in Mazar and I get on a plane in three days."

"Oh." The woman looked genuinely sympathetic. *Afghanistan* was something of a magic word in the personnel process. It was unpleasant and dangerous duty, and the system was under instructions to do everything necessary to make sure personnel assigned there got to post when they were supposed to. Mazar-e-Sharif was even worse duty than Kabul. It was the job at the bottom of the barrel that was itself at the bottom of a whole big stack of barrels. The registrar's "Oh" had somehow managed to convey all of that in a single syllable.

"Is there any chance you could contact your CDO to reschedule?" she asked.

"I don't think so," Sam said pleasantly. "The checklist for Afghan training is as long as my arm, and there's a mandatory security course that starts this afternoon and runs almost through to take-off. If I can't get this training done, it'll likely mean pushing back my departure by a couple of days."

"Well, we can't have that," the registrar agreed, and the evident sympathy in her voice made Sam feel guilty about deceiving her. "I can take your name and I'll put it into the system later to make sure you get credit for the course. Is it Christianson with an 'o'?"

"With an 'e,'" Sam replied, as though he had been answering that question all of his life.

Bill would eventually see credit for the course show up in his personnel folder. It would be months before that happened. This was the government. He might well spend the rest of his career trying to get that course credit removed from his file.

C-247 was a cross between a classroom and a machine shop. There were desks arranged to face one of the new "smart" boards that for twenty thousand dollars did the same thing as a fifty-dollar chalkboard. There were also clusters of machines arranged around the room, some of them connected directly to computer termi-nals. The air smelled vaguely of acetone and burning plastic.

Sam took a seat toward the back. He looked around the room. He was the oldest "student" in the course by at least a decade, maybe two. The Foreign Service attracted many second-career types, but the majority of entry-level officers were still somewhere in their twenties. There were about twenty people taking the class. More than half were women. The Service had changed in that respect since Sam's A-100 days when women made up a quarter of the class at most. Seventeen of the twenty students were white. Two were Asian and only one was African American. Maybe the Service had not changed that much after all.

At ten o'clock on the dot, the instructor walked in and stood in front of the class. Sam was relieved that he did not recognize him. Some of the teaching spots in ConGen were civil-service positions with the same person teaching the same course year in and year out. Some were rotational positions for FSOs, and there was always the risk that the teacher could have been someone that Sam had worked with before.

"Good morning, everyone. My name is Hal Piedmont and this is the passport class. If you're here for anything else, then you're in the wrong room. Today, we'll be learning the nuts and bolts of passports, essentially how to start with a blank book and turn it into a viable travel document. This is the practical course. Issues related to passport law and application procedures are covered sep-arately. Any questions so far?"

There were none.

"This is a blank passport book," Hal said, holding up a blue tourist passport. "Back in the days before biometrics, a blank book would have had a street value of maybe five thousand dollars. Now it's worthless without the ability to link the information about the passport holder to PIERS, which is the Passport Information Electronic Records System. This is how we know you are who you say you are. You all are the gatekeepers to PIERS. Your street value is considerable higher than five Gs."

Hal spoke for another ten minutes. Most of what he said was not relevant to Sam. The other students in the course could expect to make hundreds if not thousands of passports over the course of their careers. Sam only needed to make one.

"Now I'd like you to play with the machines for a bit," Hal finally said. "Practice making a passport or two. Take a look at how you would link the data with PIERS, but be careful not to complete the sequence or you will put Elmer J. Fudd into the U.S. consular database for real. That might be hard to explain to Congress."

It actually was not that difficult. The students entered data into the system following a series of prompts. An informal competition developed as to who could invent the most oddball characters. One group of three announced that they were issuing passports to Sheila B. Cummings, Rhonda Mountain, and Wen Shi Kum. They had to sing it before the others got the joke.

Sam laughed along with the rest, but he could feel the tension in his shoulders as he input the data for "William J. Christiansen." The program had a number of photos you could choose from for training purposes, but Sam stuck a memory stick into the computer and called up his own photo, which he was able to click and drag into the box on the form.

"Hey, that guy really looks like you."

Sam almost jumped out of his skin.

He turned to see one of his fellow students looking over his shoulder. He was a kid. He could not have been more than twenty-two or twenty-three. Maybe not even Lena's age.

"Yeah, that's why I picked him," Sam said with a smile that he hoped did not look forced.

"I made mine out to Che Guevara. You finished with that machine?"

"Almost. Give me two more minutes."

When Sam had input the data, he clicked over to PIERS and walked through the steps necessary to link William Christiansen with the database. ARE YOU SURE YOU WANT TO CONTINUE? the program prompted him. He clicked YES and was rewarded with DATA ENTRY SUCCESSFUL. DO YOU WISH TO ENTER ANOTHER APPLICANT? He did not.

Sam printed a foil that had his picture and William Christiansen's name and identifying information. He pasted it onto the first page of a blank passport book and laminated it in the machine. When he was finished, what he held in his hand looked like a genuine U.S. passport. Hell, it was a genuine passport. It was William J. Christiansen—or at least *this* William J. Christiansen—who wasn't real.

At the end of the class, Hal Piedmont had them deposit the passports they had made in a box at the front of the room for eventual destruction. It was all on the honor system. These were sworn officers in the Foreign Service of the United States who could issue passports and visas to whomever they chose. If the system could not trust them, it could not function. Sam palmed his passport as he pretended to put it in the box and slipped it into his jacket pocket.

Soon enough, William J. Christiansen would be on a plane to Mumbai.

`00:27`

When Lena was very young, maybe six or seven, she had gone through the typical princess phase. She had a collection of elaborate princess dresses in various shades of pink and purple, a silver plastic tiara, and plastic high-heeled shoes. She all but wore out a collection of Disney DVDs featuring Snow White and Sleeping Beauty and Cinderella.

One afternoon, her father found her sitting inside a fort made of couch cushions. She was a prisoner in a high tower, Lena had explained, and she was waiting to be rescued by a handsome prince.

Sam sat his daughter down for a serious talk. It was no good waiting to be rescued, he said seriously. It was up to Lena to take care of herself. If she was ever trapped by an evil wizard in a tower of glass, then it was on her to find a way out. "You make your own fate," Sam had explained. "You are not helpless. You are not a victim. You can wear the tiara if you must, but wear it with a sword."

That was the end of Lena's princess phase. She had put the dresses away, but she had held on to the lesson. Now Lena was being held hostage in a temple that looked like a castle, albeit one made of plywood and fiberglass, and built as a Bollywood movie set. Her guards, however, were both real and dangerous.

Lena hoped that her father would come looking for her. With limited time and under the watchful gaze of her captors, she had done her best to let him know where she was. There was no way to know, however, whether the message had been received and understood. It was cryptic and coded, but her father knew her well. It had been just the two of them for a long time. Even so, she would not rely on him. She would not wait passively for rescue like some damsel in distress.

She would find her own way out.

Although neither Khan nor any of her other captors had offered any insight into the reason they had kidnapped her, Lena assumed that it had something to do with her father. It had to. Why else would the leader, the one Khan called Jadoon, want her to record that message to him? It could not be about money. The Trainor family was far from wealthy. In their last conversation, her father had warned her about militants targeting an Indian city with a nuclear weapon. It had seemed so preposterous at the time that she had even worried about her father's mental state. Now she wasn't so sure. But even if he was right, what did it have to do with her? Was she just leverage to use against her father? If so, how much danger was *he* in?

For now, there was no way to find answers to any of these questions. She was a prisoner. Khan had put her in a room that looked like it had once been an office for a studio executive. It was wedged in behind the soundstage, and her captors had likely chosen the room because it had only one door and no windows. The walls were covered in framed posters of B- and C-grade musicals featuring actors and actresses that Lena had never heard of. There was a couch she could use as a bed, a cheap-looking rug on the floor, and a desk with an old-fashioned wooden swivel chair. Everything was covered in dust, as though the building had been abandoned for months.

They took turns guarding her door and bringing her food, a bland diet of overcooked rice and lentils. As near as she could tell, they were all Pakistanis. Only Khan seemed to understand English, but Hindi and Urdu were mutually intelligible, and Lena would have been able to communicate with them all without any difficulty if they had been willing. Only Khan seemed interested in talking to her.

Some of the others were clearly interested in her in a different way, however. The small man with the pinched features named Umar was the worst. Whenever he delivered her meal, he stared at her with a barely concealed lust that made her feel violated.

It was her fifth day in captivity.

Although she had nothing to do all day but sit in her cell and think, Lena struggled with a bone-crushing exhaustion. It was, she knew, the fear.

No one had threatened her directly, but the constant tension weighed heavily on her. She had little appetite. It was hard to sleep.

The fear coiled tightly in her belly like a snake, cold and scaly. If she let it, it would consume her, swallow her, trade places, and leave her trapped and helpless in the belly of the snake. She would not let it loose.

Her thoughts crossed back and forth over the same uncertainties without conclusion. The boredom of captivity was almost as debil-

itating as the fear. Lena wished that she had packed a book, anything to distract her from thinking about what her captors would
do to her. They had made no effort to hide their faces from her.
That did not bode well for the future.

Lena sat on the couch rereading a three-day-old copy of the
Times of India that Khan had given her when there was a knock on
the door.

Khan came in without waiting for an answer. He was carrying a
bowl and a plastic bottle of water.

She should hate him, she supposed, or at least fear him. It surprised her somewhat that she did neither. She had no illusions about
the danger she was in, but not—she felt—from Khan. He seemed
different than the other jihadis. Less coarse. Less brutal.

"Are you hungry?" he asked in his raspy tristate accent as he set
her meal on the desk. Lena realized that she did not know what meal
it was. It could be dinner or breakfast. She had lost track of time.

"It's chef's surprise tonight," Khan continued. "Rice and lentils
instead of lentils and rice."

Dinner, then.

Lena did not let Khan's lighthearted attempt at humor distract
her from the fundamental truth that she was his prisoner.

"Thank you."

"Can I get you anything else?"

"No."

Khan seemed not to take the hint. He sat on the couch while
Lena picked listlessly at the food.

"Just make yourself at home," Lena suggested, with a hint of
bitterness to her voice that even someone with a much more limited
facility in English than Khan would have found hard to miss.

"Su casa es mi casa."

"It certainly is."

"I am sorry about this, you understand. The circumstances made it necessary, but that doesn't make it any more pleasant."

"Why is it necessary? What on earth do you need from me?"

"That has not been revealed to me."

"Well, then, what good are you?"

"The less you know, the safer you are. I promise you that."

"Is this about my father? Are you planning to hurt him in some way?"

"I am just a foot soldier," Khan said. "All the rest is the will of Allah."

"That's bullshit," Lena said vehemently. "You are a thinking adult accountable for the consequences of your decisions. You can't just pass the buck to Allah and call it a day. How do you know what Allah wants? How does He contact you? Does Allah prefer e-mail or does He SMS with the cool kids?"

Khan looked around quickly. "That kind of talk is very dangerous," he said in a soft voice. "If Jadoon hears you blaspheme, it will become much harder for me to keep you alive."

For no good reason, Lena believed him.

"You know they'll be looking for me, don't you? My father knows people. Powerful people. Dangerous people. And then there are the people at SysNet. What are they going to think when I don't show up for work?"

"Your father has been . . . discouraged . . . from looking for you."

"Threatened, you mean."

Khan shrugged. "Whatever."

"This is all about him, isn't it? You're just using me against my father."

"I couldn't tell you."

"Can't or won't?"

"Does it matter?" Khan shrugged again.

"To me it does."

"I wouldn't count on SysNet either. Engineers here are a dime a dozen. You might already have been replaced."

This, Lena reasoned sadly, was almost certainly true. Turnover at start-ups like SysNet was notoriously high, and not everyone who left for a better offer bothered with an exit interview. "Where are you from, Khan?" she asked, changing the subject. "New York? Philly? With that accent, it's gotta be somewhere tristate."

"I'm from Quetta," Khan insisted. "Via Newark," he added a moment later.

"Jersey. What the hell are you doing here kidnapping girls who don't give a fig for geopolitics or religious wars?"

"The Quran says: *I possess no power to harm or help myself except as Allah wills. Every nation has an appointed time. When their appointed time comes, they cannot delay it a single hour or bring it forward.*"

"What about karma? I'll see your Quran and raise you the Vedanta. *According as a man acts and according as he believes so will he be; he becomes pure by pure deeds and evil by evil deeds.*" Lena had her father to thank for her knowledge of Hindu scripture. Before her mother had gotten sick, Sam had been working on a new translation of a set of ancient Vedic texts called the Upanishads, also known as the Vedanta. He had liked to read them aloud to Lena and she had liked to listen to even the ones she could not quite understand.

"We can debate theology, but I do not think it will serve much purpose. Nothing in life is simple. The choices I have had to make are complicated. I am not comfortable with all of them, but I have my mission and my mission is my guide, even as it requires me to make . . . sacrifices."

"And what is your mission?"

"Jihad."

It was an answer that stirred the snakes in Lena's stomach from their torpor and sent them crawling up her spine.

Khan's cell phone beeped. It was not an incoming call. It was an alarm. Khan turned it off and pulled on a beaded silver chain around his neck. He was wearing a plastic card under his shirt that looked like it might have been an ID card except that there were no identifying marks on it. It was just a solid blue piece of plastic. Khan removed a small manila envelope from the back and slipped it into his pocket. From another pocket he extracted a second envelope and clipped it in place behind the plastic card before slipping it back under his shirt.

"I need to take care of this," he said.

"What is that, Khan?"

"Nothing important."

This time, and for a good reason, Lena did not believe him. She knew what it was that hung from the chain around Khan's neck.

Lena supposed that it was night. It had been some hours since Khan had left with her empty bowl.

She knew that she should sleep, but she could not. The idea that her father's wild story might actually be true had taken root in her head and was branching out into a thousand different nightmare scenarios. Mumbai. Kolkata. New Delhi. Watching the first man-made nuclear explosion at the Trinity test site near Alamogordo,

Robert J. Oppenheimer, the father of the atomic bomb, had quoted from the Bhagavad Gita: *Now I am become death, destroyer of worlds.*

In the nightmares of her imagination, Lena could see the mushroom cloud spreading across the city, bringing death and destruction in the form of blast and fire and radiation. She could see the Sikh temple in New Delhi with its stunning gold dome crumbling as the nuclear shock wave swept across the capital. She could see Spencer Plaza in Chennai on fire, the silhouettes of hundreds of the dead etched into the few walls still standing by the flash and heat of the explosion. And she could see her own beloved Mumbai, the Dharavi slum blown flat and burning even as radioactive fallout scoured the district clean of life. The lives of people she loved. Lena shuddered in foreboding at the clarity of the vision. This was how Cassandra must have felt as she contemplated the fall of Troy. Powerless.

The need Lena felt to take action, even action that might well get her killed, was almost overwhelming. She had recognized the plastic badge Khan had retrieved from under his shirt. Lena had worn one herself during a summer internship at Caltech. It was a film badge dosimeter and it had only one purpose, measuring exposure to radiation.

She surveyed the room, looking for something that she might be able to use to her advantage. A weapon. Maybe something that she could use to signal for help. She knew Morse code. When she was twelve, she had built a working telegraph for a science fair and for nearly a month she would communicate with her family only in tapped-out dots and dashes. Her father had been considerably more enthusiastic about this than her mother. And much to her mother's irritation, she and her father had enjoyed long conversations rapped out with their knuckles on the dining room table or the dashboard of the car. SOS was easy. But did that mean the same thing here in India, or was it just American?

The contents of the desk drawer were not especially encouraging. There was a roll of tape that had gone dry and yellow, a movie industry magazine that was nearly a year old, a few staples but no stapler, and a small tin of paper clips. The mental image of Lena attacking a terrorist, even one the size of Umar, with a handful of paper clips almost made her laugh out loud.

Then Lena noticed something that gave her pause. The desk lamp was plugged into the wall on the far side of the room near the door. The extension cord ran under the carpet, and Lena saw that the plug by the door was the only one available.

At Stanford, she had taken as many practical-engineering courses as her faculty advisor would let her get away with. She preferred practice to theory by a wide margin. One professor in an applied-engineering class had been a stickler for safety protocols. "Do you have any idea how much paperwork I have to do when one of you baby-faced newbies kills yourself in my class?" he had asked.

Safety was just danger turned upside down, and Lena realized that she could apply one of his warnings to her current predicament.

The instructor had outlined for the class some of the more common ways people hurt themselves working with electricity. Then, for a laugh, he had offered some of the less common. One anecdote had stayed with Lena, at least in part because at the time she had found it incomprehensible.

"Someone really did that?" she had asked, somewhat incredulous.

"Right out of the gene pool," the professor had answered.

She unplugged the lamp and removed the shade. The bulb was

incandescent, which was what she needed. The fluorescent bulbs in the ceiling fixtures would not work for what she had in mind.

She unscrewed the bulb from the base and wedged the glass globe into one of the desk drawers. She hesitated, uncertain about how best to proceed. There was only one bulb. One shot. If she got this wrong, there was no "undo" button. Was it better to apply gradual pressure or crack it open with one firm shove? It was essential that she preserve the delicate contact wires inside the glass. With a mental shrug, Lena made a choice. She pushed gently against the drawer with the flat of her hand, increasing the pressure bit by bit until she heard the glass crack. She examined her handiwork. The tungsten filament that connected the two wires had disintegrated when the bulb's vacuum was broken. That was to be expected. The contact wires themselves seemed to be intact. The bulb had not broken cleanly. A few jagged pieces of glass jutted up higher than the level of the contacts. Lena ripped a page out of the movie magazine and folded it into quarters. Working slowly and carefully, she used the folded paper to protect her fingers as she pried off the bits of glass that clung to the metal base.

When Lena was satisfied that the contacts stood clear of the glass, she screwed the bulb back into the lamp. Pulling the extension cord out from under the carpet, she coiled it and left it lying in a loose pile by the door. Then she plugged the lamp back in. The lamp was a modern design with a thin metal body that was not too heavy. Grasping the lamp in her left hand, she knocked vigorously on the door with her right.

"Help!" she shouted. "I need help."

Eventually, the guard opened the door. It was Ahmedani, the big one with the wild black beard who looked like a cross between a man and a bear. He would not have been Lena's first choice. She had hoped for the vile Umar, who maxed out at about one hundred and fifty pounds.

"What is it?" Ahmedani growled in Urdu, with no attempt at pleasantries. He made it clear that he was lowering himself in talking to her at all.

"There's a spider on the wall the size of my face," she said anxiously in Hindi. Lena was not above playing the helpless female if it would help her get Ahmedani to lower his guard.

"I'm not staying in this room with that monster," she continued. "You'll either kill it . . . or you'll have to kill me."

Ahmedani actually smiled at that, and he stepped through the door into the room.

"I'll crush your little bug for you, Hindu girl. You will pay me later."

The image of the massive bearded jihadi forcing himself on her made the next part easier.

As Ahmedani brushed past her, Lena stepped back and swung the desk lamp up in a short arc, jamming the exposed contact wires of the broken lightbulb into the soft flesh at the base of his jaw right below the ear. There was a sharp popping sound like a muffled gunshot. Ahmedani straightened up as every muscle in his enormous body contracted at the same time. The lights briefly faded to brown as the terrorist's body soaked up the massive shot of 220-volt electricity carried by the slender contact wires.

"Don't ever do this," her instructor had warned the group of Stanford sophomores after the laughter had died down. "Unless, of course, you're trying to kill somebody."

I guess I am, Lena thought sadly.

Ahmedani crumpled to the ground. He was so big that he almost blocked the door. The twin burn marks on his neck made it look as though he had been bitten by an electric vampire. Lena felt for his pulse. It was weak and thready, but he was still alive. As much as he might have deserved it, Lena was glad she had not killed him.

She stepped over his body and onto the movie set. The walls of the temple were covered with plaster and papier-mâché images of the Hindu pantheon. Vishnu, Krishna, Rama, Kali, Ganesh, and a host of other gods and goddesses that Lena did not recognize looked down on her from on high.

I don't believe in you guys, or the old white man with the beard. But if you'll help get me out of this place, I will burn a pile of incense for you so large it will be visible from space.

The temple was mounted on a raised stage. At the base of the stage was an open area where the cameras would have been set for filming. In the middle of the floor was a pile of what looked like blankets. Although every part of her screamed to get out of the building as quickly as possible, something scratching at the back of her brain made her stop and look. They were not blankets. They were aprons like the kind the dentist would drape over you before he took an X-ray. Lena stripped two of the heavy lead-lined aprons from the top of the pile. Underneath was a green steel box. The place where the lock had been was now just a gaping hole that had been cut out with power tools.

I can run for help. Bring back the police, the army, scientists, somebody.

But she knew it was not true. Soon enough, they would find Ahmedani and they would move the box. No one would believe Lena's story, and if there was, in fact, a bomb in the box, it would explode as surely as day follows night.

But you would be gone, she heard the little voice in her head say. *You would have time to leave Mumbai.*

Lena opened the box.

Her heart sank.

She had hoped that she would find something relatively simple. In effect, a bomb was nothing more than a circuit. Complete the circuit and trigger an explosion. Lena knew circuits and she had hoped that she would be able to disable whatever she found inside.

Someone had gotten there first.

She could still see the part that was the original bomb and the circuitry there was relatively straightforward. Somebody, however, had connected it to a second device that was much more complicated, a rat's nest of wiring that seemed to have no sense or structure to it. The two devices were linked through a rectangular timer with glowing red letters counting down the time remaining until what Lena had to assume was detonation.

09:18:12:28

09:18:12:27

A little less than ten days.

The light was too dim to see clearly, but the tangle of colored wires and plastic switches was there for a reason. It had a purpose. Lena tried to see the gestalt, to understand how the pieces connected into an organic whole that made some kind of sense. She could not see it. There wasn't enough time. There wasn't enough light.

Maybe if she could feel with her hands, she could understand it. Lena reached inside the device that was not a bomb and ran her fingers along what looked like a mixed-signal circuit built around a comparator that could translate an analog current into a digital signal. She tried to follow the conductive wire back to its source, but her hands were too big.

"I wouldn't pull on anything in there," a voice behind her said. Lena froze. Slowly, she turned to see Khan, Jadoon, and Umar standing behind her. The man who had spoken, however, was someone she had not seen previously. He was short and almost skeletally thin with a beard that grew in uneven patches.

"That's a delicate device," the small man continued in his nasal voice. "Some of the circuits are positive and some are negative. The lack of a signal can itself be a signal or a trigger. It would not be healthy to disturb the balance of the device."

Lena understood what purpose the rat's nest was intended to serve. It was a dead man's switch, designed to make it impossible to tamper with the bomb once it had been set. It was the kind of thing only a madman would build.

Slowly, Lena pulled her hand out of the box.

Umar stepped forward and grabbed her by the wrist. She could see the lust burning in his eyes.

"I will teach this Hindu bitch a lesson for Ahmedani that she will not soon forget." He pulled her close and Lena could smell onions on his breath.

Umar twisted her wrist and tried to force Lena to the ground. It felt like her arm might snap.

"You will do no such thing," said Khan.

Umar turned on him like a striking snake.

"You're protecting this foreign whore?" Umar asked incredulously.

Lena saw his head snap back. Khan had hit him with an open hand easily and confidently as though employing only a fraction of the strength at his disposal.

"I am defending our guest," Khan suggested mildly. "And we

have orders to keep her safe . . . for now. Why don't you go see if Ahmedani needs help? That might actually be useful."

Despite herself, Lena felt a wave of gratitude sweep through her. Even so, Khan's caveat had not escaped her notice.

She was protected. "For now."

00:28

William J. Christiansen had a valid U.S. passport, but he still needed a visa for India. Sam knew that he could not apply at the Indian consulate in Washington through the regular channels. For one, it could take up to three weeks for the consulate to process the application, weeks that neither Sam nor Lena could afford. Moreover, this William Christiansen did not exist beyond the passport and the fake driver's license. He had no address, no job, no social security number, and no bank account. Most important, he had no time.

There was only one person who could help. That he wanted desperately to see her and talk to her, to hold her close and stroke her hair, offered further incentive. He did not dare pick up the phone and call Vanalika. He knew for a fact that her communications were being monitored by the NSA; and Argus, he was confident, had flagged all of her lines for special attention.

Fortunately, the Indian political counselor was a creature of habit.

The embassy was on Massachusetts Avenue near Dupont Circle, smack in the middle of Embassy Row. There was a small coffee shop on Hillyer Place only a block or so from the chancery building that served a gingerbread latte that Vanalika was all but addicted to. She and Sam had joked about her "daily fix." Unless there was some pressing business that kept her in the office, Vanalika made a pilgrimage to Grounds for Appeal every day at about midmorning.

Coffee culture had come late to work-obsessed Washington, but it had arrived with a bang. In addition to the ubiquitous Starbucks outlets, the city was dotted with smaller mom-and-pop operations that sold a break from the pace of D.C. life along with overpriced coffee. Grounds for Appeal catered to the lawyers and paralegals who were to Washington what auto executives and assembly-line workers were to Detroit: the city's sine qua non.

A day after his successful foray at FSI, Sam was sitting in an armchair covered in soft brown leather in the back corner of the coffee shop pretending to read the *Washington Post* and hoping that this was one of the days when Vanalika would keep to her routine. Consistent with its theme, the café was decorated with legal memorabilia and the bar was built to resemble a judge's bench. Lawyers on their lunch break could order a "Warren Burger" or a "Felix Frankfurter." There was also a "David Souter" on the menu, which was only identified by the cryptic note: *It's not what you think it is.*

At ten forty-five, more than an hour after Sam had sat down with a four-dollar cup of coffee, Vanalika walked in off the street.

As she waited in line to place her order, she scrolled through her messages on her BlackBerry. Sam got up from his chair and walked over to stand behind her in line.

"Why, Mrs. Chandra. What a pleasant surprise."

Vanalika started and turned to look over her shoulder. She

smiled broadly when she saw Sam and moved instinctively to embrace him. But she checked herself almost immediately. They were in public, and within shouting distance of the Indian Embassy.

"Mr. Trainor," she offered coolly, even as her eyes shone with a mixture of affection and joy at the playacting that had always been a part of their illicit relationship. "This isn't one of your usual haunts, is it?"

"No. But I had the day off and wanted to check out the new Rothko exhibit at the Phillips Collection. Can I interest you in joining me for a cup of coffee?"

"I think I can spare a couple of minutes." She winked, breaking character. It was all a game for Vanalika, and the closer they came to getting caught the more fun it was for her.

A few minutes later, she had her gingerbread latte and cranberry scone, and they were sitting together in the back of the café far enough away from the other patrons that they could speak freely.

"Sam, are you all right?" Vanalika asked. "I haven't heard from you in days. I was starting to worry."

"Actually, no. I'm not okay. Someone tried to kill me last week, and when that didn't work, they took my girl. Lena's being held hostage in India by someone who calls himself Zeno. If I go to the police, I'm afraid they'll hurt her. I need to get to Mumbai as quickly as possible."

Vanalika's eyes widened in surprise and, Sam was hurt to see, disbelief.

"What happened?" she asked. And then she said more loyally, "How can I help?"

Sam told her about the car chase on the George Washington Parkway and the mysterious message from the Stoics. He left out his trip to see Earl Holly in North Carolina. His old friend, he knew, would want to stay as deep in the shadows as possible, and his involvement did not add anything essential to the story he had to share with Vanalika. Neither did he tell her about Cold Harbor. Vanalika might feel compelled to report back to Delhi, and there was no telling where that would end up. Sam could not take the risk that it would get back to the Stoics and endanger Lena. He did, however, tell her about his foray into the FSI consular database and his new credentials as William Christiansen.

Vanalika listened intently to what Sam had to say. He was grateful to see the undercurrent of disbelief dissipate and be replaced by a look of shock and fear. She had evidently agreed to accept the fundamental truth of what he was telling her.

"What can I do?" she asked, when he had finished.

Sam pulled William Christiansen's brand-new passport out of his jacket pocket and laid it on the table between them.

"I need a visa for India. And I need it quickly. Lena's in trouble."

Vanalika picked up the passport and flipped it open to the page with Sam's picture and the data for William Christiansen. Then she slipped it into her purse.

"Is that all?" she asked.

"No. I need a plane ticket for Mumbai. I don't dare use my own credit cards, and if I bought a ticket for India with cash . . . even if I had the cash . . . it would trigger all sorts of unwelcome alarms with Homeland Security. They pay special attention to those kinds of purchases. It would be better if the flight isn't leaving from Dulles. I don't know how carefully Argus is looking for me, but if they're watching any airport, they're watching Dulles. It would be better to fly out of Chicago or even Atlanta, one of the really busy airports. Can you help me?"

Vanalika reached out and took his hand, abandoning all pretense that they were nothing more than professional colleagues.

"Of course, my friend," she said, with an expression that managed to convey both concern for Sam and disappointment that he would ever have doubted her. "It may take me a couple of days to fix the visa, and I'll book us on the first flight to Mumbai out of Atlanta. We can fly out of Baltimore to make the connection."

"We?"

"Sam, my dear, you don't think I'd let you do this alone. I'm going with you."

It took two days, forty-eight hours that to Sam seemed to stretch out into years. The waiting was painful, but Sam did not know what else to do. He had a plan, once he made it to Mumbai. Until then, however, there was nothing he could do but wait.

Between the tension of the long wait and the strain of the twenty-hour trip from BWI in Baltimore to Atlanta to Chhatrapati Shivaji International Airport in Mumbai, Sam was completely drained by the time he and Vanalika deplaned. That Vanalika had booked business-class tickets helped. She never flew steerage. Vanalika had invented a family emergency to explain her absence to the embassy. She had laughed when Sam had asked her what she had told her husband. "Rajiv doesn't care what I do as long as I don't embarrass him," she said.

There was one more hurdle ahead of them. The United States did not check the passports of outgoing international travelers against the computer database. Both the airline and TSA looked at the picture and matched the name on the passport with the name on the ticket, but that was it. Here in Mumbai, the immigration official behind the Plexiglas screen would actually run the passport through a scanner linked to a computer that would verify the legitimacy of the travel document. There was no reason that William Christiansen's passport should not show up in the system as valid. But Sam had not had the chance to test it.

He and Vanalika had to queue separately, Sam in the line for foreigners and Vanalika in the line for returning Indian nationals. When it was his turn, he stepped up to the booth and presented his unused passport to the Indian immigration officer with what he hoped was a studied nonchalance. He watched with trepidation, however, as the official flipped through the brand-new passport, studied the visa with what looked to Sam like suspicion, and then placed it on the scanner. Sam could see the bright light shining through around the edges as the computer read the lines of code printed at the bottom of the page with his picture and compared it against the information in the traveler database. Sam could not see what information appeared on the computer screen.

The immigration officer looked at him and compared his picture to what was in the passport.

"Are you here on business or pleasure?" he asked.

"Business. Just a few days."

The official hesitated. Then he stamped the passport and slipped it back through the shallow gap in the glass.

"Enjoy your stay," he said.

Sam had made it to India.

He met up with Vanalika at baggage claim. Sam caught a glimpse of his reflection in a mirror that he suspected was one-way glass with

Indian customs officials on the other side looking for drug mules. He looked like hell. Vanalika looked like a billion rupees.

"How can you look that good after a twenty-hour flight?" he asked.

"Sleep, Sam. You should try it sometime."

"I can't sleep. All I can think about is Lena."

She took his hand.

"I know."

The Mumbai airport was the same wild mix of people that Sam remembered with such fondness from his time at the consulate. An elderly Tamil woman in an ornate gold sari stood guard over a brood of half a dozen grandchildren as their parents struggled to manage a small mountain of luggage. A gaggle of businessmen in Western suits and ten-thousand-rupee haircuts checked their messages obsessively on multiple devices. And an enormous Sikh with a tangerine-colored turban and a thick black beard leaned against a pillar as though he were propping it up.

This was Mumbai. Ancient and modern. Spiritual and material. A contradiction wrapped in a paradox inside an oxymoron.

Sam saw the big Sikh again at customs. He was in the express lane for travelers without luggage. *So what had he been doing waiting in baggage claim?*

But by the time Sam and Vanalika had cleared customs, the Sikh was nowhere to be seen. Sam chastised himself for jumping at shadows. He was just nervous. He needed to stay focused. He needed to find his girl.

The terminal was air-conditioned and looked like the international arrivals area at any major airport on the planet. The moment the door to the outside opened, however, Sam knew they were in India. The heat and humidity and India's incomparable layers of smell—diesel fumes, spices, and raw sewage—hit him in the face like a blow. Even Vanalika wrinkled her nose.

"I've been in Washington for too long," she said.

"You'll get used to it again quickly," Sam promised.

They took a cab to the hotel. The cab had its own unpleasant odor that it layered on top of Mumbai's. It smelled like someone had lit a fire in a diaper pail. India had its sensual pleasures, but few of them were olfactory.

Vanalika had wanted to book them a room at the Taj Mahal Palace, Mumbai's icon of luxury. Sam had wanted something much lower profile and had been able to talk her down as far as the Holiday Inn. Camping, she called it.

They checked into their room. Mumbai was such a big city and far enough from Vanalika's social circles in New Delhi that they did not feel compelled to book separate rooms. Sam showered and changed into khaki slacks and a light cotton shirt with short sleeves. When Vanalika finished her shower, she laid a green linen shift out on the bed.

"You're going to want to wear pants for where we're going," Sam warned. "And boots."

"And just where is that?"

"Dharavi."

"How interesting."

They took a cab to the slum. The class of cabs that the hotel called for guests was a notch or two higher than what they would have been able to flag down on the street. This one had air-conditioning. Unfortunately, it also had a working radio and the driver made no move to turn down the volume on the Indian pop music he seemed to favor.

Sam rolled down the window. Vanalika looked at him quizzically.

"My daughter is out there somewhere," he explained. "I can't wall myself off from this city. I used to know it well, but it's been too long. I need to get back in touch with it if I'm going to find her."

Vanalika did not say anything in response, but she rolled down her window as well and let the smells and sounds and the feel of Mumbai waft into the cab.

The driver did not protest. He just turned off the air-conditioning and turned up the music. It would save him a few rupees.

In the rearview mirror, Sam caught a flash of tangerine in a car following two or three spaces behind them. But when he turned for a better look, he could not see anything.

"What is it?" Vanalika asked.

"Nothing. I'm just jumpy is all."

The cab let them off at the entrance to the slum that Sam had specified. They crossed a shaky wooden bridge over a canal filled with scum and garbage. At the far side of the bridge, a beggar boy with no legs plied his miserable trade. Sam knew that Lena crossed this bridge regularly on her way to work. No doubt, she passed this boy every day. Sam put some rupees in his bowl for luck.

Vanalika was putting on a brave face, but she was clearly discomfited by the squalor of the slum and the garbage piled up along the side of the narrow alleyways. This was a different India than the one she knew. An India that the elite would just as soon pretend did not exist.

"Do you want to go back to the hotel?" he asked. "I can do this next part alone."

"No," Vanalika said, visibly trying to adjust to the unfamiliar environment in her own country. "I can handle this." She lengthened her stride. Where she had been mincing on the balls of her feet, now she was walking. She loosened her shoulders, which had been tensed up. Vanalika was wealthy and privileged, Sam thought, but that did not mean that she wasn't tough too.

When Lena had decided to move back to Mumbai, she had told Sam that she wanted to live in Dharavi. Sam had tried to talk her out of it. It was no place for a young American woman, or even a half-American woman, to live. In truth, it was no place for anyone to live. The apartment right on the edge of the slum district was a compromise of sorts. Sam understood the pull of Dharavi and the hold that the district had on her sense of self. Her roots were here. Roots that she needed to explore.

He felt her absence so powerfully that he wanted to scream. That was not what Lena needed from him, he knew. She needed him to find her. *I'm coming for you, baby.*

It had been years since he had been on these streets. He had been meaning to visit Lena, but something had always seemed to get in the way. There had been changes, of course, but the basic feel of the slum was the same and the route he took was a familiar one. He had walked it many times when he had been responsible for human rights reporting in the American consulate in what had then been Bombay.

The three-story building was made from an eclectic mixture of materials, and if it had an architectural style, it would have been called "Indian Expedient." It was the home and office of his friend Jarapundi Ramananda.

"What is this place?" Vanalika asked, when Sam stopped in front of the building. "Was this where Lena was living?" The Brahmin in her clearly had trouble believing that anyone would subject themselves to these kinds of conditions voluntarily.

"No. Lena's apartment was probably not as nice as this. This is a friend's house. I think he can help us."

"Really?" she asked, with undisguised skepticism. "What does he do?"

"He's a criminal."

"How interesting."

Ramananda was sitting at a table on the first floor when Sam and Vanalika walked in. There was a glass of water on the table in front of him and a half-empty bottle. It was hot and stuffy inside. A pedestal fan in one corner tried heroically to circulate the air, but succeeded only in buffeting the flies. Sam thought Vanalika looked like she might be sick.

Ramananda had not changed much. He had put on more weight and his bald spot had expanded to creep down around his ears, but otherwise he looked pretty much the same. Sam was not surprised to find him in. It had been years since Ramananda had been outside.

When he saw Sam, Ramananda's eyes widened.

"Sam? Is it you?" he asked. The underworld boss rose from his chair with some effort and embraced his friend. Sam returned the embrace. Ramananda had been a professional contact, but he had also been a genuine friend and Sam was glad to see him.

"It's been a long time. It's good to see you, old friend."

"And who is your new friend, if I might ask?"

"Ramananda, let me present Vanalika Chandra of New Delhi."

"Charmed," the Dalit said, taking her hand and shaking it up and down as if he were painting a fence.

Ramananda sat back down at the table, and Sam and Vanalika joined him.

"Nandi," he shouted. "Bring water for our guests."

A young boy of maybe ten popped his head in from the back room.

"Right away," he promised.

Moments later, the boy brought two dusty glasses and another plastic bottle of water over to the table.

"So you got my message," Ramananda said. "I was worried when I couldn't reach you."

"What message, Rama? Was it about Lena? Do you know what's happened to her?" Sam had hoped desperately that Ramananda could add something, anything, to what Sam already knew that might help him find his daughter. It was a vain hope.

"I only know that she seems to have gone missing. She stopped coming to the school. She hasn't been home and one of the street boys says she was being followed. The Gummadi brothers swear up and down that they had nothing to do with it, and I have a few people in their organization on my payroll who back them up."

"Lena's in trouble. She was taken. But not by the Gummadis. Someone much scarier." Sam did not even try to hide his disappointment. But there had been no reason to believe that Ramananda knew any more than he did. What mattered was what the Dalit crime boss could find out.

"What's happened to her? Tell me. And tell me who." Lena's godfather was no longer smiling.

"I've made some enemies back home. People who are doing some things that I opposed. They are trying to get to me through Lena.

Someone who calls himself Zeno has kidnapped her and he's holding her here in Mumbai."

Ramananda looked at Sam thoughtfully. His expression was grim. This was a language that he understood.

"How do you know that she's here?"

"I got a message from the kidnappers. They let Lena speak as proof of life. She said that she was okay, and she was able to communicate to me that she was here."

"What did she say exactly?"

"She called me Papa Bear," Sam explained.

"And what does that mean?"

"When she was little and we were living here, we used to play a game. I was Papa Bear and she was Baby Bear and she had to sneak back into the cave when I wasn't looking. If she made it, she was supposed to shout: Papa Bear, Papa Bear, I'm home. This is the only time that she called me that other than in the taped message from Zeno. She was telling me that she's home."

"Are you sure that she didn't mean Washington?" Ramananda asked.

"No. Mumbai is her home. She's here. I know it. I need to find her."

Ramananda did not even bother to ask why Sam didn't go to the police. It would never have occurred to him to do that either. For those who made Dharavi their home, the police were just one more source of trouble. Sam left out of his story his supposition that militants were planning to explode a nuclear bomb in an Indian city. It was too far-out to present without proof and expect to be taken seriously. All Sam wanted to do was to convey to Ramananda that Lena was in danger and needed his help.

"What can I do?" his friend asked.

"I need you to lend me your network."

"What will you do?"

"I'm going to find the people who have kidnapped and threatened my little girl."

"And then?"

"I'm going to kill them."

HILL STATION PRODUCTIONS
MAY 1

00:29

Kamran Khan was praying, and he was not succeeding. From the time he found the path to Islam, prayer had offered solace and certainty. It had always been easy for Khan to slip into a state of grace through prayer, freed from earthly worries and cares, secure in the love of Allah. Now the peace and calm of prayer eluded him. He went through the motions and he said the words along with his brothers in jihad, but it was all by rote. His heart was not in it. Worldly thoughts intruded on his efforts to commune with the divine.

Lena.

As he prostrated himself in *sujud* in the direction of the Kaaba at Mecca and placed his forehead on the prayer rug, it was not Allah he thought of. It was Lena. As he reached out to God, it was Lena's face that he saw.

Khan had never experienced anything like this. It was more than disconcerting. It was terrifying. He had come to rely on prayer to keep him on the straight path, to guide him through the murky moral swamp of his mission. What was right and what was wrong? How could he know if he could not speak to God if God could not hear him?

He struggled to understand what was happening to him. It was with some chagrin that Khan, who considered himself to be fully Pakistani, or at least fully Baluch, was forced to rely on a purely American idiom.

Lena Trainor was kryptonite.

She made him weak. Uncertain. She made him feel things that he could not afford to feel, things that could endanger his mission.

He thought the others must surely see the confusion on his face as plainly as it was written on his heart. But they could not. Of course, Allah knew. The Quran said: *Truly Thou dost know what we conceal and what we reveal: for nothing whatever is hidden from Allah, whether on earth or in heaven.* And Khan had so much to conceal.

When the prayers had concluded, Jadoon called Khan aside.

"You and I have a job to do this afternoon," he said.

"Yes, Jadoon." Khan did not ask what the job was. When he needed to know, Jadoon would tell him. Asking would only have made him angry.

Khan knew that he had been dismissed, but he did not leave.

"What is it?" Jadoon asked impatiently.

"You have seen what is in the box? And the . . . modifications . . . that Adnan and I have made?"

"Yes," the HeM leader acknowledged reluctantly.

"You have seen the timer?"

"I have."

"And you know what will happen when the numbers reach zero?"

"*Allahu Akbar.* I do."

"Do you see any advantage in all of us traveling together to meet Allah?"

"What are you getting at?"

"I would volunteer to stay behind and guard the bomb while you lead the others back to Lahore. This will surely be but the first great blow in the coming battle with the Hindus. There will be other blows to strike, and there is no need for the Hand of the Prophet to lose all of its finest fighters at the outset of the struggle."

Jadoon considered this. Khan could read the eagerness on his face. He wanted to accept the proposal. He wanted to live. But he would have to be led to that conclusion gently so that he would not consider himself a coward.

"We have our orders," Jadoon insisted.

"Our orders are to carry out the mission, and to die if we must. But if we do not have to die, then it is simply suicide, and suicide is sinful."

Jadoon took his time thinking this over.

"It would be unfortunate to sully this great triumph with even a hint of sin," he offered finally.

"That's right," Khan agreed, letting the HeM commander reach the conclusions himself.

"You are the most qualified among us in matters related to the box," Jadoon said, seemingly unable to say the word *bomb*.

"Yes, I am."

"Very well. At the twelve-hour mark I will lead the rest of the team out of the city. We will go to Lahore. You will stay behind with the box. Your sacrifice will echo with honor through the centuries."

Khan bowed his head. This was his mission. This was jihad.

. . .

Whatever Jadoon's mystery job was, it involved leaving the studio. Khan had not been outside since he had persuaded—no, he corrected himself, kidnapped—Lena from her apartment and brought her here. He blinked in the unaccustomed sunlight as his eyes adjusted to the brightness. The colors of everything around him seemed intense and vivid as though he had just crawled up from underground.

The same gray panel van that Khan had used in his surveillance of Lena was parked in a garage attached to the studio. Khan drove, following directions from a GPS unit fixed to the dashboard. It took them more than an hour to reach their destination, a two-story brick house in a leafy, residential part of Mumbai. High brick walls surrounded the property.

A gate slid open to admit the van. Khan parked alongside the house.

"Stick close to me," Jadoon instructed. "You may need to translate."

Jadoon knocked on the door with his knuckles. The sound was dull and heavy. The door was painted to look like wood, but it was made from steel.

An older man with a shaved head answered the door wearing a long *sherwani* jacket embroidered in gold thread. There was a bulge under the jacket that Khan knew was a firearm.

"Welcome," he said in English. "You are expected."

The door opened to a foyer with a set of stairs at the far end. There were rooms to both sides, a living room to the left and what looked like a library to the right. The house was tastefully appointed, but it was all impersonal. There were no photographs, nothing that indicated the house was lived in rather than used.

The bald man ushered them into the library. A dark-skinned man in a Western suit was sitting on a straight-backed wooden chair. Khan recognized him. This was the man he and Masood had met with on their visit to India. He was the one who had provided the HeM with the information that had allowed them to acquire the bomb.

If the man recognized Khan, he gave no sign of it. Khan reciprocated.

There was another wooden chair and a sofa in the room. Khan took the chair. Jadoon sat on the couch. It was, Khan thought, a mistake on his part. He should have mirrored the host. The couch would make him feel soft and inferior. He thought he saw the dark-skinned man smile slightly as though some prediction had been confirmed. But perhaps he only imagined it.

"Thank you for coming on such short notice," the man said. "We will speak English. We will not use names." These were the same ground rules he had established for the meeting with Masood.

Khan translated for Jadoon.

"I am not used to being summoned like an errant schoolboy," Jadoon said irritably. "I would therefore skip the pleasantries and get to the point. What is so urgent that it calls me away from our operation?"

"This is about your operation," the man answered, when Khan had translated. "Some information has come to the attention of my organization that we must share with you."

Although he listened attentively to the translation, Khan suspected that the man understood Jadoon's Urdu perfectly. He had the advantage of listening to what Jadoon had to say twice and then having the time to formulate his response. Moreover, speaking English would help disguise any regional accent and preserve anonymity.

The bald man in the embroidered jacket entered the library with a tray of spiced tea. The dark-skinned man remained quiet while the bald man served the tea.

"The issue concerns your young guest, Ms. Trainor. You were most efficient in the way you brought her under your protection." He looked at Khan as he said this, as though he knew who had been responsible for the kidnapping. "We also appreciate the speed with which you responded to our request for a proof-of-life recording that could be shared with her father. Perhaps you know why you are holding her and perhaps you do not. It is immaterial. There have, however, been some . . . complications . . . of which you should be aware. Various members of the Dalit community in Mumbai, the group you might know better as untouchables, have been searching for her. Evidently, this young woman had an unusual group of friends and associates. The intensity they are bringing to this activity is really quite remarkable, unlike anything I have ever seen. They have a few leads, including the make, model, and license plate of your van. I do not know how they acquired that information." Khan did. It was, he was certain, the legless beggar boy. Maybe he had been wrong to let him live.

"It would be my pleasure to dispose of your vehicle for you," the man continued. "I have another car parked out front that you can take with you. It is a sensible precaution."

"Yes," Jadoon interjected. "I agree."

"Do not underestimate the Dalit," the dark-skinned man said. "Many of those conducting the search are well known to the police. Some are well connected. The line between crime and policing in Mumbai is somewhat elastic."

"So what would you suggest?"

"Give them the answer they seek. Give them Ms. Trainor."

"Let her go?"

"In a manner of speaking."

"Kill her?"

The dark man shrugged.

Khan was translating faithfully and he kept his face an icy mask, but his emotions roiled just below the surface.

"Wouldn't that just make them redouble their efforts?" Jadoon asked. "Only this time, instead of looking for the girl, they'd be after the people who killed her. I don't see the difference."

"The action would shift from the Dalit community to the police. The authorities would open a formal investigation and begin the slow, methodical work that leads to arrests. Before the lead detective had so much as filled out his first time card, the death of one American woman would be . . . overtaken by events."

Khan knew what that euphemism meant. The smoking glass crater that would be downtown Mumbai would make any murder investigation superfluous. What was it Stalin had said? *The death of one person is a tragedy; the death of a hundred thousand is a statistic.*

Jadoon understood as well.

"We will take your recommendation under advisement," he said carefully.

They drove back to the studio in silence. Their new car was an inconspicuous dark green Tata Manza. Outwardly, Khan was calm and controlled. Inwardly, he seethed. He was angry with the dark-skinned man and fearful for Lena. While Jadoon had promised only to consider the recommendation, that was likely to save face. It was closer to an instruction than a suggestion.

Traffic was heavy and the trip back to the studio was taking longer than the trip out. He realized that they were close to Dharavi, not far, in fact, from Lena's apartment. An open-air market on one side of the road covered almost half a city block. Impulsively, Khan pulled the car up on the sidewalk and parked. He did not allow himself to think about the possible consequences of what he was contemplating. If he did, he might not have the courage.

"What are you doing?" Jadoon asked, with a note of impatience in his voice.

"We need tea and rice and sugar. It will not take more than a few minutes. You can watch the car."

"Be quick about it."

On the backseat was a small pile of things that Khan had transferred from the van. He grabbed a canvas bag from the pile and slipped his wallet into its side pocket. The market was crowded, even by the generous standards of Mumbai. Here in the heart of the city, the sea breeze was too light to help break the heat. The by-now-familiar combination of alluring and repulsive smells assaulted his nostrils. A Rajasthani man with a magnificent handlebar mustache and a saffron-colored turban was selling rice from a stall not far from the entrance to the market. Different varieties of rice were displayed in woven baskets and measured out on a hanging balance scale that used metal weights. Khan picked a style of basmati rice that was similar to the Pakistani staple. He haggled over the five-kilo bag, not because he cared about the money but because it would have been strange—and memorable—if he did not. They settled on sixty rupees a kilo. It was a fair price.

It took Khan ten minutes to find the section of the market where the tea dealers set up shop. The proprietress of one of the stalls was an older woman wearing a dark-colored Indian *shalwar kameez* with a bright yellow *hijab*.

"*As-salamu alaykum*," Khan said.

"*Wa alaykumu s-salam*," she replied with a beaming smile.

"I am looking for black tea," he said in Urdu.

"You are certainly in the right place," the old lady said in Hindi.

Khan set the shopping bag down next to him on the market's concrete floor.

"You look like a strong young man. I recommend a strong tea from a Himalayan hill station in the Mahabharat Range near Darjeeling. This is a rare tea, but I have my own supplier, so I can give you a good price."

The haggling was good-natured, but Khan did not buy the tea.

When he reached down to retrieve his wallet, the bag was gone. One of Mumbai's legion of thieves had made off with it.

Khan struggled to force a complex mix of emotions into some semblance of order. As so often he did, he found comfort in a passage from the Quran.

Those who believe and do deeds of righteousness, for them there is forgiveness.

MUMBAI
APRIL 30

00:30

I t was like chasing ghosts. Ramananda's vast network of informants had produced little but rumors and shreds of hearsay that led nowhere. Lena had simply disappeared. After two days of looking and questioning, Sam was no closer to finding his daughter than he had been when he had stepped off the plane. The few leads that the Dalit foot soldiers had uncovered had been dead ends. There had been one reported sighting of the gray panel van, but the kiosk owner who had seen it had been unable to follow the vehicle. It might not even have been the right van.

Privately, Sam was also obsessively tracking the movements of Prime Minister Rangarajan. He did not know which city would be targeted, only that Rangarajan was supposed to be there when the bomb went off, assuming that the fragment of the speech he had pulled out of the Morlocks' burn bag was an accurate indication of the Stoics' intentions. Unfortunately, the Indian prime minister fancied himself a man of the people who spent more time outside of

Delhi visiting other parts of India than he did in the capital. The list of potential targets seemed endless.

They had converted the first floor of the house in Dharavi into a war room complete with an oversize map of Mumbai that they used to chart the few gossamer-thin reports that came in from the pickpockets and extortionists on Ramananda's payroll. The mid-level managers in his criminal network provided daily updates under the direction of three of the Hard Men. The Dalit enforcers did not offer Sam their names, but each sported a sizeable tattoo of a different Hindu god and he had started thinking of the three Hard Men captains as Ganesh, Vishnu, and Shiva.

Sam hunched over the laptop on the table, trying to concentrate on a press release from the prime minister's office about an upcoming trip to Chandigarh. This was near Kashmir, increasing somewhat the odds that this city could be the target for the Stoics or Ashoka or whatever militant group was playing the role of the cutout. But there was no way to know.

The air in Ramananda's house felt hot and oppressive. Sam needed a break.

"I'm going to step out for a minute to get some air," he announced.

"Why don't you take one of the Hard Men with you?" Ramananda suggested.

Sam wanted to be alone with his thoughts, if only for a few minutes.

"I'll be fine, Rama. I'm not going far and I'm your guest. No one here is going to hassle me."

Outside, the temperature was only a few degrees cooler. But there was a light breeze and walking helped to clear the fog in Sam's head.

Although it had been years since he was a regular visitor to the slum, Sam still remembered his way around. He walked toward one of the open squares where the children of Dharavi played soccer and *kabaddi*. It was late, however, and there were few people still out on the streets. The square itself was empty. Sam stood in the middle of the open area where he had the best chance to catch a hint of the breeze. A few pale beams of moonlight struggled through the clouds and smog that shrouded Mumbai in a perpetual haze to offer some dim illumination.

Out of the corner of his eye, he saw a shadow move. At an instinctual level, Sam recognized that whatever was there was a threat. Too late, he turned to run. The shadow had cut off his line of retreat. The clouds parted for a moment, bathing the figure in moonlight. It was the Sikh Sam had first seen at the airport, his tangerine turban traded in for one that was blood red.

At his belt, the Sikh wore a *kirpan*, his religion's ritual dagger. Most *kirpans* were small ceremonial objects. This one, however, was twelve inches of steel, and it made a thin, raspy sound as the powerfully built Sikh drew it from its sheath.

Sam was cornered. He had been stupid.

The Sikh closed in, confident. In his meaty hand, the long knife looked like a toy.

The shadows deepened as the moon was again obscured by the clouds.

Sam cast about for a weapon of some kind.

Without warning, the silhouette of the Sikh stiffened, and Sam heard a dull grunt followed by a thud as his assailant fell to the ground.

The moon reappeared.

The Hard Man with the tattoo of Vishnu on his forearm was

standing where the Sikh had been. The blade of his knife was wet with blood that gleamed black in the moonlight against the steel.

"Ramananda sent you to follow me," Sam said.

Vishnu nodded.

"Thank you."

Vishnu nodded again. He wiped his blade on the body of the Sikh and it vanished into an unseen sheath.

Sam looked at the corpse at his feet. The Sikhs had a proud warrior tradition that stretched back centuries. This was no street tough. This was an assassin. The Stoics or maybe Ashoka.

How the hell had they found him? And what would they do to Lena?

Two days later, they were no closer. The prime minister had visited both Chandigarh and Ludhiana without triggering a mushroom cloud. Today, he was in Mumbai, which made Sam nervous. But he had no reason to believe Mumbai was the target any more than New Delhi or Chandigarh.

He did not know what the deadline was, but Sam sensed that time was running short. He could not sleep. He had to force himself to eat.

"You can't help Lena by killing yourself, Sam," Vanalika pleaded.

"I'm fine," Sam insisted, all evidence to the contrary. He ran his hand through his hair. It was greasy. It had been days since he had showered or changed his clothes. His eyes were framed by dark circles and felt like they had been scrubbed with sandpaper. Sam and Vanalika were sitting at the small table in the war room at Ramananda's home.

"Let me get in touch with some people I know in Indian intelligence," Vanalika urged. "They may be able to help."

"We can't do that. Whoever you talk to at the Intelligence Bureau is going to communicate with others in your government over the phone or by e-mail. The NSA will vacuum that information up and put it into the system where Argus and the Stoics would have access to it. It would not take long for them to figure out that I'm in Mumbai turning over every rock I can find. Once they know, that son of a bitch who calls himself Zeno will kill Lena. I'm certain of it." The Dalit communicated face-to-face. They had no computers and few phones. In the high-tech world of twenty-first-century espionage, the low-tech Dalit were a hard target for Western intelligence.

Ramananda limped into the room, accompanied by the boy, Nandi, who followed him everywhere when he was not out on the streets plying his light-fingered trade. Ramananda sat down heavily in the third chair at the table. Nandi stood beside him.

"We have news," the Dalit leader announced.

Sam felt some of his lethargy drain away and be replaced by hope.

"Good news?"

"A lead, at least. Show him, Nandi."

The young thief put a wallet on the table. It was brown leather, worn, cheap, and stained with sweat.

"This picture was inside the wallet," the boy said, laying a small photograph on the table. It was Lena, the same picture that Zeno had posted in the self-erasing message that he had sent Sam. This was the real deal.

"Where did you get it?" Sam asked eagerly.

"One of the boys on another team . . . found it . . . at the green market in Sion."

"When?"

"Yesterday," Nandi admitted sheepishly. "The boy gave the money to his underboss, but he kept the wallet. The picture was in the wallet. He didn't know Ms. Lena, so he didn't recognize her. He kept the picture because he thought she was pretty." Nandi blushed when he said that. It was clear that he thought she was pretty too.

"Anyway," he continued, "he showed the picture to another boy this morning, someone on my team who knew Ms. Lena. He recognized her and passed the wallet on to me. Here it is."

"Thank you, Nandi," Sam said. "This is our first real lead. You've given us something to work with. I'm grateful."

Nandi bowed his head. Ramananda patted him on the back.

Sam examined the wallet. Whatever cash had been in it was long gone. There were no credit cards. A driver's license in the name of Baahir Daoud was tucked into one of the wallet pockets. The grainy photo was of a young bearded man with a serious expression, an aquiline nose, and intense dark eyes. He looked like a hundred thousand other men in this city of twenty million. Sam was quite certain that the license was a fake and Baahir Daoud did not exist. It was a cover identity.

There was nothing personal in the wallet: no pictures beyond the one of his daughter, no receipts for purchases, no train tickets, nothing.

Under a flap in the pocket for banknotes, Sam found a small sealed manila envelope. He opened it carefully.

A strip of exposed film fell out onto the tabletop. Sam held it up to the light to get a better look at the image on the film. What he saw made his blood freeze. If Sam was right that Lena was in Mumbai, she was not the only one who was in danger. He looked carefully at the film. The edges on both sides were perforated like movie film. Along one side, the words HILL ST were visible. The rest had been cut off.

"Rama, is there a Hill Street in Mumbai?" Sam asked. "I've never heard of it."

"Not that I know of," Ramananda answered. "And I'd know of it if there was."

"Vanalika, can I use your phone?"

She unlocked her iPhone and handed it to Sam.

Calling up Google, Sam typed MUMBAI HILL ST into the search box. Google offered three options to complete the search: Hill Station, Hill Station resorts, and Hill Station Productions.

"What's Hill Station Productions?" he asked.

"It was one of the Bollywood movie studios," Ramananda answered. "They went bankrupt maybe six months ago. I had lent some money at a favorable rate to one of the owners as a favor to a friend. I lost the capital and the friend."

"Show me where the studio is on the map," Sam said to Ramananda.

Ramananda pointed to a spot in Navi Mumbai on the other side of Thane Creek. Sector 18, just off Palm Beach Road.

"Jesus Christ, that's right across from the Jain temple in Trombay."

Sam felt sick. He knew exactly what was going to happen and when. There was so little time.

Ramananda looked at him curiously. "And that is significant because . . . ?"

"Because today is Mahavir Jayanti, the biggest holiday on the Jain calendar, and the prime minister is attending the festival there this afternoon."

"I still don't understand why that is important."

"I think the people holding Lena are planning to kill the prime minister and a lot of other people, and they're going to do it today."

"How?"

"With a bomb."

"From across the estuary? That is a very big bomb."

"Yes, it is. Take a look at this." Sam pushed the strip of exposed film across the tabletop to Ramananda and Vanalika.

Ramananda held it up to the light.

"There's no picture here that I can see. Just dots."

"Those dots are from neutrons hitting the film," Sam explained. "I used to work on nonproliferation issues in Washington. This is part of a tool that people use to measure exposure to radiation."

"What kind of people?"

"Dentists, for one . . . radiologists . . . and people who work with nuclear weapons."

"I don't suppose that our daughter was kidnapped by a gang of renegade orthodontists."

"I don't suppose so."

"The festival is this afternoon?"

"In about three hours."

Ramananda was silent for a moment. His expression was grave.

"Nandi," he said, turning toward the boy. "Tell the Hard Men I need them. All of them. I need them now."

He looked at Sam, who nodded in understanding and agreement.

"Let's go get our girl."

HILL STATION STUDIOS
MAY 2

00:31

The old pipes in the building carried sound with exceptional clarity, and if Lena sat close to the vent, she could listen to her captors debate when and how she should die. The dispute as to whether she should die had never really gotten much traction. That discussion had featured Kamran Khan on one side and every other jihadi on the other side. It was an unequal fight. Khan had gone down swinging, but he had lost. Lena had been sentenced to die.

All things considered, she felt surprisingly calm.

The room was dark. They would not trust Lena with another light. She sat on the floor with her back pressed up against the wall, listening to the men on the other side quarrel over her death. The small one, Umar, wanted to rape her first, of course. He had some arcane theological justification for his desire—as a captive, she was their "property" and therefore rape was not *haram*, or sinful—but it was pretty clear even to his fellow jihadis that that was just an excuse.

"If you touch this woman in that way, Umar," she heard Khan say, "I will grab you by your scrawny neck and squeeze until your eyeballs pop out and I can tie them in a bow, you brother fucker."

There was a scuffling sound that Lena imagined was the smaller Umar taking up Khan's challenge. It was over quickly, however, and she suspected that the other jihadis had broken up the fight before it became serious.

"That is enough," she heard Jadoon's booming voice command, as he sought to regain control of his fractious terrorist cell. "You, Umar, will stop thinking with your cock. And you, Khan, the strongest of us, you have been made weak by this woman." Somehow, Jadoon made the word *woman* sound like an insult. In his world, Lena suspected, it was exactly that.

"That is not true, Jadoon. I am thinking of the mission. I do not trust the Indians and I see no advantage in killing this woman. Alive, she is a bargaining chip, leverage. Dead, she is nothing."

"We have been down that road already, Khan. The woman is a liability, a distraction. You more than anyone here should appreciate that."

"The mission is all that matters to me. I have given everything to it."

"As have we all," Jadoon said more gently. "The path of jihad is rocky and steep. But you do not walk it alone."

"No," Khan agreed. "I walk my path with Allah."

"And your brothers," Jadoon insisted.

"As you say."

"But your weakness has cost you the trust of your brothers. Trust that must be reclaimed if you are to join us in fulfilling our mission."

"I understand."

"You know that this woman will die, do you not?" Jadoon asked.

"Yes."

"Do you know how?" His voice was again gentle, probing.

Khan was silent.

"Do you know how?" Jadoon repeated, more fiercely.

"Yes." Khan's voice was soft and sad.

"How?"

"I am going to kill her."

"Yes," Jadoon said, satisfied. "Yes, you are."

For the first time since she had been taken captive, Lena Trainor felt truly bereft.

Khan delayed the inevitable for as long as he could. His mind cast about wildly for some solution, some answer. There was still time to work with. The remorseless countdown clock that Adnan had attached to the bomb had more than two full days left to run before it reached zero. That could not be changed without the code known only to the diminutive physicist, and he seemed to have disappeared that morning. No one knew where he had gone. Jadoon tried his best not to show that it bothered him, but he had not been entirely successful. The entire team was on edge, which was one of the reasons they had been so quick to condemn Lena.

There was nothing that Khan's panicky thoughts could identify as a way out. Khan was compromised in the eyes of the other jihadis. He was suspect. There was only one way to prove his commitment to the mission and secure the honor of guarding the bomb. Reluctantly, Khan opened the door to the office that had become Lena's cell.

She was sitting on the floor with her legs pulled up against her chest. Her arms clutched her legs tightly, as though they could shield her from what was coming. Lena blinked in the unaccustomed light, but her eyes were dry. She cast a challenging look at Khan.

"Lena," he began, and then froze. He did not know where to begin. All of the choices before him were unacceptable.

"I know," she said. "I heard."

"I'm sorry."

"What are you going to do?"

"What I have to."

"You don't have to, Khan. You have a choice."

"What is that choice?"

"You can choose life over death. My life. Your life. The lives of hundreds of thousands of innocents that that monstrous bomb in the other room will steal when it explodes. No god could want that. Not Allah. Not Kali. Not the Christian god. No god could will what you are planning to do."

"That is not a choice" was all Khan could say.

Khan led her out of the cell and through the Styrofoam temple to the main room where the bomb was located. A slight tremble in her shoulders was the only sign she offered that she was afraid. The other jihadis were waiting. They were all armed. Not because of Lena, Khan knew, but because of him. There was a chair.

"Sit, Hindu," Jadoon commanded.

Lena sat in the chair.

The HeM leader pulled a pistol from under his robes. He handed it to Khan.

Khan stood behind Lena. He raised the pistol, pointing it at the base of her skull. It felt to him as though his arm belonged to someone else, as though it were not his hand that held the gun or his brain that would command the trigger finger. This was all happening to someone else.

He could feel his pulse beating behind his eyes, feel the blood vessels in his temples constrict, leaving him light-headed and dizzy.

His hand started to shake. He tightened his grip on the pistol, hoping that the others would not notice.

His finger tightened on the trigger. The SIG Sauer would fire at about ten pounds of pressure. Khan knew the feel of the gun, and he could watch the hammer as it pulled back, gathering the kinetic energy to strike the firing pin. It was almost at its apex now. The gun shook slightly as his finger kept the hammer poised just below the peak. Another pound of pressure, another fraction of a pound, would push it over the top and it would fire.

Khan stood poised on the edge of the precipice.

He willed his trigger finger to contract, but it did not want to obey his command.

I am Allah's instrument.

There was no choice. This was the price of jihad. The terrible price.

A phone rang.

It was Jadoon's cell.

Khan looked at him. Jadoon held up one finger.

"Wait."

He answered the phone.

"Yes."

Khan could hear the voice on the other end, but not well enough that he could understand.

Jadoon listened.

"I understand," he said, after more than a minute had elapsed. He looked at Khan thoughtfully.

"You were right, Khan. The girl is leverage. That was our Indian friend telling me that we have been discovered. But it is not the police who are coming for us. Their source tells them that it is the girl's father and his Hindu friends. I do not know why he has not called the authorities, but it is the will of Allah that we succeed. The girl may yet prove more useful alive than dead."

Khan lowered the gun and took a deep breath.

Lena felt drained, emotionally and psychologically. She had just been through the equivalent of an execution, and nothing in her young life had prepared her for that experience. *How could anything prepare you for that?* For all intents and purposes, she had been dead. Now she was not. It might have been exhilarating if Lena had any feelings left inside her. But it was as if she had used them all up and would have to wait for the reservoir to refill before she could feel anything again.

Reaching deep inside, almost unexpectedly, she found at least one emotion that pulsed like a hot coal among the ashes. Anger. Anger for what they had done to her. Anger for what they would do to her father. And anger for the hateful tool of mass murder she had seen in the steel box. Lena could still summon anger. It would have to do.

Her father was coming for her. He had found her in a city of twenty million people in a country of more than a billion human beings. She was a needle in a hundred thousand haystacks. When she was a girl, her father had diligently checked in the closet and under the bed for monsters. He had never found any. Not before today.

They had put her back in her cell. The only light was what

leaked through the ill-fitting door frame. It was enough to allow her to pace back and forth without fear of running into the walls or furniture. She was too keyed up to sit down.

The adrenaline rush of her near-death experience and the darkness of her cell played hell with Lena's sense of time. She might have been in the room for an hour or two. It might have been much longer. She could not tell.

In the dark, the click of the bolt in her cell door retracting was as loud as a gunshot. Quietly and carefully, Kamran Khan slipped into her cell.

"Lena," he said softly into the dark.

"Yes."

"I'm sorry."

She was silent.

"I had no choice."

"You do now, Khan. It's not too late. You can do the right thing. You can be on the right side."

"I am on the right side," Khan insisted. "I am on the side of Allah."

Lena could hear the pain and confusion in his voice.

"Help me," she said.

"That is why I'm here. All of my . . . brothers . . . are busy preparing to defend this place. There is no one to guard your cell. I will leave the door unlocked. When the shooting begins, leave this place. There is a window to the right of your cell that opens onto the parking lot. You have to wait for the fighting to begin, because the window is visible from the main room. If they see you trying to escape, they will shoot you. Once you are outside, the fence is climbable and there is no barbed wire. Go. Escape. Go as far as you can. Get out of this city."

"Thank you" was all she could say.

Khan exited the room as quietly and as carefully as he had entered, leaving Lena alone in the dark with her thoughts.

Her father was coming to save her, and he was walking into a trap. Lena would not allow it.

Although it was dark, she closed her eyes as she thought through the kernel of an idea that she hoped would grow into a plan. It helped her to concentrate.

The elements of the incipient plan swirled in her head as she paced back and forth. Her father would not approve of what she was thinking, but she could not bring herself to accept Khan's offer to run away. If she thought that there was any chance she could get the Indian authorities to believe her story in time to raid the studio before the jihadis either moved or exploded the bomb, she might think differently about it. Her experiences with the BMC had taught her to be realistic about the speed with which the Indian bureaucracy moved.

It was not a complex plan. That was its strength. Its weaknesses were too obvious and too numerous to worry about.

Lena was still shaking from her brush with violent death. Her hands would need to be steady for what she had in mind. Concentrating on her breathing, she willed her heart rate to slow. When she could hold her hands reasonably still, Lena went to the door and carefully turned the handle. The mechanism moved smoothly and easily. As Khan had promised, it was unlocked. She cracked the door and peered out. There was no guard in sight and the movie set shielded her from whatever preparations the jihadis were making in the big soundstage.

Lena stepped out of her cell and closed the door behind her. To the right was the window that Khan said led to the back parking lot. Until they were distracted by the fight to come, the jihadis would almost certainly spot her if she tried to escape that way. There was no door on the back side of the building. Her father and her godfather would have to come in through the front door.

Lena turned left. Near the corner of the room behind an eight-foot-tall blue plasticine Rama was an electrical panel that she had seen when the Pakistanis first brought her here. It looked to her like one of the master panels that could control every light in the studio. It made sense that the grips and lighting technicians would want to keep that close at hand.

Even better, when she got close, she saw that the switches and fuses were labeled. Without that, she almost certainly would have been forced to abandon her plan. Lena scanned the labels quickly, looking for the one she needed. It was not hard to find, a white toggle switch labeled FRONT DOOR. The fuse above it was set in the off position. She switched it to on. As long as the bulb was not burned out or missing, there was no reason this shouldn't work.

Closing her eyes, she visualized the string of letters and reviewed the combination of dots and dashes that could stand in their place. It was easy enough for her to remember. She had that kind of mind. Her mother had always said she got her prodigious memory from her father. She hoped now that that was true, that he would remember too.

Lena flipped the switch for the front-door light up and down in a set pattern. Dash. Dot dot dot dot. Dot. Dash dot dash dash.

Nineteen letters. Repeat.

They know you're coming.

00:32

The Hard Men did not look especially imposing. Subconsciously, perhaps, Sam had expected Ramananda's enforcers to look the part. Most were thin and not especially tall. Their muscles were long and ropy, a side effect of hard work rather than a vanity product derived from hours in the gym. What set them apart was the air of confidence they projected. Sam knew that look, the one that marked the bearer as the top predator in his particular food chain. He had seen it on Special Forces soldiers, experienced diplomats, and highly trained CIA case officers.

He had also seen firsthand what the Hard Men were capable of when Vishnu had handled the big Sikh assassin with such quiet competence.

They had gathered on the first floor of Ramananda's house. On Vanalika's iPad, Sam had called up a Google Earth shot of Hill Station Productions and the surrounding streets. The picture had been taken at a more prosperous time for the production company.

The parking lot was full and vendors had set up stalls on one of the side streets, probably selling street food to the film crews and extras.

On Ramananda's aging laptop, Sam had pulled together all of the information he could about the production company. It wasn't much. The studio had produced a string of B-grade flops before going belly-up about six months previously. There were rumors of mob connections and a few gossipy items about an alleged affair between one of the directors and a well-known actress.

The core group was small, just Sam, Ramananda, Vanalika, and the three nameless captains of the Hard Men.

"The complex is pretty big," Sam said. "When we get there, we may be able to work out which of the buildings are being used, but it's possible that we will have to hunt around."

"I have boys who are used to looking for people who do not wish to be found." Ganesh's tattoo of the elephant-head god on his right bicep was a crude prison design. The blue-black ink was a rough smear under his skin.

"I don't doubt it," Sam replied. "What about climbers, guys who can get up to windows on the second and third stories?"

"Rich people like to live up high," Vishnu said, as though this was the most natural thing in the world.

"Good. Do any of you have experience with this sort of thing? Anyone do time in the army?"

Ganesh nodded.

"Six years in the infantry. I was a sergeant."

"Excellent."

"He was dishonorably discharged," Ramananda said proudly. "Cracked the safe with the company's pay. It was on the third floor of a guarded facility. Hell of a thing. The army couldn't prove anything, but they did get him for hospitalizing the officer who tried to arrest him."

"Consider yourself restored in rank, Sergeant. Do you have any ideas about how to proceed?"

"How many are inside?"

"I don't know."

"What kind of weapons?"

"I don't know."

"Are they professional soldiers or muscle?"

"I don't know."

"What do you know?"

"Same as you. They have my daughter."

Ganesh considered this carefully for a moment.

"We should use multiple points of entry if possible," he said finally. "It's hard to tell from these overhead shots what the building really looks like from street level. We will have to work out the plan on-site when we can see where the doors and windows are."

"There's one more thing," Sam added. "It's possible that they also have a bomb, a very big bomb. If you or any of your men see something that looks like it could be a bomb, don't touch it. We need to get someone who knows what he's doing to disarm it."

Sam turned to look at Vanalika, who was standing beside him.

"Is there someone in the Bureau of Intelligence you trust?" he asked. "Someone who might trust *you* enough to send a SWAT team and a bomb squad to the studio even if you can't tell him why? I don't want to say too much over the phone. SMS and e-mail aren't safe either. ECHELON will vacuum it all up and I'm sure the Stoics are being hypervigilant right now."

"I think I know the right person."

"Okay. Why don't you reach out to him? It's a risk, but I think we need the help. We need to hope that there won't be enough time for word to leak back to the Stoics." Sam looked at his watch. The prime minister was expected to arrive at the Jain temple in two hours. "We don't have time to wait for the answer. If the cavalry arrives, so much the better, but we need to plan on doing this thing ourselves."

Ramananda and the Hard Men left to gather the gear they would need. That the Dalit leader had left his house was itself an unusual event. It underscored how serious the situation had become both for Lena and the city of Mumbai.

Sam and Vanalika were alone.

"Vee, I think you should stay behind," Sam said. "This is going to be dangerous and this isn't your fight."

Vanalika was characteristically blunt.

"Bullshit, it's not," she exploded. "Look, Sam. If your story is true, and I'll confess that I still have my doubts, then foreign terrorists of some stripe are plotting to explode a nuclear bomb in the center of the largest city in my country. I think that pretty much qualifies as my business. And if I buy into all the reasons why I can't report this to my government through the regular channels, reasons that are largely about the safety of your daughter, by the way, then that leaves me as the sole representative of the government of India in this little adventure. So don't go getting all fourteenth-century French nobility on me just because I have a second X chromosome."

Sam was abashed. He agreed with everything Vanalika had said. Sexism was sexism, whether the overt variety of the Persian Gulf petrostates or the more subtle form represented by outdated concepts of chivalry. It was different in form, but not in kind. Vanalika had as much right to fight for her country as Sam had to fight for his child.

"Okay, Vanalika. No argument from me. But please don't do anything crazy. Andy died because of me. I couldn't bear losing you too."

"I'll be a little church mouse."

"You wouldn't know a church mouse if it bit you on the ankle."

"Let's go."

Ramananda had arranged for two canvas-topped trucks to transport them to the studio. Black nylon bags already loaded on the trucks contained weapons and equipment. Once they had climbed on board, Lena's godfather pressed something into Sam's hand. It was a revolver that looked like it had seen better days. There were patches of rust on the barrel, and the wooden handle was gouged and scratched.

"Is this thing going to blow up if I pull the trigger?" Sam asked.

"Don't let looks deceive," Ramananda insisted. "You squeeze the trigger, the gun will fire. Aim true and someone will die. Can you handle that? For Lena."

"Yes."

The ride through Mumbai traffic took nearly an hour. It was excruciating for Sam. He kept lifting the canvas sidewalls of the cargo area to look out. At least part of him expected to see the blinding flash of a nuclear explosion each time he looked in the direction of Hill Station Productions. It would, he knew, be the last thing he ever saw.

All that he saw, however, was an impenetrable snarl of traffic that crawled forward only slightly faster than they could have walked. The Hard Men said little. Even Vanalika looked subdued. Ramananda had not offered her a firearm and she had not asked.

As they had agreed, the trucks stopped a block from the main entrance to the studios. This was a depressed industrial area of Navi Mumbai. The wide estuary of Thane Creek separated this part of the city from Trombay and the Jain temple that would soon be hosting the prime minister. By car, the roundabout trip was nearly twelve kilometers and took at least forty-five minutes. As the crow flies, however, the distance was much shorter. Sam recalled the old aphorism from the height of the Cold War. "Close only counts in horseshoes and nuclear war." For the Stoics, this was close enough.

Mahavir Jayanti was the most holy day of the world's most pacifist religion. Nonviolence was the core belief of Jain philosophy, extending even to the treatment of insects and plants. It would be a horrible irony if this celebration of peace was the focal point for the kind of senseless attack that Sam believed in his bones was already in motion.

Half of the factories in the area were dark and shuttered, a testament to misguided industrial policy. The streets here were a warren of small alleys that connected to nothing. As a result, there was not as much traffic here as in the rest of the city. By Mumbai standards, the area was deserted. The air smelled of charcoal and feces.

The Hard Men disembarked, different teams gathering around their respective captains. There were twelve of them in total. They had no idea how many men they might be going up against. It seemed unlikely to Sam that there was a large group inside. It would be easier to operate with a small team, easier to conceal their purpose and minimize the risk that one or more of their number would want to see a down payment on the seventy-two virgins before blowing himself, his brothers-in-arms, and several hundred thousand strangers to kingdom come. But that was really just a guess. Sam did not see much of a choice. They had his daughter and the clock was ticking.

Sam led them to the front gate of the abandoned studio. A ten-foot-tall chain-link fence surrounded the complex of production facilities and office buildings. A large warehouse-size building with no windows looked like the film studio itself. A smaller two-story office building was grafted onto one side of the studio.

The foot soldiers hung back as the core group that had put the rudimentary plan together stepped up to the gate. A chain looped around the posts held the gate closed. Sam lifted the lock and showed it to Ramananda.

"This is brand-new," he said.

Ramananda pointed to the tire tracks in the dust that led up to the single door in the building they had tentatively identified as the production studio. Sam could see boot prints clustered around the outside of the door. There was a light fixture over the entrance. The bulb was flashing on and off as though a contact had come loose. It took Sam a moment to realize that the pattern was not random. It was Morse code.

It was some time before he was able to dredge the simple code up from the depths of his brain. It had been many years since he had used it, but the basic knowledge was still there. He crouched in the dirt and, with a loose piece of wire that he picked up from the ground, wrote out what he saw.

U R E C O M I N G T H E Y K N O W Y O U R E C O M I N G

THEY KNOW YOU'RE COMING

The message repeated over and over. It had to be Lena. His heart soared. She was alive. He remembered how she had insisted on communicating in nothing but Morse code for weeks as she prepared for the state science fair. It had been a game for the two of them.

"Vanalika, that guy in the Bureau of Intelligence that you called . . ."

"What about him?"

"You should probably take him off your Christmas list."

Ganesh pulled out a small pair of binoculars and surveyed the building quickly.

"What do you think, Sergeant?" Sam asked.

"The front door looks like the only way in from this side. If they're expecting us, that's likely where they'll concentrate their fire."

Ganesh called Vishnu and Shiva over to join them. Shiva's tattoo covered most of his upper arm, with the god's necklace of skulls reaching almost to his elbow.

"We'll do this in three teams," Ganesh said. "I'll take my boys in through the office building on the side and look for a second entrance. You." He pointed at Vishnu. "Take the back side. Look for a window or door you can use. You," he said to Shiva. "Wait for the shooting to start, and then move on the main door. You all have hammers and bolt cutters?"

They nodded.

"Okay. It is now . . ." He looked at his watch. "Three-twenty. Take fifteen minutes to get in position. We go through at three thirty-five sharp. Hit hard and fast. Shoot anyone with testicles. If he has a beard, shoot him twice."

Sam pulled Vanalika aside.

"Vee, I'd like you and Ramananda to stay with the truck. There's at least a chance that the cops are coming, and someone needs to tell them what's going on inside. They'll believe you easier than Rama."

Vanalika's response was the maddening Indian headshake that was neither yes nor no but something closer to "I heard what you said."

Just then, the Morse code stopped. Sam felt a sudden tightness in his chest. He hadn't been tracking it, so he wasn't sure if the code had broken off in the middle of the phrase. That would have told him something about whether Lena—assuming it was Lena—had stopped of her own volition or if she had been discovered by her captors. Either way, they needed to move now.

"Let's go, boys. Remember, if you or your team sees anything that looks like a bomb, don't touch it. That's for later. I don't think the police are coming to help us. We're on our own."

The Hard Men nodded. They had expected nothing less. They had been on their own almost from birth.

The captains oversaw the distribution of the guns and equipment. There were six shotguns, two for each team. The rest of the men carried an assortment of pistols and knives. They had no grenades or explosives. It was likely the men inside had automatic rifles, maybe machine guns. The Hard Men all knew this and none of them hesitated. They were loyal to Ramananda, and if they died, they knew he would take care of their families.

One of the Hard Men cut the chain to the gate with an enormous bolt cutter. Ganesh led Sam and his team of four men around the side of the office building until they found the front door. It was locked. A sledgehammer that one of the Hard Men carried made short work of it. The man looked like he weighed considerably less than the hammer he carried effortlessly over his shoulder.

The office building was deserted. It looked like no one had been inside in months. A film of dust covered every surface and it was undisturbed. There were no footprints, no reason to believe that the kidnappers had had time to rig booby traps or trip wires. Still and all, they moved cautiously through the building. Sam glanced at his watch. They had nine minutes.

A central corridor led through the building with offices and conference rooms on either side. They swept each room as they passed. They could not afford to have an armed enemy behind them. At the far end of the hall was a set of double doors that was flush with the brick wall of the studio building. This was the point of entry. They had to assume it was locked or barred, but they would not be able to try it until it was showtime. Ganesh motioned to the Hard Man with the sledgehammer to stand ready.

Three minutes.

Sam stared at his watch, willing the second hand to move faster. At the ten-second mark, he motioned to the Hard Men to get ready. At the five-second mark, he counted down with his fingers.

The small man with the big hammer swung at the locking mechanism at the center of the double doors.

The doors exploded inward on their hinges. The man with the sledgehammer crouched down to one side as the Hard Men carrying the shotguns jumped through, firing blindly into the room.

Sam pulled the revolver from his waistband and followed them.

The room inside was cavernous, but well lit. Moviemaking equipment was piled up everywhere. An enormous mockup of a Sena Dynasty Hindu temple dominated the soundstage.

"Lena!" he called, searching the room. He did not see his daughter, but he did spot a steel box in the center of the studio painted army green. The bomb? That was for later.

The chatter of automatic weapons fire coming from the direction of the temple was a stark reminder that they would first have to earn the right to worry about the bomb.

Sam gripped the revolver and looked for a target. He thought he saw a bearded figure outlined in a window in one of the temple's turrets. He took a shot, but it was a long shot for a handgun and Sam was hardly an expert marksman. There were five shots left in the gun.

The throaty cough of a shotgun coming from behind the temple told Sam that Vishnu's team had found a way in.

Sam took shelter behind a bulky camera and looked to see how the enemy was covering the front door that Shiva's team would assault at any moment.

The Hard Man standing ten feet to Sam's right raised his pistol at something up above, but the bottom half of his face disintegrated before he could take a shot. Sam looked up and he could see someone on the catwalk dressed in a white *shalwar kameez*. Pakistanis? Sam shot twice at him and missed.

Three.

The Pakistani on the catwalk recognized the new threat and turned, swinging his Kalashnikov around to center on Sam's chest.

Sam dove to the left just as the front door slammed open and two shotgun-wielding Hard Men jumped through. He felt rather than heard the Kalashnikov rounds that slammed into the floor no more than six inches from his head. Chips of broken concrete lacerated his cheek.

The Hard Men concentrated their fire on the catwalk, and Sam saw the bearded jihadi spin in place and fall over the rail. He hit the floor with a dull thud and one of the Hard Men moved in quickly to claim the Kalashnikov that was still in his hands.

Sam's job was not to kill jihadis. He had to find Lena.

As the fighting descended into chaos, he moved along the wall calling her name.

He could not see Vanalika anywhere either, and he hoped that she had decided to stay outside with Ramananda.

The Pakistanis had set up the temple as a strong point. The Hard Men had to assault the position as though they were attempting some kind of medieval siege.

Sam saw two more Hard Men go down, caught by automatic weapons fire. The Dalit could not match the jihadis' firepower, but it was apparent even to Sam that the attackers had the defenders outnumbered. They were taking casualties, but they were pushing the Pakistanis hard.

An explosion ripped through one group of Hard Men who had gathered together to charge the defended temple. Men screamed, and Sam saw one young Dalit street tough choking on his own blood.

Sam did not want to think about what might happen if a grenade went off near the big steel box in the middle of the room.

One of the Dalit attackers went to the aid of the boy who had been injured in the grenade explosion. Sam was surprised to see that it was Ramananda. His love of Lena, Sam knew, was strong. It was why he had come. But if Rama had come inside, where was Vanalika?

A bearded man wearing a *taqiyah* prayer cap popped up in one of the windows of the temple and aimed an AK-47 at Ramananda. Sam fired two shots at the jihadi, forcing him to take cover before he could shoot at his friend.

He had one bullet left.

When the temple fell, it fell from behind. Vishnu's team succeeded in driving the Pakistanis out from the cover of the fiber-glass set.

Sam counted three Pakistanis who escaped from the temple and took shelter behind a stack of wooden crates. Sam thought one of them looked like the man he had seen in the driver's license photo from the wallet that Nandi had acquired.

There was a break in the shooting, a pause as men stopped to reload and catch their breath.

Into that pause came a single gunshot directed at the ceiling that seemed to demand attention.

Everyone in the room turned to look. Sam saw Lena coming out from behind the temple. She was not alone. Vanalika was with her.

It took a moment for Sam's brain to process what he was seeing.

Vanalika—his friend, his ally, his lover—was standing behind his daughter with an arm wrapped around her throat and a pistol pointed at her head.

00:33

You're one of them, aren't you, Vee," Sam said sadly. "One of the Sons of Ashoka. The Indian Stoics."

"I'm a patriot, Sam. And I'm not hung up on labels. But, broadly speaking, yes. So put the guns down all of you or I will put a bullet through the skull of this beautiful girl . . . and that would be terribly sad."

Sam was pointing the revolver at Vanalika's head. It was a makeable shot, for someone who knew what he was doing and who had an accurate weapon. Sam had already missed with his first five shots and the margin of error had been measured in feet rather than in inches. Moreover, Vanalika was turning side to side, making it hard to aim.

He had no doubt that she was serious. Vanalika was nothing if not fiercely determined, and for the first time, Sam could see the glint of fanaticism in her eyes. These were the mysterious depths that Sam had sensed in Vanalika. How well had he really known her? Not well at all, it seemed. Vanalika, he could see, was in the grip of a belief greater than herself, greater than Lena or Sam or the untold number of innocents whose lives she was prepared to sacrifice.

Sam did not lower his gun. Neither did the Dalit who were locked in a kind of Mexican standoff with the jihadis. They all stood there frozen in an absurd tableau, no one daring to move or break the delicate balance of terror that had been struck. None of the Dalit had an angle on Vanalika as good as Sam's. It was on him.

"Was it all an act, Vanalika? Were you using me from the very beginning?" Sam was stalling for time, but he also desperately wanted to know the answer to this question. Not two minutes ago, he would have given his life for this woman. Now he wanted nothing more than to take hers.

"No, Sam. You weren't important until you made yourself a problem. No, I genuinely like you, which is what makes this so hard, but I love India. Country comes first, I'm afraid."

"For love of country you would kill hundreds of thousands of your own people? That's insane. You must see that."

"You're exaggerating. This is a relatively low-yield weapon. Models put the death toll at well under one hundred thousand, and thanks to our American friends, we have run that through one of the most sophisticated computers in the world. India can spare a few tens of thousands. It's a rounding error, really. Now, put the gun down." Her expression hardened and she pressed the barrel even more tightly to Lena's temple.

"You'll just kill us all if we drop our guns. Your big Sikh friend sure wasn't looking to talk."

"That wasn't my decision. It was a mistake, a waste of valuable material. I can still use you and you're worth considerably more to us alive than dead. But if you don't believe me, go ahead and shoot. Maybe you'll kill me, but I think it's more likely that you'll kill your little girl. I don't think you'll take that risk."

Aim true, Ramananda had told him. Squeeze the trigger. And what you are aiming at will die.

Sam's finger tightened on the trigger. He held the gun with both hands, the way the State Department had taught him in Crash-and-Bang. In the training course, they had shot at paper targets. This was profoundly different.

It was Spears's damn trolleyology test made real. What if you could sacrifice one to save five? What if you could sacrifice one to save one hundred thousand?

What if the one was your daughter? Your only daughter.

He couldn't do it.

Sam looked at Lena. He had been so focused on Vanalika that he had not really looked at her. He could see she was scared, but she would not let herself panic or lose control.

God, she looked like her mother.

He felt a warmth flood his chest at the thought.

"Lena, baby . . ."

"Dad."

"I love you."

Sam started to lower the gun.

Vanalika's left eye exploded. She arched backward and collapsed to the floor. A pool of blood framed her head like a halo. Lena fell to the ground as well, gasping for air. Sam ran to her and gathered her into his arms even as he was dimly aware of the exchange of gunfire around him.

. . .

Khan saw the opening he had hoped for, a brief window of possibility. There were only three of them left standing: Khan, Jadoon, and the little turd Umar. He knew what he had to do.

Without the slightest compunction, he shot Vanalika in the back of the head. Before her body hit the ground, Khan had pivoted and put two rounds from the SIG Sauer into Jadoon's midsection. The big jihadi leader looked at him as if seeing him for the first time. He tried to train his Kalashnikov on Khan, but there was no strength in his hands. Jadoon fell to his knees and then slumped forward as though in prayer.

Umar was as quick as the weasel that he resembled. He beat Khan to the draw. The bullet from his Kalashnikov shattered Khan's forearm. The SIG Sauer fell from Khan's nerveless fingers to clatter on the concrete.

I have failed, Khan thought. *I am dead and my mission is over.*

But Khan did not die.

A dozen bullets from the guns of the Hard Men slammed into Umar. The jihadi crumpled to the ground as if he were made of straw.

The Hard Men pointed their weapons at Khan, who again was certain that he would die and who was again spared.

"Stop!" Ramananda called, freezing the Hard Men in place. "I don't think this man is our enemy."

Allah be praised, Khan thought.

His arm was spurting blood. The bullet had severed the radial artery. He might not need to be shot again to die.

Khan stripped off his shirt and wrapped it around his right forearm as tightly as he could.

The pain was white hot and Khan feared for a moment that he might pass out. He felt nauseous and dizzy. His field of vision had contracted. The edges were fuzzy and gray. A disinterested part of his consciousness recognized that he was sinking into shock. But he needed to check on Lena to make sure that she was unhurt.

Lena was sitting up now. A man Khan assumed was her father was wiping bits of blood and brain off the side of her face. Her breath was coming in rapid gasps.

"Lena," he said gently. "Are you hurt?"

She looked up at him and shook her head, but did not try to speak. Khan felt that her being alive validated every choice he had made no matter what happened next.

"Who are you?" the man kneeling beside her asked.

"I'm an American," Khan said. "I'm a government agent who works—used to work," he corrected himself—"directly for White House Chief of Staff Solomon Braithwaite."

"Which agency?" the man asked.

"One you've never heard of. One that doesn't exist. How is she?"

"Unhurt. Thank you. Thank you for what you did."

"You're her father?"

"Sam Trainor."

"Kamran Khan."

"You need to get that arm taken care of."

The simple act of breathing was a struggle. Her lungs did not seem to work right, and the numb tingling in her hands and feet made it feel as though they were being deprived of oxygen. Lena let the muscle spasms run their course, let her breathing slow on its own, let the feeling return to her fingers. It was the second time in three hours that someone had held a gun to her head and threatened to kill her. It was not the kind of thing that you could get used to.

She clung to her father as he wiped the blood and slime from her face and hair. He had come for her. Somehow, she knew that he would.

A part of her listened to the exchange between Khan and her father. He was not one of them. Somehow, she had known that too.

Khan was hurt, something about his arm. She hoped it was not serious.

Lena pulled back from her father far enough that she could turn and look at him eye to eye. She was breathing almost normally now.

"I knew you'd find me," she said.

"Every time, honey. You're my girl."

Lena looked to Khan and saw that the erstwhile jihadi was sitting on the floor. His face was gray. His clothes were red with blood.

Lena released her grip on her father and struggled to her feet. She was a little unsteady, but she made it to Khan's side and kneeled down alongside him.

"Kamran," she said. "You did it. You saved us. Now we need to get you to a hospital."

"Lena," her father said gently. He was standing behind her and put one hand on her shoulder. "We'll get help for Khan, but first we need to do something about what's in the box."

The expression on her father's face was grave. Lena tried to sound reassuring and confident in her response.

"It's okay, Dad. I saw the timer. We have almost two days before it's supposed to go off."

"I don't think that's right. Everything I saw, everything that led me here, makes me think that the target is Rangarajan. He's here in this city for another couple of hours at most. They wouldn't miss this window."

Lena looked at Khan.

"Is that right, Kamran? Do you know what the plan was?"

"We never talked about the bomb or the goals of the operation. We followed orders. Jadoon was the only one who knew the big picture." Khan nodded his head in the general direction of the big jihadi he had shot after he had killed Vanalika. "But Lena's right about the timer. I watched Adnan, the physicist, set it."

"And where is he now?"

"Gone," Khan said. "I don't know where."

"Like a rat jumping ship?"

"Maybe."

"Come with me, Lena," her father urged. "Let's look inside the box. When we're sure that's secure, we can figure out who to call for help."

After what they had been through, Lena could not doubt her father. How could she ever have doubted him? If he had reason to be afraid, then so did she. The box sat in the middle of the room, undisturbed by the firefight that had so recently raged around it. Sam lifted the lid. Lena could see the confusing jumble of wires and circuit boards that made it look as though the bomb had been turned inside out.

"Why did they do this?" she asked.

"Adnan came here from Lahore with instructions from Masood," Khan said. Lena turned and saw that he was standing up and making his way painfully over to the bomb. He held his injured arm up against his chest, and Lena could see blood leaking through the improvised bandage. He needed a hospital urgently. "He made the modifications, allegedly because the warhead was configured for airburst and controlled by an altimeter rather than a timer. He also entered some kind of code that is supposed to make it tamper proof. The new circuitry is deliberately complex and, according to that little shit Adnan at least, loaded with traps. Doing anything to the bomb without the right code or cutting the wrong circuit is supposed to trigger the warhead. I doubt very much that that was part of the original design."

Lena looked at the circuitry. It was a mess. Figuring it out would take considerable time. The digital timer affixed to the side of the bomb offered some reassurance even as it counted down the seconds. The angry red letters flashed 02:00:25:47.

"The timer shows a little more than two days before the bomb is supposed to go off," she said to her father. "Do you think it's a trick of some sort?"

"I think it's a lie. It's one thing to be a martyr in the abstract. It's quite another to watch the last seconds of your life count down. The only one who knows for sure is this man Adnan, and he's mysteriously disappeared. Rangarajan is the target. He's here now. He won't be here two days and twenty-five minutes from now. Something's not right."

"Fuck me." What little color was left in Khan's face seemed to drain away.

"What is it?" Sam asked urgently. "What do you know?"

"There were two pieces to the timer when Adnan assembled it," Khan explained. "I saw him fit them together like a sandwich. Two layers, each with a screen. Why would he do that, unless . . ."

"They show a different time," Sam said, finishing his thought.

Once more, Lena reached inside the bomb as if she were a surgeon reaching inside a patient's chest. Her hands were shaking.

Calm down.

She pulled her hands back, squeezed them into fists, and then extended them as far as she could. A few repetitions of this exercise helped dampen the shakes. If she pulled the wrong wire loose, it would be the end of everything.

Patiently, carefully, Lena examined the timer. It was chunky, thicker than it needed to be. A line bisected the device all around the outer edge, and the connecting wires were attached to the lower half of the timer. At the top right corner, she found a small notch. It was just big enough for her fingernail. She hooked one nail into the notch and pulled up. With a sharp click, the top of the timer detached. It was battery-powered and not connected to the rest of the circuitry. Underneath, there was a second timer. It was counting down and Lena had no doubt that this one was real.

00:00:21:19

00:00:21:18

00:00:21:17

Oh God.

"Adnan knew," Khan said. "Masood was going to kill us all." He was not surprised. The HeM leader was as cold-blooded as a cobra.

"Sure looks like it," Sam said grimly. "And he may get his way yet."

Khan kneeled down next to Lena and looked intently at the weapon in the box. His arm throbbed, but there was nothing he could do about that. "Lena, I worked on a bomb-disposal unit with the U.S. Army. Let me help you."

"I'll take any ideas you have," Lena said.

"I think most of the complexity here is just for show. It's smoke.

The timing circuit should be relatively simple and straightforward if you can identify it. Remember that it needs to link into that timer."

"What are the buttons on the timer?" Lena asked.

Khan looked where she was pointing. There was a row of ten black buttons along the bottom edge of the timer labeled 0 through 9 and one larger green button with a Greek delta, the engineering symbol for change.

The timer itself flashed 00:00:19:37.

"I think that's to enter the code. It's a PAL, a permissive action link. You need the code before making any modifications to the bomb. In a normal situation, the PAL is supposed to keep someone from arming the bomb without authorization. Adnan has rewired it so that you need the authority to disarm it. If you don't know the code, you can't deactivate it."

"So what do we do?"

"I don't know. Why don't you take a look at the circuitry and see if you can figure out how to stop this thing. I'll see if I can work out a way to get around the code."

Khan and Lena knelt shoulder-to-shoulder beside the box as they searched desperately for a way to halt the countdown. Blood from Khan's wounded arm stained Lena's clothes.

The timer was remorseless and implacable as it counted down the seconds.

00:00:18:12

00:00:18:11

With his good hand, Khan examined the timer, looking for some kind of answer in the physical object. It offered few clues. The timer itself was a solid block of steel and glass. There were no markings on the casing and no instructions. When he hit the green button, the screen would toggle back and forth between the count-down and a row of nine blank boxes where Khan would have to enter the code he did not know.

Good security practice would have been to use a random series of numbers as the code. If this is what Adnan and Masood had done, they were all as good as dead. But Khan did not believe that the code was random. Adnan had looked in his little black note-book before entering the code. He had gotten his instructions from Masood and Masood, Khan knew, was a mystic. He believed in the raw power of numbers. The numerical key code for this—the Hand's most ambitious operation; perhaps the most ambitious operation by a nongovernmental actor in all of human history—would not be left to chance. Masood would not accept that. It would not be a random number. It would be carefully chosen. Symbolic. An act of worship.

Khan tried to recall the details of what Masood had told him about numerology. Masood chose him for the mission as a good-luck charm with the right combination of letters in his name. Could his name be the key? The mullah had his own unique numerological system, and there was no way to know the values he had assigned to the alphabet. Moreover, Kamran Khan did not have the right number of letters. There were ten letters in his name and nine digits in the code. It didn't fit.

Nineteen was a critical number, he remembered. *Over it are nineteen. And we have set none but angels as the guardians of the hell-fire.* That's what the sura said, and the code was certainly the guardian of hellfire. But again, it didn't fit, not neatly. If he entered the number 19 five times, he would leave a dangling "1" at the end of the string. It was not, Khan understood, beautiful. The code would have nine digits. It could not be split evenly in half. But it could be divided.

Nine.

Three times three.

Could it be?

The answer clicked into place. There was no way to test it, but it had to be right. It felt right. It was all that they had. If Khan was wrong, the city of Mumbai would die. They would all die.

"I know the code," Khan said to Lena. *I think.*

She nodded, but did not respond. There was a thin sheen of sweat on her forehead.

Lena was at a loss. The circuitry was so complex and so dense that she could not understand it. She could not *see* it. It had always been easy for her to visualize systems. That had always been her strength as an engineer. But she had never before tried to apply this skill to a system that was deliberately obtuse. Most of the loops she identified and tracked were connected only to themselves. Some looked like traps, triggers that would set the bomb off if the circuits were disrupted. What she could not find was the central circuit, the one that controlled communication between the timer and the warhead.

Lena looked inside the bomb, maybe there was something there, a more obvious vulnerability that she could exploit. But there was not, at least not that she could see.

She looked at the timer. That was a mistake, the equivalent of a rock climber halfway up the cliff face looking down.

00:00:12:35

00:00:12:34

00:00:12:33

I can't see it. Where is it?

"I know the code," she heard Khan say.

She nodded. *That's good. But it's meaningless if I can't figure this out. There isn't time. I need more time.*

00:00:11:49

Her hands started to shake again slightly with the strain.

Khan must have seen it. He reached out with his good hand and took hold of one of hers. His grip was strong, the skin smooth and cool.

Lena closed her eyes and took a deep breath. When she opened them, the circuitry in front of her was less of a tangled mass than it was a set of complete loops and circuits laid one on top of the other. She could see it. She could see the central trunk and the wires she would need to cut to interrupt the critical circuit. It was clear to her. If Khan had, in fact, solved the puzzle of the code, she could deactivate the bomb.

And they had better hurry.

00:00:08:35

00:00:08:34

"Okay," she said. "I'm ready. Let's do it."

Khan used the green button to switch from the countdown screen to the row of nine empty squares. They blinked at him impassively, arrogantly. *Do you think you can defeat me? I contain one billion possibilities . . . and only one truth. Do you really believe you can find me?*

He entered the code.

786-786-786.

The Basmala. *Bismillah ir-Rahman ir-Rahim.* In the name of

God, the most gracious, the most merciful. Masood had called it the most sublimely beautiful of numbers, representative of the divine. "Never forget this," he had told Khan, as they dined on red beans and rice. Khan had not. The HeM leader believed in magical numbers and 786 was the most magical of them all. It had to be right.

The screen went blank. For a moment, Khan expected the bomb to explode. *Would he see it? Would he feel anything as his body was atomized? How would he explain his failure to Allah? Was this, in fact, His will?* Khan felt the icy grip of doubt.

The screen flashed back to life.

CODE ACCEPTED.

Khan could breathe again. He was ashamed of his doubt, of his weakness. It was not Allah's will that a city should die.

He pressed the green button and toggled back to the countdown screen.

00:00:06:27

00:00:06:26

He looked at Lena.

She was composed and beautiful.

"Finish this." With his one good hand, Khan pulled the razor-sharp knife out of his boot and handed it to her. When she looked at him, he could see the doubt in her eyes that mirrored his own.

"Do not worry. You know what to do. Your instincts are right and Allah will guide your hand."

Lena took the knife and picked up one of the loops of wire coated in pale blue plastic. She crimped the wire in a half loop and inserted the tip of the knife. Khan put his hand lightly on her shoulder.

"Make the cut."

Lena drew the edge of the knife up inside the loop and severed the wire. Moving quickly, she picked up a red wire that ran parallel to the blue wire and sliced through it neatly.

The timer flashed.

00:00:05:17

00:00:05:17

00:00:05:17

Her father hugged her. There were tears in his eyes and an expression that Lena recognized as neither relief nor joy but rather pride.

Khan slumped down beside the box. His complexion was pallid. He was dying.

"We need to get an ambulance for him," she said.

Ramananda pulled a phone out of his pocket.

"I will call one now," he promised. "We will meet it out by the gate."

"Who do we call about the bomb?" she asked her father.

"I don't know," he conceded. "The people who orchestrated your kidnapping call themselves the Stoics. They have high-level government connections and access to the raw feed from ECHELON. I don't know who to trust in either the Indian or the American government at this point." He looked at Vanalika's body, and there was a deep sadness about him that Lena knew would take a long time to heal, if it ever would.

"These Stoics are all national-level politicians? Not state or local?"

"So far as I know."

"Then I know what to do."

"What?"

"I'm using Uncle Ramananda's phone . . . and I'm calling city hall."

PHILADELPHIA, PENNSYLVANIA
SEPTEMBER 15, 1777

00:34

T*he war is not going especially well, is it?"*

It was the kind of understatement for which Colonel Benjamin Tallmadge was justly famous. George Washington's army had been soundly defeated at Brandywine Creek only four days earlier, and William Howe's redcoats were advancing on Philadelphia with the grim inevitability of a river rising to break its banks.

Tallmadge sat with two other men in the back room of the Bull and Barrel drinking weak ale out of pewter mugs. Although the Bull was considered a respectable establishment, there were rooms upstairs where at least a few of the barmaids plied a parallel and considerably more lucrative trade. Doubtlessly, Tallmadge thought, they would service the British officers with equal enthusiasm once the redcoats took the city, even if the more patriotic among them could be counted on to charge the occupiers double the rate for the Continentals.

Officially, Benjamin Tallmadge was an officer in the regular Continental Army attached to the Second Light Dragoons. In reality, he was the head of General Washington's military intelligence operation and a spymaster of some skill. His companions at the Bull were Robert Livingston, an influential New York politician, and Hugh Mulligan, an Irish trader who owned a controlling interest in a small fleet that operated just barely on the legitimate side of the triangle trade in molasses, rum, and slaves. They were all three patriots, and they shared a growing conviction that the Continental Army was losing the war.

"Brandywine was a bloody disaster," Livingston said vehemently, snatching the bait that Tallmadge had dangled in front of him. "How many days until Howe marches into Philadelphia?"

"Two weeks at the outside," Mulligan offered, his County Cork brogue softened only slightly by twenty years in the New World.

"Desperate times, desperate measures," Tallmadge suggested.

Livingston eyed him skeptically.

"What exactly do you have in mind, Colonel? Your invitation was circumspect to the point of conspiratorial."

Tallmadge raised an eyebrow.

"Was it now? I do apologize for that. It's so hard to know who to trust these days. Just look at what happened to my man Nathan Hale. Betrayed by his own cousin and hanged by the neck until dead. Poor boy."

"So, what is it then, lad?" Mulligan asked. "Something that involves a little trading, I'd wager. Otherwise, what would I be doing here?"

"This is partly about your ships," Tallmadge admitted, "and your financial resources, Livingston. But, ultimately, it is more about you. What I have to suggest requires a certain intestinal fortitude, a willingness to think through an issue with clarity and act as pure logic dictates in the finest tradition of Pericles or Zeno. In this regard, I find both sentimentality and a surfeit of religiosity to be considerable handicaps. And I do not believe that either of you gentlemen suffers from one or the other of these maladies."

Mulligan and Livingston nodded at this characterization, acknowledging the accuracy of Tallmadge's assessment. Both men were classically educated and understood the allusion to the Athenian luminaries.

"We're listening," Mulligan offered.

"We are at some risk of losing this war," Tallmadge said, "and most likely hanging for it in consequence. But there may be a way to tip the balance and hurt our enemy sore in a manner that he does not expect, albeit at a not inconsiderable cost to ourselves."

"What is the nature of our mysterious benefactor?" Livingstone asked.

"Smallpox."

"An indiscriminate killer," Mulligan said, shaking his head. "It would lay low at least as many bluecoats as red."

"Not if Washington can be persuaded to inoculate the army in advance of the outbreak," Tallmadge explained. "I would propose to import blankets, linen, and mattresses from the hospitals at Guadeloupe that even now are filled to overflow with the victims of a smallpox outbreak. We consign the shipment to the British port authorities in New York and here in Philadelphia, and then help our enemy bury his dead with a glad heart."

"Washington would never agree to this," Livingston said dismissively.

"No, he would not. Which is why I will tell him that my spies have learned that the British are planning to use smallpox against us. I am confident that I can persuade the general to order the entire Continental Army inoculated against the disease and to even accept a certain necessary rate of fatalities among those treated."

"And what of the civilian population?" Livingston continued. "Those without the resources or organization to effect quarantine in the period when the inoculated are most infectious."

"There will be losses among the civilians," Tallmadge admitted.

"Maybe even considerable losses. But their sacrifices will be in the service of liberty."

"And I will lose the crew of the ship that carries the consignment," Mulligan said.

"Almost to a man," Tallmadge agreed. The negotiations began in earnest.

It took time, but by nightfall, the three had agreed on the outlines of a plan. There was only one more matter to be resolved.

"You should know that I do no business in Guadeloupe," Mulligan said. "I have no connections there to make the necessary arrangements."

"I have already contracted with a young man whom I consider sufficiently resourceful to serve in that capacity."

"What is his family name?" Livingston asked.

"Smith," Tallmadge replied. "Should he prove equal to the task, it may well prove that we should wish to procure his services again. Our new nation will, from time to time, find itself in need of the kind of guidance and clear thinking that only men such as we can provide."

"True," Livingston agreed. "So very true."

CUMBERLAND, VIRGINIA
MAY 4

00:35

I t was raining and the roads were slippery. Spears was glad that he had taken the Mercedes rather than the Porsche. The 911 was a beautiful piece of machinery, but it didn't handle well in the rain. An unobtrusive brown sign with gold lettering marked the entrance to the OAKHURST CONFERENCE CENTER. Spears turned off the rural highway and followed the narrow road to the main building.

The Oakhurst was one of several conference centers and sylvan retreats of indeterminate ownership scattered across central Virginia and Maryland's tobacco country. The especially curious would find in the county records that the Oakhurst was the property of a holding company registered in Richmond that was itself a subsidiary of a Singapore-based shell corporation that had a history of association with the Central Intelligence Agency. Among the Oakhurst's less public features was a safe house where more than a few Eastern Bloc defectors had spent their first six or so months under guard in the land of liberty.

It was unusual for the Governing Council to meet outside the

Beltway, but these were unusual times. The failure of Cold Harbor had left the Stoics more exposed than they had ever been in their history. They were suddenly vulnerable. The klieg lights of a government investigation were probing the shadows that they had made their home.

Spears drove up to the front of the main building and parked. Like the other buildings on the Oakhurst's expansive and well-manicured grounds, it was built in a faux Tudor style with a steeply pitched slate roof. It looked expensive, and since the ultimate source of financing was the CIA's black budget, it almost certainly was. The Oakhurst was a little twee for Spears's taste, but they would not be here long.

The staff had made themselves scarce. Even the cleaning crew at the Oakhurst was cleared Top Secret/UMBRA, but there was no point in taking chances. The members of the Council could pour their own damn coffee.

The expressions around the table in the main conference room were grim. All of the Governors appreciated how much danger they were in. Commander Weeder was already there, sitting with the other backbenchers in the outer row right next to the door. Spears nodded at him as he entered the room, and Weeder acknowledged his existence with the slightest movement of his head. His scarred face was otherwise immobile and all but impossible to read.

Legal and Vice were the last to arrive, just a few minutes behind Spears. The Chairman quickly gaveled the meeting to order.

"This may be our last session for some time," he began. "The Lord administration has rediscovered its spine after the fiasco in Mumbai and is trying to walk the cat back on our operation. The odds that they will succeed in following the trail back to this group are not negligible."

"What happened in India was absolutely unacceptable," Plans said indignantly. "Moreover, it was amateur. We need to do our own internal assessment to establish accountability."

About half of those at the table looked over at Spears expectantly. He was Operations and it was on him to defend his actions. For the Stoics, "amateur" was among the most vicious epithets.

"Mumbai was a setback," Spears agreed. "At first we thought the problem was with Ashoka, that the Indians had been penetrated. That frankly wouldn't have been a huge shock. Their OPSEC was always a weak link. But it looks like the problem was with our instrument rather than our partners. Somehow, Braithwaite got an agent inside the Hand of the Prophet. That agent insinuated himself into the operation and disrupted it from the inside. After the fact, it appears that this same agent was able to connect the Indian services with the Ashoka leadership. Our Indian counterparts were picked up in sequence. Ashoka has, for all intents and purposes, ceased to exist.

"There was no way we could have foreseen that, and we could not vet individual members of the HeM team. The whole idea was to do this through cutouts so we would have distance and deniability, but we paid a price in terms of control and visibility. It's something we should factor into future planning."

"There will be no future planning," Plans said vehemently. "Your fuckup has left us bare-assed in the wind and the president's people are crawling all over this. We'll be lucky if we don't all end up sharing a maximum-security wing in Leavenworth. If we're unlucky and they're ballsy enough, they'll just kill us and feed us to Lord's fucking labradoodle."

"One thing at a time," Legal interjected. "We can still benefit from a more complete understanding of what happened before we write our own obituaries. For example, how did Braithwaite get control of his own stable of operatives? He was the White House chief of staff, not the head of CIA."

"We're still trying to piece this all together," Spears replied, "but it looks like Braithwaite was not only aware of our existence he had also picked up enough data to realize that a major operation was under way. He didn't trust the established intelligence agencies and had good reasons for that." Spears nodded in Reports's direction.

"Braithwaite's been around D.C. for a long time. He knows how things work. Our understanding is that he managed to carve off a piece of the black budget to set up his own in-house intelligence agency and recruited operatives who reported directly and exclusively to him. One of his agents was assigned to penetrate the HeM, which was one of the prime suspects as a subcontractor in our operation. He wasn't the only one. Braithwaite had other agents in other likely organizations. Not all succeeded. Not a few are dead. Our misfortune was that the agent in HeM seems to have been especially resourceful and was able to continue his mission even after the line back to Braithwaite was . . . cut."

"Clearly, then, none of this can be laid at your doorstep," the Vice Chair said sarcastically. "What about your own little renegade? Trainor. You deny all culpability for him as well?"

"Trainor was a nuisance," Spears acknowledged, "and a threat. But he was a containable threat. If it hadn't been for Braithwaite's agent inside the Hand, the ghost in the machine, Trainor would not have been a problem."

"But he was, wasn't he?" Vice continued, evidently unmollified by Spears's cavalier dismissal. "He was more than a fly in the ointment. He brought armed men to ground zero and started a firefight with the jihadis, killing our liaison to Ashoka in the process.

Do I have that about right? And this was your man. You hired him. You gave him access to the Panoptes material. Do I have that about right as well?"

Once, at the early stage of his career before he had discovered that his real talent for combat lay in the bureaucratic and political battles of Washington, Spears had been deployed in an anonymous war zone in some steamy tropical hell when a sniper had zeroed in on his unit. For Spears, it was like a red X had been painted on the back of his head, and no matter which way he turned, the invisible sniper was sighting in on the target. He had not enjoyed that sensation, and he had never forgotten it. For the first time in a long time, he felt the stirrings of that same feeling again. A little tickle of fear, an unscratchable itch at the base of his skull.

"Argus Systems hired Trainor because he was the best South Asia specialist available on the market and we needed credible product to provide cover for our extracurriculars. At the time, we were unaware of his relationship with Vanalika Chandra, as was Ashoka. It was unfortunate, but it was not foreseeable."

"Unforeseen and unforeseeable are not synonyms," Finance chimed in, and Spears could feel the loop tightening. "It seems to me that you were in a position early on to identify Trainor as a problem and nip that problem in the bud. You failed and the debacle in Mumbai was a direct result of that failure."

"It was the Commander and the operations group who failed in that respect," Spears insisted, and he hated himself for the whiny note that he could not quite keep out of his voice. He was a SEAL, dammit, not some grade-schooler. "The Council ordered the ops group to take care of Trainor. Experienced black-ops professionals went up against a middle-aged academic and failed. That was most definitely unforeseeable as well as unforeseen."

"That failure has been recognized," the Chairman observed. "Those responsible have been separated from the organization."

"Separated?" Spears asked.

"Separated," the Chairman confirmed.

"There is clearly a rich vein of self-criticism to mine here," the Vice Chair said, "but this is not an accountability review board. We need to consider our course of action over the short and medium term, and address the clear and present threat posed by the Lord administration's aggressive investigation. The floor is open for suggestions."

There was a pause. The only sound was the scratching of the Librarian's pen as his note taking caught up with the conversation.

"I think we should begin with a formal decision to terminate Cold Harbor," Legal said, breaking the silence. "The operation has become a liability. It was ambitious. It was in the finest tradition of our organization, but we need to cut the cord and make sure that Lord's people can't follow it back to us."

There was a murmur of assent around the table.

"Legal is correct," Plans offered. "The organization comes first. Cold Harbor should be canceled."

"Let's vote on it for the record," the Chairman said.

Spears voted yes.

It was unanimous.

"I don't think that's enough," Legal continued. "Throughout the history of the Republic, our contributions to our nation's health and well-being have been anonymous. It is that very anonymity that has enabled us to play the role we have at critical junctures. Now that anonymity is in danger of being stripped away. The public that benefits from our guidance and oversight would not understand what we do . . . nor would they welcome it. I am proposing an operational pause in all of our activities. No operations, no meetings, no recruitment, no communications of any kind, nothing that the investigation can lock in on. That is the only way to preserve the capability we represent for the future. If we are ever exposed, I doubt very much that anything similar could again be assembled. New safeguards would be put in place in the policy process specifically to prevent that."

"I agree with that," Reports said. "There's the question not only of institutional and organizational vulnerability, but also of personal risk. It's better that we go to ground and wait for an operating environment more conducive to our activities."

"How much time are we talking about here?" Finance asked. "Months? Years?"

"Years, for certain," Reports replied. "Decades, if necessary. The logic of the situation mandates patience and fortitude. At a minimum, we should be prepared to outwait Emily Lord and her left-wing administration."

"Lord is only two years into her first term," the Vice Chair observed. "If she wins a second, and her poll numbers look pretty good right now, that's a minimum six-year hiatus. Can we afford that?"

"We've been around for more than two centuries," Legal replied. "If we aren't greedy, we'll make it through the next two in a position to make a difference. But only if we aren't greedy."

"What about the Indians?" Vice asked. "Can the Ashoka people finger any of us when they crack under questioning?"

"No," Reports insisted. "The link between us and Ashoka was Chandra and she's unlikely to break. Being dead and all."

It was gallows humor. No one bothered to fake a smile.

"What about Argus Systems?" Finance asked, looking pointedly at Spears. "That would seem to be the most obvious point of entry for the investigators."

"That's a reasonable concern," Spears acknowledged. Unconsciously, he ran one hand across the back of his head, trying to brush off the imaginary target.

"What have you done about the computer systems?"

"Scrubbed clean and wiped down to the bare operating systems. There's nothing there."

"There's no such thing," Reports said contemptuously. "Not for people who know what they're doing." It was clear from her tone that this group did not encompass Garret Spears.

"Argus needs to be removed from the equation, including the physical plant," the Vice Chair suggested. "I know someone who can take care of that at a reasonable rate."

"I propose we vote on that," Legal said.

"Seconded."

It was unanimous.

"What about personnel?" Legal asked. "What connections are there from Argus that could lead back to us?"

"Just the Commander and Ops," the Vice Chair replied. "No one else was looped in on Cold Harbor or the organization."

"The Commander can disappear," the Chairman suggested. "A new face. A new identity. We have done it before, and the Commander has a unique skill set that we will almost certainly want to draw on in the future once we resume a normal operational tempo. Would someone care to make a motion?"

"I move that we authorize the Commander's disappearance and make available the necessary financing to support that operation." Finance made the motion and it would be his responsibility to identify the financial assets that would be employed.

"Seconded," said Vice.

Spears voted yes.

Again, it was unanimous.

"Which leaves Operations," Reports said, with just a hint of regret in her voice.

"I could disappear like Weeder," Spears said. Even to himself he sounded desperate. He had also, he realized, violated Council protocol by speaking Weeder's name out loud. It was one more strike against him. "I could make it to Mexico and use that plastic surgeon we contracted with for the Bolivians. I have contacts in South America, a network. No one would ever find me."

"It seems an unnecessary risk," Legal commented.

Spears pushed his chair back slightly from the table, calculating the distance to the doorway and wondering if they had disabled his car. He was too late. Weeder's meaty hand settled on his left shoulder, and Spears felt something cold and hard pressed up against his neck right over the carotid artery. He did not need to look to know what it was. A jet injector. Powered by a cartridge of compressed gas, the jet injector would drive a narrow stream of liquid straight through the skin without the need for a needle. Charged with sodium thiopental or another fast-acting barbiturate, it was the weapon of choice for SEALs in snatch-and-grab operations. The jet injector could also be charged with other drugs that served other purposes.

There was nothing Spears could do. He was pinned at the table and Weeder had every conceivable advantage of position.

"I'm sorry, Ops," the Chairman said. "But while the talents that the Commander brings to the organization are all but irreplaceable, your particular abilities are more . . . shall we say . . . commonplace."

"I have important friends," Spears protested. "Congressmen. Committee chairs. People who matter in this town. You need me."

"You do understand," Plans said, "that there are fifteen other people in this room whose security and well-being are at risk as long as the Lord administration's investigation is focused on you. The math is really quite simple. If you could sacrifice one to save fifteen, why wouldn't that be the optimal solution?"

"The logic does seem unimpeachable," Finance added.

"Do we have a motion?" the Chairman asked.

For Spears, everything seemed be moving as slowly as though they were underwater. His mouth felt dry and cottony. Even if he had known how to plead his case effectively, he did not think he would be able to speak.

"I move that the current chief of operations be removed from his position on the Governing Council and then neutralized as a threat to the organization's future." Reports made the motion, but she seemed to take no pleasure in it.

"Seconded," said Plans, who did not bother to disguise his own eagerness.

"We will have a vote on the motion," the Chairman said. "Ops, at this point you are still a member of the Governing Council and entitled to vote, but I would ask that you do so by raising your left hand and I caution you to move slowly."

Spears voted no.

Otherwise, it was unanimous.

00:36

H ow's the arm?"

"Getting better. I've had three surgeries and the rehab's a
bear, but I'd be lying if I said it was the hardest thing I've
ever done."

Sam smiled at that.

"I'll bet."

The last time Sam had seen Kamran Khan, the American mole
in the HeM was being unceremoniously shoved into the back of a
Toyota panel van outfitted as an ambulance. One of the paramed-
ics had told Sam that Khan's chances were no better than 50/50.
Khan had beaten those odds, which were far from the longest he
had faced that day.

Khan's arm was out of the cast, but still in a sling. He had abandoned Pakistani dress in favor of a tan summer-weight suit. Sam
had to look closely to spot the slight bulge on the right side of his
suit jacket. Khan was armed, but he would have to draw with his
off hand for a while. His beard was trimmed short, and he wore

fashionable rectangular glasses with gold wire rims that made him look more like an art history teacher than a secret agent.

Sam's feelings about Khan were complicated. This was the man who had both kidnapped Lena and protected her; killed for the Hand of the Prophet and taken a bullet to save the city Sam loved. He was, at a minimum, a complex person.

"What do the doctors say?"

"They tell me I'll get back full use of the arm with three or four months of physical therapy. There's no nerve damage, so there shouldn't be any lasting effects."

"And then what?"

"Then it's back to work."

"Well, I'm glad you were able to make it today. Lena appreciates it as well."

"She's something else," Khan said admiringly.

"Yes, she is."

Sam could see his daughter standing about fifty feet away talking to one of the BMC officials. She laughed politely at something he said and lightly touched his arm. She would have been a hell of a diplomat. She was dressed formally in a sleeveless *choli* with a vermilion sari draped over her left arm. The chain across her throat was a thick braid of gold in three different colors. It had belonged to her mother, a gift from Sam. Her earrings were small golden hoops and there was a gold pin in her thick, lustrous hair that a high-end stylist had spent hours fussing with earlier that morning. He loved her so much and the knowledge of the danger she'd been in because of him clamped on to his heart like a vise. When he thought about what a near-run thing it had been, it was hard to breathe.

It was a sizeable crowd. There were at least several hundred people gathered alongside the freshly cleaned and scrubbed canal that divided the slum from the rest of Mumbai. Two square blocks on the Dharavi side of the bridge had been cleared and leveled. Half would be for new housing, a mixture of middle-income homes and subsidized apartments for the residents of the slum. The other half was set aside for a new school: the Janani Trainor Technical Academy.

In less than half an hour, Lena and the mayor of Mumbai would be breaking ground for the school construction with a gold-colored shovel. Until the school was built, Lena would continue to teach the children of Dharavi out of her old building, albeit with brand-new computer equipment donated by the city. What happened at the Hill Station Productions studio had been kept out of the newspapers, but the commissioner knew what Lena had done and just how close his city had come to annihilation. Approving a new, more sustainable plan for the development of Dharavi was the least he could do.

There would be time enough to speak with Lena later. Right now, he had some questions for Khan.

"I wanted to ask you about the status of the investigation into Argus and the Stoics. I've learned a few things over the last weeks, but this is all being kept very close and I suspect that your sources on this may be a little more direct than mine."

Khan smiled ruefully at that.

"That's probably true," he admitted.

"So what's the latest?"

"It's not easy. The president has given the FBI the lead. The agents involved have been handpicked and then polygraphed about any connection to the Stoics or Cold Harbor. Argus Systems and its leadership are the most obvious places to start, but the Argus building in Arlington burned down before the investigators could go through it. There's no lead on the arsonist. It was a real professional job."

Sam knew about the fire. It had made the news, and he had spoken to Shoe, Sara, and Ken, who had already all found positions in rival firms.

"What about Spears?"

"They pulled his body from the Potomac just a few days after we interrupted Cold Harbor. He drowned. Kind of ironic for an ex-SEAL. We're keeping it quiet for now, and when it comes out, it'll officially be an accident of some kind. The currents up by Great Falls can be pretty treacherous."

"We?"

"Yeah. My organization has loaned me to the investigation."

"You're still not going to tell me what that organization is, are you?"

"No way. You're not cleared for it. I'm in it and I'm hardly cleared for it."

"So what are you doing here? Isn't the investigation in D.C.?"

"In between my PT sessions, I've been helping the services here roll up the Sons of Ashoka, the Stoics' Indian counterparts. They've had more success than we have. I was able to ID the go-between who met with Masood and Jadoon, and he rolled over on his comrades in conspiracy faster than Sammy the Bull. Turned out he was an Indian Air Force general with access to the nuclear weapons codes. He and the rest of Ashoka were ready to sacrifice Mumbai if it meant we'd step in and strip Pakistan of its nukes. It's hard to believe some of the people who were in that group. People you'd never imagine."

"Tell me about it."

Khan looked abashed.

"I'm sorry about that. I wasn't thinking."

"It's okay. It's something that I'm going to have to come to terms with. You know the irony of it is that Vanalika really did make the phone call that started all this. She had a satellite booster up in the cabin where we were staying. I thought the intercept of the call was fake, and when I went looking, Andy Krittenbrink and I found other reports that had been falsified by Weeder and his people. Argus was salting the Panoptes material with real intel products that were consistent with the messages they were trying to send to Delhi and Islamabad. But if I hadn't been suspicious of the Vanalika intercept, I never would have found the others."

"Good thing you did. And I know the price was high."

"How did your organization learn about Cold Harbor? Was there a leak of some kind?"

"Truth is, we didn't know about it. We had picked up some signals that some big op was under way, but the details were fuzzy. We knew it involved a Pakistani extremist group. The Hand of the Prophet was just one of the organizations we were tasked to penetrate, and it was far from the most likely source of the threat. I drew that particular assignment, but I had colleagues targeting other groups. Some made it in. Some are dead."

"I'm glad you're not. It was a hell of a thing you did."

"Infiltrating HeM was my mission. My form of jihad against the barbarians and wackos who have hijacked my religion. That's what jihad means, at least to me. Jihad is struggle, the struggle for the future of Islam being waged between the modernists and the medievalists. I saw for myself what that meant when I was stationed in Afghanistan. There was a local, a Pashto translator who worked with my unit. I was invited to his wedding. The Taliban exploded a truck bomb during the reception to punish him for collaborating. That was the point where I focused my jihad on the struggle within my religion."

"Civil wars are always the bloodiest. No one can hurt us like the ones closest to us."

"Ain't that the truth. The medievalists hit their high-water mark on 9/11 and the Hand was determined to do them one better. But by the time I was able to put the pieces together, Braithwaite was dead and I didn't know who I could trust. The communications were all compromised, and there was no way to know if I would be accidentally alerting the Stoics to my presence in HeM. I had to figure something out on my own. But I wouldn't have made it without you and Lena. I thought I had it set up so that Jadoon would leave me alone with the bomb at the end, but with the fake timer, I was never going to get that chance."

"How did you know that your wallet would find its way to us and that we'd be able to follow it back to you?"

"I didn't. I had to trust that I knew the will of Allah."

"Cast your bread upon the waters?"

Khan shrugged.

"Something like that, I suppose."

"How's the hunt for Weeder going?"

"He's disappeared. We can't find him and we don't even know where to start looking. The guy has had the same training I have and then some. If he wants to stay lost, it'll be very, very hard to track him down."

"We found bin Laden."

"After ten years and ten billion dollars. And then we only caught him because he was still part of an organization that needed to communicate with itself. We found a loose end and we were able to follow it all the way back to his compound in Abbottabad. Weeder's a lone wolf. Meanwhile, the Stoics look like they've gone to ground and we may never know who besides Spears and Weeder were part of it."

"So what are you going to do?"

"When my arm heals, I'm going to join the task force full-time."

"To what end?"

"John Weeder murdered Solomon Braithwaite, my friend and mentor. I'm going to find Weeder, and I'm going to kill him."

Sam looked at him appraisingly. Kamran Khan was dead serious. Sam suspected that he would somehow find a way to succeed.

Lena broke away from the city official she had been schmoozing to join them, linking arms with Sam and leaning into him slightly in a gesture of affection. Sam knew what this meant. She wanted something from him. This was his daughter and he could read her moods like an experienced sailor could read the sea and sky.

"Dad, could I ask you to give Tahir a hand?" she asked. "I want to make sure he gets a good seat."

"He'll get the best in the house," Sam promised.

That was what she wanted, he understood, time alone with Khan.

He picked his way through the crowd, moving in the direction of the bridge that the boy called home. He couldn't begrudge her some private time with Khan, her captor and her savior. It was complicated. No doubt, they had a lot to talk about.

Besides, she had earned it.

This was Lena's day. Her victory.

Sam was immensely proud of her.

. . .

Although surrounded by people, Lena and Khan were now effectively alone for the first time since her last day as his prisoner. Khan looked different, of course. The jihadi disguise was easy enough to peel off with a change of clothes and a haircut. But his eyes were the same. Intense. Bright. Clear. Lena knew there could never be anything between them. The distance that separated their lives was too great. But if not Khan, she also understood that this was the kind of man she could love. Still, there was something that she needed to know.

"I want to ask you something."

"I think I know what it is," he replied carefully. "But I don't know the answer. That's the truth even if it isn't especially satisfying. It was right on the knife edge. It could have gone either way."

"So why did you hesitate?"

"All is according to the will of Allah. If I had shot you, the bomb would have exploded and Mumbai would have been destroyed."

"That only works as an explanation after the fact. It's not much of a guide. You still need to choose. Life is about choices. And karma," she added. "Good karma, in this particular case."

"Yours or mine?" Khan smiled.

"We'll see."

Lena looked out over the crowd. She could see her father standing in the front row with Tahir perched on his shoulders smiling broadly as only a ten-year-old can. Sam held on to his legs to help him stay balanced, clearly unconcerned that they both ended at the knee. He was good about things like that, and Lena loved him for it. There was a bandage on Tahir's neck where a local surgeon Sam had known for years had removed a fibrous tumor as a favor to her father. It was a first step. Eventually, she hoped to get the boy off the streets and into her school.

It was almost time for the official ceremony to start. Uncle Ramananda was already on the dais with the mayor and the commissioner. The commissioner was a wily fox of a politician, and he had forged an alliance with Ramananda that Lena hoped would help the Dalit to move away from the margins of Mumbai society and create opportunities for kids like Nandi and Tahir.

The Gummadi brothers had secured seats on the stage as well. As a consolation prize for losing the permits to the Five Star development, they had landed the contract to build the school and the first tranche of housing.

That was not the only reason for the Gummadi brothers' flattery, however. In addition to her own standing, Lena was the only daughter of Emily Lord's nominee as the next United States ambassador to the Republic of India. Political appointee ambassadors were typically big-money campaign donors who had essentially purchased their new government jobs—not for the meager salary, but for the grandeur of the title. Sam had earned the job. He deserved it.

Lena was immensely proud of him.

EPILOGUE

Alejandro Vargas rolled his copy of *El Tiempo* into a tube and, with a casual flick of the wrist, crushed the fat fly that had been creeping greedily toward his fried plantains. When he unrolled the paper, he noted with some satisfaction that the greenish guts of the fly were smeared across the face of Emily Lord. The story that accompanied the picture was about the president's valedictory tour of South America. Lord had only a few short weeks left in her eight-year, two-term presidency. Like most of what the spineless Latin American press wrote about her, the article was laudatory, highlighting the Lord administration's determined efforts to promote trade and investment in South America, and to reframe what it called the unwinnable and morally bankrupt war on drugs as a challenge to be met more through social programs than through military might.

Vargas was unimpressed. And the American people seemed to agree with him, having elected Lord's most consistent opponent in the Senate, Harrison Fletcher, to succeed her in office. Fletcher was a dyed-in-the-wool neocon, which was not ordinarily Vargas's preferred flavor of conservative. Too ideological. But the president-elect was also, by reputation, a little on the slow side and relatively easy to manipulate if you knew which buttons to push. That was most definitely a combination Vargas would have used to his advantage. At least back in the day.

He reached up to touch a rough patch of skin on the side of his neck where the doctor had removed the tattoo, and for a brief moment, he was once again Commander John Weeder, USN. The moment passed quickly. He had gotten used to thinking of himself as Alejandro Vargas, and he was reasonably content with the life he had carved out for himself in Colombia. The old cartels had been pushed out of the drug business by a group of newcomers known loosely as *bandas criminales emergentes* or BACRIM. Emerging criminal organizations. They were not afraid of violence and had need of the kind of services that Vargas could provide. The BACRIM paid handsomely in cash or cocaine or gold depending on the circumstances. If you had money and status, the señoritas in Colombia were beautiful and willing. So were the señoras, for that matter, if their husbands were away. Or dead.

It was a good, comfortable life, but he missed the sense of purpose he had found through his work on the Council. Maybe Fletcher's ascent would open up opportunities that the stunning failure of Cold Harbor had foreclosed. Vargas could only hope and wait.

He took a long swallow from the bottle of cold Cerveza San Tomás. For all of their trigger-happy shortcomings, the Colombians sure knew how to brew beer.

He unrolled the newspaper, turning from the fly-stained global affairs pages to the sports section. His football team, Atlético Nacional, had battled the Patriotas to a 1–1 draw at Atanasio Girardot Stadium. Vargas could not allow himself to follow the real football scores, it would draw attention to his Americanness. He had learned to like the South American variety well enough and to appreciate the passion that the players and fans brought to the sport. Some years ago, a star defender for Atlético had been gunned down in the streets of Medellín after accidentally scoring on his own team. It was, perhaps, a little extreme, but Vargas could admire the enthusiasm of the fan base.

On the table next to the half-eaten plate of plantains, his phone buzzed softly. A text.

He picked it up.

Where the incoming number should have been, there was just a line of dashes. His pulse rose. The message confirmed his hopes.

> *Navy Yard; Building C; Room 467*
> *December 17; 1500 hrs.*
>
> *Congratulations, Mr. Smith.*
>
>   *—The Chairman*

Alejandro Vargas dropped a ten-thousand-peso note onto the table to settle the bill, and James Smith walked out of the café with a spring in his step. Six years in Colombia was long enough. It was time to get back to work.

KASHMIR—THE REAL STORY

Bill Clinton once called Kashmir "the most dangerous place on earth." In part, this was in recognition of the reality that Kashmir was—and still is—a violent place where a host of armed groups with irreconcilable visions of the future compete for influence. President Clinton was also, however, concerned about the nearly seventy-year-old Kashmir dispute serving as a catalyst for conflict between those fractious neighbors, India and Pakistan. Adding nuclear weapons to the mix, a spark struck in Kashmir is one of the more plausible scenarios leading to a nuclear war, albeit one that would most likely be limited to South Asia.

The roots of the Kashmir conflict are deep and date back to the 1947 partition of the British Raj into the Dominion of Pakistan and the Union of India. The two nations suffered through a violent birth. Millions, most of them Muslims, were displaced. Hundreds of thousands died in widespread violence. The territory of Kashmir was a prize that New Delhi and Islamabad fought over from the very beginning. Under the terms of the partition plan, the maharaja of Kashmir—Hari Singh—had the option to join either Pakistan or India or remain neutral. He opted for neutrality, doubtlessly hoping to parlay that into his own little absolute monarchy.

The Hindu Singh, who ruled a princely state that was largely Muslim, was riding a tiger. Within a few weeks, Muslim tribesmen under the direction of the new authorities in Pakistan were at the gates threatening the Kashmiri capital of Srinagar. Singh fled to India, and in exchange for Delhi's protection, he turned over the keys to Kashmir. Fighting between India and Pakistan continued until New Year's Day in 1949 when a UN-brokered cease-fire froze the situation on the ground with India in control of some 65 percent of Kashmir and Pakistan in possession of the rest. It was meant to be a temporary solution. Seven decades later, however, the Line of Control between the two—so familiar to Sam—is still the effective border between India and Pakistan.

Since 1947, India and Pakistan have fought three wars, two of them triggered by disputes over Kashmir. While tensions have eased some in recent years, the situation is far from stable and the underlying causes of the conflict remain unresolved. It is easy to see how these two South Asian giants could stumble blindly into a war that neither wants, locked in a violent struggle conducted along the very edge of the nuclear abyss. It is even easier to see how a major war on the subcontinent would undercut fundamental U.S. interests, including, in particular, in Afghanistan.

Pakistan has long been a prickly partner for Washington, jealous of its prerogatives and unhappy with the line it is forced to walk between its commitment to the alliance with America and the political problems posed by their homegrown Islamic extremists. Pakistan is an exceptionally difficult place to govern, and many observers are deeply concerned about the growing influence of the Islamists, including, it is rumored, in the military.

The "loose nukes" scenario is a real one, at least among war gamers and planners. There have been reports that the Pentagon has contingency plans in place to "snatch" Pakistan's nuclear weapons should it look like the Pakistani military can no longer ensure the integrity of command-and-control. This would be an enormously risky thing to do, but the prospect of one or more of the hardline groups in Pakistan's tribal belt gaining control of a nuclear warhead has the power to concentrate the mind.

The Cold Harbor protocol that Earl briefs to Sam is fiction, but the fears that underpin it are very real.

As the Afghan war winds down, there will be a temptation on the part of policy makers to turn away from this exasperating region and invest U.S. political capital elsewhere. This would be a mistake. South Asia is a volatile but vital region that merits a major investment on the part of the United States. America's diplomats, Sam Trainor among them, are at the pointy end of the spear.

Secrets of State is a work of fiction. The opinions expressed in the novel are those of the characters themselves. The views offered here are my own and—as always—do not necessarily reflect those of the Department of State.